Lee Ann

AND

Stanley

Also by the author:

Fiddler: A novel

Fiddler: A screenplay

Lee Ann AND Stanley

A NOVEL

JQ Gustin

ISBN: 0989621405
ISBN 13: 9780989621403

For

Ben and Nicholas

Stars

Vintage juice squeezer, manufactured in West Germany, circa 1950

Part 1: Morning

1.

It rained in the night, a hard driving rain that had soaked the pavement and rooftops. A city stood steaming in the first light of dawn. Stanley saw none of this. He was teetering on that ledge between sleep and waking, drifting with his first fully conscious thoughts, neither judging them, nor staying with any one longer than it cared to stay. Mysterious aromas came to his senses. Not the iodine laced mist of morning San Francisco. No, the air was heavier, earthier, carrying with it scents of fresh brewed coffee, rain soaked timbers, and musty masonry. It was an older air, more layered with history and human habitation. His first waking thought was that he must not be home, because now, along with these pleasant aromas, were old familiar, but not hometown sounds: mule hooves clip-clopping on cobblestones, a saxophone heard somewhere far up the street, a strange bird song. And what was that? A steam calliope? He lay for a moment longer with eyes closed, enjoying these scents and sounds. Enjoying the fact that he must be lost in a place so far from home.

He opened his eyes. A white plaster ceiling soared high above. New Orleans. It came back in a flash. He was in New Orleans. And, he rolled his eyes to one side, there was the back he expected to see. A back he'd seen many times before on mornings of his life.

Lee Ann did a sheet bound one-eighty roll and slammed an arm into his face. Feeling Stanley's sharp morning stubble on her skin jarred something deep inside. Her eyes snapped open. He managed a soft "mornin" but it was stabbed through by a piercing shriek. She leapt from the bed, took two strides

1

across the spacious hotel room floor, and disappeared behind a bathroom door.

"Lee Ann!" Stanley called after her, but to no avail. He heard the tub filling, the sound of a small transistor radio, a muffled male voice delivering the morning news.

"Good morning New Orleans... here's the news this morning May Fifth. This morning in Topeka, Kansas the Kansas State Board of Education begins hearings on creationism, intelligent design versus the theory of evolution. We're still debating this in 2005? It has been reported that Kansas Citizens for Science is threatening to boycott these proceedings...."

Lee Ann was never far from the news.

Stanely tuned it all out. Seemed like a headache he didn't need here in the twenty-first century.

"Good mornin', New Orleans," he mused to the vaulted ceiling. He closed his eyes, opened them again. Yup, still New Orleans. He'd been putting some miles on these past few weeks: New York, Minneapolis, Chicago, St. Louis, Seattle, and back to San Francisco.

Things had been going well in the art market and that was good, because he'd been mucking around in the mud for almost twelve years now. Throwing pots, plates, and vases until the tips of his fingers bled. And of course there had been the inventions, the sculptures of God knows what. People had called them everything from disembodied organs to blobs from hell. Even he wasn't sure what they were, apparently apparitions that grew out of his imagination. He liked them. No one else did. They were costly to construct, fire, and display, and they brought no return; so much for unbridled imagination. But the plates and pots and vases had kept him in T-bones and cheap red wine for years now. Even though he'd been going nowhere. Then he'd found it.

Mythology.

"Grab your coat...don't forget your hat...leave your worries on the doorstep...just direct your feet...to the sunny side of the

2

street!" He heard Lee Ann's atonal alto coming from behind the bathroom door. Shower, listen to the news, sing while you're putting on your lipstick and makeup, take mental notes for the upcoming day, review scripts, and generally crank up the brain, the mouth, the body. Oh yes, she could do all this and more before her morning coffee. Lee Ann Barnes, cohost of KPIQ's *Good Morning San Francisco*.

She came through the bathroom door without ceremony. "Stanley! You still in bed? Come *on* man, New Orleans is out there!"

It would be tiresome to see exclamation marks floating in the air punctuating everything Lee Ann said—though Stanley thought it would be appropriate. He saw them floating now, hanging up there in the air, decorating the ends of all of her bubbled sentences. She, of course, remained oblivious to her cartoon character as she rummaged through her suitcase for her jeans, sandals, and this day's cotton blouse—mouth working all the time. "So it's Brennan's for breakfast, then could we do a little browsing before...let's see, we need to leave by four-thirty to make it out to Poteet Porcelain. That would mean..." He tuned it out as he pulled his stiff, somewhat stocky almost forty-six-year-old frame out of bed and lumbered in the general direction of his morning shower.

"Stanley, I'm going to square some things away with the station, and then I'm going on down to lobby...see what's shakin...so if you're not out of the shower by the time I finish here, then I'll be down there, okay?"

He managed a muffled "I'll find you," disappeared behind the bathroom door, and cracked a high window. Air rushing in was as humid as air rushing out. A New Orleans steambath May morning. He stood for a moment trying to decide whether to shower or bathe. In this air, one could take a morning bath just by standing in one spot and sweating.

He stepped into the shower, adjusted the tap a few degrees colder than usual, and stood cooling off. What a shock it had been, Lee Ann suddenly appearing at the gallery last night. She in her slick green full-length gown, mahogany-red hair done up in some egg-beater, wind-tunnel affair. And of course when she breezed in, you could just as well be part of the furniture. People soon forgot that it was your show, your genius that people had put on their tuxes and tutus to come out to see. So he'd done that, melded back into the white plaster walls of Genoa Gallery and watched as she'd promenaded from group to group, sipping champagne from one of his ram horn goblets, watched as she'd peddled his wares. Oh, not overtly, mind you, but with a style and grace—not to mention savvy—known only to Lee Ann Barnes. Listen.

"How long have I known Stanley? Just about all my life. We went to the same grade school together...Glenwood Springs Consolidated. Daddy drove a beef reefer out of Denver...he was gone most of the time...Stanley's mom and dad might as well have been my own. Well, I do love my daddy Sherman, though..."

"A beef reefer?"

"You know, a refrigerated meat...you know...transporter. He called it his beef reefer."

"Oh yes, of course," said a withered prune of a woman.

He turned his face to the cool flow pulsing from the shower nozzle. So good to be able to stay in the better hotels now, ones with pulsing showerheads. That old biddy "oh yes of coursing" Lee Ann had been an ossified case of uptightness. She'd been put off by Lee Ann's direct delivery, a candid manner that had endeared her to thousands of San Francisco morning viewers. Lee rarely missed a beat, always plowed full steam ahead.

"I think Mr. Hochstetter's finally hit his stride now, don't you?" She'd swept her champagne glass (now) around taking in the various mountains of mythology that Stanley had fashioned from common clay. "I'm going to get these on the show as soon as I can. You certainly couldn't describe this stuff in words, could you?"

He turned a squeaky valve and stood drip drying in the steamy bath. The last of his shower water gurgled down the drain and all fell silent. Yes, it *would* be difficult to describe these creations of his that were currently drawing buyers to the galleries. He thought it was probably the cartoon character of the pieces that enchanted them. Or maybe it was their strange condensation of history. He drew his subjects from all of western civilization: Egyptian, Greek, Roman, Gothic, Celtic and Nordic; all were represented. There were boatloads, bridgeloads, towers and long processions of demigods, maidens and sprites, along with their mythical beast companions: centaurs, minotaurs and pans, unicorns, gargoyles and griffins. All were thrown together by some mad mythical storm. A storm possessed of strong torrential winds that pulled and sheared all the figures of all the compositions so that they seemed to lean and strain against its fury. As if their sole reason for trudging along together was to weather this weather—was to weather this storm—wind torn.

This windtorn illusion was not easy to effect. It took hours to sculpt, all the delicate ears, eyes and noses, lips, maws and claws, mandibles, tails and scales. But it was worth it when he unveiled one of his masterpieces to the incredulous oohs and aahs of an appreciative audience. And the patrons paid well, very well. Last week he'd had an offer of $87,000 for a piece he'd entitled "Lief Ericson's 13th Dream." A placard by that piece gave credit to Bob Dylan for the inspiration.

Eighty-seven thousand.

He stepped out of the shower and began toweling off. Yes, it looked like the days of barely making ends meet were just about over. Last night the show at Genoa Gallery had grossed a tidy $122,000. Half of that would be his. It boggled his mind. Just last year he'd been hard pressed to meet the monthly mortgage. Now his monthly bills seemed a pittance. At last he could expand his digs and find a place where he didn't have to be constantly surrounded by mud: mud in the dirty dishes, mud in the mail, mud in the clothes closets, mud everywhere and in everything. Yes, as soon as he returned to San Francisco, he would go hunting for a place where the studio could be apart from the house.

A dream coming true.

He shaved, put on some cool cottons, and made his way down to the lobby. Lee Ann, as he expected, was sitting in the bar nursing a virgin mary and holding forth to a group of California compatriots and fans; two older couples who no doubt had recognized her familiar face and were engaging her in a little inside conversation. Lee Ann, she never tired of people. Stanley wondered how she did it. Oh well, it was her business. People that is. It's what she did. People.

One of the older women is speaking. "Oh my dear, I just don't know how you do it...I mean put on that show day after day, week after week, always interesting, always current, always entertaining."
Lee Ann. "Well, I have a lot of help you know...I'm just the tip of the thing. And, course, Bradley and I are a team."

"Stanley!" She brightened as she saw her frumpy, lumbering friend entering the bar. He was quickly introduced to everyone around the table. Lee Ann knew all first and last names. How did she do it? He, of course, cared little about the names of these people he would never see again and remained standing as a signal that he expected to be leaving as soon as possible for Brennan's. "Nice to meet you...pleasure...oh, you're from the Bay Area? How long are you staying in New Orleans? How nice...boy, Lee Ann, I'm starving..."

Lee Ann stood, made some parting remarks, then the two of them made their way out to the street. "Stanley, I don't see why we couldn't have sat for just a bit with those people. You know Tom is a retired importer...connections worldwide...could have been some help in exploring the foreign markets for your wares. You're *so* asocial. Oh well, you've always been a snob now that I think about it."
It was so easy being with Lee Ann; she would more often than not answer her own questions. And he liked that, someone

who not only carried on her side of the conversation, but his. This was appealing to a muser like Stanley.

They made their way down the rain drenched streets of the French Quarter, window shopping as they went. He'd been along these streets before, many years ago, and they hadn't changed that much since then. New Orleans, like San Francisco, was layered with strata from every era of American history. The antique shops were the best; they held the flotsam and jetsam of the years. He snapped pictures as they moved along. There were objects whose forms he could use—windows into the past.

Lee Ann stood gazing into one of these windows three doors up. He could see, even from where he stood, that something was making Lee blue. Something about Lee Ann radiated emotion like Sutro Tower. She had at least 50,000 watts of power.

He moved to her side and saw immediately what was causing her melancholia. There in the window of a second hand store was a maroon and lime green 50's vintage juice squeezer.

Without moving her eyes, she whispered, "Do you ever think of Bird?"

Stanley: "Every day."

"Bird..."

"Baby Bird..."

Out of all the toys and playthings their two-year-old son, Bird, could have been attached to, he'd fixed on a strangely art deco juice squeezer. A squeezer identical in design to the one that now seemed to occupy a position at the center of their universe in a dusty secondhand storefront window in New Orleans, Louisiana. Lee Ann slipped an arm around his stocky waist. It seemed they couldn't move, couldn't shift their gaze from the deco squeezer that, like a black hole, drew them into the past.

"Remember how he'd drag that damn thing around by the handle? Remember how he'd try to crush anything he could fit into the breach of that thing?"

"Mmm...Bird. Where is he Stanley? Where is our little baby Bird?"

"Don't know Lee…wonder every day."

"He's almost twenty-seven years old now you know. He must wonder, he must remember something about us even though he was only five when he…" She couldn't finish.

They stood a moment longer in silence, remembering the child that had so magically and serendipitously blessed them when they were young. A child they had found sleeping in a wicker basket at the foot of an ancient eucalyptus in Golden Gate Park. Years ago when their world was young.

And then at five years of age, as mysteriously as he had flown into their lives, Bird had flown away.

Bird…Baby Bird.

A full house at Brennan's Restaurant was enjoying a bright May morning. Stanley, with his new found wealth and panache, slipped the head waiter a twenty and requested a table in the open air atrium by the fountain.

Stanley had known Lee Ann nearly all her life. They'd been playmates, runaway lovers, parents, parted partners, and now just friends. They had more history than they knew what to do with. So he knew one thing without a doubt about Lee Ann, she loved a surprise—because *she* always seemed to be three beats ahead of the action.

"Whoa Stan…never seen you do that before."

"Hey, how often do I get to take my ex-wife out to breakfast in New Orleans?"

"Mmm…" She felt something stirring inside. What was this? Stanley! A man of the world? No, just couldn't be.

He noticed a soft sheen coming into her eyes. "What? Why are you looking at me like that?"

"I've never seen you do that before."

"What?"

"Slip sugar into the palm of a…maître d'."

"Well, I haven't seen you for…let's see…been about five years now hasn't it?"

"About."

"Funny you should suddenly show up just about the time I start getting rich and famous."

"Famous people *are* my business Stanley...you know that." She lowered her eyes and smiled broadly, then raised them to drill him. My how the woman could glow. He held his ground.

"Hmm, well, glad to see you again, Lee, even if it did take money and fame to get you back around." He shifted in his chair. "You know, you haven't really been away from me. Handy thing about having an old friend...ex-wife...on TV. You can turn on the tube any morning at 9am and there she is in living color."

"Uh huh...I'm sure every morning you're glued to the tube watching *Good Morning San Francisco*."

"Not every morning, but enough to keep in touch. Time moves more quickly for you, Lee, than me. I'm pretty much the same person you left down on the Embarcadero five years ago. But you, you've changed, and I've had the pleasure of watching it all happen on local TV."

She took a sip of her ice water, smiled slightly. "Hmm...how? How have I changed, Stan?"

"Well let's see"— he looked her over— "you're better looking for a start."

"HA!"

"I'm serious, Lee, you don't have as many freckles as you used to. I thought it might be TV makeup, but no, your skin tones have melded nicely in your old age. And you've darkened your hair, not such a carrottop now."

Her eyes flashed round and wide. "Old age?"

"What are you now? Forty-four? Uh huh, you were forty-four on June twelfth last year weren't you?" He couldn't resist twisting the blade. "Let me tell you, Lee, take it from one who's a year your senior, forty-four is...well...getting there."

A silence fell between them. And then the waiter came to take their order. Or so they thought.

He told them Brennan's didn't serve breakfast in the fountain area, but that he did have a nice table on the second floor inside, overlooking the fountain. Stanley grumbled and said he thought he remembered eating breakfast in the fountain area years ago.

Lee Ann waved it on and suggested they climb the stairs. He followed along behind, grumbling about wasting twenty dollars on nothing. She gave him a look over her shoulder and he fell silent.

They were seated in the air conditioning, as promised, looking through pane glass windows at the flowers surrounding the tables and chairs in the outside courtyard below.

A double dollop of eggs benedict seemed to be the choice of the day (one of the few things they'd always agreed on was food). Stanley ordered champagne. Lee Ann said he would have to drink it himself, seeing as how she'd floated through the Genoa Gallery opening on a wave of very good French bubbly and then caught another wave of that same elixir on the red-eye flight down here to New Orleans. He canceled the order.

"Stan, I got a bitching hangover, *don't you?*"

"Don't remind me."

She rummaged in her purse, found some aspirin, gave him three, said, "I gotta hit the head," and suddenly was gone. Witchcraft.

Stanley sat watching a dessert chef preparing bananas foster with all the liqueur and brown sugar and sliced bananas going up in flames. He swallowed the aspirin with a healthy shot of water and let his mind drift back to the events of late last evening when they'd become a little too celebrant on champagne. And when the doors of Genoa Gallery had closed for the evening, and all the patrons dispersed with receipts for their selections of his mud mythologies, he and Lee Ann had sat sipping a final glass with Evie Ester, proprietor of Genoa, who was running tallies on her Mac. It was then that they'd had the crazy notion to run away to New Orleans. Evie had Continental on the line in a keystroke, New Orleans in another, booking them at Le Richelieu via the last flight east.

So they'd fled to New Orleans, the land of dreams...you'll never know how nice it is, or just how much it really means. New Orleans.

Lee Ann had rejoined him, and the eggs benedict had come too, although he wasn't sure when.

"Why did you scream and jump out of bed this morning?" he asked as she put her napkin back in her lap.

"Why did I what?"

"This morning, when you woke up, why did you scream and jump out of bed?"

"I sleep till I wake up."

He processed the response, but something didn't click.

"I sleep till I wake up?"

"Yeah." She stirred a fork in her eggs and hollandaise sauce.

"Oh."

"It was a shock. I was shocked. I woke up with my ex-husband's grizzly face in mine. I was..."

"Repulsed?"

"Stanley."

"What?"

"Nothing. No," she softened, "certainly not repulsed. I was... well...it was just sort of weird when I realized what...what..."

"We'd done?"

"Yeah."

"Did we do something?"

She lowered her eyes. "I don't remember...do you? I mean I was so bushed and sloshed when we got into bed, I think I fell asleep right away. Didn't we just fall asleep?" She looked up wide-eyed in anticipation of what he was about to say. He poker faced it for a full five seconds while he considered whether or not to tease. Without averting her eyes, he smiled.

"Stanley, don't you dare tease me about this. *C'mon,* what happened?"

"Nothing Lee, absolutely nothing. We were tired and lubed. And we aimed our bodies at the bed, tilted at the heels, and fell asleep before we hit the sheets. There...satisfied?"

The flush drained out of her face like someone emptying a cooler full of raspberry punch. She released a breath that she'd been holding for too long.

"So we're here for another three days at least. Probably going to be hanging out together for that length of time. One hotel room, one bed. Or we could find a room like the one Evie *said* she reserved. You know, one with twin beds. Or we could get separate rooms, or we could even go to separate hotels, or cities or..."

"Don't make it complicated," she said softly.

"You're right." He changed the subject. "Daughter Claire called last week."

"From Crete?"

"Yes, said she was enjoying the dig she was on, was finding some incredible Minoan artifacts...but was ready to get back to Toronto. Said she was missing Jackie...which I thought was cute. They're still roomies you know. A couple of bookends those two."

Lee nodded. "It was good she called, yes?"

"Uh huh, she didn't ask for money this time. She seems to have called just to talk. We kept it light, current affairs and such. You knew that she's working for the Royal Ontario Museum now. You knew that?" Stanley waited for Lee Ann who seemed to have cruised off on some other sea of thought.

"Is this a beginning then?" she asked.

He wasn't sure what she was referring to so responded in kind. "Isn't everything? I mean isn't every bloody nanosecond a beginning?"

"Her birthday is coming up you know."

They blurted it out almost at the same time. Laughed.

"Haven't found anything to give her." Lee Ann grew pensive.

"Neither have I."

They finished breakfast and decided on a return walk to the hotel with a side tour of French Market. He threw an arm around her shoulders as they moved off down Toulouse Street. Some difference in the cadence of their gaits made for a jarring sensation that resulted in their giving their Parisian lovers routine the toss. Stanley moved along the street alone now, marveling as Lee Ann ranged out a half block ahead, fell behind as much, was lost from view for a moment, then magically reappeared to the fore again. Lee Ann the quantum leaper. How audacious of him to think that he could have moved along arm in arm with Lee Ann Barnes.

2.

As they approached French Market they closed ranks and walked along the narrow sidewalk side by side—occasionally dodging other Saturday morning sojourners.

"I read somewhere in the *Chronicle* that you've been flirting with NBC? Any truth to that, Barnes?" He extended an imaginary microphone in her direction. She smiled and pushed it away.

"More like they've been flirting with me."

"So what's the prognosis? You going up to the big show?"

"I can't say it wasn't an interesting offer." She sighed. "They wanted me to host a TV news weekly aimed specifically at global environmental issues. It was tempting."

"But you turned them down, didn't you?"

"It would have meant literally moving to New York. Being out of the country for long periods of time. You know me, Stan, I'm a westerner, a homegirl. Besides, I don't really know all that much about bugs and animals and trees."

"Would you need to? You're a meteorologist, a weatherwoman; that's a good background for a science reporter."

"I know, that's what NBC kept saying, but there was something else that held me back too..."

She took a moment out to wave back at a group of tourists in a mule drawn carriage, then continued.

"You know, I've been a KPIQ girl from the beginning. I love my little show and all the great people who help put it on. It's a jungle out there in network land. It's easy to get eaten alive and quickly join humus on the forest floor. Speaking environmentally of course."

He smiled. "I know, I spend a lot of time in the mud myself."

14

She bumped him good-naturedly with her elbow. They walked in silence for a moment, then he asked.

"So, Lee...what made you come down to the gallery last night? It's been what, almost five years? After Embarcadero I thought you were going to hate my guts forever. Why the sudden reappearance?"

She studied her feet as they moved along the wet pavement— mumbled, "I got your printed invitation. I promised Claire..."

"Oh"— he processed her response for a moment—"but I've sent you invitations to all my openings. It was Claire's idea?"

"Yes. She said I was going to start feeling more and more stupid as time went by if I kept up this alienation thing. Course, she was...*is* right. As usual."

They'd reached the market and stood looking down an aisle of haggling produce and trinket merchants. Stanley, hands in his pockets, moved into the crowd feeling pensive—slightly defensive. Somehow he couldn't buy Lee Ann's explanation for her sudden reappearance back into his life. Claire, she said it had been at Claire's urging. But that didn't seem likely. Even though things were improving between his estranged daughter and himself, why would Claire be encouraging a reunion of her parents? Claire had always played them off one another so successfully. Why would she be urging a truce now? Something didn't ring true here. Lee Ann wasn't coming entirely clean.

"So how do you want to do the market, Stan?" Shouting over the din of the crowd, she brought him back.

"I guess at our usual pace, Lee. You cover the whole place and get everyone's name and complete life history while I look over the first stall...and then we go home. Isn't that the way we usually do a flea?"

She paused to take in her old trail buddy. She could tell by his tone of voice and body language that he was feeling funky about something. She knew that *he knew* that Claire wasn't the whole of her reason for looking him up. And he was right. She would tread lightly now until she could reveal her true motive. And that would have to be soon. He was growing restive.

"I'll stick with you, Stan. Lead on."

If it killed her, she was going to do it at *his* pace this morning.

Events are shaped long before they happen. Shaped in space to occur in time. If someone could sit high above and *watch* in all directions and times at once, then that someone might rule the world, heal the sick, do great works, maybe even write a little novel. In the case of our story, that set of omnipresent eyes would have seen the nefarious note that Lee Ann carried in her handbag...would have seen the stevedores now loading a heavy pile of produce pallets onto a forklift.

And now the young driver is moving them over to a flatbed truck. Innocently enough he pushes a wrong lever—the pallets are released—fall freely—come crashing to the concrete floor with a resounding, *CRACK!*

Suddenly a woman twenty feet away, a woman with tasseled red hair and that note in her purse, whirls in the direction of the sound. Eyes rolling wildly, breakfast threatening to leave her stomach, she rag dolls onto the cold concrete floor of French Market.

3.

She wasn't unconscious for long, but long enough for an initially startled crowd of people to regain their wits and move quickly to surround the fallen woman. Stanley was the first to bend over the prone and unconscious form of Lee Ann Barnes. He shouted for someone to call an ambulance, checked her pulse, cradled her head, and motioned for a vendor selling Mexican blankets to bring some over to keep her warm and pillow her head. And now her eyes snapped open and took in the eerie sight of faces circled high above her. And there were Stanley's eyes again, for the second time this morning, closer than she cared for them to be, peering intently into hers. But this time the face that housed those eyes was etched with concern and, yes, more than a little fear. She heard him speak as if for the first time.

"You all right, Lee? What happened?"

It was too soon to converse, and certainly not Lee Ann's style to be lying prone on a concrete floor in some ethnic market with the whole world staring down at her. In one martial-arts-like motion, she tucked at the waist, rolled forward onto her feet, straightened her knees, and stood wobbly but upright, nervously smoothing and adjusting her clothes. Stanley stood behind her, at the ready to catch her, should she regret her too rapid recovery. The ambulance arrived.

"Oh man, Stanley, is that for *me?* Please, tell it to go away. I just fainted...I'm fine. God, this is *so* humiliating."

He had to reflect a moment. Yes, he had yelled for someone to call an ambulance. And four minutes ago it had seemed like the right thing to do. But now there was Lee Ann, back on her feet, straight in her clothes—soiled as they were from the grit of the market floor—Lee Ann, back up and ready to roll, although not moments before she had been passed out cold on the market floor. The woman *was* a living segue.

She moved quickly out of the market onto French Market Place and headed west. He gave his hotel name and room number to the ambulance driver and set out on a trot to catch up. Out of breath now, he finally drew abreast of his flustered friend.

"Lee, you okay honey?"

"God Stanley, this is *really* humiliating you *know.*"

"It's okay, I just want to know if *you're* okay. What happened? Why did you...you..."

"*Faint*, Stanley...the word is *faint*. I don't want to talk about it. I've already ruined our day. We were having such a great time, and then I have to go and make a fool of myself. God, this is so *humiliating!*"

"Come on, Lee, forget it. It was just a bunch of strangers. You'll never see them again."

"Well, yes...yes I will!" She paused to catch her breath. "I'm going back to the market, Stan. *Did you see those African bracelet?* I've *got* to get Claire one of those bracelets for her birthday, Stan. She's been wanting one like that forever. And so I..." She broke off midsentence and collapsed on a brick ledge along the sidewalk. A trembling woman sat hugging her own shoulders as if to contain a body that refused to be still.

He sat down beside her and put his arm around her shoulders. Something was wrong, but he knew he couldn't pressure her into telling him what it was. He took the oblique approach. Stanley was very good at the oblique approach, at least where Lee Ann was concerned.

"Yes, I did see them, they were fine, better workmanship than what you usually see in that category of crafts coming out of Kenya." They were quiet for a moment. He could feel her still shaking, so drew his arm more tightly about her shoulders and felt her slowly relax into him.

"Feels good, Stan. I'm scared shitless. Give me a minute to calm down a bit, 'n'then I'll tell you what's happenin. Just give me a minute..."

Stanley savored a moment of hearing Lee Ann rounding her n's like the cowgirl he'd known so long ago back in Colorado.

"Take your time."

It was Thursday. He would sit with his arm around Lee Ann Barnes until the sun went down if that's what it took to calm her. She felt small and almost childlike as she melted into his ample frame. Being a man of moderately generous proportions himself, he had always enjoyed the feel of her small body pressed against him. And then too, she had always been a bit warmer to the touch than any woman he'd ever known. Probably a manifestation of her sprinting metabolism. The feel of Lee held fast now beneath his wing brought back a flood of memories, sweet reveries. He wondered how he felt to her, what was going through her mind. What was so dead wrong that she would faint dead away at the sharp report of some crashing pallets.

She was falling still now in the crook of his arm. The trembling was subsiding, and he knew as soon as it reached full ebb, she would be back on her feet, ready to hit the track and rejoin the race.

He spoke softly. "Can you tell me now?"

She turned and looked him straight in the eyes for a moment. He wondered for that moment if she might be going to kiss him. That *was* her look—a prelude to a kiss. But no, she turned away quickly and began rummaging in a cluttered shoulder bag. A well-handled piece of paper came to her grasp. She unfolded it with jerking hands and held it out to him. "Here."

He took the rumpled piece of paper and read a short message composed of letters clipped from magazines. The message was chillingly succinct.

"If I can't be inside your body...I'm going to send a bullet to be there for me."

Stanley read the note two times, because it simply didn't register on the first pass. Finally, on the third reading, he grasped the full meaning of the message and felt his breakfast lift in his stomach. He straightened his back, narrowed his eyes, and read the note a fourth time just to make sure he was getting it right.

"If this is some kind of joke, it's fucking *sick*."

"It's not, Stan. I'm afraid I'm nutbait at the moment. I thought that loud crack...what was it?"

"Some pallets got loose from a forklift driver and crashed to the floor."

"It was a loud sharp *cracking* sound...I thought it was a gunshot...a fly buzzed by my head at exactly the same moment. I thought I was deadmeat." She paused for breath. "Wow."

"Sssssssss." He couldn't suppress the reptilian hiss that emanated from some snakepit in his libido. Lee's characterization of herself as "nutbait" and "deadmeat" was so like her, but it wasn't funny; she was the target of some very sick person.

"Tell me everything you can. How serious is it? How long has this been going on?"

She started hesitantly. "About two weeks now...but it seems like about two years. I've been petrified out of my wits. How am I supposed to work when I have to look over my shoulder every two seconds!" She had to stop to catch her breath again, then went on. "It started off fairly innocently, but it's been getting more pathological with every note. Man, this last one's *not* one bit amusing. I want to kill this sick clown, whoever he is." She gulped air. "And when I find out *who* he is, and I *am* going to find out, he's going to be the one who's soaking up a *slug*."

Stanley knew from her cold intonation that she was probably serious with this gangsta talk of hers. Her father, the driver of that eighteen-wheel "beef reefer", had taught her to shoot his .357 Marlin with great proficiency. More than one weekend he and Lee, and Lee's daddy Sherman, had driven up high into the Rockies to camp, hunt, and shoot a freezer full of venison. She turned out to be a much better shot than he, so during their married years, it was always a joke that the Beretta lived in a drawer on her side of the bed. You didn't mess with Lee Ann Barnes. Sherman had taught her well.

"Okay," Stanley had recovered some semblance of mind, "how did it begin?"

Lee Ann's body had finally stopped trembling. "I'll just have to tell this a little at a time Stan. You know? It feels so good to just sit here and be quiet for a minute. I feel safe with you. Man, you can't imagine the stress of this situation. I feel like a walking target."

"All right by me, Lee...we sit."

So they sat in the shade of a magnolia tree on the corner of Ursulines and Decatur streets. And as they sat, they silently shared a comfort and tranquility that only the years can bring.

They'd spent their early years growing up as playmates on Stanley's parent's ranch, a thousand acres of Roaring Fork River Valley grassland. The summer after he'd graduated from high school, and Lee Ann was two short months away from finishing, they'd celebrated and become lovers.

Up in the barn, up in the hayloft, the way everyone remembers it at least once in his or her life, Lee and Stan had come to each other for the first time, and it had been with searing passion and haste. She missed her next period—and the next. She was pregnant. Well, it might not have been that first time in the loft. There was a second time, within twenty-four hours of the loft, down under the cottonwood tree by the river. And after that, the fast one in the pickup truck alongside the road, some road, somewhere back up in the mountains. Oh, and the time alongside the highway with traffic whizzing by. As a matter of fact, once the floodgates of young lust and passion had been flung open, they'd been totally irresponsible about their sex. There was no going back, there was no going slow. There was no "being careful," because, you see, they really didn't care; they were in love, and that strange power, the one we all know so well, was sweeping them along. Like tubing on the rapids of the Roaring Fork River, they'd been swept along.

The sun had moved a short distance in the sky, so they shifted back into the shade of the tree. Lee straightened and looked at him. "Stan?"

"Yeah."

"We've been some miles...huh?" She paused. "Do you remember when we ran away to San Francisco?"

"No Lee, I don't remember the summer of seventy-eight, music in the park, you pregnant, us the runaways. No, dumped it all from the banks."

"Stan."

"Yes?"

"I want to kiss you."

"On the lips?"

"Yes...on the lips. I have need to."

"Sure...what the hell."

She turned under his arm, put a small face to his, and kissed him gently. A short, soft, and loving kiss. Then she moved back to fix on his dark eyes.

"That was nice," he said, nodding.

"*Nice?*"

"Uh huh. Nice."

"They shoot us for saying *nice* in the broadcasting business. Strip off our buttons and gun us down at dawn. And *you* say it about our first kiss in five years." Her tone was soft but direct.

"Full," he said.

"Full?"

"Yeah, you don't like nice...how about full?"

"Full is better..."

"So...we've got some business to discuss here don't we?"

"Unfortunately."

Lee Ann slid out from underneath his arm and straightened her spine, breathing deeply. Satisfied that everything was still in working order, she started in.

"Okay...so Stan, about the seaman. That's what he calls himself ...seaman. Anyway it all started about two weeks ago when I get to my car and there, sitting on the hood, is this long wooden box in the shape of a thin white coffin..."

"Whoa...*whoa!* Backup...*hold it.*" He strained at the pole to haul her back to the boat. "Semen? S-e-m-e-n, as in cum? A thin white coffin? Whoa, I see why you fainted!"

"Yeah, well you haven't heard the half of it yet. No, he spells his name s-e-a-m-a-n, as in sailor, thankgod, but yes, it was a box containing three long-stemmed callalilies, and it was in the shape of a thin white coffin. It was lined with white satin. It was beautiful."

4.

"Beautiful?"

"The way it was made. The craftsmanship and proportions of the coffin. Very fine work, you would have appreciated it."

"And was there a note with this charming little bouquet?"

"Yes, it said something like 'Dearest Lee Ann, you've stolen my heart...I know you'll be mine till death do we part.'"

"Jesus," he hissed, "what is with this guy's *death* thing?"

"Well, he definitely has that; it's a big thing with him. And you know, Stan, I don't know how long he'll be able to keep it up without it becoming a parody of terror. I really don't." She paused to consider. "Except, right now, he certainly has me scared out of my frigging wits."

"So, what happened after the coffin?"

"Lots of stuff. Stuff like a video DVD, shots with a telephoto lens as I moved around various places in San Francisco. He, or whoever was shooting me from a nearby rooftop, covered me doing an interview with Amy Tan in Chinatown. Oh... and then, you know...mundane stuff, like me driving to work, going to lunch, waiting for the cable car, shopping. You know, just moving around shots. He even recorded me one evening leaving for and coming back from a dinner date. It was creepy." She shivered. "But then again, the quality of the work was very fine. There was even a music track on the piece: Nat King Cole singing 'Darling Je Vous Aime Beaucoup.'"

"How suave."

"Yeah...suave. So...this DVD came through the mail, wrapped in red paper with a white label. Just your standard DVD disk video of someone watching me...almost like a movie. Want to hear what the message was enclosed with this little beauty?"

He nodded.

"The DVD was labeled 'My Aurora Borealis,' as in Northern Lights? And the note enclosed was sort of an incantation. I memorized it because, again, it was really rather beautiful in a dark sort of way. It went:

Aurora Borealis
Reflections from a chalice
of fathomless blackness
you dance in a dream

Aurora Borealis
Dim light in the palace
of fathomless blackness
and visions never seen."

She recited the verse softly, with tenderness in her voice, almost as if she were lulling a child to sleep.

"Whew...you dealin with some arcane dude here, Lee, but yeah, I can see that he's got class. Too bad you can't somehow communicate *back* with him, ask him if he'd like to step out of the shadows, be more of a regular guy, maybe just go have dinner some evening."

They sat in silence for a moment, then Stanley went on. "Were there things other than the DVD sent through the mail? What were the postmarks?"

She apparently hadn't heard his last question, so went on with a previous train of thought.

"I know, sometimes I actually find myself wanting to just *know* this person...without all the melodramatics. Right now, though, he's totally controlling the show. And you know, I think he wants to keep it that way. And he really hasn't become overtly vicious or homicidal till this last note. I found this one"—she waved the bullet note in front of her—"inside a hollow, black granite egg sitting on my doorstep two nights ago when I got home from work. Lovely little thing to find on your front steps.

Postmarks? Everywhere in the USA: New York, Seattle, Santa Fe. So that takes in some territory, huh?"

"Mmm...what else, how else has he communicated with you?" Stanley was developing a morbid fascination with this poetically perverse terrorist.

"He's faxed me things. A rather beautifully rendered etching of *Venus on the Halfshell,* with the inscription: 'Venus pales in your light...I made love to you in my dreams last night.' See, when he gets off his death kick, he's rather charming." Her face clouded over. "This last little lovenote however"—she waved the seaman's bullet note before her again as if to air some bad odor out of it—"no, I'm afraid, not funny." She folded it and put it back into her bag.

"Obvious question," he began. "Have you contacted the police? Have you told anyone else what's going down?"

"No, I haven't reported this to the police. I did tell Maureen Palmer, my boss at the station. She had to know. She's cutting me quite a bit of slack that she wouldn't be able to cut me under normal circumstances. Yeah, she knows about everything...is pressuring me to contact the police but says she'll let me play it the way I see it. It's my life that's in danger she says..." She paused to consider for a moment.

"And Claire knows about it."

"You've told Claire?"

"Yes...she's known about it since the first contact of the callalilies in the coffin. I told her because it seemed an innocent enough gift. But then...I felt slightly uneasy about it...I wanted her opinion as to whether I should be concerned or not."

Mmmhuh...okay, so Claire knows."

"Yes...I've spent a fortune on calls to Crete." She frowned. "I haven't told her about the bullet note yet, though. Don't think I will. She'd worry."

"Good reason to."

"The thing that gets me more than anything is...I can't know how long this will go on. How am I suppose to carry on a normal life, and *work,* with this fruitcake in my fridge! And after that last note! Man, I knew I had to get out of town *fast!*"

Stanley fidgeted for a moment on the hard tile ledge.

"So *that's* why you looked *me* up? That's why you came to the opening last night at Genoa? That's why you were so pliant about running away with me to New Orleans?" He sighed. "Should have known...once again...a pawn in your game." Stanley was disgruntled, wondered now what she would say, or if she would simply do her famous avoid-the-issue routine and cut to commercial.

"Come on Stanley...let's walk."

There, he had his answer.

They moved off up Ursulines Street in the direction of Le Richelieu. No, he couldn't let her get away with it. "So, Lee, c'mon, is that why you wanted to run away with me again?"

She knew she was cornered. She'd slipped out of one corner, only to find herself in another. And she was growing weary of corners—very weary. She considered getting mad but knew that Stanley, of all people, would see through that. Besides, she really was enjoying his company. She was feeling for the first time in two terror filled weeks that she could breathe freely, not have to be continually snapping her head around to check her hindside. Well, what the hell, that's what she'd tell him then, the straight-out truth. "Stanley...oh Stanley," she began."

"Yes?"

"The kiss was *nice.*"

"Full," he said, somewhat appeased.

They hurried through the lobby of Le Richelieu and, much to Lee Ann's relief, found themselves to be the only people on the elevator. "God, Stanley, I look like I've been scoopin out the horse barn, need a shower, need to change, need a drink now... need a little nap. It's eleven-thirty...we've got six hours before we appear bright and shining to Mr. Jean Paul Poteet. Won't it be fun to meet him? Those pictures you showed me of his place were breathtaking."

Stanley had never known anyone who could cram as many words into one breath as Lee Ann Barnes. Of course she had started out her television career as a weatherwoman and, as everyone knows, weather people are full of wind.

"Poteet," he mused, "the consummate southern aristocrat, living the plantation life on a bayou island no less! Did I tell you he's a direct descendant of the pirate Jean Lafitte? Do you know about Lafitte, Lee?"

The elevator reached the second floor and stopped with a juicy bounce.

"I've heard of him, but no, nothing specific do I know about Jean Lafitte. Brief me." Lee Ann assumed her television anchor persona and became all ears. She was already intrigued by this man they would soon be meeting. Who knew, maybe Poteet would be show material. She stalked show material like she used to stalk deer. Her hunter instinct was highly refined.

Stanley started in. "Well okay...let's see...Jean Lafitte lived in and around this area in the early eighteen hundreds. He and a band of around a thousand men sailed the waters at the mouth of the Mississippi doing a fair share of pirating. He had a bounty on his head, but he was such a brilliant naval tactician that they could never catch him. But then, during the War of 1814, the United States forces were short on men to defend New Orleans against an invasion by the British. So somehow Andrew Jackson got word to Lafitte that he wanted to cut a deal."

"Good 'ol boys, huh Stan?"

"Right...anyway, the deal was that Lafitte and his men would be given a full pardon by the US government if they agreed to do battle with the British, in favor of Uncle Sam. Payment being booty captured, in addition to the pardon."

"Such a deal is this," she broke in. "The man gets to practice legal piracy! He should be so lucky! Yes?"

"Yes, he certainly was, because Lafitte and his crack core of cannoneers and musket men, along with another three thousand thrown together troops, defeated the British army of nearly eleven thousand. Good work, Jackson. Good work, Jean Lafitte!"

"I'd say so...those are some stiff odds."

"They were, and so, after the war, Lafitte enjoyed the good life of New Orleans for a few years, not only a pardoned man, but also a hero. Yes! the man was a cunning customer."

They'd made their way into room 201 during his rather lengthy but concise telling of the pirate Lafitte's story. Lee Ann wanted to hear the conclusion of his little dissertation, but she wanted her shower more. And knowing Stanley, he would be getting into the details next, and that would take some time.

"Stan," she began, "I want to hear what finally happened to him, but I need to freshen up, way up. Why don't you find us a bottle of gin, some tonic, and limes...I'll shower...n'then we'll kick back out on the porch and sip a bit."

"Read my mind, Lee. Get pretty. You know...wet hair, no makeup, your best terry robe." He made his way back to the door.

"Hurry..."

On his way back down to the lobby, he couldn't help thinking about what he'd just heard. There'd been something in Lee Ann's tone of voice when she'd said, "Hurry..." that was making him break a cool sweat. He knew the woman, knew she had something on her mind that he wasn't so sure about. She wanted more than a shower and a drink—she was in the mood. But he wasn't sure he was. It could get complicated. Nearly thirteen years had passed since he and Lee Ann had been lovers—if you didn't count that sad six months, five years ago, when they'd made an honest but ill-fated attempt to rekindle the flame. That time had ended with Lee jumping out of his car down on the busy Embarcadero, wandering across traffic, and being run down by some innocent motorist who couldn't swerve fast enough to miss her. Two weeks in traction for her, but luckily no permanent damage.

He'd called for the ambulance that night too, and ridden with her to the emergency room at San Francisco General, only to be turned away at the desk because he was no blood or legal relative of hers. It didn't matter they shared a daughter. Hospital policy: husbands or blood relatives only could accompany patients beyond the door. He could have lied, told them he was still her husband, but he hadn't known their silly policies. So he'd gone to the outer waiting room to sit and pray while they set her bones, stitched up her lacerations, and wound her in gauze and white plaster. *That* had been a night. And all because they'd had another one of their epic arguments over the daughter they were trying to save.

He'd sent flowers, magazines, and notes to her during her recovery. He'd tried to visit, tried to phone, but she'd left instructions with the desk that she didn't want to see him, even talk to him on the telephone. The woman could be cold. And so he'd put his tail between his legs and hunkered off to lick his wounds. Okay, he'd concluded, if that's the way she wanted to play it, okay, he could be cold too, though not as convincingly as Lee Ann.

The desk clerk, waving a piece of paper, motioned Stanley to his station. It was a message from Claire, via her roommate Jackie, for Lee Ann. She was to call a Toronto telephone number that he recognized as Claire's. Lee Ann must have tried Claire when she'd come down to the lobby this morning before him. And not reaching her, must have left a message on Claire's machine? A message that Jackie, not Claire, was now returning? He thought he smelled a rat, but then decided he was over reacting, stuck the memo in his pocket, and made his way to the bar.

The room was filling with a late morning crowd so he quickly made arrangements with an amiable female barkeep to have a bottle of Bombay, tonic, and limes sent up to their room. The young woman behind the bar went on mixing drinks as she took his order.

"Got a hot date, Stan?" the girl teased.

"Whoa! How did you know my name?"

"Heard that pretty lady friend of yours this morning say it out. Is she really a TV talk show host?"

"Local morning show in San Francisco."

"Wow, lucky girl, I'd love to get into that kind of work."

"Ask her about it next time she's down," he offered. "That is if you have a couple of hours to spare. Lee loves to talk about herself...as you might have noticed if you were listening this morning as closely as it sounds like you were." He said it with a smile and dropped a ten on the bar as a tip. It was fun to tip big, a luxury he could, after twelve years of poverty, afford.

"Thank *you*, Stan, my man." The affable young bartender scooped the ten into her apron and threw back her shoulders. He couldn't help noticing that this robust woman was a statue waiting to happen.

"Can't keep the lady waiting; see you later." He turned to go.

"No sir, not wise to keep a lady waiting. Oh, name's Lisa Lynn, pleased to meet you." She extended her hand. He took it for a short businesslike pump.

"Pleased to meet you, Lisa Lynn...later." He smiled his warmest smile, noticed it was returned, then turned once again and walked from the bar feeling slightly flushed and overheated—and it wasn't just the New Orleans humidity. Lisa Lynn was the kind of woman who had always struck a glancing blow to his psyche: long legged, well endowed, sociable, perfectly at ease in her body. Only one problem now: Lisa Lynn was young enough to be his daughter. He winced at the fact that he was approaching forty-six. Nature was so cruel.

"Pick on someone your own size, Stanley," he mumbled to himself as he entered the elevator and pushed the button. He wondered what Lee Ann was up to right now. Twenty minutes had elapsed since she'd smiled and said, "Hurry..." with more than a little suggestion in her voice. Knowing her as he did, she could be in an entirely different frame of mind by now. And besides, he still wasn't sure that this impending business was to his liking. He wanted Lee, had always wanted Lee, and supposed he always *would* want Lee. Reason enough for him not to *have* Lee. He would wait then, wait and see. But he knew, if she made a move, he would follow her lead. He'd always been powerless against her sexual advances, had scorned himself on more than one occasion for being such an easy lay.

As the elevator hoisted him ponderously up to the second floor, he was lost in thoughts. Thoughts of Lisa Lynn and her broad white smile. Thoughts of Lee Ann and the kiss she had given him earlier this morning. And last but not least, thoughts of the note he now carried in his pocket: a hotel memo—a bomb—sitting there waiting to go off and ruin everything.

But Stanley was also very good at waiting. So he would wait. Wait and see.

5.

Considering her current state of mind, he called to her before he started to keycard the door. "Just me, Lee...big bad old Stan."

"Come in, I'm thirsty!"

She was propped up in bed reading a paperback when he walked around the corner and into the room.

"Hey...Miss Muffet on a tuffet?"

"Oh man, Stan, I must have been in a mild state of shock this morning after that faint. I feel like someone's worked me over with a rubber hose."

He moved over and sat beside her on the edge of the bed. "You want a backrub?" He said with no innuendo.

"I'd die for one, but where's our drink?"

"They're sending it up. This is a high-class joint, babe, don't like people wandering around the lobby swilling bottles of gin."

There was a soft knock on the door. "That was fast," they said in unison and laughed. After a brief exchange with the bellboy, and a quick mix on the dresser top, he returned to the bed with a matched set of gin and tonics. Lee took down half of her glass in two gulps and set it aside on the nightstand.

"Now, about that backrub...oil or no oil?"

"*You have massage oil!* Why are you packing massage oil?" She stared at him in amazement. He stared straight back.

"Hmm, well, you never know when you're going to get lucky...do you?"

"Stanley..."

"No...I carry it for my hands. If you had your hands in mud and water as much as I do, you'd understand. Besides, I don't like those perfumed hand creams. You go around smelling like

33

a French cat house. Massage oil is light, scentless, the perfect balm for my poor beleaguered paws"

"Hmmph." She wasn't convinced but also not in the mood to pursue it. Lee was ready for her rubdown, and massage oil would be...okay...*nice*. Without hesitation she unbuttoned her light cotton blouse; she was braless—slid it off both shoulders, threw it across a chair by the bed, rolled over, flopped facedown on the sheets and said, "Oil me."

He walked to his suitcase across the room and rummaged about for the oil. The sudden and unexpected flash of Lee Ann's breasts, fleeting as it was, had made his blood rise more than a few degrees. He spent a little longer than necessary locating the oil. A sea of ambivalent feelings were churning in his head and chest.

"What're you doing, Stanley? You can't find it?"

Lee Ann's voice, coming from behind him, brought him back.

"Oh...it was buried...no, I found it."

Back at the bed, he squirted a generous portion of oil into a cupped palm, held it for a moment, warming it, and said. "Ready?"

"Ready," came a muffled voice from a face inside a pillow.

Very slowly he inverted his hand and let the oil drip onto her bare skin. She shivered as he spread it lightly about her skin from waist to top of shoulders.

Her back glistened now with the light, scentless oil as he moved his fingers lightly over her bare skin exploring for knots; he found a few and then proceeded to knead the long muscles from the base of her spine up to the fleshy masses at either side of her neck. She moaned in appreciation and near ecstasy as she felt his familiar hands squeezing the tension from her body. She felt as if he was kneading her like a large lump of clay, shaping her to his liking. She'd always loved Stanley's hands. How could you not love the hands of a man who molded common clay into objects of stunning beauty? His hands had range, from a gentle caress to a powerful pressure that he could concentrate at the very tips of his strong fingers. She felt his hands now, once again on her body, and the years melted away.

Too soon he'd finished with her back. She could tell because he was relaxing his pressure and softly caressing her to a finish. Then his hands were still. Then gone.

"Want me to do your buns?" His voice came softly from somewhere above her.

She clutched a pillow and rolled over, eyes wide in mock consternation. *"Stanleee!"*

"Well, do you? You always loved that as I remember. Besides, by the feel of those knots in your back, bet your butt and legs could use some work too. Purely a professional opinion mind you."

"I'm sure."

"Well?"

She rolled back onto her stomach, kicked the sheets off her legs and mumbled, "What the hell."

He looped his index fingers through the waistband of her briefs and said, "Lift." She obliged him by raising her hips slightly off the sheets as he gently eased them down. Down below her waist. Down over her long legs. Down over her well traveled heels.

And then his breathing ceased, for there she was: Lee Ann Barnes, in all her birthday glory, lying there on white hotel sheets. Lee Ann with her still girlish figure, and yes, he was right, age had mellowed her skin tones, blended some of her freckles, and brought a creamy glow into her flesh. He still hadn't drawn a breath—felt he didn't want to touch her lest she disappear like the apparition she appeared to be. A vague fear suddenly stirred in him. He lifted his glass off the bedstand and moved quickly to the French doors.

Lee Ann, feeling his sudden departure, rolled over slowly, gathered the sheets about her, and watched as he moved off. He didn't see the quizzical expression crossing her face, only heard her voice come softly from behind him. "Hon?"

It was the first time she'd called him "hon" in longer than he could remember. He was comforted that she was feeling that way toward him. It would make what he was about to say—easier to say. That one term of endearment had posed a multitude of questions. He would answer with another.

"Yes?"

"What's wrong?"

"Oh, I don't know..." His voice followed his eyes as they ranged out over the city. "It's just...just that you are so damn beautiful to me." He felt a heat welling "It's been a long time for me, Lee. *Long* time."

"C'mere, Stan."

"No...I need a minute here."

Without taking his eyes off the skyline, he held an index finger up and out in her direction.

In an apartment across Chartre Street someone was practicing "Mood Indigo" on a tenor sax and making some painfully cacophonous mistakes. It struck him funny—brought him back. He turned and faced her.

"What's going on...what're we *doing* here, Lee?"

She was sitting up in bed now, propped up against the pillows, with the sheet pulled up just below her chin, confusion darting about her eyes. "I know..." She let out her breath. "This isn't fair to either of us, is it?"

"Least of all me." Stanley looked up sharply. She turned away.

"Hmm...*you* again. Well, how original...you know..."

"Wait a minute...*wait*." He interrupted her.

"No...you *wait*." She swung her eyes back around and tried to back him down.

They locked for a moment, then both softened.

"I'm waiting..."

"*I'm* waiting..."

"We need a chairperson."

"We need an ambulance."

"Speaking of ambulance...it's been a long time since Embarcadero, Lee."

"I knew it. I *knew* you were going to bring that up." She shook her head, reached for her drink, took a sip. "Well, okay Stan, let's have it out." She propped herself higher in the pillows and tucked the sheet under her arms. "You mind if I don't get

36

up? It was a long hard night...*and* morning. I'm going to need a nap after we finish with this. Aren't you tired?"

"Yeah...I'm tired." He wished he was the one lying down now.

"You want to come over here?" She patted the bed.

"No."

"Suit yourself. Okay"—she shifted her eyes to the wall—"Okay, Embarcadero. You want to start? Why don't you start?"

"Thank you madame, chairperson, the Stanley from California appreciates that." He turned and moved back to the window, needing the distraction of the city as he launched into these waters. He'd been waiting almost five years to say what he was now about to say. And now it had to be good. He decided on an oblique approach. Claire's style.

"Did Claire really tell you that you were pushing the estrangement thing past the point of credibility? She was at least *part* of the reason you came down to Genoa Gallery last night?"

"Yes, Stan. And yes, you were right, I was going crazy with this seaman business, and it had become pathological fast. And I needed to get out of town just as fast to figure out what I was going to do. So...when I heard you were planning a trip down here to New Orleans to pick up some clay, well...you know me... little kill-two-birds-with-one-stone Lee Ann."

He laughed. Oh, she was right about that. He'd watched her on more than one occassion take two mating pigeons out with one well-placed glance shot from her sling.

"I always thought that was cruel when you'd shoot those pigeons when they were fucking."

She looked over at him. "Yeah...and how many times did I have to tell you it was a lovely way for them to die. And besides, who liked pigeon pie more than anything in the world? YOU!"

"Guilty as charged." He sighed and moved back on track. "Why should Claire care if we get back together or not? She certainly hasn't done anything in the past to promote our reconciliation. Why now...what's she got to gain?"

"Why don't you ask her that yourself."

"I just might do that...but now I'm asking *you*. Any theories?"

"Doesn't even have to be a theory. She's told me flat out that she's tired of refereeing our pain about it. Our estrangement, I mean." She paused. "And she thought I was carrying it...our *alienation*...to the point that it would soon seem like bathos. You know, pathos that has tripped over the line and become comedy?"

"So what do *you* think?"

"I told you. I think she's right...was right...so here I am." She patted the bed one time with the palms of both hands.

"In all your birthday glory." He shook his head. "You know, I know you live in the fast lane, Lee, and you have to segue between an axe murderer and Bozo the Clown. But, Lee, I'm a transition man...I need little periods of time to adjust to the fact that one minute I'm cancer and the next minute I'm the lottery. Know what I mean?"

She'd grown attentive. A rare moment of listening, he thought. Finally she answered.

"I know, Stan...I know. What can I say here? I'm sorry? I don't feel like saying I'm sorry. I had my reasons for going away when I did." She looked away. He waited. She continued.

"After being run down on the Embarcadero, not only was my spirit broken, so was my body. I was at wits end with you. Nothing I said or did seemed to get through to you."

He stood with head bowed. "We're talking about Claire here, of course."

"Yes...we're talking about Claire here."

He leapt in. "The girl was running wild! You were mollycoddling her! I was telling her the way it was. That she was ruining her life at an early age. That she would regret it. You know...it had to be like, good-cop mom...bad-cop dad."

"Except it wasn't working...was it, Stan? *We* weren't working. And Claire was going down fast. And we were panicking. Would you say that was a fair assessment of the situation?"

"Yes."

There was a long silence between them as both tuned in to the bustle down on the street. A woman was singing "Stormy

Monday" in a rich black contralto. Her voice pushed up on the early afternoon humidity like a mushroom popping through humus. Stanley walked over to the bed, took Lee Ann's hand in his. "I missed you, Lee," he said softly.

She swallowed hard and looked up at him. "I missed you too Stan...I did." She shut her eyes. He bent down and kissed her on the forehead, then turned and walked back to the middle of the room.

"Lee?"

"Yes?"

"Can we decide something about the sleeping accommodations... right here and now? Because the ambiguity of our situation here is making me feel more than a little uncomfortable. In more ways than one."

"I know...we've...well...*I've* been doing some flirting, haven't I?"

"Have I?" he asked.

"No...not really. You've been really..."

"Nice?"

She laughed huskily. "Mmmhuh...very nice."

"So...you're a flirt. You've always been a flirt. I suppose you just can't help it. I mean you're so good at it that you can't help wanting to do it. Right?"

"Stanley." She looked off to the side.

"So...we going to do it? Or are we going to decide right here and now that we are a little fresh out of the starting gate? Might be good to just cool the jets a bit, get a room with separate beds. Or maybe even separate rooms?"

She considered it for a moment, "Separate beds yes, but do you really think we need to go to separate rooms? That's no fun. I've bunked in the same room with guys on location lots of times. I *do* know how to behave, Stanley. I'm a big girl."

"You can say that again." He walked over to the phone, picked it up, and waited for the desk to come on.

"Uh, hello, this is Stanley Hochstetter in room 201. I was wondering if you might have a room available, similar to this one, on the street side, with twin beds? Our room has only a queen sized bed and we're both restless sleepers..." Pause.

"Hmm...well...all right...if anything opens up, could you please let us know? Thank you." He replaced the receiver in its cradle.

"Okay...so much for that plan. She said that it was Jazz Festival Weekend and it was only due to a late cancellation that we were able to get this room. The Quarter's booked. So...that's that. We're going to be sleeping in the same bed, I guess. Or...we could take turns on the floor."

"Stanley, would you please come over here and sit down? I have something I need to tell you, and I don't want to shout. Please."

Tall French doors led out of their room onto a broad wooden deck. As Stanley was relating the details of his unproductive conversation with the desk clerk, he'd wandered out to the railing to see if he could catch a glimpse of the singer down on the street who was now offering up some improvisations on "Stormy Monday." No, he couldn't see her; she was somewhere out of sight. So he made his way back into the room and sat down at the foot of the bed. Lee used his brief absence to put on her blouse. She sat leaning forward now, her eyes fixing on him flatly. "Okay...okay," she began, "*I'm* going to behave...and *you're* going to behave. We're not going to flirt. We *are* going to be sleeping in the same bed, because I know neither one of us is going to be bedrolling on the floor. Right?"

"Right."

"Right. So...what I need now is a little friendly hug of truce, and then as long a nap as we can salvage from the time that's left. What time is it?"

"Going on one pm." He moved up the length of the bed into her waiting arms. They held each other for a moment.

"At Poteet's by five-thirty? How long does it take?"

"Looks to be about forty-five minutes on the map, barring traffic."

"Forty-five minutes plus another forty-five minutes to dress and be out of here. That puts us at four pm blast off time, and out of the hotel at four forty-five pm. Three hours of blessed sleep. Oh God, Stanley...I need it."

"I know you do babe. Me too." They rubbed each other's backs for a moment and then mutually released and moved back to shake and close the deal.

Then Stanley moved off to change into some light cotton sweats. Lee Ann grabbed hers off the back of a chair sitting beside the bed and pulled them on. He kept his back to her as she did this. They were entering the polite mode now—a combined (but silent) sigh of relief from each. They were dog tired, needed a nap, and needed now to be free of the sexual jeopardy that had been brewing between them from the moment Lee Ann had entered Genoa Gallery the previous evening. He moved back over to the bed and laid down facing friend Lee. Her eyes were already secreted away behind closed lids.

"What're you looking at, Stan?" She whispered without opening them.

"A monkey."

"Monkey, huh?"

"Yeah, monkey."

"Tired?"

"Yeah...exhausted."

"Feels good, huh?"

"Mmm."

They felt themselves drifting off.

So we'll drift off too, across the street from Le Richelieu, to hover and peer into the window of an apartment building where a young lad is sitting on the side of his bed, chewing his fingernails, and studying his now silent saxophone, wondering if he'll ever be able to play "Mood Indigo" before his solo recital on Monday.

And there below, down on Chartre Street, a homeless woman, dressed in layers of rags, is picking up her beggar's cup of change, packing up her "Stormy Monday," and making her way down the sidewalk to find another corner where she'll sing the blues to a new crowd of passing tourists.

Or maybe we should gain some real altitude and drift much higher above, up to a place where we can see Crescent City stretching off to a humid horizon—a silver slash of river curling through its core.

New Orleans...the land of dreams...

Stanley dreamed his favorite dream again. And yet another variation on the theme of his first time with Lee Ann, up in the hayloft of the barn, back home in Colorado, a lifetime ago.

But now he felt himself surfacing, swimming upward out of his sleep, all was sanguine behind closed lids. He opened his eyes only to find them blinded by a shaft of light that fell through the fenestrations of the high French doors. He rolled over and saw that Lee Ann was lying on her side, facing away from him, still asleep.

She rolled over, face up, still deep in slumber. Very carefully, without rocking the bed, he moved his head to shield her eyes from the brilliance behind him. She was perspiring; a fine mist seemed to lift around her face. A mist rising like a halo.

She opened her eyes slowly, drowsily. This time, seeing Stanley's face above her didn't seem to rattle her china. She smiled sleepily. "Hi."

"Hi."

"Who are you?"

"My name is Stanley. I'm your ex-husband."

"Oh...right." Another smile. "What time is it?"

He glanced at his watch, "three forty-five."

"Fifteen minutes before we have to get up, Stan. Man my whole body feels like I've been marathon bungee jumping."

He smiled at her fresh description of post shock syndrome.

Lee's cell warbled.

6.

It was Jackie in Toronto saying that Claire was in jail, being held on suspicion of art smuggling. Lee Ann took the call. She wasn't too happy about it. Wasn't too happy about the fact that Stanley hadn't told her that Jackie had returned her call. He had to level and tell her that he'd forgotten to give her the message, the one still ticking away in his trouser pocket. He had been right; there had been a bomb lurking in that slip of paper the desk clerk had handed him. And also right that it'd been waiting to go off and blow their little dream cruise out of the water. Claire. What's new?

They showered, donned evening dress, and took the lift to the lobby. Highly disgruntled, Stanley wandered off to the bar while Lee Ann talked with the desk clerk, probably something further to do with Claire. He really didn't care. Lisa Lynn was still behind the bar. He stood for a moment watching her as she moved efficiently here and there, watering down the patrons. Lee Ann joined him; they emerged from Le Richelieu at 5:15, and moved to their rental car, a blue Mustang convertible.

"We're going to be late by about a half hour. We said we needed to leave by four forty-five to make it to Poteet's by five-thirty."

"You want to drive? I'll navigate."

"Good idea."

Lee Ann swung behind the wheel, and he took up his position shotgun on her right. She fired the engine of the small car and did a couple of wheelies out of the parking lot.

"Okay, give it to me, navigator."

"First, I'd say...reduce your altitude."

"Oh right...no New Orleans moving violations, huh?"

"Huh," he agreed. "Okay take a right up here at Chartre and then a quick left onto Esplanade. Head north until I tell you to turn."

"Okay." She made a civilly obedient but crisp right onto Chartre, then left onto the tree-lined Esplanade as instructed— kept her speed five miles over the limit until he called right again.

She wheeled it right and they kept on going.

"This place is pretty far out on the bayou," he said.

"You said forty-five minutes; how could you know that?"

"Map reading 101. And I have been to New Orleans before you know." He glanced over at an intent Lee Ann and saw she was apprehensive. "You know, if it looks like we're not going to make it, we'll just call. No problem."

Silence from the driver. Lee Ann was considering. Well, he was right—they could just call. It wasn't like you had cameras and sound crews and guests waiting. In the telecasting business, you had to be on time. No room for sluff, either in the big sense or the small. You had to be there and hit your cue. Could he know this? Probably not. His world was a stop-action land of formulation in clay. There really was no clock running when you were pulling forms from the mud.

A storm was brewing to the southwest. White cumulus clouds rose in round towers against a stormy black panther creeping in from the Gulf. The Mustang plunged headlong into its claws. Lee flipped on the headlights.

"Does that thing look as nasty to you Ms. Weatherwoman as it does to me?" Stanley was fidgeting in his seat.

"Ain't no little spritzer; good thang the top's up."

He heard Lee Ann now, back out on the highway, trucking with her daddy Sherman from the Blue Ridge Mountains of Tennessee.

"Okay," he said, "you'll just keep going on this road for another ten miles before we need to make another move. Steady as she goes."

She nodded, yes, as they entered the storm. Sheets of rain pummeled the car.

"Yikes!" she shouted over the roar of the rain on the vinyl top, "I'm thinkin', I'm puttin' in to the first place we come to. I cain't see sheeeit."

The glare of oncoming headlights was cutting visibility nearly to zero. And now a series of potholes in the road, sent the Mustang bouncing hysterically this way and that on its rental car shocks. Lee Ann was in her usual form—dealing with it. Stanley was in his usual form, uttering such supplications as "Jeeesus!" and "Muuuther!"

A blur of blue neon appeared out of the downpour a short distance ahead. Lee Ann had the car going in the direction she wanted it to go now, so she swung it into a roadhouse parking lot, shut off the engine, and flopped back against the headrest. Her breathing sounded short to Stanley, or was that his? He followed suit and sank back into the cushions. They sat for a moment in silence, letting their pulses slow, listening to the rain drum on the roof of the car.

"You know, Stan, I may have to leave for Toronto tomorrow. Claire's in a heap of trouble. Someone's got to be there for her."

"She's got Jackie, doesn't she?"

"Well, of course..."

She fell silent, wondering if he knew yet how close Claire and Jackie were now. A closeness that she was still having to adjust to. Claire and Jackie were lovers. She studied him for a moment. No, he didn't know, otherwise he would have discussed it with her by now. She went on. "Yeah...I'm sure Jackie is there for her; it's just that Jackie is her roommate, and I'm her mother. You know I'm right, Stan." She was testing the waters, watched him closely...no, he didn't know.

"Yeah, Lee Ann, I know you're right, but can we talk about it later? I just want to enjoy this evening without Claire continually coming up. Then tomorrow we'll talk about it. Maybe there'll be some new developments by then."

"Mmm..." said Lee Ann, lost in her own battle plan, "want to check this place out while we're waiting for this rain to let up?"

"Uh, sure...ready?"

She grabbed her handbag. "Ready."

"Go," said Stanley.

They jumped out of the car in unison, made a dash across a flooded parking lot, and pushed through the roadhouse doors. Silence now, except for the sound of rain drumming on a metal roof.

They stood in the tile entryway drip-drying and looking around. Nothing about the outside of the Inn spoke to what they found inside. The decor was more like the living room of a rustic hunting lodge than that of a restaurant. A mammoth limestone fireplace with tiers of candles flickering in its gaping black mouth was central to the room. Grouped around its hearth were three overstuffed leather couches and beyond these, tables set with flowers and candles. A room arranged to feed fifteen or so families.

A short, matronly woman with dark hair and Indian skin appeared out of nowhere. "Good evening...could I show you to a table?" she asked. Her voice was a low contralto—her tone flat but cordial.

Lee Ann jumped a foot and turned to face the voice greeting her. "Oh"—she caught her breath—"actually we're just a couple of cats climbing on your roof to get out of the flood."

The woman smiled and nodded.

"What do you think, Stan? Some bread and water while we wait for this thing to blow over?"

He nodded yes.

"To be sure," said the woman as she turned and led them to the couches by the fireplace.

"Any idea how long this thing is going to last?" Stanley asked.

"Be a short storm, followed by clear skies into the evening. I consulted my crystal ball. That would be the satellite map on TV," the innkeeper intoned with dark intrigue. But as she spoke the words "...on TV," she broke into large, loud black laughter. Lee Ann smiled; weather was something she knew about. Stanley joined the hostess in good-natured laughter, ordered rhubarb juice and some bread, inquired about the use of a telephone, and watched their hostess as she moved off to fetch the fare.

"Stanley, why don't you use your cell?"

Stanley stood dumbfounded, staring at Lee Ann.. Really? She hadn't noticed that he still didn't have a cell phone? Until now?

"I don't have a cell phone, Lee Ann."

"You don't......"

"No, I don't have a cell phone yet."

Lee Ann took pity and quietly held hers out to him.

"No, I like pay phones. I know how to use them."

She waved him off. She was impatiently awaiting this intriguing host of theirs. Some amazing bloodlines there.

Stanley made his way over to a pay phone alcove, consulted a card in his wallet for Poteet's number, and very shortly had a late-working secretary on the line—or so he thought.

"Poteet Porcelain, may I help you?"

"Yes, this is Stanley Hochstetter. Mr. Poteet was expecting us for an early evening dinner engagement...?"

"Yes?" came the soft-spoken voice on the other end of the line.

He continued. "My friend Ms. Barnes and I are being delayed by the storm, but we're not over fifteen minutes from you, and we'll be on our way again as soon as the rain breaks. Could you relay this information to Mr. Poteet please?"

"Ah, Mr. Hochstetter, Stanley Hochstetter, the ceramic artist from San Francisco?" The voice on the other end of the line had shaded from polite official to warm and friendly—with a gild of excitement and anticipation.

"The same," he said.

"Mr. Hochstetter, this is Melissa Frank, a friend and associate of Mr. Poteet's. I'll be joining you for dinner this evening. I'm looking forward to meeting you. Jean Paul's shown me the photos of your work; I love it!"

So pleasant being known, thought Stanley. He was enjoying the reception he was receiving on the other end of the line. Not just the reception but the feeling in the voice behind it; these southerners could be charming. "Well..." he resumed, "thank you, and I'm looking forward to meeting you. We shouldn't be more than half an hour. And please... call me Stanley."

"Of course. I'll tell Jean Paul you're soon to arrive. Actually he was tied up with some business and asked that I greet you until he could join us. So... everything is working out fine Stanley." Melissa Frank didn't have to say his name, but she did, with a subtle but distinct southern drawl.

"Great, we'll see you shortly then Melissa...Ciao."

"Shortly then, goodbye."

Yes, thought Stanley, he was looking forward to meeting Melissa Frank. He returned to the dining room to find Lee Ann and their Creole hostess sitting face-to-face on one of the couches near the fireplace. The woman was holding Lee Ann's hand palm up, studying it. He watched them for a moment before closing ranks—they were obviously enjoying their exchange. Lee Ann saw him coming.

"Stanley! Meet Claire Leveau. Claire, Stanley." Claire offered her hand. Stanley took it, shook it, and noted its warmth.

"Pleasure to meet you, Claire Leveau. We have a daughter named Claire. I'm sure Lee's told you."

"Ayee, she did indeed, and I hear that you are a famous artist Monsieur Stanley!"

"Whoa! Lee Ann, you been exaggerating again?" He threw her a lopsided grin.

"Ah, yes," Claire went on, "she has been describing your work to me, and it sounds as though you are a magician with the earth you mold."

"Hmm...well, people seem to like what I'm doing at the moment. And I like the things I'm doing at the moment. So...a brief moment of success. Not sure about the famous part though. Lee, I'm going to look outside, see what's happening."

He grabbed a piece of bread and a glass of juice and made his way to the door. The two women went back to what they were discussing before he'd rejoined them.

Outside the rain had subsided to a soft drizzle. The air was fresh and light, scrubbed by a Gulf breeze, a welcome relief from this afternoon's oppressive humidity. Some early diners passed him on their way into the Inn as Lee Ann came through the door heading in the other direction. "Ready to go?" she asked.

"Yeah"—he downed the last of his juice—"I'll just return this glass and say goodbye to Claire."

The innkeeper was busy with her newly arrived patrons, but he caught her eye as he set his glass on a ledge inside the door. "We'll come for dinner; nice meeting you."

She smiled and nodded. "Yes! Please do...soon!"

Lee Ann was standing in the middle of the parking lot looking up at the sky when he rejoined her. "Fascinating woman," she said softly. "Wait till you hear about her lineage...and her sister Jahna who lives in New Orleans...a voodoo woman! Claire gave me her address, said we should go for a reading."

Stanley took her arm. They moved off in the direction of the car.

"This is such a different place, isn't it, Stan? These people have such a rich heritage. You know what I mean?" She didn't wait for him to answer. "Claire is African, French, Irish and Choctaw Indian! How's that for a bloodmix?"

"Well...it's common down here, Lee. New Orleans is a melting pot of melting pots, ethnically speaking."

"I've got to figure out how to get some of them on the show."

"You've always got to figure out how to get some of *them* on the show, Lee."

She smiled over the top of the car as she opened the door. "Yeah...I suppose I do."

The rain had stopped completely now, so they put the top down and continued on their way. "I love the side roads that life sometimes sends you down, don't you, Stan?"

He considered it a moment. "You know, sometimes I think my whole life has been spent over here on the side roads.. and you know what, Lee? I really don't care if I ever get to the freeway." He shook his head at what he'd just said. "Although...

lately it seems I've been spending a lot time out on the old four-laner."

"You mean with the new found fame and all?"

"Yeah, the new found fame." He looked over at her. She kept her eyes on the road. "And don't go telling people I'm famous, okay? It's not true, and I get embarrassed."

"Oh *kay*, Stan, I *won't*." She looked over at him. "But it's fun. Why can't you just have fun with it?"

"I am, Lee...at my own pace."

"Mmm."

"Hey, you want to hear the rest of the Lafitte story before we join his great-great-great grandson?"

"Yeah, sure. I almost forgot about that. Can you get it all in before we get there?"

"I'll talk fast." He took a breath. "Let's see, where were we?"

"Lafitte had just kicked the British army's butt, I think, is where you left off."

"Right...okay..." And Stanley was off and running. He told her that after the war Lafitte had settled in New Orleans and lived the life of a military hero. But it wasn't long before he tired of this and went back to sea. Soon he'd pirated enough ships to put together a fleet of his own, but now he was a wanted man again, so he sailed over to Texas and settled on an island off the coast of what is today Galveston. On that island he built a royal compound he called Maison Rouge, and a surrounding village housing his men and their wives and women and children.

"The womenfolk, right, Stan?"

"You got it. Anyway...life and the pirating business were good for a number of years. But soon he'd made too many enemies for his own good. Those he'd plundered had had enough, so they put together an armada and went to clean out the den Lafitte called Maison Rouge."

"Pressed his luck a little too far?"

"I guess so. But listen to this! Lafitte's spies got word of the impending invasion and notified their leader. Lafitte flew into a rage and ordered his entire settlement burned to the ground. He also ordered all but several ships to be burned. So when the armada arrived, they found little but smoldering ruins. And Jean Lafitte was never heard from again..."

"Really?"

"Really. Some historians say he fled to Central America, or even farther south to South America, but there really is no official record of his operations subsequent to the conflagration of Maison Rouge. End of story. How'd I do? Brief and to the point?"

"Great job, as usual Stan. Jeez, what a guy." She glanced over at him. "And so how does Mr. Poteet trace his lineage back to a man who lived so far outside the law? Does he have papers?"

"You'll have to ask him that yourself, Lee. And I'd say it could be soon. We're here."

They had been paralleling a low stone fence for a quarter mile or so and were now approaching a gatehouse. "That's it. Pull in and stop. We'll need to talk to the troll."

After a brief exchange with the pleasant woman on duty, they were on their way again up a narrow asphalt road vaulted by arching cypress trees. The moss-hung trees followed the lane around several sweeping curves, and suddenly there it was, an antebellum southern mansion, complete with high Doric columns enclosing a broad front portico. It was shortly before sundown, but with dark clouds still trailing the storm, the light had grown frail. The mansion seemed to glow from within, welcoming them.

"Wow, Stanley," Lee Ann whispered, "you really know how to take a girl to dinner." She pulled into a paved area at one side of the colonnade and parked beside a lime-green Bentley. Engine off, they sat for a moment settling in. Stanley had seen the pictures of this estate that Jean Paul had sent him during their short time of corresponding—and he had shown them to Lee Ann—but neither of them was prepared for the historic grandeur they knew they were about to experience. Lee Ann took a compact from her purse, turned to her navigator, and said flatly, "Want to kiss me before I freshen up this war paint? We gotta look good kemo sabe."

"Sure...give me a peck." He puckered his lips like a fish, she pursed hers; they touched ever so gently and moved back laughing conspiritorially..

"Last time we get to act silly for the next few hours, huh?"

"That's right, so paste on that TV cohost smile of yours, and lets rock and roll."

She obliged with a wide-but-not-too-wide, bright-but-not-too-bright smile, and said without moving her lips, "How's this?"

"You're good."

A short walk down the portico found them standing before some ten-foot-high coffered doors that stood open to sweet evening breezes. Lee Ann pushed the doorbell. They stood peering inside.

A spacious oval entry hall containing an obligatory curved white staircase and perfectly centered chandelier met their gaze. Suddenly a woman appeared from a side hall and walked to greet them.

"How are you? Stanley and Ms. Barnes, I presume? I'm Melissa Frank."

Lee Ann was closest and held out her hand. "Lee Ann, please, call me Lee Ann. Pleased to meet you, Melissa."

The woman, smiling and nodding, shook Lee Ann's hand and then shifted her eyes to Stanley and extended her hand palm down, as if to be kissed. Stanley surprised himself by taking her hand in his and raising it lightly to his lips. "Yes," he said quietly, "Stanley Hochstetter, pleasure to meet you in person, Melissa."

Melissa, a woman in her late thirties but with much older eyes, smiled slightly and drew her hand back slowly from his kiss. She was statuesque with Spanish black hair and smooth bronze skin. She showed not the slightest trace of surprise at his greeting. No little relief for Stanley, as he couldn't remember ever having kissed a woman's hand upon meeting her. For Melissa, Stanley thought, this was standard procedure. And this told him she was a woman who traveled in circles higher and wider than he ever would. He was immediately intrigued by Melissa Frank, was looking forward to knowing her better. Lee Ann sensed something was brewing already between these two. And to her absolute horror, she felt the ugly green dragon of jealousy leap from the baseboards and nip her sharply on the heel.

Melissa said, "Come...let's pass this time in the library. Jean Paul will be joining us soon, I'm sure." She turned and led them through another set of double doors under the upper landing of the circular stairs. They entered a spacious book lined room complete with hearth and a blazing fire.

"A little cold front's trailing the storm...it often does. I like that...it means we can enjoy a late season fire. I love fires, don't you?" Melissa turned, spoke softly, addressing both of her guests in a gracious manner.

"I guess we're lucky out in San Francisco," Lee Ann began. "We can enjoy a fire in the fireplace year round." She paused, listening to the log crackling beyond the hearth. "You know that statement Mark Twain made about San Francisco's summers? 'The coldest winter I ever spent was a summer in San Francisco.'"

Melissa had busied herself for a moment tending the small blaze. She looked up in surprise and amusement. "No." She smiled, "I hadn't heard that one. Thank you, I'm a big fan of Mr. Twain. Yes, I know what he meant. I also spent a cold summer in your city. I loved it, wearing woolens in the summer...so chic." The southern accent gently rounding all of Melissa's syllables mesmerized Stanley. He would have to ask Melissa Frank to come sit by his bed and read the New Orleans telephone directory to him—maybe even Proust. She went on.

"As I said, I think Jean Paul will be with us shortly. He's very busy at the moment...many projects culminating all at once. And, of course, he has to keep the foundry on schedule. Time's precious. But he's so fond of your work, Stanley! So looking forward to working with you as you explore this new clay we've formulated. I've worked with it some already and I can assure you that it is delicate and responsive...but very tolerant in the kiln." She paused, seemingly out of breath.

"I'm looking forward to it." Stanley could sense her excitement.

"Would you care for some sherry? We just received a case of very fine private reserve from your California. I've been dying to sample it. Sherry by the fire, my favorite...oh well, I'm talking too much, aren't I?" She turned and moved to a small corner wall bar. The two guests agreed that sherry by the fire would be just the thing, and a party of three settled into some deep leather cushions to watch the flames and await the arrival of Jean Paul Poteet.

"So..." Stanley began, "you've worked with the clay? I trust we're going to get a peek at your projects?" He looked directly at her and thought he saw a blush beneath her burnished skin.

"If you like. After dinner we'll take a tour of the foundry, and I'll show you my little pets." She smiled. "But don't expect thunder and lightning; I'm much more of a traditionalist when it comes to my subject matter and style than you Stanley. I'm currently doing genteel little figurine scenes of pre-Civil War plantation life. But you! You and your savage mythology. The rage you pull from clay astounds me."

"I hope you see the humor too. That's part of what I'm going for right now."

"Yes...a nice balance to be sure. Mad mythology with a measure of mirth. It works. Don't you think?" She addressed Lee Ann.

"Never ceases to amaze me," agreed Lee Ann smiling warmly at the artist.

"And you said your newly formulated compound is very tolerant in the kiln, as far as large masses go?" Stanley was weary now of being the center of attention.

"You won't believe the forgiveness of this clay. Well...really it's more a porcelain, you know. We've fired some rather large free-built urns and not a crack or a spall in the lot. It's amazing."

Sitting beside Stanley, Lee Ann could hear the conversation drifting off to shop talk. She didn't mind, always found conversations between artists some of the most stimulating.

And she could see the chemistry between Melissa and Stanley bubbling along nicely. She'd recovered from her initial bout with the green dragon and had settled in to watch the action. After all, what right did she have to be jealous? But there had been that moment, and she couldn't deny it. Best just be amused that she could still feel this way for old Stan. Tuning in to the conversation, and knowing she would need to interject something soon just to keep the flow going, she indulged herself a moment of scrutinizing the library walls. There were books, of course, and some very fine oil portraits. And here and there, tastefully spaced and lighted, were trophy heads of several large African mammals: a water buffalo, a cheetah, a wildebeest. She wondered who had murdered these—hoped it hadn't been Poteet. Suddenly her eyes fixed on a series of three red lights blinking above what appeared to be a set of sliding wood panels. Before she could ascertain what mystery this arrangement might hold, the third light in the series lit solidly and the panels parted in the middle to reveal a small, well-lighted cubicle containing the figure of a man in a wheelchair. He appeared as a dark figure against a brightly lit background. Stanley and Melissa, still engrossed in their conversation, hadn't noted his arrival. The man wheeled his chair from what Lee Ann could now see was a domestic elevator, and silently crossed the room to join them by the fire. Melissa and Stanley now noticed him at the same tiime and broke off talking—midsentence. She could see his face now. There was no mistaking who it was.

All three rose to their feet to greet, Jean Paul Poteet.

"No need to get up," Poteet chimed jovially. "You all look so comfortable there by the fire, and I come rolling in here and interrupt such camaraderie? What nerve!"

"Jean Paul." Melissa smiled warmly, moved to his side, and kissed him lightly on the forehead. "I know you know Stanley Hochstetter from your correspondence with him, and this is his..." She paused, searching for a term. Lee Ann came to her rescue.

"Good friend and traveling companion."

Melissa nodded to her guest. "Yes...Lee Ann Barnes."

Poteet looked from one to the other nodding to each as they crossed the distance to his chair. Stanley reached his chair first, so Jean Paul took his outstretched hand and pumped it firmly. "So good to finally meet you, genius," he said straightaway to Stanley. Then he swung his eyes around to engage Lee Ann's.

"He is a genius, don't you think, Lee Ann?"

Lee Ann, for some reason unbeknownst even to her, presented *her* hand, palm down, to Poteet. "Yes I do...pleasure to meet you, Mr. Poteet."

Poteet took her hand gently for a moment and fixed her with his gaze.

"Well, that's not going to work, is it? I call you Lee Ann and you call me Mr. Poteet? I believe Jean Paul would be fair." A mischievous light came into his caramel brown eyes. He kissed her hand and released it. She blushed and had to exercise no little restraint in drawing her freshly kissed mitt back as slowly as Melissa had. She could see how you could get into this hand-kissing business, but then again, it sort of gave her a gooey feeling inside. She was a western girl, but she could learn.

"Jean Paul it is," she said matter-of-factly.

"We're sampling the sherry that arrived last week from California," said Melissa, addressing the debonair man in the wheelchair. "Would you care for a glass? It's a trifle sweet, but woody the way you like it."

"Yes, wouldn't want to be sitting out any rounds of that, Lissa, my dear."

Melissa moved off to the corner bar and returned with a tray, another glass, and a crystal decanter. Jean Paul, not one to leave an awkward silence in the ebb and flow of conversation, had addressed Stanley. "So, sir, I know a bit about you, but how is it that you find yourself in the company of this charming and beautiful television personality, Ms. Barnes?" He smiled warmly at Lee Ann who looked up sharply. How had he known that?

Stanley, also surprised, kept it to himself. "Hmm, let's see, would you like me to start when we were kids playing in a hayloft back in Colorado?"

"Start wherever you like. We have all evening." Jean Paul's tone was jovial. He sounded truly intrigued by what he was about to hear.

"You want to do the honors of our bio?" Stanley turned to Lee Ann, then to Jean Paul. "She's much better at summation than me."

Lee Ann hit her cue running. "Childhood playmates, lovers, husband and wife, parents...and now just friends. That's pretty much it in a nutshell."

That's new, thought Stanley. He'd never heard that wrap-up before, and it was definitely brief and to the point. She certainly had her host's attention.

"But now for the details." She continued on. "It's true, I grew up with this guy here...was raised by his mom and dad on a ranch outside of Glenwood Springs in Colorado. My mom died shortly after I was born and my daddy drove a semi and didn't think the cab of a Peterbilt was any place to raise a daughter...bless his heart. I went trucking with daddy Sherman in the summertime, but wintertime I lived with Stan, here, and his family, and, well, we grew up like brother and sister."

"You traveled in a truck all summer with your father? Did you drive it?" Melissa seemed excited and didn't let Lee Ann answer. "I've *always* wanted to drive one of those big rigs, but Jean Paul won't give me the keys...will you, dear?" She smiled over at him. He smiled back.

"Come, Melissa, they don't want to hear our domestic squabbles." He turned to Lee Ann. "You see we have a fleet of our own trucks down at the foundry. Melissa keeps threatening to run away with one, so we keep the keys in the safe. Melissa," he looked back at her, "you've shamed me into it. Tomorrow I'll have Henry give you a first lesson."

Melissa's eyes sparkled for a moment and then fell back behind sleepy southern lids. Her smile warmed as she sipped her sherry.

"I'm sorry, Lee Ann, we interrupted your story. Please, go on." Jean Paul spoke over the rim of his glass.

"All right," she paused, "or do you want to do it Stanley? You take it."

Stanley pulled himself up. "Okay..." He also sipped for a moment collecting his thoughts and then went on. "So...one spring just before Lee Ann graduated from high school, we...for some reason...fell madly and passionately in love, made a baby, and ran away to San Francisco."

"With the baby?" Melissa asked.

"In here," said Lee Ann, patting her stomach.

"You were pregnant and you ran away to San Francisco? What year was that?" Jean Paul felt a need to place this story in time.

"Summer of seventy-eight, in the Haight....with all the druggies."

"Fascinating." Poteet leaned forward in his chair.

"We lived a little too hard and too poor, and we lost the baby." He paused. "But several weeks after that we found an infant lying in a wicker laundry basket under a eucalyptus tree down in Golden Gate Park. There seemed to be no one looking after him, so we took him home."

Laughter and amazement from Jean Paul and Melissa. He had them.

"Well, not right away, mind you. We stayed with him for an hour, then two hours, then Lee Ann went back to our place and got some blankets and a thermos of coffee. Night was falling. It can get pretty cold in Golden Gate Park after sundown with the fog rolling in."

"And still no one had come?" Melissa asked.

"No, no one came all that night and not in the morning and not into the next afternoon. No one came."

"So you took him home, notified the authorities, and turned him in?" asked Jean Paul.

"No, we just took him home and raised him for five years... called him Bird, in honor of Charlie Parker, the jazz sax genius, and the fact that he just flew into our lives."

Lee Ann was squirming in her seat.

"Yes?" Stanley asked.

"Well...it was extremely hard on us losing our baby. Even though it was hardly there yet, it was there for us, so when we found Bird, we felt that some divine providence had sent him our way. We really did, and we were just hippie kids. We left a note on the tree with our telephone number and a message that said something like 'If you've lost something here and want it back, call this number and tell us what it is, and we'll give it back to you.' We got a couple of crank calls, but no one claimed Bird."

Stanley nodded.

"What a lovely story," mused Melissa. "And you say you raised him for five years? Oh, I'm almost afraid to ask. What happened then? You were found out? His parents showed up?"

"No..." said Lee Ann in a barely audible voice, "he was abducted."

"Pardon me?" Jean Paul, now leaning even further forward in his chair, strained to hear.

Stanley continued. "Lee Ann was bringing him home from preschool one afternoon and stopped at the store to pick up some things for dinner. Bird walked around the corner to an adjoining aisle...and never came back."

"Holy Mother of Jesus." Jean Paul registered genuine shock. "What did you do?"

Melissa's eyes narrowed.

"What could we do?" Stanley continued. "We couldn't report it to the authorities, having acquired Bird as we did. We lived with the pain."

There was a moment of silence in tribute to every parent's worst nightmare.

"But then I got pregnant again, right away, and Claire, our daughter, was born in 1984. She'll be twenty-one in a few days, lives in Toronto. But...we never really did get over losing Bird, did we Stan?" She looked over at him. He looked up, met her sad eyes.

"Not something you *would* ever get over," Jean Paul said softly.

"Well...so...we seem to be monopolizing the conversation with our little tragedy. How about you two? How long have you known each other?" For Stanley, it was high time to shift focus.

Melissa deferred to Jean Paul. He took the oblique approach. "Well...I think forever, don't you, my dear?"

"Yes, Jean Paul," she returned, steady eyes looking into his, "sometimes I feel it has been forever, but"—she turned to her guest—"it has been actually fifteen years. We have two daughters together, Jacquel and Stella. They're presently in Rio de Janeiro for two weeks visiting their grandmother...my mother."

Lee Ann looked over at Jean Paul and saw the muscles along his jawline rippling as they will in the face of a man who is suppressing some kind of what? Rage? A storm had blown into his light brown eyes rendering them dark and menacing. What was this? Stanley saw it too.

"I suppose we're all wondering at this time why, being two couples who share children, we all have different last names?"

Way to go, Lee Ann, thought Stanley. A cut to the chase girl if there ever was one. Everyone looked at one another a bit sheepishly—including Jean Paul. Good, thought Lee Ann. She didn't like those ugly little ripples along his jaw, but she did make a mental note to find out what was causing them.

"Okay, since I brought it up...I'll tell first," she offered. "Stanley and I are divorced. We split when Claire was eight. I went to weatherschool and started my career in telecasting... as you know Jean Paul." She lobbed a sly smile of her own in his direction. He nodded. She went on. "Stanley and I have... *had* Claire to raise. We decided right from the beginning to do as good a job as possible. And now that that's basically done, sometimes we are in each other's life more than others. Huh, Stan?"

"You could say that, Lee." He glanced at her, and then turned to his host and hostess. "How about you two?"

Melissa nodded to Jean Paul.

"Melissa and I were married for five years during the time Stella and Jacquel were born. But then we separated, and she

60

took the girls back to Rio." He sipped shortly from his glass... went on. "As you did, we decided that it would be best for them to have two active parents. So Melissa moved back here. We have re-established our,"—he searched for a term, finally found one—"friendship...and will take our combined parental duties through our daughters' graduation from high school." He looked over at her. "Did I explain that correctly, my dear?"

"Quite," said Melissa crisply and stood to pour another round of sherry.

"Oh, not for me," Lee Ann declined. "I'm feeling a bit light headed here...better save up for dinner. You know," she turned to Jean Paul, "what I really want to know right now is...how did you know I was..."

"A television personality on KPIQ in San Francisco?"

"Yes, how did you know that?"

It was a smile Lee Ann would see often in the future, Jean Paul's parody of sinister amusement. Yes, she thought, he must have some lineage back to Jean Lafitte; how else would one come by such a swashbuckling smile?

"Rather than answer that, let me show you...Melissa, what say we move to the study and then to the kitchen to treat our guests to some of your cooking from Cajun heaven." He turned back to his guests with a normal smile now. "No one cooks like Melissa, so we've let the Kenyans go for the night and asked her to do the honors. My favorite place anyway, the kitchen. Sound all right to you two?"

Lee Ann glanced over at her compadre. A quick look between them was enough to say, "Yes!" Stanley summed it up for both of them. "Sounds like our kind of evening."

"Well then, we're off to the study. I'll show you a bit of what I'm working on these days, and then we'll have a peek at that new clay and the magnificent little treasures Melissa is fashioning with it. Is it a plan?"

They toasted to newfound friends. The sherry was warming their cockles as they boarded the small domestic elevator bound for the third floor of the mansion. The floor Poteet referred to as "the study."

On the short ride up, Lee Ann stood behind Jean Paul's wheelchair, which put Stanley side by side and slightly in touch with Melissa. Was it just his imagination or was she emitting some sort of energy? An aura that barely brushed his physical being but radiated like the warm fire and the sherry, straight to his core. He felt it, his core, a poor old core that had lain dormant and cold these last few years, but now with the appearance of Lee Ann and Lisa Lynn and now Melissa, seemed to be warming nicely. The cesium rods were being pulled at every turn and the old reactor was heating up. His only concern now was to avoid meltdown, and Melissa wasn't helping. In the next instant, he decided he was overreacting to a mere touch. Try to sober up, Stanley, he admonished himself, lest this obviously perceptive woman pick up your licentious vibrations. Grow up Stanley, try to muster the class act. He pictured someone throwing a bucket of ice water over his head to bring his temperature down, and shuddered imperceptibly as his potent imagination threw him into reverse. It worked. As the elevator glided silently up to the third floor, Stanley came down.

The lift stopped smoothly, the doors parted, and they stepped into a spacious area with a towering coffered ceiling. French doors reaching to the full height of this flat but ornate vaulting opened onto small balconies overlooking the portico. Here and there, at the center of comfortable seating areas, were large antique walnut desks equipped with electronic work terminals. The room looked like an executive loans department of a very prosperous and well-established Southern bank.

"This is the slave galley," announced Jean Paul. "Come... follow me." He wheeled off ahead of them through a door in a wall at one end of the room. His three companions followed and found themselves in an office that was a smaller version of the one they'd just passed through. Jean Paul moved over behind a massive walnut desk—a larger version of the ones in the galley—and invited them to sit in chairs facing a wood-paneled wall.

"Now, Lee Ann, let me answer the question you asked earlier." And with that he pressed several keys on his terminal and the paneled wall slid silently aside to reveal an array of nine television screens: three rows of three. With the stroke of another key, the screens lit simultaneously with programs currently in progress on nine different channels. "Don't you just love the satellites?" marveled Poteet. "In addition to all the local channels, national networks, and cable accesses, we also subscribe to one local channel in each of nine major US cities." He glanced over at Lee Ann. "Just so happens that KPIQ in San Francisco is on the list. I very much enjoy your morning show, Ms. Barnes."

With raised brows she nodded in the direction of his Cheshire smile. "HA! Well...thank you very much."

"I *am* a fan." Jean Paul's tone was one of quiet sincerity. "And then, of course, once in a while I have to do some work, so these monitors also let me keep in touch with the foundry out back." He pressed another key and the screens filled with static black and white shots of several locations around what resembled a large factory area. Another keystroke and he'd summoned up the view seen by the security cameras on the grounds.

"And now for the show. Melissa, would you get us a glass of water? We'll clear our palates here before we lay siege to the cellar and decide what varietal delight we wish to sacrifice with dinner." Melissa obliged as Jean Paul turned once again to face his keyboard full on and type some instructions to the television array. Behind the scenes machines whirred and clicked, and one by one the screens lit with images of whales, manatees, and sharks, and others with views of rainforests and rivercourses teeming with life. Now all the screens faded into the African savannas thundering with herds of migratory animals, and following these, as they have for millenniums, the predators, the scavengers, and the groomers. Jean Paul wheeled around to see that he had the rapt attention of his guests. "This is what I do when I'm not working...take these little home movies"

A little more than home movies, thought Lee Ann. The production value of all the work was extremely high.

"You may have noticed the trophy heads hanging about the library?" Poteet went on. "My grandfather bagged those. I was along on some of those hunts...even took a shot or two, though I never hit anything...much to the old chap's consternation. Grandpa Jacques, I mean. No, I've always loved animals, even as a child. Don't know why I keep those heads around really, except as a reminder that the beautiful creatures of the earth have a hard enough time surviving against the crush of us avaricious homosapiens, without having their heads shot off. So...I sponsor a foundation that promotes and facilitates communication among organizations worldwide whose aim is the conservation of endangered species...and soon to be endangered species. You may have heard of it, *One World Incorporated?*"

He paused, saw no recognition from either of his guests, so went on. "Well, you will. We're new, but we're growing fast, and so far, cross your fingers, we've been successful in funding our foundation entirely from television documentaries that we ourselves have produced. That telemontage we've been watching is some of the work we've done. I never tire of watching it, but you must be starving. I want to show you something coming up here, and then we'll adjourn to the kitchen."

The San Franciscans sat watching, enthralled by the majesty of the beasts that ran, swam and swung across the nine screens before them. "Okay..." said Jean Paul, "here it comes. Watch the center row of three screens. This was a three-camera shoot."

As he spoke, the screens above and below the center row went to blue, but the center screen, screen 5, came alive with a full-front telephoto shot of a large male rhino. The huge animal filled the frame. "I was operating the camera that took this angle. As I said, we had three cameras working on this shoot, so what you're about to see is something we edited together as a little photo album of...well, just watch."

The rhino filling screen number 5 was pawing the dust, obviously agitated and about to charge. Screen 4 came on, showing another angle of the beast. It was also a telephoto shot that pulled back to show him from the side and facing a camera-equipped truck not thirty yards away. Poteet said, "Remember, that's me operating the camera on that flatbed truck facing off with Old

Jack. That's the rhino's name...Old Jack. Watch, and you'll see what I saw." Screen 6 now came on showing an overall scene of the two camera trucks that were shooting the scenes on screens 4 and 5. On screen 5, Old Jack had begun his charge, so the telephoto pulled back slowly to see him coming on. There was a lurch now in the picture on screen 5. Poteet interjected, "That jump in the picture is where my driver panicked, popped the clutch of the truck, and killed the engine." Up on the screen, the thunderous approach of Old Jack and the sound of the driver frantically trying to restart the engine foretold of what was to come.

"I was watching all this and there was really nothing I could do but keep taping and hope Sunjab, the driver, would get us started and get us the hell out of there before Old Jack reached us. Wrong." As Poteet finished saying this, Old Jack hit the side of the stalled truck sending cameraman and camera wheeling through space. The camera hit the ground, and there was a split second of fractured black lines on the screen as the unit died and Screen 5 dissolved into snow. But Screen 4 and 6 continued to cover the action.

The melee lasted no more than a minute, but long enough to tell the tale. Camera crew 3 on screen 6 got it all. The rhino rounded the stalled truck as Sunjab leapt from the cab and ran to the aid of the fallen cameraman—Poteet. But not before the one ton beast had taken swipes at Poteet with his horn and trampled him beneath his massive front feet. On Jack's last pass, Poteet was literally thrown into the air like a rag doll and came to rest on his side, clutching at his legs. The rhino moved off to paw the dirt and consider the other truck that was now bearing down on him. Quick thinking on the part of camera crew 2, appearing on screen 4. As camera 2 continued to roll on the back of the moving truck, it covered the scene of the rhino, and a few yards off from him, Sunjab running to Poteet, flinging him over his shoulder and up onto the bed of the truck. The tall black man then jumped up into the cab, successfully fired the engine, and this time left Old Jack in the dust as the truck exited the frame. Then camera crew 2 moved off to follow, still covering the befuddled and angry rhino. As the action concluded on screens

4 and 6, screen 5 faded back in to show Poteet, later at camp, lying on a cot with two fully splinted legs.

Poteet hit a key that turned all the screens to solid blue. Blue faded to black and eventually cooled to gray. "Well, that's it. Thought you might be curious as to why I am wheeling about these days. I still have my legs, but they're not much good for walking. Doctor said if I worked on them for several thousand hours I might get some strength and mobility back, but...I'm lazy." He punched a few final keys on the console. "Well, what say we adjourn to the kitchen. You must be ravenous now that you've seen a man mauled by a rhino."

Poteet twisted stiffly in his chair, moving his body to direct his eyes—like Dr. Strangelove, Lee Ann thought. What a bizarre piece of footage to show your dinner guests. But then again, she could see how he would do that—to explain his confinement to a wheelchair. There was a long silence in the room.

"I know what you're thinking," Poteet said quietly. "But you must know that I still love that old boy, Old Jack, the rhino, I mean. He's a radio-tagged specimen and we're tracking him for study. I mean how could you hold a grudge against a beautiful creature like that? He's one of just five hundred such beasts left on this planet. Just glad it wasn't a shark. Something less romantic about losing it to a shark, don't you think? Rhino, now that's romantic. Ha!" He gestured towards the door. "Well, we're off to the kitchen." And with that he wheeled from behind the desk and headed in the direction of the elevator. The others followed along behind. This time Lee Ann hung back with Melissa and asked a question that had been on her mind. "Melissa," she whispered, "do you think it would be all right to ask Jean Paul about his...who was it...great-great-great grandfather, Jean Lafitte?"

Melissa nodded. "Oh, surely...but I warn you, once he gets started, he may not stop. That's his favorite ancestor you know." Lee Ann nodded, acknowledging Melissa's gentle warning, and began framing her questions. The kitchen would be the place to ask them.

7.

The kitchen was out back in keeping with most antebellum southern mansions.

Our dinner party exited the elevator on the dining room side of the first floor, moved quickly around a banquet sized table, and found themselves in a short connecting hall leading to the galley. Full length glass on either side opened onto small and meticulously kept miniature fern gardens.

Stanley, pushing Poteet's wheelchair along, said, "Made some modifications to the original I see. Is the kitchen the original?"

Poteet smiled proudly. "Oh many, many, but what you're about to see is the original structure, erected almost two-hundred years ago. The trusses and walls and decking are entirely original, as is a beautiful brick bread oven, which you'll soon be sampling...I mean the fruits thereof. Melissa has some dough rising. And, oh yes, you would like this...the floor we're crossing? It is the original Spanish tile floor that was laid when this house was built by some of Lafitte's people in the early eighteen hundreds. Did I mention Lafitte in that last fax?"

"Yes, you did. Jean Lafitte you say?"

"The same."

A moment of silence passed between them as Stanley, rolling Jean Paul along, recalled a fax he'd hurriedly read, which arrived on the machine that Evie Ester insisted he install in his paltry digs. Evie, a tireless tripper with technology was helping him plod technically fatigued into the twenty-first century. "Yes, Jean Lafitte, I remember." Then under his breath Stanley whispered, "Lee Ann is crawling out of her reporter's skin right now wanting to know about your family's connection with Lafitte. Expect to be interrogated."

"Aye, mate" came the gravely response from a transformed voice ahead of him. Stanley liked this guy.

Brick red tiles were passing beneath his feet. And here and there he could see a square that looked newer than the others. Apparently one that had become too badly cracked to repair and had been replaced. But overall it was a magnificent floor. Old, worn, and well traveled. He could spend hours staring at every tile in it. After all, it was made of the earth—fired clay—and Stanley had a penchant for fired clay.

Poteet was speaking again. "Well, you know, up until the time I took over this house after Grandpa Jacques died, the kitchen had stayed pretty much the same since the time it was built, as I said, two centuries ago. But you know, I love to cook, and Melissa loves to cook, and we spend a great deal of time out here. *And* we have a great bunch of people working and living around here to socialize with." He faded off.

"Employees?" Stanley asked.

"Well yes...but more than that. These people are my friends, compatriots, people I've hand-picked over the years on my various expeditions to Africa. My friends and bearers from Kenya...beautiful people." He paused. "You'll meet them all, I'm sure, in the future. Tonight we wanted to have the place to ourselves."

Melissa and Lee Ann, who had been tagging along behind holding their own little powwow, closed ranks. Melissa had heard Jean Paul's reference to the Kenyans. "Yes, Lee Ann, you and Stanley must come back before you leave New Orleans and spend an evening with our friends from Kenya."

They entered the kitchen. Lee Ann made no attempt to muffle a little cry of delight. "Stanley! This is a dream!" She looked at him, saw his eyes also sweeping this way and that, trying to take it all in. The kitchen was immense, at least fifty by fifty feet square in plan, with an exposed hand-hewn, rustic trussed ceiling soaring high above. Stanley, wide eyed, looked down and saw that the floor in the connecting link fanned out to be twenty-five-hundred square feet of two-hundred-year-old tiles. He was momentarily overcome, but quickly recovered and said to the back of Poteet's graying head, "And where might I take you, sir?"

"Let's set a course for the refrigerator," said Poteet. "That sherry was fine but a shade trampy. I need a beer to freshen up for the eighty-five Rothschild we'll be having with dinner."

Stanley wheeled Poteet to the refrigerator and pulled open a four-foot-wide, industrial-sized, stainless steel door. Inside was an assortment of bottled beverages that could have stocked a convenience store. "And...what can I get you?"

"A Beck's would be my choice...and help yourself."

Stanley grabbed a Beck's for Poteet and a small bottle of Evian for himself. He saw an opener hanging unceremoniously on a chain by the frig, popped the top on the beer, and handed it to his host. "I'm a happy man now," said Poteet, waving the green bottle in the air. "Go find the girls. I think they've gone exploring. Let them wander off too far and we may never see them again."

While Stanley had been attending to his bartending duties, he'd noticed that Lee Ann had made a short phone call, but now she and Melissa had moved off, as Jean Paul had put it, "to explore."

It was obvious that Melissa loved showing off her kitchen to someone as enthusiastic and appreciative as Lee Ann. Stanley joined them and tagged along behind. Lee Ann kept rolling her eyes up to the open trussed ceiling above where, suspended below skylights, potted ferns, spider plants, and philodendrons hung. These hanging plants made the room feel as much like a greenhouse as a kitchen.

The threesome moved over to one corner of the room where a large round table, surrounded by a dozen or so high back chairs, waited for diners. Off to the side was a comfortable sitting area with a fireplace that appeared to be a modified beehive-shaped bread oven. Stanley thought he could very easily live here and work here and never leave here and never want for anything more in his entire life. What would it be like to have a studio like this?

Melissa spoke softly as she moved gazelle-like about the area. She was explaining that they often entertained as many as fifty people at a time, that the kitchen staff varied anywhere from two to twenty depending on who wanted to spend time socializing there.

"So, as you can see, we knocked out these walls and put in sliding glass doors." She moved over and opened one of them. "You know, I think it's warming up a bit now. Let's open these up and see if we can get a little air moving through."

Melissa and Stanley unlatched and slid four of the glass panels aside. She flipped a switch, and to the rear of the kitchen, a garden lit up like a stageset from *Gone with the Wind*.

Jean Paul busied himself putting the bread into the beehive oven as the other members of the dinner party moved out onto the patio.

"These cypress trees, it's said, were planted by Lafitte himself when his people acquired this mansion and lived here in the early eighteen hundreds." Melissa swept her hand around. "Of course there are no records or diaries documenting this, but the family he started here has stayed intact since that time. And family history has been passed down for five generations, so, it's probably true. These trees are close to two hundred years old."

"Well, I think I'll join you in a cold Evian, Stanley," she said as she turned to go back inside. "Could I get you something Lee Ann?"

"The same please...would be fine, thank you."

"Good, let's freshen up for the Rothschild. Perhaps some cheese..." She said it almost to herself as she turned and led them back into the kitchen.

"That would be a plan," said Lee Ann as she set off quickly to follow. She was already mentally interviewing Poteet. He would be on her show, oh yes, he *would* be on her show—particularly with the *One World Incorporated* angle. That was the ticket; that was the key. And the rhino story and lineage from Lafitte were simply delicious icing on the cake. She couldn't wait. Poteet, a man who was dedicating a considerable portion of his resources to the preservation of the world's animal population, finds himself a victim of one, attacked and crippled by a rhino, and put in a wheelchair for perhaps the rest of his life. Now *that* was a story, *that* was news—though she would never in a million years let them present it that way.

She was organizing it in her mind, timing it, pacing it for greatest impact. The monitor in her head was rolling. She took the Evian that Melissa had poured into a tall glass tumbler and garnished with a sprig of mint...and sipped.

Her cell phone warbled. She grabbed it from her jacket pocket, excused herself, and answered it. It was Claire. "Claire," she said softly, "are you all right?"

"Yeah, Mom...yeah, I'm fine," came a sarcastic twenty-year-old voice from above the border.

"Are you still in Toronto? Are you still being held?"

"I am in Toronto. I am *out* of jail..." She paused. "I had someone help me make bail, and I'm looking for an attorney...I think."

"So..."

"So everything is fine, but...I miss you. Can you come up and see me? We'll hit my arraignment together...have a good old time." Her delivery was sardonically droll. Lee Ann was more than familiar with it.

"What did you do?" she asked.

"Oh..." Claire went on ever so lazily, "I brought some art objects into Canada that I should have run through proper channels. And I didn't and...I got caught. You'd think with drugs and weapons and illegal aliens and all, the redcoats would have better things to do with their time than bust some little chick smuggling artifacts."

"You know it's against the law, Claire."

"Yeah, I *know*, Mom, I *know*...but anyway...I want to see you. Can you come up?" Pause. "Then I'll fill you in on all the details.

But I want you to know that I'm fine. And I appear in court next week to see if this bad little girl should be sent to the brig."

"You mean prison!" Lee Ann was having a difficult time processing this possibility.

"As in prison, Mom...but let's not get ahead of things. A law student friend of mine says I can get off with a fine and probably deportation. So relax, come on, let's go have some fun. I'll show you Toronto before they throw me out of Canada forever. What's a girl gotta do, get herself thrown in jail before her famous mom will come and visit her?"

Lee Ann wasn't about to take Claire's smart-ass lip, but she decided it was best to keep it cool. Claire had always been a punk. She wondered if Claire would ever grow up and join the civilized world. "Come on honey...don't...don't get going on me right now."

"Sar...reee," said the voice on the Toronto end of the line. Lee Ann felt the hair on the nape of her neck bristle.

"Anyway, Claire, I called Continental before we left the hotel this afternoon." She lowered her voice to almost a whisper. "And if I can get a flight, I'm going to be up there by tomorrow evening to see you...uh huh...yes... I'll have to call you a little bit later to give you my flight number and time, but I'm pretty sure I'm going to get on. They're optimistic. So we better not talk anymore right now. Your dad and I are in the middle of a power dinner. Know what I mean?"

"Oh, Mom...you're always in the middle of a power something, aren't you?" Claire knew she was pushing buttons, so she rushed ahead with all the sincerity she could muster. "So you and Dad having some fun down there on the bayou, huh? How's the old guy doing? Hear he's getting famous!"

"He's doing great, Claire. Looking great...has lost some weight..." She trailed off.

"Great, that's great. Well, give him my love." She sounded almost sincere now.

"I will. Listen...I'll call as soon as I know about my flight. Just leave your machine on tonight and I'll leave a message. It could be late. Are you at home?"

"Yeah, Jackie and I are staying in this evening. We've had enough excitement these last few days to last at least for the rest of this week, huh?"

She heard Claire turn and say something to Jackie, so shouted into the receiver to draw her back.

"OKAY! WELL MAYBE WE'LL TALK AGAIN..."

Claire broke in. "It's okay Mom. You can stop yelling. I'm back."

"Okay honey. Well...can't talk anymore right now. I love you...glad you're safe...bye."

"Love you too, Mom, bye." Claire hung up.

Lee Ann kept the phone to her ear for a moment, pretending to be still connected with her felonious daughter. Thank God, at least Claire was not sitting in some cell somewhere. She could breathe easier knowing that. Discreetly now, so as not to be noticed, she scrolled to Continental Airlines, had a short conversation with a clerk, gave them her number, and hung up. Business complete, she turned and returned to her hosts.

"Anyway, I don't care what you say, the man was a common criminal."

"A common criminal my tush, Melissa, the man took the skills he had mastered and made a very comfortable and rewarding life for himself!"

"Laaafeeet," said Melissa. "Hmmph."

Lee Ann studied Stanley as she closed ranks on what appeared to be an old debate. Her saddlepal was taking it all in with a sly grin that told her he was enjoying Melissa and Jean Paul's diverse and confrontational views on family history. She wondered if it was just their act for him.

They stopped talking as she approached. Melissa, clad in an apron, stood at a sprawling island cooktop and continued to fling greens and other vegetables into the air, letting them fall sizzling and crackling back into a skillet. She wondered if Stanley had filled them in concerning Claire's situation. If so, now they would want to know the latest developments. She hoped he hadn't. She would rather talk about that other smuggler, Lafitte.

"That was Claire, and she's all right Stanley. She's all right." She glanced quickly at Melissa and Jean Paul. "Did...uh...Stanley tell you that she was being held on a customs violation?" They nodded in the affirmative. "Well yes, she was in jail for a couple of days, but she made bail, and she's home and doing fine. But...I'd really rather not talk about it right now if you don't mind. It's a little embarrassing actually."

"Well..." Poteet began in a fatherly tone of voice, "I'd venture to say that there are few people in this world today who have not in some way transgressed the law...as it is." He looked around, saw that he had agreement from all. "It's just that your daughter was unlucky this time. And after all, who did she really hurt? No one...just a little ill-fated smuggling I'd say."

"I'd agree with you, Jean Paul," Stanley broke in, "it's just that we have a number of ill fated transgressions back there, including but not limited to drug possession, reckless driving with a close-call DUI. Let's see..."

"*STANLEY!*" Lee Ann was mortified that he'd flung the doors of the family armoire so wide to the room. "I can't *believe* you..." She glared at him.

He knew she was right. He'd lifted the corner of the rug a wee bit too high. "Sorry," he said somewhat chagrined.

"Oh...it's quite all right." Poteet waved it off. "Melissa and I have our hands full with Stella...wouldn't you say?"

Everyone glanced at Melissa. She seemed to be comfortable with the question.

"We do have our moments," she said, wistfully stirring a roux. "She loves her daddy...she doesn't love me so much..."

"That's not true dear...it's just a phase she's going through you know," Jean Paul consoling.

"A phase she's been going though ever since she was born Jean Paul...she's fourteen now, remember? Hardly a phase. Oh well, we'll muddle through somehow..."

She continued to work as she said this, combining ingredients and splashing wine into skillets filled with fish and vegetables. Her motions were fluid, efficient, and graceful. And what was that strange twist creeping into her pronunciation? Stanley wondered. A slight Spanish accent? Was it Spanish? Not quite.

"Ees just about time to eat all of this." There it was again.

Lee Ann, who had dropped over to the sidelines to watch the action, was still recovering from the fact that Stanley had rolled out Claire's record—well—part of it. Thank God he hadn't mentioned Claire's short bout with amateur prostitution. *That* had been the killer.

She jumped in to help Melissa serve the plates, cover them with large silver steamers, and load them onto a serving cart. Stanley was sent to fetch the bread from the oven. Poteet had already uncorked the wine and now loaded it onto the cart. With all in readiness, they fell in single file and proceeded to the dining room. In the lead Lee Ann pushed Poteet. Next came Stanley, propelling the serving cart. And bringing up the rear, Melissa, carrying the hot bread, wrapped in a linen towel like a freshly bathed baby.

"Lee Ann..." came a commanding voice from their leader rolling out ahead, "are you comfortable with talking about Claire? There are a few more things I'd like to know."

"Mmm, yes...what would you like to know?"

"So...am I to understand that your little girl stuffed some Picassos into her pack and swam the river into Canada?"

She was amused, "Ha! No, I don't think anything as exciting as Picassos. But, who knows, Claire does have connections. No...she'd been working in Knossos, Crete, on a temple dig. She didn't want to go into it on the phone, which I can understand, but I'd say that she found some small objects, wrapped them in her clothes, and tried to fly them back home to Canada to sell them. But...she got caught."

"My family has a long tradition of smuggling," Poteet said thoughtfully.

"You can say that again," chided Melissa from the rear. Jean Paul ignored her and went on.

"You say Claire was apprehended in Toronto?"

"Yes, Toronto."

"Well, you know, I am French...I suppose it doesn't show."
She heard him chuckling up ahead. "But aah, Montreal...Toronto.
Vive le Quebec...vive l'Ontario. I know some people up there.
I'd be glad to do whatever I can to help," — she couldn't see him
smiling now— "within reason, of course."

Lee Ann was feeling better by the second, and so was
Stanley, who'd been listening from behind. He'd been feeling
Lee Ann's sudden departure for Toronto looming ominously.
He had felt it ever since he'd read that note the desk clerk had
handed him this afternoon. He knew Lee would be out of here
tomorrow if Claire was still in jail. But now with Claire out
on bail, and Poteet offering to help, and with her interest in
getting Poteet on *Good Morning San Francisco*, well, he felt they
might be able to relax and enjoy the remaining few days of this
sojourn that was currently bearing beautiful fruits. He glanced
back at Melissa. She smiled warmly at him. They entered the
high-ceilinged dining room.

"Oh Jean Paul, this room is entirely *too large* for four people;
can't we please move back to the kitchen? It's just so huge!"

"No, Melissa...we'll just use all of the table. See here...Lee
Ann...you and I have the loudest voices, so you go down to the
other end there, and you two"—he motioned to Melissa and
Stanley—"take port and starboard...and we'll have a merry little
feast."

"Jean Paul, you know I don't like this game. *Please*..." Melissa's
tone was cold, even, firm.

"Nonsense, my dear. Come! Let's set the table."

Jean Paul seemed to be feeling his grape. He appeared almost
ribald to Lee Ann. She hoped he wasn't an obnoxious drunk.

There seemed to be no doubt about it, an expansive oval
mahogany table, six feet wide and sixteen feet long, would be
set on its quadrants. Poteet positioned himself at the head of the
board, while Melissa, Stanley, and Lee Ann set all four places
with linens, silver and crystal taken from an antique sideboard.

You know, Jean Paul, this is *extremely* cumbersome without help."

"Come, my dear, you're all doing splendidly! You know how I love this room!"

Lee Ann's cell warbled again in her jacket pocket.

Melissa, already overworked, looked up, slightly annoyed. Lee Ann saw it and said, "I'll make it short."

She moved to the sideboard, punched talk, and put the phone to her ear. "Hello."

"Hello, is this Ms. Barnes?" came an efficient metallic voice on the other end.

"Speaking."

"Yes, Ms. Barnes, this is Continental, and we have confirmed your flight tomorrow morning from New Orleans to Toronto. That's flight 937, departing New Orleans at 9:15am, arriving Toronto at 2:35pm, with one transfer at Chicago O'Hare. We'd like to ask that you be at the Continental desk an hour before flight time to check luggage and pick up your ticket, and boarding pass."

"Thank you, I will," she said softly.

"Fine. Thank you for flying Continental."

The voice hung up. Lee Ann breathed a sigh of relief. All right, she could go then if she decided to. But she hadn't decided yet whether she would. Things were too intriguing around here at the moment, and it felt so good to be lost from the seaman—if only temporarily. That was one intrigue she was happy to be without. As she stood for a moment with her ear still pressed to a purring receiver, she moved her mind back on track. She needed to get some kind of a tentative commitment from Poteet to appear on the show. At least that would justify her abrupt leave of absence. And more immediately she needed to make up some excuse for this last call. She didn't want to tell Stanley yet that she'd confirmed her reservations for tomorrow morning. That would surely spoil his evening. And she didn't want to do that. He was having such a good time and so was she. All right then, she decided on a little white lie. She knew how much

Stanley hated her "little white lies." Her *blanc de blanc* lies, he said often, in his estimation, shaded to midnight *noir*. But it was either that or ruin his evening. She rejoined once again the program in progress.

"Claire again?" Stanley asked as she packed away her cell. "Is she going to do this all evening?" he added under his breath.

"No Stan, that was Continental Airlines."

He fixed her with narrowed eyes.

Oh boy, this was it. So much for his brief few moments of companionship. Claire! Damn her hide; she'd been doing this to them since she was a baby. "No, Stan, that was Continental Airlines," Lee had said, and his sweet little pot had buckled and fallen onto the wheel. He'd always hated when that happened. "And...?" he asked.

She passed him on her way to rejoin Melissa in preparing the table. "I'm having them check on some times, some regular flights up to Toronto. In case Claire needs me. Remember I mentioned I might have to go?"

He looked up sharply, a million thoughts flashing through his mind. But yes, she was right about one thing. At least one of Claire's parents had to be there for her. He had such mixed emotions about all this. He wished he could be there for Claire, but it seemed that every time in the past when he had tried, she'd kicked him in the nuts. So good luck, honey, good luck. Such a punk, a brilliant little punk. She had her mother's street savvy, she had his art; she'd put it all together and become an art smuggler. Way to go, Claire. Oh, this little girl of his, would they ever meet on the bridge? Would they ever work it out?

"Stanley...?" Lee Ann, standing at the head of the table with Melissa and Jean Paul, held a glass of wine out to him.

"Oh, sorry," he said, walking over to join the three of them. He took the glass from her hand. "Thank you."

Poteet was about to make a toast, as soon as Stanley had returned from his pout. And there he was again, thought Lee Ann, old Stan, ruminating in the midst of a gala social occasion. Well, she knew exactly what was on his mind, and so did the hosts, so they had busied themselves pouring the wine and indulging him in a moment of funk.

Poteet raised his glass. "To newfound friends and future found good health and fortune." They all agreed heartily and took communion.

And so dinner began, with Lee Ann and Poteet booming to one another down the length of the table, and Melissa and Stanley attempting a more civilized volume across it. Occasionally those two found it necessary to shout something to their counterparts down at either end. They all agreed it was fun—even Melissa was being a good sport about it—but finally decided that the shouting had become tiresome. So they convened at Poteet's end of the table and finished the blackened redfish dinner with a bit more decorum. A second bottle of wine was evenly distributed to the dregs as they sat relaxing and digesting. Stanley looked at his watch: 10 pm.

"Melissa," he began. "I'd very much like to see the foundry and your work before we call it an evening. Could we do that while there's still time? I could get very comfortable very fast if I don't get up and move around." He looked around at the other faces at the end of the table.

By that magic known only to Lee Ann, she had, during the course of the dinner, alluded to the fact that she would like to have Poteet appear on her show. Poteet had been receptive to the idea. After all it would be excellent exposure for the foundation he considered his most important work. And so an informal negotiation and contracting had gone on throughout the delicious blackened redfish.

A negotiation that Stanley had watched with interest and secret amusement, just as he'd watched Lee Ann plying his wares two nights ago at Genoa Gallery. Such a girl.

There was an awkward silence at the table following his proposal of a visit to the foundry. Poteet certainly didn't want to go to the foundry, and Lee Ann, he could tell, wanted to talk to Poteet alone to cinch her deal. He wanted to talk to Melissa alone for whatever reason might ensue. And he definitely wanted to see what kind of work this graceful, gracious, and beautiful woman was doing. So everything worked out fine. Melissa and Stanley saw Jean Paul and Lee Ann off to the library, left the big house and walked on down the road—to the foundry. A lazy Louisiana breeze brought fragrant bouquets up from the bayou.

As hard as Stanley tried, he couldn't stop admiring the woman walking at his side. Though he knew she flew in the upper troposphere, and he was still dusting crops, they were both pilots of a sort; they were both artists. Melissa had a warm genuine quality about her that suggested some strong beginnings. Among other things, he wanted to know about those. He wanted to know about Melissa's childhood, her family. She was speaking softly at his side. He lowered himself into the warm bath of her voice.

"If you could name one thing...one thing that keeps you and Claire apart, what would it be? I know what my answer to that question would be concerning Stella and myself, and I'll tell you what it is, but...you go first." She stopped in the road, turned to him, and looked him straight in the eyes. "What would it be?" It was like looking into a fire—looking into Melissa's flickering brown eyes.

He took her arm, turned her, and resumed walking. They were arm in arm now, matching each other step for step in a flowing stride. It was a fluid, floating sensation that he'd never felt with Lee Ann. He would do nothing to disturb the calm. "Let me walk here for a minute and think about that. Such an honest question deserves a considered answer."

And so they walked in silence. Ten paces...twenty...thirty, still not a word from Melissa. My how this woman could wait. Finally, just as what he hoped was the foundry came into view, he said, "Our similarity."

Melissa let out her breath and without breaking forward stride nodded yes with her whole body. "Yes, I'd have to say that's what it is with Stella and myself...our similarity." She grasped his arm more snugly.

Back in the trees, at either side of the path, he could see little bungalows, some with dimly lit porches. He didn't want to pursue this issue of their estranged daughters any further and was curious about these rambling but trim cottages. "Who lives out here?" he asked.

"Our Kenyan staff" came a short reply.

"The Kenyans? Explain to me now about the Kenyans. Just a bit more, I mean."

"Well...they are...as we said, people of Kenya, in Africa, who Jean Paul has come to know over the years. You know...on his various cinemagraphic expeditions to their savannas. Some of the older ones he's known since he was a boy."

"Really."

"Yes, when he joked that they had made him an honorary member of the tribe, he wasn't entirely joking. He loves these people, and they all love him and profit considerably from their association with him."

He didn't remember Jean Paul joking about being an honorary member of some Kenyan tribe—must have been some previous recent dinner guest. He let it pass. "Don't they miss their homeland? Are they naturalized citizens or still Kenyans?"

"They're still Kenyans, always will be." She paused. He waited. She went on. "With the help of Jean Paul, they own and maintain a compound in their home country, almost a village, but with all the conveniences of the twenty-first century: a church, and their own schoolhouse, a satellite dish for TV reception, a clinic.

"It was a big game hunting lodge, established by Jean Paul's grandfather Jacques, but over the years since Jacques's death, Jean Paul has converted it into a village studio to support his work with the wildlife conservation effort there. The people who live in those cottages you see, will rotate back to Kenya at the end of a six-month stay, and the group that is in Kenya now will come over here to work in the foundry and around the house. Works out well that way in terms of work permits and such. The children, of course, come for nine months when they come. It gives them a full year of school here in the States."

"What a guy," Stanley said quietly. "Saving the wildlife of the planet, making reparation in his own way to the people who his people once enslaved. Making beautiful social art out of everything he touches. I'm envious."

"Yes, he is a good man...he has his strange side too. If you get to know him, you'll see it. It's difficult to be a man with as much wealth and power as Jean Paul and not find yourself sometimes abusing it. But yes, you're right...bottomline...he's a fine man." She pulled up short, gestured forward. "Well...here we are."

They'd reached the foundry, which, from the outside, was little more than a large, nondescript tilt-slab concrete building. Surrounding this concrete box were remnants of the old operation: some behemoth beehive kilns, some ancient limestone outbuildings, and here and there, tastefully placed, a piece of vintage machinery set out in the weather to rust away and give testament to a porcelain factory that had been here for over two hundred years. On a large expanse of crushed oyster shells in front of the crumbling kilns stood three gleaming silver and green eighteen wheelers. They were trimmed in white with a flowing script that read: *Poteet Porcelain*.

"Better not let Lee Ann see those rigs," he said, motioning in the direction of Poteet's armada. "She'll sign on to make your next delivery."

"Can she really drive a rig?" Melissa asked, wide eyed.

"Her father, the trucker, taught her how. Yes, Lee Ann can drive a rig."

"What a girl!" Melissa was obviously amazed and amused. And, Stanley imagined, a shade envious.

"Yes, mame, Lee Ann can ride, shoot, rope, spit, and swear all at the same time...you'll see."

Melissa smiled appreciatively

They moved through a small, light green pedestrian door at one side of a broad loading dock and found themselves in a dimly lit cavernous room. Melissa flipped a bank of switches and a modern porcelain factory sprang into full view. At the opposite end of the highbay, Stanley could see the faces of some industrial-sized gas-fired kilns. Extending out from the doors of these giant ovens were long tables with over twenty potter's wheels. And neatly arranged in heavy metal shelving along one wall were all shapes and sizes of plaster casts. An overhead crane, large steel carts, and conveyor belts served to move the porcelain in progress from one processing area to another.

Aside from the white grit that unavoidably accompanies such an operation, the area was a picture of efficient organization. Stanley stood and took it in. His eyes kept moving back to the roll-in kilns at the far end of the room. "Those beauties down there are a potter's dream, aren't they?"

Melissa, standing quietly at his side, knew that he was a bit awed by it all so she was patiently letting him feast his eyes and take it in. "Yes...I certainly do avail myself of those ovens... baking my bread." She stood quietly for a moment longer and then, motioning to a far wall, said, "There are some rooms on the other side of those doors, but basically it's just glazing and shipping...not too exciting. This is really the nucleus of the operation. We can look in there if you like, but time is growing short, and I'd like you to see my little pets."

"Lead on," said Stanley.

Melissa turned to the bank of switches and returned the foundry to its slumber. They left by the same door they had entered and walked a short distance across the drive to one of the ancient outbuildings. She pulled a key off a lanyard around her neck and let them through a heavy oak door and into a room that was bathed in a lunar glow that fell in shafts through windows and skylights.

"Do you mind if we stand and look at it this way for a moment, before I turn on the lights? I love to look at my babies in the light of the moon. They seem to come alive." She was almost whispering now. Stanley felt a cool tingle trickle across his scalp.

"Please, whatever you do, don't turn on the lights. This is magic."

He saw immediately what she was referring to. He knew that he himself liked to look at his work in the light of the moon. But he had always used a dark-colored clay, so his pieces would take on a ferocious, brooding quality. Melissa, on the other hand, had been using her marble white formulation to fashion her works, and in the high contrast of the moonlight, they seemed to glow—as if emitting their own interior light. He stood transfixed by the magic of this menagerie. She touched his hand. "Go ahead, walk around, but watch your step; this floor is very uneven."

He moved off slowly, carefully, to survey the collection of what she had modestly described as "little figurine scenes of pre-Civil War plantation life." They were consistently a quarter life sized—larger than he expected—and sat on sturdy, rough hewn timber pedestals about the room.

Suddenly his heel snagged a crack in the flagstone floor and he was thrown forward, off balance. He recovered quickly but not before Melissa gasped.

"Are you all right?"

"Yes, but you're right, this floor is tricky...best turn on the lights now. Though I want you to know I could stand in one spot, and turn, and enjoy this until the moon sets."

"Well, do then...take your time."

So he did just that, stood in one place and slowly made a full turn, taking it in one more time. And as he turned, he formulated questions in his mind about areas of the work that were lost in shadow. Questions that would be answered as soon as the lights came on. Finally he'd come full circle and stood once again facing a woman lost in her own deep shadow. She was barely visible across the room. "I'm in awe," he whispered.

"Well, best I burst your bubble then." She put her hand up to a wall switch. "Ready?"

"No, but go ahead."

With a single tiny movement, she revealed her magic. The overhead lights rudely dispersed the lunar glow, and they found themselves in a room now full of frozen though expressive life-forms.

Little figurines, my ass, thought Stanley to himself. Melissa's work was more, much more than that. There was a sinuous, lifelike quality to her figures, even in the full light of the lamps blazing overhead. They seemed to twist and always move upward.

She walked to his side. They stood facing the first assemblage.

It was of an old black fisherman walking along with what Stanley imagined were his grandchildren: a boy on one side and a girl on the other. The three of them were moving along, engaged in some mutual amusement that was causing the old man's eyes to squint in mirth and his semitoothless grin to spread like a piano keyboard across his face. The boy had his hand up to his mouth as if to hide his grin, but the young girl was looking up in admiration at the ancient one. The work astounded Stanley—shook him to his core. He felt his eyes well up, burn, and threaten to spill over with tears of pure admiration. Melissa smiled warmly and took his hand. "I know," she said, "it's happened before."

He put his arm about her shoulders. "Yes...I'm sure it has."

8.

"You cause a lot of people to break down and cry?"

"Only people who see what I do."

"And you like my stuff? Gargoyles and griffins, crude plodding Nordics, all lost in some sort of metaphorical mayonnaise?"

"Don't you see, Stanley?" She looked up at him. "We're so opposite."

It hit him like a ground-to-air missile. He hadn't even seen it coming.

All night, ever since the phone call when he'd talked briefly with Melissa, he'd been setting himself up to fall in love. And now he just had. He could just hear Lee Ann right now. "You know, Stanley, your problem is you fall in love with every skirt that passes you on the street. *Get a life!*"

But it had happened again. He felt the body radiating beside him. He felt the mind spritely and light. He'd felt the glide of their stride on the path down to this place. And now, unfortunately, he felt the hook in his cheek.

"NOOOooo!" The spirit screamed and went tumbling off... down into a dark abyss.

Well, yes, one could see it that way, he thought, but come on, he'd been on the course, he knew the waterholes and sandtraps—didn't he? She'd said, "Don't you see, Stanley, we're so opposite."

"You could say that," he said softly.

Melissa turned her back on the fisherman and his grandchildren and moved off in the direction of the next piece. It was a southern belle reclining on a couch with an expression on her face that could only be brought on by Gulf Coast humidity. There was even a frosted glaze about her eyes that spoke of heat. The coloring of the whole work, for that matter, was very unusual. For the most part, it was just white matte porcelain, but here and there a subtle hue crept in. On the belle's face, pinks and peaches played peek-a-boo with her expression. Melissa did some strange and chancey things.

Stanley glanced back at the fisherman and his grandchildren. The old man was carrying a ceramic bucket, but out of his clenched fist grew a real cane pole. Not of clay, of cane. He was less impressed with the belle. He had little sympathy for feigning females, though the expression on the face before him begged service of a kind he wouldn't mind giving her. He surmised it was just something Melissa had to do. "That cane pole"—he motioned in the direction of the fisherman—"it intrigues me."

"Do you know how long cane lasts?"

Yes, he did know, as a matter of fact. Claire had told him that they had found perfectly preserved objects made of cane in the pyramids and mastabas of Egypt. He hadn't checked it out but couldn't think why Claire would make up such a story. So, it must be so. "Mastabas," he said.

"Mastabas?" Melissa whispered.

"Haven't they found objects made of cane...very well preserved...in Egyptian tombs dating back to three thousand BC? So that is five thousand years."

"And some in the Himalayas that date from eight thousand BC, that's ten thousand years. If my work is around in ten thousand years, I'll leave a little note giving them permission to replace the cane. Of course, I'll expect them to be respectful of the original for at least that long."

"Yes," he said, "know what you mean. Eight thousand BC, huh? Well, you know how those Dalai Lama's lie."

They cracked up. It was spontaneous and unexpected—felt good, because things had been getting a bit too heavy.

The next piece was something Stanley could relate to. It was a mule pulling a buckboard wagon. In the seat a black man was driving. His wife, staring straight ahead, sat on the seat beside him. In the back of the wagon, draped over boxes of canned goods and bags of corn and beans, were four children and two dogs, all with limbs intertwined, all fast asleep.

He turned and looked into the artist's eyes. "They are inspired. I didn't expect this." She returned his appreciative gaze. A gentle smile warmed the corners of her mouth and eyes. She said.

"Alright, I've shown you mine, now can I see yours?"

They both laughed.

"Well, you've seen the snaps."

"But I want to see the living works. You know what I mean."

"Mmm."

Yes, he would like to spend more time with this Melissa, maybe even work with her. And he felt that she was feeling the same. But he knew she was somehow mated with Poteet—not married, but still mated. And he was mated, no doubt, in some new and yet undefined way with Lee Ann. And though he felt that Lee Ann would let it all go in an instant if something better came along (hell, he wasn't sure what she felt, if *anything*), it didn't really matter. He would not cross any lines where Melissa and Poteet were concerned.

You do not cross a pirate's path without signaling far in advance for quarter.

9.

You do not cross a pirate's path without signaling far in advance for quarter. The words screamed in Stanley's brain like a boatswain's whistle.

He had *met* Poteet now. And such a rich picture he now had of the man.

Of course he'd talked with him on the telephone as they'd made arrangements for his pickup of the clay, but he'd had no physical picture of the man. Now he did. Poteet was indeed the many times great grandson of the pirate Lafitte; Stanley had no doubt about that. The long strong jaw, the deep-set eyes, the hair that swept back from his face as if combed by a Gulf Coast gale. It was a face reminiscent of Hook's, though he would never say that to Poteet's. And the voice and the words and the timing—the sense of complete control of his domain—Lafitte's blood ran in Poteet's veins. This could *be* Maison Rouge.

Melissa turned and moved off to inspect her latest work, one that appeared to be half finished. Stanley noticed it on his three-sixty turn of the moonlit room, but it had been draped in muslin so he'd had no idea what it could be. In the moonlight it appeared as a long horizontal object shrouded in white. Melissa delicately folded the damp cloth back, as if turning down the spread of a bed. And slowly, ever so slowly, he saw what was on her mind. It was an old black man, reclining on a narrow cot—a very, very old man. The veins and vessels and bones stood out in a hand that was draped across his chest. His head was thrown back, with lower jaw jutting skyward.

He moved over cautiously so he could see what was happening. The man was obviously in the throes of death. But due to the tilt of his head, he was unable to see the expression on the old man's face. Now he saw it. Despite the rakish angle of the head and jaw, the old man's face spoke of bliss and contentment. That was a surprise. He had expected anguish and pain. He looked up at Melissa who was standing off to one side. "Is this it?" He spoke softly.

She looked away, startled by the perceptive nature of his question. "No," she answered, "this is only the center of it. I'm planning an assemblage here." She held out her hand, palm up, and gestured toward the old man. "There will be a whole congregation of people gathered about the cot. Some will be facing away, some will be facing him. Those facing away...as if they haven't the slightest idea what is going on behind them. Those looking on will have that hollow expression of grief. And some in either situation will have those expressions reversed. Do you know what I am trying to explain?" She didn't wait for his reply, but went over, put a hand out to the old man, and said, "But look at *his* face."

"I did." Stanley spoke softly, as if in prayer. "He'll soon be free."

"Yes."

She retrieved the shroud and carefully retucked the old man in, and then, using a garden hose with a spray attachment, rechristened the cover with the finest of mists. Satisfied that all was once again in order, she walked back to his side. "So... we have things in common, Mr. Hochstetter." He nodded in the affirmative, holding his breath. She was standing very close to him, her eyes dancing about his face. Some of the mist from the hose had fallen on her bronze skin and black hair. He wanted to take a soft towel and gently pat her dry—see how it felt to touch her, if only through a towel. What was she thinking? There was such serenity there behind her eyes.

"We should get back."

"Yes."

They walked back to the big house talking the technicalities of working with clay, talking about the clay that would soon be delivered into Stanley's possession. She said the clay was her secret and so had ruminated long and hard after Jean Paul had shown her pictures of his, Stanley's, work, deciding whether or not she wanted to share it with him. Finally, she said, she had agreed that Jean Paul could contact him and make it available. She told him again how much she admired his work. He told her again how mutual that feeling was. She said if his work—subject matter—had been anything similar to hers, she probably would not have consented to share the clay. After all, there was only so much of a market out there for large ceramic assemblages. And then she said something that surprised him, yet made perfect sense. She told him that she had to meet him first, see what he was like as a person, before she made the final decision to share.

"So, did I pass?" he asked.

"With flying colors" came the music of Melissa's voice at his side.

They walked a moment in silence, then Stanley said, "I don't mean to be rude or forward here...but I need to ask you a question."

"Yes?"

"You and Jean Paul were...separated? I believe that was the word he used...after five years of marriage...are you..."

"Still married?"

"Yes. That was the question I was having difficulty with..."

"I understand...Jean Paul has a genteel way of putting things where we're concerned. No...we're not married. We divorced ten years ago before I left with the girls for Rio."

He let out a breath that he'd been holding. "And so you are now..."

"Very good friends Mr Hochstetter. Raising our two daughters through their most formative years."

He could tell by her polite but firm tone that he had reached the gate and it was swinging slowly shut. But he had his answer for now.

They'd reached the veranda behind the kitchen. "Well, shall we see what that ex-husband, very good friend of yours, and ex-wife, very good friend of mine, are up to?" He knew he was teasing, taking a chance here, but needed to stay in the game.

"Good plan," intoned Melissa with mock intrigue.

Safe! She could take a joke. He needed that in a woman, if she was to become a "very good friend."

"Where do you suppose we'll find them?" he asked.

"Those two mediaphiles? Well, I'd venture a guess they have adjourned the library by now and moved off to the study... where all those TV screens are kept. That's where I usually find Jean Paul this time of night."

"Let's go."

They moved through the kitchen, back through the connecting link and the dining room, and on into the library. The fire was cold in the hearth, the room was empty. So they boarded the elevator and waited for it to reach the third floor. As the lift's doors slid aside, they could see a rectangle of light radiating from the doorway to Jean Paul's study and the sound of television and French being spoken—then laughter and more French—and more laughter. It was Lee Ann and Poteet conversing in French. When had she learned that?

"Sounds like they're having as good a time as we," Melissa said with a trace of merriment in her voice. "Let's sneak up on them."

Stanley nodded. Sure, what the hell. He liked this woman's sense of play.

They moved silently to the office door and stood for a moment eavesdropping. Stanley wondered for what purpose. He knew not a syllable of French. Melissa turned, cupped her hand, and whispered in his ear. The feel of her warm breath and lips so close to his ear sent a cool wave washing from the top of his head out through the tips of his toes.

"They're talking about Lafitte...best not press our luck." She backed up a few paces, walked directly to the door, and stood by the jamb. Stanley followed her lead and came to rest slightly behind and to her side.

Poteet looked up calmly and, seeing them, put his finger up as if signaling "...one moment please."

Lee Ann was seated in an Eames chair at one side of the big desk. Her feet were propped up on an ottoman, wineglass in hand. She was surveying the bank of screens opposite her. Stanley looked around Melissa into the room.

More beasts of the wild. Poteet and she were no doubt reviewing more of his work, while carrying on a side conversation about Jean Lafitte—in French. Up on the wall of screens, the animal show concluded and the screens went to blue for a moment. Then a face appeared on the centermost panel—not Poteet's—and began addressing the viewing audience.

They moved farther into the room to get a better view. Poteet had signaled, one moment, because the show they were watching had arrived at the beginning of a final pitch. The man of the moment, a very distinguished older man with a white mustache, was appealing to all the people of the earth to send him information about their various organizations: which organizations should be dedicated to the preservation of wildlife, in any form and at any level. Any organization from small groups through international consortiums were welcome.

An 800 number and an address flashed across the screen for several seconds under the title, *One World Incorporated,* and then the center panel went to blue. Poteet left the monitor on blue and swiveled to face them. "Good timing!" he boomed to the wandering Stanley and Melissa. "So, that is my appeal to the people of the world. Planet Earth for *all of us.* No small order." He paused; everyone was silent. "Sounds a bit pompous doesn't it?" There was a round of good-natured denial.

"Well," Stanley offered "Melissa and I work in the mud every day. It's a dirty job, but someone's got to do it." It was an obtuse comment but one that served to leaven the prodigious task Poteet had seen fit to assign himself.

"Ha! So...you've been down to the foundry now...no doubt Lissa has shown you her little pets. What do you think?"

"The foundry? Very impressive. Melissa's work? I can only say that I was stunned and amazed."

Poteet smiled warmly and nodded.

"And now," Stanley continued, bending slightly at the waist and addressing both of them, "may I have my load of clay?"

Poteet's eyes sparkled, his thin mouth curled upward. He said, "Melissa, has this man passed your muster? Do you consent to his being entrusted with your magic earth?"

The sculptress smiled slightly and glanced at Stanley. "Yes Jean Paul, he does...and I *do* very much want him to have it."

"Well...I could tell early on that she would let it go. So sir! You will find it resting on the trunk of your car."

How had he managed that, wondered Lee Ann. Poteet had not been out of her sight all evening. Such a mysterious chap was this. A silence fell between them for several seconds. Poteet knew the hour was late and expected his guests' next move.

"Sir..." Stanley began, feeling a need to remain formal, "you've been most gracious. It's been a memorable evening, but now we must be going."

Poteet looked at his pocket watch. "Eleven-o-five," he said, "near twelve bells. And you are speeding back across the bayou to your hotel room in New Orleans? Wouldn't you and Lee Ann prefer to stay for the night and drive back in the morning? I'm sure we've got an extra room around this barn we could freshen up for you..." He left it dangling, looking at both of them.

Lee Ann sprang from her chair. "Oh, you know, Jean Paul, you've been most gracious, but"—she moved over and took Stanley's arm —"we gotta' be hittin' the trail."

Jean Paul smiled in appreciation of her informal decline. He had come to know her over the past few years in her television persona, and now this evening in the flesh. He was amazed to discover that these two were exactly the same person.

"So go then...get out of here!" he boomed and slapped the desk with the palms of his hands. It was a spontaneous and loud gesture that caught everyone off guard. He softened immediately and went on.

"I can't remember when I've enjoyed an evening so much. But you must come back at least one more time before you leave New Orleans. Meet the Kenyans...all of them." He paused, looked at Stanley. "Well then, I don't mean to press, but please, after you've had time to consider it, call tomorrow and tell us when you can come back. We'll have a big party next time. You must promise!"

"Promise," they agreed in unison.

"Done then!" Poteet raised both of his hands as if releasing a pair of doves.

They made their way back through the slave galley, down the elevator to the library, through the towering oval entry hall with the curved stairway (where Stanley imagined Jacquel and Stella had played as young girls), and out onto the dimly lit portico of the mansion. Just five short hours ago they'd looked up at these high Doric columns and swallowed hard at the thought of penetrating this fortress. Now it was just the grand home of Jean Paul and Melissa, friends from Louisiana. Well, not yet, but they were both sure it would come to that.

Melissa stood by Jean Paul's chair as their guests walked to their car and deposited two twenty-five pound bricks of Melissa's clay in the trunk. They all waved one last time as Stanley started his turn down the cypress canopied lane.

"CALL!" Poteet boomed one last time before they were out of earshot.

"PROMISE!" Lee returned, and then they were gone.

Poteet and Melissa stood watching red taillights disappear down a tunnel of trees. "Well, Melissa...what thinks you of our new California friends?"

"What thinks you, Jean Paul?"

"Ah, I asked you first."

She grew reflective, was silent for a moment and then said, "I think, if you take away all the trappings, they are very much like you and me. Except...reversed in gender."

"Ahhh...my wonderful, perceptive Melissa. My feelings exactly. It will be fun having them for friends, won't it?"

"Yes," she said without elaboration, and thought...very good friends, I'm sure.

10.

And so the sound of Lafitte laughing echoes down the dark streets of the the French Quarter as our dinner guests speed away from Poteet's compound: one of the many Maison Rouges that our naval privateer established.

"I wonder how many Lafitte had?" Lee Ann mused. "You know...I'd like to know the number."

"How many what?" Stanley asked, jumping into the middle of her thoughts.

"Children...I wonder how many children Jean Lafitte had?"

"I'm sure many, but then there was only one recorded. A boy named Pierre, born out of wedlock to Lafitte and his mistress Catherine Villars.

"How did you know that?"

"I read it in a biography of Lafitte written by a man named Lyle Saxon." He paused for a moment to consider something and then went on. "Almost nothing is known about that son, Pierre, except that he was born and named after Jean's brother and lifetime comrade in arms. Brother Pierre, on the other hand, had nine children of recorded birth...one son who he named Jean, reciprocating the honor. Since I read that, I've been curious to know how Poteet traces his bloodline directly to Jean...if nothing is known about that one son of his."

"Good question."

"I thought maybe he might actually be descended from brother Pierre's passel. They were a tight unit all through life, as you can see...Jean and Pierre, I mean. Did he say?"

"No...hmm, that's interesting. I wish you had been there to ask. No, he just showed me his family heirlooms and such, authenticated by some outfit in Paris. I really didn't have enough information…or for that matter…the inclination to probe. Would have seemed inappropriate. But, you know…you've made me curious. See if you can find out, why don't you."

"Hmm, I will." Stanley swerved to avoid hitting a turtle crossing the road. Lee Ann moaned and grabbed her head. Uh-oh, a little too much fine French wine? He decided to keep going and keep her mind off of it. "You know…Saxon gives the impression that Lafitte wasn't really a womanizing kind of guy. He loved power much more than women. Who knows, maybe he was gay."

"You think so? Have you read that somewhere?"

"No…I don't know that, and I've never read anything to that effect, but maybe he was. He was a man of the sea; he spent most of his time with men. Maybe he was lost in naval tactics and power… partied once in awhile but basically just liked to pirate." He looked over and saw Lee Ann's head rolling about on top of her neck—propelled by every sweeping turn of the levee road.

"Talk to me, Stanley…" she said.

"What would you like to discuss, my dear?" He considered asking her if she would like to drive but reconsidered. She was in no shape to negotiate this narrow two-laner.

"Tell me about Melissa's stuff, any good?"

"Very," he said quickly.

He paused to reflect now and choose his words carefully to describe Melissa's work. Lee Ann shut her mouth and let him ponder. Hurry up, Stanley, let's keep it rolling. Oh boy, she *really* didn't feel so good now. She pressed herself deep into the cushions and hoped he would get on with it; she needed to keep talking, keep her mind off a stomach that was swilling about below like a backyard pool in a San Francisco shaker.

"I don't know," he began tentatively. "I don't know exactly how to describe Melissa Frank's work. It's very good, technically…I'm sure you'll agree. Subject matter? It's very much about slavery. She's doing a complete set of figures of black people, slaves, as seen prior to the time of the Civil War. And they *are* beautiful. They have a sinuous Thomas Hart Benton feel to them. If he sculpted as he painted, that's what I think his work would look like. You know, all the lines of all the figures flowing into one another. Some distortion, yes, but not as much as my work. Not to the extent of a cartoon. Just a twisting and a pulling of the figures. And the expressions on the faces are excellent...full of life."

"What....what are they of?"

He thought he'd answered that. He looked over at Lee Ann, saw that she was turning green. She'd even let a preposition dangle. That wasn't like her. "Um...people. Old people, young people, kids, families. Basically everyone looks as though they're having a good enough time. Not suffering all that much."

She spoke softly, "I think I should drive now, Stan. I'm feeling kinda woozy."

He could tell by the way she was slurring her words that she meant business. She needed to stop, but it wasn't to switch drivers. "Sure thing," he said, "first wide spot in the road we come to."

"You know, I wouldn't mind just walking around for a bi..." She gulped off the end of her last word.

He saw a gleam of crushed white oyster shells in the headlights ahead—that wide spot in the road they so desperately needed at this moment in time. He pulled off the asphalt and onto the shells. In the light of some old streetlamps he could see a picnic table or two. Lee Ann didn't wait for the car to come to a full stop; she bulldogged down out of the passenger's side door—wedgy heels sending up a hail of clams—and made for the trees. He parked the car, shut off the engine, grabbed his sportcoat from the backseat, and set off after her.

"I'm okay now Stan, just give me a min..." she didn't finish the word.

He winced as he heard her gag. Yes, she did need a minute by herself here to be sick. And she did that, grandly he thought, and with a minimum of cursing and groaning. Then she came running back to the car for a few Kleenexes, a spray of Binaca, some mints, and a swig from a bottle of Evian. She hated to throw up. He knew that she would do anything to avoid it, but now she had, and it was over, and he knew she would be glad she had, as soon as she'd freshened up again.

Somewhere from the deep recesses of her handbag she produced a scrunchy, pulled her now frizzy hair back into a ponytail, and stood mopping the perspiration from her brow. "Man Stan, I hate to do that. It makes me sweat like a mare in foal. You think the water down at that spigot is okay to drink?"

"Hmm, this is a picnic ground, so I'd imagine if it wasn't, they'd have a sign to that effect. Let's check it out."

They put an arm about one another's waist and set off in the direction of the spigot. "You tired?" he asked.

"No, not at all. You?"

"No."

There it was again, that jarring, out of synch sensation, every time he tried to move along arm in arm with Lee Ann. What *was* the problem? Was it that her legs were so much longer than his? Was it that she simply was oblivious to the fact that it should be comfortable, flowing and smooth when you walked arm in arm with another person? He'd tried hard, and now he tried again to match *her* gait. No use. It simply would never happen. Was it her? Was it him? What *was* it? He thought of Melissa.

He let her go as they approached the spigot. She swung her long legs from the hips and strode out ahead of him. Lee was back, feeling strong again; he could see it in that cowgirl stride of hers. She reached for the handle, turned it on, bent at the knees, balanced on her toes, set her elbows on the tops of her thighs, and began splashing off her face. Melissa had disappeared somewhere back into the steamy bayou midnight, so Stanley fell in love again with Lee Ann. Well, not so much in love as into the past. He'd seen her do this so many times. Lee Ann, squatting on the tips of her toes, washing her face like one of the ranch hands. Washing her face like one of the boys.

"Crossfire," she heard him say behind her.

"Wha..?" she said, still scrubbing.

"Oh, I don't know...can you spare some of the agua, senorita?"

"Oh, sorry, let me get a couple of handfuls here and then you've got it."

She cupped a palm, slurped up a couple of mouthfuls, and flung her hand off to one side. Bright diamonds of light shot from her fingertips and disappeared into the trees where Melissa had disappeared just moments ago. She stood and started mopping the last of the water off her face with the tail of her blouse. Stanley splashed off his face, took a couple of long pulls on the spigot, and turned it off.

They moved to a picnic bench and sat down side by side, elbows resting on their knees. It was a position they'd brought with them from riding coral rails out on the ranch—back home. Lee Ann leaned back, shifted her elbows to the table, arched her back, and stuck out her chest.

"Lee," said Stanley, looking full on at her breasts, "how do you keep those things ridin so high?"

She snapped her shoulders forward and sat staring at him out of the corner of her eye. "Crossfire?" she asked, "what did you mean by that?"

"Oh no. You have to answer my question first."

She looked at him as if she thought she was really tough and said, "Well you know Stan, there never really was all that much to fall in the first place, hmm?" She elbowed him. "And you know...we have to flex our pecs a lot in my business. So I'd say you have your answer there as to why these little beauties— HA—are a ridin so high." She bounced them several times in the palms of her hands as if to prop them up even higher.

He felt it all getting back to normal again—and it felt good. Poteet and Melissa had been an acid trip into aristocracy, and then Lee Ann had lost her wine, but now it was time to settle down again and enjoy this humid Louisiana night. Lee was feeling playful. So they'd play.

"Crossfire, Stan, I'm waiting..."

"Okay, fair enough." He wondered how honest he was going to be. Not very, he decided.

"What I should have said is braintied." He paused, took a breath. Lee Ann hadn't the slightest idea where he was going with this, but her interviewer instincts were relentless, and she wouldn't let up. She knew, and he knew, they had something they needed to talk about right here and right now, and the band had started to play, and it was time to dance. She waited. Lee Ann was not very good at waiting, but she did now. Finally, he went on.

"Been kind of a hermit these past five years, Lee. Oh, not a monk, but then again, almost. Celibacy, you see."

"Five years!"

Well, I cheated there a little bit last year, but yeah, Willy's been sleeping like a bear for most of five years. Oh, he's come out of his cave and taken a hand ration now and then, but..."

"STANLEY! Let's not get too graphic here."

"Oh...sorry." He bumped her with his shoulder. "Anyway... suddenly this morning, I wake up in New Orleans with my ex-wife's back in my frame. And this afternoon...boy...this afternoon." He pulled her in sideways.

"Mmm," She made that sound, slipped a hand around his waist, and fell into him like a bale of alfalfa.

"So, here I am falling in love with you again, and I'm feeling some good things coming back from you...old shoe...and then we head out to Poteet's, and Melissa comes smoking up my tail like a heat-seeking missile..."

She pulled away quickly and gave him a look. "She flirted with you! What did you guys do down there at the foundry? Flounder around a little?"

"No, I didn't mean to implicate Melissa. She's all lady and loyal, in some way I haven't figured out yet, to Poteet. But now... yeah, now that I think about it, she does flirt. Discreetly...oh so discreetly...but she flirts. Anyway, it's probably that I'm in love with her work." He was out of words, thought it was time to lob the ball to Lee Ann who was dancing around in the flat. "Sounded like you and Poteet were getting along *marrrvolously.*"

"Are we through with you and Melissa, and me and you, and you being a naughty horny little boy?"

"Uh huh...for now. Hey, when did you learn to speak French?"

"Helping Claire with her homework. She's a hopeless Frankophile you know."

"I know."

"I don't speak much. But it's a fun language to play with. Somehow Jean Paul and I started talking about Lafitte, and we lapsed into French. I think I started it and he quickly picked it up. Soon left me in the dust. But he was patient and amused.... and so we made a joke out of it. That's when you and Melissa returned from the *fouuundry*."

"So...did you fall in love?"

"Tsssss..." She let about that much air out from a space between her tongue and the roof of her mouth, and then looked at him sideways and smiled.

"Madly Stan...hopelessly...desperately...terminally in love."

"Exaggeration will get you nowhere, Lee Ann, fess up."

"Well, it's hard for you not to fall in love with lovely Melissa, the very fine artist, isn't it? Jean Paul is a well-connected media freak with some rather good intentions, wouldn't you say? Yeah, I was entertained, amused, enlightened, saw a potential personality for the show, saw a mutually beneficial symbiosis kind of thing. Yeah, Stan, I was attracted...fell down a couple of stairs."

"Mmmhuh."

"Oh, Stan, you know us gals in those high heeled shoes. We're just always a–catchin' those little old heels on the treads and snaggin our little ol' nylons on the table leg. We're just always a-dodgin' that *crossfire*." She slung an arm over his shoulder.

"What say we do some ridin', partner?"

"Yeah," said Stanley in his best desperado, knowing that their trading time was done. "Let's ride."

11.

The Louisiana bayou night was steamy, but the air between them had been cleared. Now the humid breeze rushing about the passenger compartment of the Mustang was cool and invigorating. Things were back to go. Lee Ann was driving, and because the road was narrow and winding, and patches of fog lifted here and there over the asphalt, she was taking it easy. She wanted to know about the one time out of five years of celibacy when Stanley had "cheated."

"So, you had a hot one there last year?"

He wasn't sure what she was referring to. Then it occurred to him. She was asking him about that sad little time last year when he'd come out of retirement and tried to get it right. She was talking about Kathleen. "Oh," he said, "wanna hear a war story? Long or short version?"

"Hmm, well, just take off...if you wander too far, little dogie, I'll nudge you back home."

He smiled. "Just keep that lariat off my hams, hear?"

"Deal."

"You remember Kathleen? Kathleen and Jackson Jerek? We were just sort of getting to be friends when you and I split up again...five years ago?" He needed to know that she remembered them before he went on.

"Yeah, Jackson, the young assistant DA, and Kathleen..."

"Became a casting agent...still is...doing very well."

"Stanley! Did you ruin their happy home? Shame on you!" Lee Ann, making one of her quantum leap assumptions.

"*Au contraire* dearest...you want to button up and listen?"

"Tell me, tell me, I won't tell." There she was, his bratty little sister bouncing in her chair.

"All right...so...Kathleen and Jackson split shortly after we did."

"Didn't know that...lost track of them. I liked Kathleen, but Jackson was kind of a pompous little ass, didn't you think?" Lee Ann leapt again. "Oh, so you were the consoling friend and ended up in bed with Kathleen! Stanley, did you fall in love with Kathleen Jarek?"

"I'll tell you what, Lee Ann, why don't you tell the story?"

"Sorry...shut up, Lee Ann...listen."

He waited and then went on. "Yes...to answer your question, I did fall in love with Kathleen. And it was hard, baby. Hardest since you." He poked her in the ribs with his index finger.

The Mustang swerved momentarily...dangerously close to a steep shoulder.

"HEY!" she shouted, pulling it back on track. "There are creepy, crawly things with big teeth on either side of this road. I'm not in the mood for a swim." She looked at him and then quickly swung her eyes back in the direction of the road. "Okay, so you fell...then what happened?"

"Gotta double back here a bit, Lee. You're always jumping out ahead of the action."

"I always got a commercial coming up, cowboy. *Yippee yi ki yay, git along little dogie, 'cause you know that Gillette will be your new foam.*" She sang it in her best cowgirl alto.

Stanley could only marvel. Was this girl ever "off"?

"So you wanna do the shaving cream slot, and then come back for the conclusion of Kathleen and Stanley?"

"Naw, Stan, you just keep going. Sounds like a close shave." She cracked up at her own joke, and her friend just shook his head. Lee Ann, stand-up comic.

"Somehow, you are usurping all the pathos from my story. And if you don't stifle, Edith, I'm just going to have to back up, *way* up."

Lee was still writhing, trying to contain herself. "Okay... promise...I promise Stan. I'll quit."

He looked over at her—chewed his gum. "Let's talk about something else."

"Oh no...come on, Stan, I'm sorry. I promise I'll quit. Tell the rest of it."

"Okay. I was going to give you the semi-long version, but I've lost heart for it, so here's the bare-bones version. I fell in love with Kathleen and stayed friends with Jackson. Because I was talking with both of them about their past problems with the other, I figured out what had gone wrong with their marriage. So I told them both what I'd come up with..."

"You figured out their problem? Were you doing it with her at this point in time?"

"*Doing* it, Lee? Yeah...we were *doing* it. Their problem? Yes, I did. I figured it out. Some of it stemmed from the fact that she was black and he was white. That was easy, and I told them they couldn't make that go away. But what was really at the bottom of it all was their self-centeredness... what's new? They just hadn't taken the time to work out how they would handle two extremely demanding careers colliding. Well, there were specifics, domestic things, you know...we isolated those...too detailed to get into here." He dug in her handbag, looking for another mint. "And I know you're waiting for the punch line."

She nodded but kept her lip zipped.

"Very strange...they decided to have lunch, and after lunch, well not right after but shortly after, they decided to fly off to Rio." He paused, thought of Melissa, went on. "And a week after they got back, they got remarried."

"What!?"

"They redid it and are presently enjoying marital bliss...as far as I know."

"Too much! I suppose that sweet little Jackson asked you to be his best man. He's such a...why-just-stick-the-old-DA-blade-in-and-give-it-a-twist-kind of guy. Creep!"

"God...you really didn't like him, did you? No...actually they were about as empathetic as two people could be. Both came and talked to me after the honeymoon and asked if they could come over some afternoon and talk. Both wanted to remain my friend. I said yes, but said it would have to be in the next ice age...or some time around then."

"Good for you Stan." Lee consoled. She could tell by his expression and tone of his voice that Kathleen had been more to him than a flight to the moon on gossamer wings. That Kathleen had been more than just one of those things.

She yawned. She could listen for only so long without nodding off, especially at this time of night after only six hours of sleep in the last forty-eight.

"Wanna hear my story, Lee?"

"Wanna hear my story, Stan?"

It was their way of passing the ball.

"Yeah, Lee Ann, tell me your story."

Without taking her eyes off the road she said, "Okay"

She softened, became radiant green in the lights of the Mustang's dashboard. A mist formed about her face and eyes, telling Stanley that this must be a doozy. "...okay," she'd said, and her voice, in that brief consent, had grown husky and, he thought, a little sad.

"We can talk about something else if you like."

"No, this'll do me good to tell you...old historian. You'll like this one."

She took a deep breath.

"His name was Miguel...Miguel Costos Ramone. His people in Colombia called him *Alondra*, 'lark', in Spanish. He'd played the flute since he was a little boy."

"A musician?" Stanley asked.

"Yes, a musician...like you, Stan. Not professional but just enjoyed it. No, he was a doctor. I wish you could have known him." She looked at him, he nodded, she went on. "He came into my life about two months after Embarcadero. I was just out of my casts, trying to do the weather at KPIQ. Miguel was, among other things, a physical therapist. And man, oh man, did I need one. So I dropped into his office one day for my first session. He lived in a penthouse on Russian Hill."

"Russian Hill penthouse, huh? Way to go, Lee."

She smiled. "All very innocent though...and ethical and proper. Yeah Stan, if ya gotta know, I fell in love with him the minute he opened the door and said. 'Senora Barnes...?'"

"He wasn't all that handsome really, not tall, not distinguished in any way, except for the simplicity of his Indian face. And his eyes...eyes of age..."

She went on to tell him that Miguel treated her all that next year. That she would look forward to her Tuesday and Friday sessions like a schoolgirl because she just kept falling more and more in love with him. He, however, gave off no sign that these feelings were mutual, always remaining the gentle caring physician that he was.

At the end of a year's time, after he had quite literally put her back on her feet again, he'd told her one day that he could no longer treat her. "Why?" she'd asked. "Because...I have fallen in love with you, Lee Ann," he'd said in that polite Indian manner of his. She said that it had astonished her, because for a whole year, he hadn't given off the slightest hint of these feelings.

She said she'd confessed to him then that the feelings were very mutual. So they'd celebrated by going to lunch at the Japanese Tea Garden in Golden Gate Park. After lunch she'd taken him to the eucalyptus tree and told him the story of Bird. He'd told her then about his wife, who had been abducted from her parents' house in Bogata one day never to be seen or heard from again. "We held then," she told Stanley, "and cried a little for each other."

Three happy years passed. She said that Miguel and his young children, Pedro and Lita, had become part of her life: a new family. She said she loved the children and spent time with them even when Miguel was away in Colombia on various medical missions. He'd been setting up clinics in the jungle to take care of those wounded in the drug wars. It was a mission that would cost him dearly.

"He was such a good man though...always having to straddle some kind of medical/military metaphor. It was an interesting but, at the same time, painful, thing to watch that..."

They were exiting Interstate 10 now, heading back into the French Quarter. Le Richelieu was only a few short blocks away. Stanley yawned and nodded. He'd been listening carefully to Lee Ann's telling of this tale, interrupting only to ask a question or two. He'd liked her characterization of the man, somber as it was. He wondered what had happened to Miguel. But he would wait. He could tell that she was nearing the wrapup.

"...I guess I'm having to tell you enough so that you will see, without a doubt, that I loved the man and his children and his work very much. Can you see that?" She looked over at him with plaintive eyes: a little sadness, a little indignation, a little pain.

"Yes love, it's most evident."

They'd reached Le Richelieu. Lee Ann, now in a deep funk, found a space in the parking lot, swung in, and cut the engine. "Need to sit here for a minute, Stan, while I have a cigarette and finish this."

"You smoking again?"

"Only when I'm about to be executed." She looked over at him, pushed in the lighter and fished a cigarette out of her bag—all in the same motion. The lighter popped out, she lit, the end glowed, and she said, "That's what happened to Miguel." Deep drag—exhale. "He was executed." She said it coldly, with more anger than he'd seen from her since she'd told him about the seaman.

"He was *executed?*"

"That's what I've been told...what I could learn from his family, and they'd received only sketchy details. Basically, it went like this: He was at some outpost back in the hills, taking care of the wounded from the fighting, when he was captured by some splinter group of the FARC guerillas. The leader of the group recognized him as the son of a wealthy Bogata physician, Miguel's father, and held him for ransom. The ransom money was somehow diverted, so the FARC commander ordered Miguel's execution." Her voice had grown hoarse. "A medical doctor tending the wounded, shot in cold blood." She shook her head and put a hand to her brow. "They sent his head home to his family...in a box."

The smoke from her cigarette curled like intertwining serpents—like a caduceus—into the early morning darkness. Stanley, feeling slightly sick to his stomach, sat in shocked reverent silence for a moment then began softly.

"A man dedicating his life to the preservation of wildlife on this planet is gored into crippledom for the rest of his life by an angry rhino. A woman returns to her husband, thanks to the work that her lover has done to reconcile them. A man building hospitals to take care of the wounded of some jungle struggle is gunned down by a roving petty guerilla. Huh, my story sounds pretty mundane in comparison, doesn't it."

"What is this"—Lee Ann glared at him—"some kind of competition?" She was still feeling incensed, taking it out on him. Well okay, he could field it.

"No Lee, just seems I'm picking up a theme of rescuer becomes victim."

She softened, then smiled sadly. "No, Stan, I don't think your story is mundane in comparison. We both lost a love. Mine just moved off a little bit farther into the hills than yours."

"Sorry."

"Me too." She stubbed out the cigarette and covered her mouth with her hand. "Whoa, I think I'm getting tired now, how about you?"

"Yeah," He nodded, his limbs had grown leaden at the sight of her cavernous yawn. "I'm exhausted."

They closed up the car, made their way to the room, let themselves in, and there, straight ahead of them on a small wall table, was the bouquet.

12.

It was an arrangement of gardenias, with leafy sprays all done up in a very oriental way. But it was a southern spring bouquet and so fragrant that it laced the air in the room with a sweet spicy perfume. Lee Ann made it to the table in three long strides, picked up the card, and read it. Her already naturally light complexion turned chalky white. In a Kabuki face, hazel eyes glowed vermillion. She handed the card to Stanley. He took it and read the brief message:

The seaman sends you his love.

Lee gasped. "Christ, Stanley, how did he find me? How did he know I was *here?*"

Stanley sat down slowly on the edge of the bed, card still pinched between his index and second finger. He twiddled it and snapped it several times with his thumb. "Unbelievable."

"The man is spending an *awful* lot of money watching me, Stanley. An *awful* lot of money." She stood, breathing deeply... went on. "And he's obviously very well connected, as you might have noticed. *And"* —she motioned to the bouquet—"you gotta admit, he has class." She laughed the silly giggle of a condemned person.

"Sick...but yes, great. Beautiful bouquet."

"Beautiful...always beautiful," she said softly, "Maybe he isn't so bad after all. Maybe he isn't a bad person...just some lonely old rich guy out there who...*no*...he's weird." She scrunched her eyes. "He's weird...I don't like someone telling me they are going to put a bullet in my body because *they* can't be there...

that's just jack *sick*." Her tone of voice had slowly descended into pure disgust.

"Yeah, sick...so, he's having you followed. But you already knew that. But, of course, didn't think his help was this good."

Lee walked back over and sat down on the edge of the bed. She laid an arm over his rounded shoulders and thumped his clavical with her fingernails. "Yeah, he's good ...I wonder if this could have something to do with Miguel?"

He shook his head. "No...it's not that. I think it's someone you don't know, some wealthy, lonely man out there who has seen you on TV every day. I've been known to fall in love with newsladies on occasion. Know what I mean, tellybean?" He laughed, gave her a squeeze. "Even a few after you..."

She pinched that clavical hard now. Hard. Stanley took the pain. They sat in silence for a moment.

"So I think...so I *have* to confess a lie to you," she stammered.

"It's okay if I confess it before you find out about it isn't it? Then you're not so mad that I lied?"

"Oh sure," he mumbled, drawing in his breath. Boy, never a dull moment with L. A. B. around.

She blurted it out. "I've confirmed reservations for tomorrow at nine-fifteen am to fly to Toronto."

He looked over at her out of the corners of his eyes. "You *what?* I thought you said you were just checking. But you'd already confirmed!"

"I know...I lied. I didn't want to spoil your evening. That's okay isn't it?"

He pulled her in sideways. "Yeah...it's okay. I'm just having to shift gears a little bit here. I suppose..."

She interrupted. "You know, I might not have gone...you know? I was teetering. I was thinking about all the great times we've been having down here on the bayou...as they say. And I wanted to go back out to Poteet's, investigate Claire Leveau, spend the rest of the time with you. I *love* this town, Stan... but now I can't stay...I've *got* to give this guy the slip...you understand, don't you?"

He nodded, shuffled his feet. He knew she was right. She continued.

"But this time...this time you'll have to cover for me, because I need to lose whoever's following me. Even if I have to work out some kind of disguise." She spoke softly now to her old sidekick, almost in a whisper. "I *need* to lose them Stanley."

"Do you think there's a mole at the station?"

"You mean at KPIQ?"

"Yes, you know, someone there always knows, or practically always knows where you are...where you're going...where you'll be. You know, phone calls come in, where's Lee Ann, when's she coming back...ta da, ta da, ta da. You know what I mean?"

"Brilliant Stanley."

"Well? Do you think there is an informant there? Someone paying someone to feed them inside information as to your whereabouts?"

"Makes sense doesn't it? God, you don't suppose they've bugged my house and tapped my phone do you?"

She was getting slightly hysterical, but he could see why. "No," he began quietly, "that requires a fair amount of costly equipment and risk. And it wouldn't be necessary if they had a mole at the station. It could be that someone is slipping a receptionist or line producer a couple of hundred to give them some rather innocent information. Maybe this receptionist or producer has been told that it's someone at a rival station who's interested in keeping track of you." It sounded weak. "I don't know, I'm not a PI, but those guys can come up with six hundred innocent reasons why someone should spy for them... for money."

"So you think this morning when I called Maureen at the station, someone was eavesdropping and relayed that information to someone who relayed that information to the seaman!?"

"Or maybe someone was watching when we left the gallery last night, followed us to your house while you got your things, and followed us to my place while I got my things. Followed us to the airport, saw what flight we got on, got on a later flight, paid someone at the rental car company to tell them where we were staying...no, the mole at the station is more expedient. And you did call Maureen this morning and tell her where you were, didn't you? That's the way I would try to work it...infiltrate the station..." He was almost mumbling to himself now, but Lee Ann heard him loud and clear.

She sprang from the bed, flew to the French doors, flung them open and screamed.

"HOW LONG AM I SUPPOSED TO PUT UP WITH THIS FUCKING SHIT, STANLEY?"

He patted the air with his palm—believed that was the correct signal for take the "fucking" volume down. She did and went on in a frustrated whiny voice. "I'm just a little working TV talk show host trying to make a living! How am I suppose to be cheery little Lee Ann, shooting from the hip, with this creep licking my neck like some fucking slimy lizard?" She didn't like to use the various conjugations of the word fuck, liked to save them for special occasions. He could tell she was furious. He would be too.

"I'm sick of it Stanley; I'm going to the FBI. There must be a law against this, isn't there...stalking across state lines or something? I have nothing to lose, I have nothing to hide, I'm the *victim!*" She screamed the word in a whisper and collapsed into a chair. He was glad she'd thrown her tantrum. Was even happier that now it seemed to be over. She could get loud when she was angry and frustrated. It was going on 12:45am and even in the French Quarter of New Orleans, one or two people were sleeping.

"FBI might not be a bad idea Lee. You are a personality, they probably would...oh, I don't know though...they probably *wouldn't* do much for you. They have a lot bigger fish to fry, especially in this neck of the woods. No, to tell you the truth, I think somehow you're going to have to get in touch with this seaman person yourself. Say...before you put a bullet in my little bird body, can we talk, face to face, just you and me...see if we can strike some kind of a bargain...work something out?'" They were silent for a few beats and then he continued with a new idea.

"Why don't you do it on your show? Go back to San Francisco, put it on the air, and get back out again, and don't let *anyone*, not even Maureen know where you're going. Or...better yet"—he was making this up as he went along—"why don't we videotape you giving a message to the seaman? You can send it to the station with instructions to run it on your show. Go public, pull in popular support, turn the seaman's shit back on himself. I don't know... makes for some rather exciting material, pays the bill for your absence. Action journalism...and all that."

Lee Ann had been listening to him intently as he pulled all this out of his ass. "Stanley, I love your mind. You should have been a spy. You'd have to learn to drive faster, and lie a little bit more convincingly, but you really *should* have been a spy."

"Oh, you know...I am a spy, Lee Ann...in my own mind."

"Hmmph."

"You know how much I love le Carre...and now Grisham. I've learned so much from those guys. Great writers you know, really know how to spin a crystal web of intrigue and then shatter it with some single shot of realization."

"Don't really want to talk about shots right now, Stan, if you don't mind. We've got work to do. Did you bring your video equipment?"

He stared at her incredulously. "Uh huh, Lee Ann, I haul the old Betamax recorder and separate dino camera with me everywhere I go. Got it right over there in my suitcase. He motioned to a black bag in the corner that was really more a large carry-on case. In these last few months on the art circuit, he'd learned to travel light.

"Stan, I didn't mean your old dinosaur. I just assumed you'd have bought yourself one of those zippy little camcorders that pack away in a dopp kit."

"No."

He looked at her for a moment, and then said, "No Lee Ann, I didn't bring the dino, and I haven't yet purchased a 'zippy little camcorder.' Just sorta left the TV work to you.

"Hey... doesn't your cell phone do video?"

"Not yet, Stan, not yet."

"Well then, where're we going to find a camcorder at two am ?"

They made a plan. Lee Ann would stay in the room and work on her message to the fans of her San Francisco morning show. Stanley would go downstairs and start with the night clerk to locate a camcorder. If that didn't pan out, he would go from there, but he would somehow acquire a camera and return to the room.

In the room they would tape Lee Ann's message, and it, along with a letter in her hand, would be mailed by Stanley the next day to KPIQ in San Francisco. Attention: Maureen Palmer: URGENT! After it was in the box, he would call KPIQ and tell Maureen personally that it was coming. Only that.

After the taping, Lee Ann would pack and disguise herself in some way. He would leave the room first and move to the car in the lot. If someone was watching the door to the room, it was assumed that someone would follow him. Ten minutes after he left the room, Lee Ann would exit via the front entrance. She would walk to the corner of Royal and Ursulines streets where Stanley would pick her up. They would drive twenty-four miles across Lake Pontchartrain Bridge in the early morning darkness, watching their tail all the way. If a person was being pursued by a single PI operator, that bridge across miles of open water was a dream come true. Additionally, they decided that Lee Ann would not cancel her reservations with Continental out of New Orleans, but simply not show and forfeit her fare. She would, however, board the earliest commuter flight out of Baton Rouge and fly to some larger airport somewhere connecting to Toronto. If anyone could follow her through that maze of maneuvering, he deserved to catch her, she said.

They hugged and congratulated each other on their ingenuity.

Stanley said, "And besides Lee Ann, I don't feel this guy would harm you in light of all his earlier feelings of needing to charm you. So, though we...*you* do need to lose him and go on the offensive, I don't think there is too much *real* danger in all of this."

"Well good Stanley, I'm glad you feel that way, because as long as you're with me, you are in as much danger as I am. Who knows, maybe this guy is a really lousy shot."

"I don't think there's too much *real* danger in all of this." It had sounded oh so comforting, when he'd said it, but Lee Ann couldn't quite buy it.

"You know Stanley, one thing I've learned in the news business is that people will say one thing with their mouths and do something entirely contradictory with their actions. I can't really buy your lonely, rich pussycat theory. It could get me killed. I mean that. That's how I feel." Emeralds sparkled at the center of her dead earnest eyes. He knew better than to argue.

"You're right, Lee. Let's go."

They discussed one last detail before he departed on his mission. And that was whether or not to approach the desk clerk for the camera. If the clerk was watching for someone, he would report this. They were donning the cloak of the spy and had started suspecting everyone and considering every movement. They quickly decided it didn't make any difference if it *was* reported. He would return to the room with the camcorder and in two or three days—they hoped—the seaman would see their handiwork. By that time Lee Ann would be long gone. They marveled again at the silly, potentially lethal, game "he" was making them play, and then Stanley departed for the lobby leaving Lee Ann, steno pad in hand, scribbling away in bed.

Before Lee and Stan left Genoa Gallery the night before last, Evie Ester had walked to the wall safe in her office, punched out a combination on a digital keypad, and returned to the desk with a neatly banded packet of eighty one-hundred-dollar bills.

She insisted they take at least this amount of cash with them down south "...'cause you just might find some little side trip y'all might want to be takin." Evie was Jewish but could do a convincing Scarlet O'Hara. Stanley had thought, what the hell, she owed him $110,000 from the haul of the show that evening. He would take eight on the barrelhead. The eight thouand rested now—tucked away—sleeping soundly in the house safe of Le Richelieu.

He approached the night clerk, a kid barely out of high school, and said, "Good evening." Giving his California driver's license to the kid, he said, "My name is Stanley Hochstetter; I'm in room 201, and you're holding some cash for me in your safe. I'd like to get that money now please."

The clerk looked at the license, then up at Stanley, then down at the license, then up at Stanley. "Wull, I don't know, kin it wait til morning?"

Uh oh, he thought, this guy doesn't know the combination to the safe—and he needed the cash tonight. "Can you access the safe?" he asked, holding his breath.

"Watt?"

"Do you have...do you *know* the combination to the safe?"

"I think so. They made me memorize it. Hope I can remember it."

Was this kid fishing for a tip or was he just slow? Stanley pulled a twenty out of his wallet and laid it on the desk. "It would be worth this to me if you could remember."

The kid's eyes grew wide. Just a bit slow Stanley decided. The young night clerk turned to a small connecting room and worked on the safe for a full three minutes while Stanley paced the lobby. He looked out the windows to see if anyone was watching, then walked in the direction of the bar. It was dimly lit and empty, but he'd heard someone closing up. Keeping his eye on the still empty front desk, he ducked his head around the corner and saw Lisa Lynn battening down the hatches. Stroke of luck! He would skip asking the kid for a camcorder. He didn't have imagination enough to tie his shoes. He would go directly to Lisa Lynn, who he suspected was resourceful as hell. Paydirt. Where *was* that kid?

The clerk finally returned to the desk empty handed. Stanley's heart fell. Damn! He walked over to the desk with the twenty still in hand and said, "No luck?" The kid looked at him for a long moment then answered.

"No, I got it, but I'm suppose to ask you your mother's maiden name."

"Iris Mulholland," he answered quickly.

The clerk pulled an envelope out of his baggy pants and looked at the information printed on the outside. "Rawht," he drawled.

Stanley pushed the twenty over to him, took the envelope out of his hand, and exited quickly for the bar. "You done good, kid," he said and left him wondering if he had. The kid had looked into the unsealed envelope and seen a pile of hundreds—a whole lot of money. If he'd screwed up, he'd be working for this hotel for the rest of his life. "Oh, mister! You're suppose to count it after I give it to you and sign a release." Stanley heard him but decided the kid could chase him into the bar if he wanted to. He couldn't afford to miss Lisa.

She'd finished mopping up and hanging glasses and had gone on to shutting down the till. She had her back to him as he entered the bar. The comely little bartend was wearing a black-scoop neck tank top and snug, but not too snug, Levi's. Her long brown pony tail was swishing back and forth on the nape of her neck as she looked back and forth, back and forth, from till to tally tag. Without turning from her work she spoke—Texas all the way. "Closed for the evenin, Stan ma man, but I could spare y'all a soda."

She turned and blinded him. He felt like a Rocky Mountain buck caught in the headlights. This morning she'd been wearing a baggy blouse tied at the waist over that tight black tank top. This morning the blouse had been unbuttoned enough to hint at the glory, but now there it was in *all* its glory. He hoped she didn't, but knew she did, see the flick of his eyes.

"Rawght kindly of you, got a nasty mouth fulla traildust. Glass of sody with some eyes'd do me fine." He could overdo Texas; it wasn't that far from Colorado.

Lisa Lynn, thoroughly accustomed to people making fun of her accent, produced a glass, scooped some ice into it, pulled a spigot from a console, and bubbled him up. "This is good for that wee bit too acid stomach that comes with fine French wine. Heard you went out to Poteet's this evenin."

What? He flashed. This girl knew everything. "How in hell did you know that, Lisa Lynn?" he asked and pulled a swizzle stick out of a drink that didn't need stirring.

"Little lady of yours gave your life story to those Californians this morning. I heard Poteet this, and Poteet that, and Poteet Porcelain this evening for dinner. Put it together." She folded her arms in front of her and smiled as wide as a West Texas prairie. "Lisa Lynn, little law student at Tulane, workin bar at Le Richelieu, hears all...sees all...tells nothin."

Stanley wondered. "I'm impressed," he said flatly.

"What you doin prowlin round this time a night?"

"I might ask you the same. You were here this morning. What're you doing...two shifts today?"

"Yeah, Thursday's my long day, need to rack up the bucks."

Bet she's racked up a buck or two in her day, he thought and smiled. "Know what you mean...uh, Lisa, I'm kind of in a hurry here and you probably want to get on home, so I'll get to the point." She nodded, he went on. "I was wondering if you or any of your friends have a TV camcorder I could borrow for...say, till...well, I could get it back to you tomorrow by noon...give you a deposit if you'd need one, whatever, but I need it now, and it would be worth this to me to have one for that short a time." On the way into the bar, he'd fished a hundred out of the envelope. He pushed it now, across the mahogany, in her direction. "I could go more, if you need to collaborate."

Lisa Lynn was going to be a right fine lawyer. She looked at the hundred without expression, thinking how she might scoop it up—smiled. "You and that little Lee Ann makin home movies this evenin? Boy, do you Californians *ever* sleep?"

"Whoa, Lisa Lynn, y'all got a dirty little mind?"

"Well...are you?"

"None of your business, can you do it?"

Lisa was going through the Rolodex she kept in her brain. Had to be someone nearby, someone who might be up this time of night.

"Got a friend named Amanda who lives a couple of blocks from here. She's a party animal by night, and her old man's a musician...among other things. I think they might be up. I think they might have one." She hesitated a moment, then went on. "You say, you could go a couple of hundred on that? I'd want to share. Amanda and Clay are a couple of poor street kids. Don't mean to be greedy, but you know what I mean?"

"One fifty," he said, digging another bill from his pocket and laying it on the bar. "Done," said Lisa and scooped up the money. "I'll need this to close the deal, but you can trust me. Say you can get it back to me tomorrow morning?"

He would be on his way back from Baton Rouge tomorrow morning, but he could make it by noon. "How about noon?" he asked.

Lisa bit her upper lip. "Noon would work. Okay...meet me back in the lobby in about fifteen minutes. I'm not sure this is going to work, but I'll give it a shot."

"That's cutting it pretty close, isn't it, lass? What say you try for a half-hour, and could you bring it up to room 201? That way I won't have to wait, and you won't have to wait.

Lisa pulled up one side of her face in a cowgirl grin and walked out from behind the bar to join him. They moved off in the direction of the lobby.

"Okay, see you at the door of room 201 within the half hour."

"Right." He watched her move off on her Lone Star legs. She'd ride right high and handsome on a red roan pony. Clem the clerk waved a release at him as he reentered the lobby. He signed it quickly, thanked the guy, and made his way to the elevator. Good work, Stanley. Good work.

13.

Lisa Lynn hurried down a slick black street that curved away from the French Quarter. She hoped she'd find Amanda home. It would be an easy seventy-five for her, and an even easier seventy-five for her starving artist, flea market, vagabond friend. She hoped that Clay hadn't returned home yet from the club. She didn't want to see Clay. She *really* didn't want to see Clay. But she knew she would be seeing Clay as she climbed the stairs of their ramshackle house and heard voices coming from inside. The angry voices of Clay and Amanda fighting. They were always fighting these days it seemed. Good little budding lawyer that she was, she stood for a moment trying to hear what it was they were battling about. Clay was speaking in that measured way of his, but with anguish in his voice.

"I can't believe you did that Amanda. I can't believe you took all that stuff and traded it for twenty-five bucks! That was my stuff!

"We gotta eat, Clay; we gotta pay the rent. You need a root canal...I thought..." Amandaa broke off. Lisa could tell her friend was nearing meltdown. Clay spoke softly now, and she couldn't make out what he was saying. Good timing, she thought. They're arguing about money, and here I am! Money Woman to the rescue!

Knock, knock. Pause. "Who is it?" Clay's impatient voice came from inside. "Just little ol' Lisa Lynn, paying you a profitable visit." She hoped that would work. There was a long pause and then Amanda's round hippy face appeared in the crack of a narrowly opened door. Her large blue eyes were ringed with red.

"Bad timing Lisa," she said.

Lisa knew that she had to talk fast. She pulled the money from her jeans. "I know it's late Amanda, but I've got a little business proposition for you this evening. A painless one-fifty for the use of your camcorder until...say three tomorrow afternoon?"

Clay came and stood behind Amanda in the crack. His face warmed at the sight of her. He was a thin six feet two with a huge mop of curly brown hair, an angular musician's face, and a two-day-old growth of beard. Lisa melted a little every time she laid eyes on him. She thought that lately she'd been getting some signals from him too. But he was Amanda's old man so, in her mind, that was that.

"A hundred and fifty till three tomorrow? Come in, come in," he said, and opened the door wide.

"I'm in a big hurry Clay," she puffed. "Gotta get back to the hotel in"—she glanced at her wrist—"fifteen minutes. Oh, and if you've got a blank tape, could you throw that in?" The guy hadn't asked her for that, but she didn't want to make two trips so took out some insurance.

Clay moved across the small but well kept living room to a wall closet. He opened the door, grabbed a small black bag, and returned to the two women. "What's up? Why do you need a camcorder pronto this time of the morning? You're not PI-ing again are you, Lisa?"

"No, *Clay*, nothing like that. Some people in the hotel need it for something. They're not saying what."

"Some *other people* are going to be using it?"

"Clay...I said I would have it back by," she thought a moment, "early tomorrow afternoon. Either this one or one just like it. You know I'm good on my word. I'm in a hurry here. Are the batteries charged? Blank tape? Connecting cables?"

"Everything's in the bag...but I'm not so sure..."

Lisa slapped the money into Amanda's hand and said. "Call you, or see you, around three this afternoon. Gotta run."

She made her way around Clay who was still fretting and closed the door behind her. Should she listen a minute and see what they said after she was gone? Well maybe, for just a second—time was growing short. She put her ear to the door. Clay immediately opened it. She bolted.

"What'd I tell you about that snoopy stuff, Lisa Lynn? You gonna get yersef killed someday with that shit." He was smiling. He rarely called her by both of her names, saved it for when he was teasing her and needed to mimic her twangy Texas speak.

"Yer right, Clay," she said turning red. "I'm a clod."

"Night," he said, "Take care of that thing."

"I will...promise."

He closed the door, and she set off in the direction of Le Richelieu—feeling stupid.

She was right; she *was* a clod. She'd given Amanda and Clay the whole hundred and fifty and would show nothing for her efforts here. Well, they needed it worse than she did, and besides, she wanted to talk with Lee Ann before she left about the TV business. What she was doing right now would certainly endear her to those two midnight movie makers. She wondered again what they were up to at this hour of the morning. And why couldn't it wait until tomorrow when they could rent a camcorder for a lot less than one-fifty? And as she hurried along the street back to the hotel, she wondered about that Slav, Audid, who'd been hanging around the bar this afternoon asking after a stocky middle-aged man and his "stylish" red headed female companion. He'd walked into the bar with a large arrangement of gardenias and told her that the desk clerk was away from her post and could a bellhop please run these up to their room? Lisa wondered what slimy Audid was up to now. She knew damn straight he wasn't a florist.

14.

When Stanley arrived back at the room, he called to Lee Ann again before slipping the card into the lock. She called back, He let himself into the room and walked to the dresser in quest of tonic and lime: no gin. He didn't bother Lee who was still sitting in bed, yellow pad still on her knees—still scribbling furiously away. "'Bout got it, Stan... how'd you do?"

"'Bout got it, Lee...keep your fingers crossed."

"You got a camera?"

"I said keep your fingers crossed. I've arranged for one, whether it gets here is contingent."

"On what?"

"On how resourceful Lisa Lynn is."

"Lisa Lynn?"

"Lisa Lynn, purveyor of the libations this afternoon. Barkeep downstairs. You talked to her?"

"No, but I know who you mean...long stemmed Texas rose who makes those mean bloody marys. Stan! You dog! You tell her you were her long-lost daddy?"

He smiled. "Man's gotta do what a man's gotta do." He paused. "No, I'm sure she's heard even that before. No, I was straight as a hundred-and-fifty-dollar arrow. And she caught that old Apache shaft right in her perty little teeth."

"Stanley, when did you become such a little operator?"

"My latent Jewish blood, Lee Ann. Hochstetter, remember."

"What are you making?"

"Tonic and lime, no gin."

"Sounds good, could you?"

"Sure." He filled another glass and squeezed the last wedge of lime over the fizz. "So...what do you have? Can I hear it?"

"Yeah, but let's sit out on the balcony...kind of stuffy in here."

"Sounds good."

They picked up their drinks and moved out onto a balcony that was really more a painted board roof over the sidewalk below.

"Should we set up the lights?"

"What?"

"Should we set up a place with a chair and move some lights around before we settle down out here?"

"Uh yeah..." he said, "and I've got the makeup girl coming in at"—he glanced at his watch—"one forty-five. And the hair guy at one-fifty. So let's keep up the pace people, we've got a show to do here."

"You making fun of my craft, Stan?"

"Yes."

"Okay well...do you think we should do that?"

"Well I don't know. I mean, what's the use of setting up the set before we know if we've got a camera or not?"

He had a point. She hadn't even considered that the camera might not show. Camera crews got fired fast if they didn't show. But this wasn't KPIQ, and she sure couldn't fire Stanley.

"God, Stanley, I'm *such* a spoiled bitch."

He turned quickly to face her. Had he really heard Lee Ann say that? "Spoiled bitch?"

"I didn't even give a second thought to the fact that the camera might not be here...that all that tech stuff might not be taken care of." She put her hands to her face. "I'm a bitch Stanley. I've become an imperious bitch!"

He stepped toward her, took her loosely in his arms. "No, Lee...no. You're not a bitch, honey. You've got a lot on your mind..."

She sighed, and turned away.

"It's okay...c'mon, let's get comfortable for a minute here before Lisa Lynn descends."

They sat down Indian style on the painted boards of the deck. He glanced at his watch. "Moving up to two am, Lee, best be ready when the camera arrives. Let's hear it."

Lee Ann took a sip of her drink and held it in her mouth as she flipped backward through the pages of the steno pad. She reached page one, swallowed, and said. "Okay...now you've got to understand that I've written a long letter to Maureen, which she will give to Bradley and Laura, my sub...God, Stanley, that woman scares me."

"Stay on track Lee."

"Right, okay, so the hosts will set this up, saying something like, '...and you all know that we've been saying Lee Ann Barnes is on special assignment these past few days, but that's not entirely true. Lee Ann Barnes is currently running for her life.'" She stopped. "They may want to soften that, but I doubt it. Then they'll explain why and say that they have a tape sent to them from New Orleans by yours truly, and they'd like to play it at this time. And that's where I come on and, as briefly as possible, plead my case. How's it sound so far?"

"Great. So, what do you say?"

"Okay, I gotta rehearse this anyway a few times, so this will be take one, okay?"

There was a quiet knock on the door. "Lisa Lynn," he said just as she'd taken a first big breath to begin her spiel.

"*Damn!*" she mumbled under her breath, and then, "Oh... good."

He heard it. "It's okay, this won't take long. She's either got it, or she's come to say she couldn't get it and has brought the money back. But I think she's got it. I have a feeling she's a resourceful gal."

"Getting to know this 'gal' pretty well, huh, Pops?"

"Stop," he said in earnest and turned toward the door. "Come on, meet this girl. She's been telling me how much she wants to meet you. And she *is* fetching us a camcorder." There was another knock on the door. "Hang on, I'm on my way." He shouted as loudly as he felt he could—considering the hour. "*Come on*, Lee, get up off that spoiled bitch ass of yours and come and meet our tech support." He set off in the direction of the door.

"Who's there?"

"Lisa Lynn" came a husky whisper from the other side.

He opened the door. God, she was beautiful in all her youth, standing there in the doorway with a small black camcorder bag over one barely clad shoulder.

"You got it!"

She beamed like a prairie sunrise. "Yessir, partner, I rounded this little critter up for you." She slung the bag down off her shoulder and, by the strap, held it out to him. "Got some blank tapes in there too. I know you didn't specifically ask for that but thought you might need them." She paused, seemed reluctant, but went ahead and said it anyway. "Stan, you suppose I could get some kind of deposit on this thing...I trust you and everything, but you can see my point."

He reached for the envelope in his jacket pocket and peeled eight hundred off the deck. "This do it? That's eight."

Lisa took the bills, fanned them, counted them, and stuck them into her jeans. "Eight," she said, "you're a gentleman Stan...pleasure to do biz..."

She startled as Lee Ann suddenly appeared behind him. The red head was still dressed in evening clothes and so was he. They appeared to be in the middle of some kind of project. "Whoa..I can see y'all are busy. See you tomorrow. Noon?" She turned and started to make her way off down the hall.

"Whoa yourself," he whispered after her. "Come back here...I want you to meet someone."

Lisa turned, took two long strides back down the hall, and ended up centered in the doorway.

The two women practically knocked him over, moving toward one another to shake hands and greet for the first time. He drifted back to the dresser for another virgin ginny, but shit, no lime. So he stood for a moment in complete awe of the assemblage of long legs across the room from him. Leg overkill. He looked at his watch: 2:05 am. Damn, he felt these girls might go on for hours at the rate they were going. He wanted to make sure that Lee and he were well on their way within the next few hours. Best to cross Lake Pontchartrain at night—keeping track of headlights as they moved along.

He moved over to the women. His plan was to infiltrate their conversation and then politely suggest that Lee Ann and he get back to work. They fell silent as he approached—knew what he was going to say—so closed up their conversation with that timeless female, "...finish this later." And, like a dustdevil in September, Lisa was gone. Lee Ann stood with her back to the closed door and asked, "What?"

"What, what?"

"Why are you looking at me like that?"

"Women...they never cease to amaze me."

"I hope not."

They got to work, moved the furniture around, propped the camera on a just-the-right-height burea, set up a chair with some well adjusted lights—and decided they had it. It had to look like New Orleans, because, Lee explained, it *was* New Orleans. Stanley asked if she wanted to rehearse once before they rolled the tape. She declined, saying that she wanted to catch the urgency of a first take so she'd try to nail it on the first run. "But," she said, "there are some things I want to cut in. So here they are, Mr. Cameraman." He was all ears. She went on. "When I hold up the *'bullet to be there for me,'* note, I want you to *slowly* zoom in on the message at the same time I'm reading it. Use the motorized zoom. All these camecorders have little motorized zooms. Okay, got that one?"

"Yes, I'll have to find it on the camera, but that sounds feasible."

"Okay...and when I tell the audience that we returned to the room and found this bouquet"—she motioned to the gardenias—"then I will pause and you will press pause at that time..."

"Check."

"Then we'll set the camera up to take the bouquet while I do the voice over. When I pause again, you'll press pause again, and we'll go back to me in the chair concluding my message. Can you see all that? It will look professional even when they view it at KPIQ. And the editors can tighten it up when they transfer it to the broadcast tape. Does all that make sense?"

"Roger, Cameraman Hochstetter...ready to commence firing."

"Okay, let's do it."

He reviewed the simple controls on the camcorder, while Lee Ann machine gunned through her lines several times at high speed. He'd watched her do this before to warm up her brain and her mouth: recite at high speed so when she did it at a normal pace it would be there for her. Finally, they were ready. He pushed the record button on the camera and said quietly, "We're rollin."

She took a deep breath, looked directly into the camera and began her pitch.

It went smoothly with all camera directions incorporated. She finished up with:

"We need to talk seaman...get human. And until we do, I guess you won't be seeing me on TV. That's the deal." She paused a long moment and fixed the lens—a hazel-eyed newshawk. "This is Lee Ann Barnes, in New Orleans; good morning, Mister Seaman, wherever you are." She looked into the camera to accommodate a fade. She had an "...I'm a cat and I just ate a canary" look on her classic cowgirl face. A few seconds of that, then she sliced her hand across her neck and Stanley hit *Stop*.

"Flawless," he breathed, and Lee Ann said, "Yes, I think that should do it."

They celebrated by raiding the courtesy fridge for a couple of Squirts. Then hooked the camcorder up to the TV in the room. Confident they had the show in the can, they settled back on the bed to watch it. It was going on 3:30am Exhaustion was overtaking them, but the *Lee Ann in New Orleans* spot was a hit. Even Lee was impressed with what they'd managed to produce with the little camera. As a reward, they decided to give themselves an hour of sleep before going to phase two of the great escape.

Lee Ann set the travel alarm for 5am. They could clear the hotel at that early morning hour before sunup when few people were up and about. But it would be growing light out on Lake Ponchartrain about the time they started their crossing. The cover of darkness out on the lake wasn't as much of a priority now as some much needed sleep. "And besides..." Stanley reminded Lee Ann, "Pontchartrain is so beautiful at dawn!"

After separate showers, they hit the sheets spooning and fell immediately to sleep. Sleep was so welcomed by both of them that descending into it felt like pressure on a funny bone.

Part 2: Light

15.

Friday, May 6, 2005

5:55am, New Orleans, Louisiana

....listen to Jesus...*LISTEN!*...to Jesus
..and so...what we've been talking about this early morning hour brothers and sisters...is this

....on those mornings of darkness...when the sun is not shining in your heart

...on those mornings of darkness...when a tired and aching body is all you can offer the day

...ON THOSE MORNINGS OF DARKNESS!

(clapping and yea saying)

...when you awaken and wonder what next calamity is going to *PULL YOU BACK DOWN INTO THE ABYSMAL BLACK HOLE OF NIGHT!"*

...on those mornings...brothers and sisters

...I would say to you

(long pause)

...look to the light

...look *to* Jesus

...*Listen!* to Jesus

...look toward the light.

...amen

...amen.

And now we'd like to ask that you stand and raise your voices in song and join with our glorious choir, The Morning Glory Singers, as they offer up a hymn of praise. A beautiful hymn of lament and of praise brothers and sisters...entitled, "Were You There When They Crucified My Lord?" And we ask all of you out there in our radio audience to please join us later for our 8 o'clock service. This is brother Elijah Hamble... wishing you a...

Somewhere in another land Lee Ann and Stanley heard the call.

It was the sound of a Southern Baptist choir breaking into a much-loved spiritual. They were lying face-to-face in the pillows. At the first lines of the hymn two sets of eyes snapped open, and panic set in.

Both startled, sat bolt upright in the bedsheets, and looked at each other in horror. Stanley swung round and fixed on the clock radio: almost 6am. It was getting light outside. He was the first to speak. More like shout.

"JESUS...WE BLEW IT...WE BLEW IT! IT'S SIX...THE DAMN SUN IS COMING UP!"

Lee Ann groaned and rolled her back to him. She buried her head in the pillow. He heard a muffled scream. Then she flopped back onto her back, staring blankly at the ceiling. "Oh shit."

"Oh man, I can't believe we did this. Didn't you set the alarm? I thought we agreed on five." He grabbed the travel alarm sitting beside the clock radio and saw that it was set for 5am, but the alarm switched was not pulled to the ON position. "The switch isn't pulled, Lee Ann...shit!"

"It wasn't?"

"No."

"I blew it. I've flunked spy 101. I'm a failure." She continued to stare at the ceiling.

He set the alarm back on the nightstand, turned the radio off, and sank back into his pillow. The two of them laid there for a moment watching the light come up in the room, wondering which one of them would finally speak. Lee Ann had always had a greater aversion to dead air than Stanley. Finally she could stand the silence no longer. "You pissed at me, Stanley? I know...I blew it. I was sure I pulled the switch on when I set it. Besides, I can't believe I didn't wake up before now..."

"The maids must have been listening to the radio and accidentally set it to auto on. I didn't set it for"—he squinted at the dial—"around six, did you?"

"No."

"I wonder how long we would have slept if it hadn't gone off?"

"I can't believe I didn't wake up on my own. I always do that." Lee Ann was talking to herself as she rolled onto her side to take in Stanley who remained lying on his back studying the cornices.

"You mad at me?"

"Nah...it was an honest mistake. Besides, now I get you for another day...don't I?" He rolled over to face her.

"I don't know...what do you think we should do?"

"I'd say lay low for another day and take two tomorrow morning, same time as planned, five am. *I'll* set the alarm this time."

He felt a bare foot come up and kick him in the shin. "Hey!"

She put her hands in front of her face, karate style. "Don't you dare hit me...don't you *dare* hit me."

"Stop kicking me then." He was smiling as he rolled back onto his back. She followed suit. They went back to their own jumbled thoughts.

Finally he asked, "So does that sound like a plan? Hang out until tomorrow morning and try again? Take two?"

"I guess so. Too many people up and about now. We could be followed and not even know it."

"That's the problem."

"Maybe we'll hear from the seaman again. Maybe he'll call and say, 'Oh let's just forget this stalking thing...let's just all go out to breakfast together.'" She wiggled under the sheets.

"Would be good if this thing would go away that easily, wouldn't it?"

"Yes, it would." Another long pause. "You mad at me, Stan? For blowing the great escape?" Lee Ann, at the corner of her eyes, saw him shaking his head.

"Nah, we'll just do it tomorrow morning. Enjoy another day together. Actually I'm happy it turned out this way."

"Mmmhmm...but I'll have to get in touch with Claire somehow and let her know what's happened. Make new plans. Except I can't call her from my cell. He knows I'm in New Orleans now. We don't know who's listening. Maybe you could call her from a pay phone..."

"Make you some new reservations and give her a ring?" He spoke to the ceiling. "Need to talk with that little poacher anyway."

"Stanley?"

"Yes?"

"I know this is off the subject, but I've been wondering... well, this is kind of personal. Um...what were you and Kathleen doing about..."

Time went by; she didn't finish. He asked. "About what? Birth control?"

"No..."

"AIDS?"

"Yeah."

He hesitated for a second and then decided it was best just to answer the question. "We were both tested, and tested again six months later. We came up clear both times. We promised each other to be monogamous. Neither one of us particularly liked...*like*...latex sex. Defense rests."

"Yes, but you said that she was seeing Jackson too."

"Oh that wasn't until after we were tested. Then, of course, they ran away to Rio and that was the end of me. How about you, Miss Suzy Q?"

"Miguel and I were tested several times and came up clear." Lee Ann had that sadness in her voice again at the mention of Miguel. They were silent for a moment.

Finally he spoke. "Why did you want to know that?"

"Oh, I don't know, in case there's an accident and I have to give you mouth to mouth artificial resuscitation."

"Lee Ann, stop goofing. Why did you want to know that?"

"I don't know, just curious, I guess. I just wondered how you'd handled it with your last liaison. I guess...I don't know. Something you just ask people these days when you're occupying the same bed with them. Case there's an accident."

"Is there going to be an accident?"

"I don't think so. What do you think?"

"No, I don't either. I'm pretty happy with our agreement. I mean, I guess I hoped at first that, well..."

"We'd maybe be doing it?"

"Sure. It was feeling comfortable...could have drifted in that direction. Didn't you feel that certain drift?"

"Mmmhuh, I did. Strangely enough, after coming completely from the other side of having those feelings, I did. Funny how that works."

"Funny." There was a silence as they both absorbed what had just been said. Then Stanley went on. "But with everything else going on, you the victim of a stalker, Claire in jail, I mean out on bail..." He took a breath. "I've thought about it, and I'm comfortable we're not heaping *that* layer on top of everything else. Kind of have to keep our heads here for awhile."

"I agree." She paused for a beat. "But you're kinda horny, aren't you? I can feel that."

"What's new? I'll live."

She giggled at his side, rolled onto her side to face him. "Man, we, I mean *I* really blew our great escape, didn't I?"

"Don't worry about it." He found her hand and patted it. "I'm glad we've got another day together. We were getting some good work done...don't you think?"

"Mmm, I think, long overdue work."

"Speaking of work," he began, "we need to get the tape in the mail and pick up some supplies. One or both of us will have to do that. I don't mind. Wouldn't mind a little solo time out on the streets. So you want to stay here and relax, maybe stretch out those shock-sore muscles while your big warrior hunter goes out to forage?"

He patted her on the hip, bent over, and kissed her on the temple, and quickly rolled out of bed.

"Hey! Where you going?"

"Gotta hit the shower, Lee, feelin' kinda sticky. We need to mail that tape ASAP." As he began making his way to the bathroom, he heard her voice coming from behind him.

"Wait!" He pulled up short and turned to face her. She was sitting up in bed with no makeup, her rusty hair tasseled about her face.

"Thanks for not being mad at me, Stan. I love you sometimes for how you are with me."

He smiled. "I love you too, Lee. Sometimes..."

She threw a pillow at him. He caught it in one hand, tossed it back, and took refuge behind the bathroom door.

The shower went well. It was cooler this morning so the steam rose up and flew out the window. He scratched himself down with a loofah, sudsed up his body, took care of himself, rinsed off, and turned off the tap. Ah, that's better. So it was obvious to Lee that he was horny. That was a fair assessment. He was. It always helped to take refuge in hand rations when the fire was starting to rage down below.

He dressed, picked up a pile of hundreds, the camcorder, and the tape to KPIQ, and gave Lee Ann, who was sitting up in bed going over some notes on her laptop, a good-bye peck. On down to the lobby where he asked a deskclerk if the hotel could find an independent carrier to get a tape to San Francisco: ASAP. She told him that it would be no problem. Twenty-four hours, she said. With one down, he walked through the bar and saw that Lisa Lynn was not tending this morning. So he deposited the black bag in the trunk of the Mustang and was soon on his way out of the hotel parking lot.

He would be watching in all directions today as he moved about the Quarter. Watching for anyone who might be watching him watching for them.

It was still early, so he drove around for an hour or so, enjoying the people of New Orleans greeting a bright spring morning in May. But it was more than idle meandering. He kept one eye firmly fixed in the rearview mirror so that, by the time he stopped for breakfast, he was satisfied no one was tailing him. Or if they were, they had to be ghosts.

After breakfast at a sunny corner cafe, he walked about looking for a boutique. Lee had asked him to buy her the largest white scarf he could find. "You'll see it later," she'd said. At a store whose sign was written in Arabic, he found a large white linen shawl and decided that it would do nicely.

It was time to see if Wayfarer's Antique Shoppe was open. On his way there, he was hit by a chilling notion.

It was an uncomfortable hunch that had been bubbling below the surface of his thoughts ever since they'd returned to the hotel last night and found the bouquet. Now, alone, he let it come to full boil.

Could the seaman be Poteet?

It all fit so well. The dark romance of it, the class act, the wealth to pull it off, the DVD so professionally done, the

141

seaman, the pirate Lafitte—*his descendant Poteet!* Stanley's spy mind scrambled to assemble a scenario that made sense. By the time he'd reached the store, he'd put together a rough sketch. It went like this:

Poteet, in perusing his local channel accesses, had come across Lee Ann Barnes doing her *Good Morning San Francisco* show. He had become fixated and infatuated. So he'd hired someone to get background on Lee Ann. A bio. PI work. The "researcher" had come across the fact that she had been married to Stanley, a ceramic artist! Perfect connection. So Poteet had made his first communication—a letter to Stanley—saying that he, Poteet, had seen his work in *Ceramics* magazine, and was very impressed, and wondered if he might be interested in trying out some new porcelain clay that an associate—that would have been Melissa—had formulated. Would Stanley like to come to New Orleans, see his operation, and pick up a few pounds?

Stanley could see how the timing of that letter coincided with the chronology of the stalk Lee Ann had described yesterday. Yes, it fit quite well. The thought of Poteet's cunning gave him chills for a full fifteen seconds. Well, there are orgasms and then there are orgasms. Yes he would definitely discuss this theory with Lee Ann upon returning to the hotel.

An elderly woman was just unlocking the door when he approached the antique shop. The maroon and lime-green juice squeezer was still in the window so he bought it immediately for forty bucks—without haggling. Then he came across an old but mint condition King alto saxophone. The proprietor had some new reeds and let him step into an adjoining rear courtyard to try it out. The horn, priced at $500, was a sweetheart. He talked the owner down to four-fifty on the barrelhead. The woman was not happy, but let it go for that. He left the shop with the squeezer and the horn feeling wise for having tucked eight hundred in his pocket this morning before leaving the room.

He picked up a Kenyan bracelet at the French Market, satisfied for a second time that the workmanship was very good for twenty-five dollars. Lee would be happy to have her birthday present for Claire. Claire would be happy to finally get it. He wanted to keep his girls smiling. Things were looking up.

At a corner liquor store he picked up a fifth of Tanqueray, a couple of six-packs of tonic, some limes, a bottle of expensive champagne, a cheap styrofoam cooler, a six-pack of Squirt, two deli ham-and-cheese sandwiches, and a *Times Picayune*. Shopping complete, he returned to Le Richelieu. It was half past noon.

Lisa Lynn's big cheerleader smile greeted him as he approached the bar with the little black bag. Then she looked at her watch and frowned. "Thirty minutes late, Stan, 'fraid I'm going to have to charge you another one-fifty. Did you get what you were going after?"

"On the first take, girl. Went like a dream."

"That's what your friend said when she came down to the bar awhile ago. We weren't that busy so had about a half hour to talk. What can I get you?"

"Glass of ice water, please. What did you talk about?"

"TV business mostly. How I might go about breaking in. She's a great lady, Stan; you're a lucky man." Lisa slid a tumbler of ice water across the bar in his direction. Stanley took half of it down in one gulp.

"Yeah," he said smiling slightly and thinking a multitude of muddled thoughts. "So, Lisa...I want to thank you for fetching this little beauty for me on such short notice this morning." He slung the bag onto the bar and laid a fifty on top of it. "Really helped us out." Lisa nodded, pulled the case off the bar and pocketed the cash—all in one motion.

"Pleasure to do business, Stan."

He waited while she took a drink order and then jumped in. "Um, Lisa, do you ever do any guide work? You know like show out-of-towners around your city? We're looking for a guide. You be interested? Say a hundred bucks for the evening. We'll throw in water and a feedbag?"

Lisa went on making drinks for a moment, considering it. "You and Lee Ann want to see where the natives hang out? That it? Maybe hear some jazz?"

"You got it."

The bar was nearly full. Lisa was hustling and unable to have a real conversation. He knew it was time to wrap it up. "Say tomorrow evening, if you're not working, which it seems you always are." He slid off the bar stool and finished his water.

"Have to let you know a little later, Stan. I'm not sure if they're going to need me here or not. But if they don't, sure, that sounds like a plan. When you guys want to light out? Tomorrow evening you say?"

"How's eight pm sound? We'll sightsee, eat some local cuisine, and then I think we'd like to, as you say, hear some jazz."

"Let you know before I get off at five, okay? Will you be in your room?"

"Waiting by the phone...oh, thank the guy who loaned us the camera. Much appreciated."

"Let you do it yourself if we go out tomorrow evening. He's a musician over at the *Arabesque*. A great combo, he plays sax."

Stanley had the alto case in one hand, a fat shopping bag in the other.

"You play?" Lisa said, looking at the case.

"'Bout thirty years ago. Played sax in highschool band. Some after that." Stanley hurried on. "Pretty rusty now though...I'd imagine."

Lisa smiled. "Know what you mean. Bad sax sounds like a goose with its neck in a wringer."

"You got it...better get going here. I can see you're a bit backed up. But call this afternoon okay?"

"*You* got it, Stan." She turned quickly to tend some impatient and thirsty customers.

Stanley left the bar wishing he had a cell phone as he drifted across a hallway to the pay phones. He called Maureen at KPIQ and left a message with her secretary that an extremely important tape from Lee Ann would be in around noon tomorrow. Then he called Continental and made a reservation for tomorrow for Lee Ann to connect to Toronto via Baton Rouge. Finally, he punched in Claire's number. After three rings, Claire's voice came across the line sounding husky with sleep. It was quarter to one in New Orleans, quarter to two in Toronto.

"Hullo..."

"Hi, kid. It's your pop. How you doing?"

"Dad!"

"The same."

"Wait a minute...I just woke up. Had a late one."

"I can tell." He heard Claire rearranging herself in bed.

"So I thought Mom was coming up today. Did I miss something?"

"No. You won't believe this, but we've had *quite* a couple of days ourselves. We overslept this morning, as in over schlepped."

Claire giggled. "Okay, so, is she coming today? You two doing it again? Having fun?"

"Having fun...*not* doing it."

"Clever Daddy."

"Okay, Claire so...some business here."

"Right..."

"Got a pen? Here are the details."

Stanley rattled off Lee Ann's flight number and arrival time as Claire copied them down. She said she would be there to pick up her mom. They chatted briefly about her current predicament. He gave encouragement and signed off, not mentioning anything about Lee Ann's stalker. Lee had asked him specifically not to. It had gone well—the conversation, that is. He never knew with daughter Claire.

On the lift, on the way back up to the room, he thought about the possibility of seeing the town with Lisa the following evening. He hadn't mentioned that Lee Ann would be in Toronto and that it would be just the two of them. He couldn't help feeling dirty and old again—but he was getting used to it. He wondered if Lisa would consent to guide him if she knew Lee would not be with them. Well, he would wait and see.

He called to Lee Ann before slipping the key card into the lock. She called back and he let himself into the room.

Lee Ann, in peach-colored leotards, was sitting spread legged on the floor doing some yoga moves.

"Hi, honey, I'm home."

She groaned. "Oh man, Stan, am I a stiff little puppy. Give me a minute to get healthy here..."

"You got it, girl. Bought some deli sandwiches. Are you hungry?"

"Starved!" Lee Ann was always starved. "Did you get ahold of Continental? Claire?"

He chuckled. "Yes, I did get ahold of Continental Claire, as a matter of fact. You leave from Baton Rouge tomorrow morning at nine-o-five am, and arrive Toronto at three twelve pm EST. Claire will be there to pick you up."

"Did you talk with her? How did it go? How did she seem?"

He stepped over her long legs on his way to drop his load. "Got a lot of stuff, Lee. My little shopping bag's just a-bulging at the seams. Right now though I'm headed for a shower. Humidity's got me stuck together like a wet phone book. She sounded fine. It went well."

"Know what you mean. God, it's hot and sticky. Good...good to hear you two are getting along...*finally!*"

"Really." He off-loaded his cargo and disappeared behind the bathroom door.

Lee studied the two shopping bags and the brown battered case the cat had dragged in—and considered peeking. Then she remembered how pissed Stanley got when she did that so she went on stretching. She could wait.

Stanley adjusted the tap to luke-cool and stepped under the flow. It was early May in New Orleans but a particularly muggy early May. The extra weight that he carried around with him, and the adjustment from San Francisco's light spring breezes, was making him sweat like a plow horse. Showers helped. He hoped he'd acclimate soon.

"It's beautiful Stan, just the one I had my eye on. She'll love it."

After he'd finished his shower, Lee had taken one. They sat now, wrapped in heavy terry hotel robes. Lee was drying her hair with a towel and he was rummaging in his shopping bags for the next item. He'd just handed her the Kenyan bracelet that he'd bought for Claire. Lee Ann was examining it from every angle.

"I think it should be a present from both of us, from French Market in New Orleans...where her parents started talking to one another again."

"Yes? But you know Stan...I think *you* should give it to her. You know...just from you. And write her a little note. I'll take it to her. You know, something light to let her know you are on her side through all this legal mess she's got herself into. Could you do that?"

He considered it a moment. "A letter? You know how I am about letters. I hate to write. I would just as soon pick up the phone."

"That's the point, Stan." She looked at him. "It would surprise her."

"She thinks I'm old, boring, and predictable, huh?"

"Sort of."

"I am old, and I am boring, and I am...

"Predictable?"

"I wouldn't say that."

She laughed. "No, I wouldn't either. Maybe a little set in your ways, but you still surprise me at least once every five years."

He shook his head. "Okay, I'll do that. I'll jot a note, but it's going to be a short one."

She turned quickly toward the relic sitting beside the shopping bags. "What's in the case? Looks like a...sax?"

Stanley grabbed the case and placed it in front of her. He quickly threw the latches and lifted the lid. Inside, an old silver alto lay sleeping in its green velvet bed.

Her eyes squinted down to take in the detail of the old King.

"You're going to start playing again!"

"Certainly not around you...least not this trip. I blew it out back of the antique shop where I bought it, just to test the action and hear its voice, and I'm rusty as an old pump. But yeah, I'm going to get back to it. Sounded like hell but felt good to be making that noise again."

"Mmm, I know how much you loved it." She paused, took him in. Perhaps they were both remembering it was shortly after Bird had disappeared that Stanley had packed away his sax for what seemed like might be forever.

She wanted to move quickly now—beyond that sad memory. "What else you got in dat bag, boy?"

He grabbed the white linen shawl wrapped in turquoise tissue. Lee took it, unwrapped it, and spent a moment letting the material slip through her fingers. "Perfect," she said as softly as the fabric she was feeling. "Just perfect."

"Are you going to tell me what it's for?"

"Later."

"Okay, I've got one more thing, but it has to wait till later. What say we grab some Squirts and head out onto the deck for a sandwich and a chat...do some business...been thinking..."

She studied him for a moment. "Good, because I've been thinking about things too this morning, and I've got something I want to discuss with you."

She moved some wicker chairs out onto the deck while he popped some tabs and grabbed the sandwiches. They settled back under a threatening spring sky to sip, munch deli fare, and talk.

"Okay, ladies first. What's on your mind?"

"Sure you don't want to go first?"

"Nope...you go."

"Okay," she paused, frowned, and went on. "I don't know where this notion came from...intuition...somewhere I don't know...but this morning when I was thinking about all that's happened in the last week or so, particularly last night, I was hit by the crazy notion that...now don't laugh at me okay?" He nodded. "That Poteet *might* be the seaman." She searched his face for a first reaction. There it was, the lopsided grin she hoped she'd see.

"Great Lee! We came to the same conclusion independently. That's what I wanted to discuss with you. I had the same hunch this morning about halfway through my shopping. Couldn't get it out of my head. Even came up with a possible scenario."

She stopped chewing and drew a bead on him with her right eye. The same one she used to sight in her .357 Marlin. He wasn't sure what she had in mind by this look. She bit her bottom lip. Hunter Lee, ready to squeeze. "A scenario...that's something I couldn't put together because I didn't have enough information." It was that cold tone of voice again. "I knew I needed to talk with you first to find out how your correspondence with Poteet started. Did he contact you first?"

He saw her wheels spinning. So good to see that. He was afraid she wouldn't be receptive to his current notion. But now it seemed she'd reached the same chilling conclusion. "Good question, Ms. Investigative Reporter. Yes! The answer is yes; it was Poteet who wrote to me first saying that he had seen my work in *Ceramics* and had some clay that I might be interested in trying. Would I like to come down and see his operation, take a few pounds home with me..."

She was listening intently but couldn't resist interrupting. "Another question. Did *he*...or did *you*...ever mention my name in any of your correspondence?"

"No, you never came up. I didn't mention you, and he didn't mention you, though, as you know, he did know about you before he met you last night because he had watched you doing your show."

"So how does this all connect? That's what I can't figure out. How did I just fall into his hands like so many pieces-of-eight?"

He smiled at her maintenance of the pirate motif. "That's a difficult one, Lee, but this is the way I've got it figured. First, he saw you on TV and became infatuated, you know, fixated, the way compulsive people become. So being the wealthy man he is, he hired a PI to do some digging and put together a bio on you. And then, in reading that bio, came up with the fact that you were, at one time, married to me, a ceramic artist. Bingo! He dug a little bit more, found me, sent me that letter saying that he admired my work and was interested in meeting me in person..."

She picked it up.

"In meeting you, he felt he would eventually, and naturally, through the association, meet me! Brilliant. But why didn't he just contact me directly? You know, say that he was starting, *One World Incorporated,* and would I be interested in covering it on my show?"

"And what would you have said to this stranger from Louisiana?"

She thought for a moment and then responded. "That I did a show dealing with things happening in the San Francisco area and environs. Sorry, but no thanks."

"Exactly. So, anyway, I contacted him by phone about two weeks ago, said I would like to take him up on his offer and pay him a visit around the first week in May after my show opened. He said fine, just to let him know when I would be arriving."

She picked it up again. "He took a long shot and sent me the bullet note to scare me in your direction. In this case, your opening, knowing I would run to a trusted friend who *he knew* was heading directly in *his* direction. He knew that note would scare the shit out of anyone, and that particular 'anyone' would be looking to get out of Dodge pronto!"

"Exactly! That's exactly the way I had it figured."

"This man really does have pirate blood in his veins, doesn't he?"

"I'd say so. It was a long, long shot, but he elevated his best cannon and took it. Pretty good shooting, huh?"

"Excellent. Not to mention brilliant strategy. So...what now?"

"Well, it's still just a theory...but a fairly plausible one." Stanley finally caught Lee Ann's darting eyes. "And, after having met the man..."

"Yes, that little pirate smile of his...seaman...give me a break!" She smiled. "I feel fairly certain about this, Stan."

"I do too, Lee, but we can't go sailing out to Poteet Porcelain with *our* cannons blazing. What if we're wrong? Then we've alienated what we both decided last night after dinner was a potentially valuable friend. Two friends counting Melissa."

"Wouldn't want to alienate Melissa, would we, Stan?"

He narrowed his eyes at her little smirk. "No, Lee, *we* wouldn't."

"What do you think *we* should do?"

"Proceed as we have been proceeding, see if we can lure him out of his den. You go to Toronto, help Claire out, see what his next move is. You know the tape will probably be airing day after tomorrow. I'll make sure Poteet is watching."

"You found a courier for the tape delivery in twenty-four hours? You called Maureen?"

"Yes, the people at the desk said they'd see to it. Twenty-four hours. And I left a message with Maureen's secretary to be expecting it."

"How did you know it would be on Monday's show?"

"I read the letter you wrote to Maureen while you were in the shower this morning. When I should have been checking to see if the alarm was armed and ready."

"God, Stanley! And you call me a snoopy dog."

"Hey, Lee, we're in this thing together. Remember? He might miss and hit me, so I feel entitled to keep abreast of developments."

She scowled. "This is just a big joke to you, isn't it?"

He rallied. "I'll say it again, Lee. I feel strongly that the man doesn't want to harm you. He just wants to get to know you personally...for whatever reason. And maybe now that he does, and has an in to you through the show, he will cease and desist with this seaman bullshit."

She fell silent—sullen. He could tell that something was bugging the hell out of her. Her white skin had taken on an ashen hue. It went with her hazel eyes, but it didn't look good. She looked as though she might be getting ready to throw up again. "Lee?"

"I don't want to talk about it anymore, Stan. I need to sit alone for a minute and think. I really do need to get to the bottom of this...form some kind of a plan of my own. I really don't appreciate being terrorized."

It was the cold tone of voice she used when she wanted to squelch. But he knew he wasn't the object of her disdain this time, so nodded in deference to her request for privacy and stepped back into the room to begin his letter to Claire. Let's see, what should he say to his outlaw daughter. Keep it light, Lee had admonished. Okay, that would be a challenge wouldn't it? Let's see...

Dear Claire,

HAPPY 21ˢᵗ, you little smuggler. So they caught you swimming the river with priceless works of art did they? What now?

He smiled. Maybe that was what he wanted to say, but it wouldn't be what he would say. He began again in his mind. In a half hour, with a first draft in the wastebasket, he folded a single sheet of hotel stationery and sealed it into an envelope bearing the crest of Le Richelieu. That should do it. What was Lee Ann up to? Still ruminating out on the deck? He looked out the French doors. Yup, she was sitting slouched down in her chair—staring straight ahead.

"Lee?"

Her eyes flashed up at his. Machine Gun Mouth formed the next words in approximately the next five seconds. "Enough pouting, huh? Jesus Stanley, I just want this thing to be behind me. I just want to get on with my life. This whole thing is sapping my mental energy! It's bad...bad!"

He extended a hand, helped her to her feet, and took her loosely into his arms. "Got a little surprise for you. Want to see it?" He bit one of her earlobes. She giggled and squirmed as she broke loose of his grasp.

"Yikes! Oh gods, Stanley, that gives me chills down to my toes."

"I knows. Well, do you want to see it?"

"Segue time?"

"Yes...segue time. I'm tired of this seaman clown ruining our fun, aren't you?"

"Thoroughly."

"Okay then, take a look at this."

She followed him into the room and sat on the bed. He moved over to the antique store shopping bag, took it by the handle and held it out to her. She looked inside and saw something wrapped in a brown paper bag. Pulling one bag out of the other, she cautiously opened the top and looked inside. Tears suddenly welled up like a mountain spring and spilled over her lower lids. She didn't sob; she made no sound at all, as she pulled the maroon and lime-green juice squeezer from its wrapping. He grabbed some tissues from a box on the nightstand and held them out to her.

"I couldn't resist it, Lee; somehow I knew we needed to have this and keep it."

Lee clutched the hard metal object to her breast, curled over it, and began sobbing like a baby. She rocked back and forth as if she was cradling one. "Oh man, Stan, oh man, oh man...just give me a minute here..."

He moved around to her side and sat with his arm about her shoulders, drying her eyes, and holding her nose with the tissue so she could blow. She would not release her grip on the squeezer. It took a minute or two, but she finally recovered and laid the machine lovingly on the bed. "I need a long hold Stanley. I know I've reached my quota on holds for this week, but can I have some overtime... puleeze?

He kicked off his sandals, helped Lee Ann out of hers, and the two of them laid back on the bed with the cold metal squeezer lying between them. "Was this a mistake? Is this too painful? Maybe I shouldn't have bought..."

"Stanley?"

"Yes."

"Shut up."

"Yes'm."

The squeezer was digging into the place between them now, so they set it on the nightstand and clutched one another like frightened monkeys. Lee started shivering again as she had yesterday morning after the faint. He pulled her in as closely as he could and held her fast.

"Uh, Stan..."

"Yes?"

"I can't breathe, honey."

"Oh, sorry." He released some but not all of the pressure.

"That's better." She gulped a couple of much-needed breaths and began hesitantly. "Do you remember that Bird"—another pause, another long breath—"that Bird had his squeezer with him when he disappeared?"

"Yes I do. He had it in that tan gym bag he carried every day to preschool."

"Do you remember what color his squeezer was?"

"Uh huh, it was originally white, but when we bought it down at the Sausalito flea market it was...someone had painted over the white enamel with bright blue paint. Why?..."

They released and jerked their heads back to fix on each other's eyes. The thought had occurred to them simultaneously—like a flash of lightning—or was that outside? The world had started to spin—out of control—too fast—too fast. He rolled over, grabbed the squeezer by its long neck, pulled the car keys off the nightstand, and came to rest in a cross legged position sitting on the bed. She sat bolt upright and faced him. "You want to do the honors?" he said, holding the squeezer and the keys out to her.

"No...you do it. I'm shaking like a leaf. I can hardly breathe..."

He put a key to the lime-green body of the contraption, applied pressure, and pulled down once. Twice. Three times. The paint spalled off, and underneath little flecks of blue appeared. They looked at each other for an infinite second, and then he repeated the process on the long maroon handle. More flecks of blue, and under that, the original white enamel.

"I'm not going to cry...I'm not going to cry...I'm not going to cry," sobbed Lee Ann as she had years ago when she'd been his little sister. And then she broke into uncontrolled wailing that convulsed her whole body. She buried her face in her hands. He had no strength left to comfort her. He decided he might as well follow.

It lasted a full two minutes; two people sitting on a bed down in New Orleans, clutching a maroon and lime-green deco juice squeezer between them, sobbing like babies. It was Lee who finally dried Stanley's nose and managed a weak but earnest: "Does this mean what I think it means, Stan?"

He shook his head. "How many '50's juice squeezers do you think there are in this world that are white, blue, maroon, and lime-green? In that order."

"One," she said, praying.

"Probability is high that you are right."

"Then this is...was...Bird's squeezer?"

He nodded, couldn't quite believe it himself. "I'd say so...I'd say so."

16.

Had fate twisted the blade, or had Providence smiled brightly on their faces? They were at a loss to know, but they did know they were completely drained from absorbing this latest salvo—this latest broadside. Or was it a blessing? A sign? The blue paint raised a multitude of questions that set their minds scrambling to sort out countless permutations in possibilities. They couldn't possibly know, but hoped against hope, that Bird was nearby. That was their not so silent prayer. But then, in twenty-two years, maybe Bird had drifted up to Alaska and the squeezer had wandered down here to New Orleans of its own accord. That could have happened. It made as much sense as their thinking its one-time owner was here in this city. And even if Bird *was* nearby, how could they possibly ever find him? And if they did find him, what would they do with him? And what would he do with them?

Hi, we're Lee Ann and Stanley, we raised you from an infant to five years of age. We became very attached to you, and then you disappeared. This has haunted us for years now—twenty-two to be exact. Now we want to get attached to you again so you can assuage our guilt about having lost you. Sound like a plan son?

They lazed on the bed for awhile. Then, weary of the gravity of it all, did this comic scenario of their hoped for, sometime, future reunion with the one they called Bird. It helped.

Around six in the afternoon, with a light rain padding about on the deck, Lee and Stan reviewed their plan.

They would follow through with their earlier scheme for Lee Ann to fly out of Baton Rouge and disappear in Toronto.

They would try again to make sure the alarm was set so they could make their early morning escape and drive across Lake Pontchartrain: twenty-four miles of open water over a four-lane causeway. Stanley reminded her that, at mid-span, no land could be seen in either direction—only water. She asked if there would be enough light to see that in any kind of detail.

"The sun was coming up around six this morning wasn't it?"

"Yes...six."

"That's about the time we should be hitting the bridge." He thought for a moment and then went on. "And that's good... because then we'll be able to tell if were being followed out there. And if someone *is* tailing us, we'll lose them."

"*We'll* lose them, Stanley?"

"You drive, Lee, *you* lose them."

"Deal."

A sun peeking in and out of the storm clouds now dropped below them. Low light lancing through tall French doors was casting golden patterns on the walls. They sat sipping a gin and tonic—a balmy Gulf breeze was trailing the rain.

Euphoric and confounded: two words that described how they felt about all that was happening to them. As much as they both felt they would like to celebrate, they wouldn't. There was still a degree of sobriety and wit required to deal with all the possibilities now crushing down upon them—and yet at the same time, buoying them up. It was a light and a lightheadedness they both agreed was reminiscent of times back in the psychedelic seventies. A maroon and lime green juice squeezer sitting in the slanting rays of a late afternoon sun was a catalyst for a million old memories. It had to be Bird's.

Stanley moved over to the precious idol, grabbed it by its long green neck, and held it up like a victory cup. "I'm going back to Wayfarer's Antiques tomorrow and ask the lady who sold this to me if she knows how she came by it. Even if she got it at a fleamarket... anything...any lead will do." He was pacing around the room now. "She wasn't too happy with me when I bargained her down to four-fifty on the sax. We both knew it was worth at least that...or more...five-fifty...six? She looked healthy. So..."

"STANLEY! GET ON WITH IT!!"

"Okay, I'm going to do what I can to trace it. I'll ask if she knows anyone who goes by the name of Bird. I wonder if he still does? Anyway, I'll keep you posted."

"Please do."

"We need to stay in touch while you're in Toronto. We've got a lot of business boiling...caldrons bubbling"

Lee, nodding yes to all of this, walked to his side, and circled her hand around the neck of the squeezer just below his. She looked up at him sleepily, her eyes still slightly red from her cry.

"Yes, we'll be in touch now."

"You hungry, Lee?"

"Famished."

"Let's get out of here."

Warm and inviting the Vera Cruz Cafe was pleasantly congested with an early evening crowd of tourists and locals. Lee Ann sat hunched over her plate, devouring a taco and scooping black beans into her mouth all in one continuous motion. When she was this hungry, she could eat like a ranch hand and didn't feel a need to apologize for it. She liked to groan too when she was eating something that was sending her to Mexican heaven. And this food was doing that.

"Mmmm, ahhhhh, gawwwd. This food is so good, Stan. Isn't this food to die for?"

"Don't talk, Lee...just eat.

"Tired?" he asked after a few more bites.

"Not at all."

"We have to get up early tomorrow."

"You have to get up early Stan. Me? It's just a normal day."

"Oh right. Forgot."

"What did your letter to Claire say?"

"That's between Claire and me. And don't peek. I'm going to be asking her whether it was steamed open in an airline bathroom."

"Okay, I won't. But if she wants to read it to me, can she?"

"Sure, absolutely." He considered it a moment. "You know, Lee...Claire and I have to develop a bit of a communication on our own now. You can't always be so threatened. What's that all about? Just the little news snoop in you?"

"I guess so...but yes, you're right, Stan, I know."

After dinner, they took a stroll around a washed down and abandoned French Market and then walked up onto the levee and on out to the river. They'd not come over to the river until now, and they'd been in New Orleans for over thirty-six hours. Amazing. But now they sat by the side of the Mississippi, watched the boats come and go, and talked. It was a little review of what had happened and then a gentle foray into their futures. Both agreed that one day at a time was the way they would do it. It had been a long ride, and neither of them felt they wanted to put the bit back into their mouths—maybe *ever* again. That settled, it was back to the hotel for a final run-through of procedure, packing of bags, and a little time Lee said she needed to spend in the bathroom preparing her "costume." She told him not to peek. He didn't protest. Stanley had entertainment cranked up to eleven. Within three minutes she emerged fully disguised, and he roared. "Fantastic!"

The alarm was set and checked by both of them. They climbed into separate sides of the bed, settled in back to back, and drifted off to separate dreams.

A cloud of giant black locusts came whirling down out of the sky to greet her. She heard them coming from far off. She was walking down a fenceline out on the ranch in Colorado. Stanley was walking behind her. And there it was, coming around her shoulder; one of the insects—mutated to human proportions—had a sharp claw around her neck! She screamed in her sleep, realized that she was asleep, realized that she was dreaming. Run! Run from the claw! Get free! She twisted and kicked, even though now she knew it was only a dream. It was too real! Too real!

"Lee! Lee! Wake up!" came an urgent but hushed voice from behind her. The insect still had its claw on her shoulder. Her mind screamed for help and then she screamed, but it was only Stanley, shaking her. And the travel alarm was still buzzing. She rolled over and buried herself—literally let her self be absorbed into—the body of one Stanley Hochstetter. He felt her strength as she clung to him for dear life.

"Oh God, Stanley. I was having a nightmare about some locusts who were coming over the mountain like a giant black cloud...buzz'n like a big generator. And then one of them grabbed me from behind with this obscene black claw and it was all oily...*Jesus!*"

"It's okay now," he whispered. "You must have heard the travel alarm. And that was my oily mitt on your shoulder. See... there...it was all a bad dream." He released her slowly. She settled back into her pillow as he shut off the alarm. They lay in silence for a moment, realizing what they were about to do.

"Oh man, Stanley, I'm in pain. I need to sleep another twenty-four hours. Can I do that?"

"Nope...we gotta rock and roll. Claire's expecting you... remember?"

She let out a deep breath. "I remember."

He took his wake-up shower first, hurriedly dried off with an already limp towel, and moved back into the bedroom. Lee rushed past him, throwing him a "mornin" and a kiss with her lips. He returned the "mornin'" but not the kiss. There was no time; she was behind the door before he could get his lips puckered. Morning was not a good time for Stanley. Especially mornings before the sun had come up. Especially mornings when he knew he would not get his first cup of coffee for some time. But he rallied and dressed quickly. He would just imagine it to be one of those spring mornings when he and his dad and Lee Ann and her daddy Sherman had risen before dawn, downed a heaping ranch breakfast, and mounted up to drive the cattle to spring pastures high in the Rockies. A little bit of danger, a little bit of feeling like a real cowboy. But there would be no time for breakfast or reminiscing this morning, at least not until they were on the bridge—safely on their way to Baton Rouge.

Okay, he was dressed and ready. Lee Ann had finished her shower and came through the door wearing only a towel, another wrapped around her head turban style.

"Okay babe, I'm outta here. I checked the synchronization on our watches again. You're a minute slower than I am, but I decided to leave it that way because it would take too long to fix it; a minute doesn't really matter anyway, and it may be the only time in my life when I'm faster than you."

She was already rummaging about for her clothes and waved him off. "Stanley, go on, get on out of here. I gotta get ready, and you gotta take the lead, remember."

He stepped to the door, opened it, and looked both ways down the hall. "Clear," he whispered. "Be careful, Lee; watch everything."

"Same to you; now get *out* of here."

Little bossy Lee Ann. She'd always been that way for as long as he'd known her, little bossy Lucy Lee Ann. But there was no time to muse; it was RoboCop time. He moved from a hall elevator through an exterior passageway and out into the parking lot—encountering no one. He tossed Lee Ann's bags into the trunk of the Mustang and shortly was on his way out of the lot and onto Barracks Street. Still no one. No, not correct. He glanced into the rearview mirror and saw a car pull out of a parking space a half block down from the entrance to the hotel lot. Shit. The car's headlights bobbed behind him. Shit!

He took the first right onto Chartres, gunned it to the next intersection and took another right, repeating this around the block until he'd arrived back at the hotel. As he pulled in and off the street he swung his head around to see if his tail had come around the corner yet. No, not yet. Yes! He found his old space, luckily in a far corner of the lot, and swung in. Through other car's windows, he watched as his pursuer, in a dark green Datsun Z, passed the entrance to the lot and continued on down the street. "Brilliant," he whispered, full of himself, "...but not where I'm *supposed* to be." He glanced at his watch. 4:40a.m. In exactly five minutes he needed to be at the corner of Royal and Ursulines streets. It would take him less than a minute to reach that destination from here. He would wait then. Well, this was certainly the perfect time and place to wait.

Stanley wasn't a smoker, but right now, watching the seconds tick by on his watch, feeling the breezeless spring night hold him a bit too tight, he wished very much that he had a cigarette.

17.

At exactly 4:40am. a very pregnant Arab woman emerged from the front entrance of Le Richelieu. She was pear-shaped in the right place under her full-length dark-blue caftan. She stood adjusting her handbag and the large white head scarf that was drawn up across the lower half of her face. Her eyes peered out from under the scarf and saw nothing out of the ordinary—not a single living soul on the street. She glanced at her watch and began walking in the direction of the intersection of Royal and Ursulines. It was Lee Ann, pillow safety-pinned to the bottom of her bra, head wrapped in the white linen scarf that Stanley had bought her yesterday morning, and, of course, the full-length dark blue caftan she never went anywhere without. Lee Ann, pregnant Arab woman. She smiled behind her veil, wondered if they or he or she were watching her right now, would they know it was she? No, she doubted that very much.

She rounded a corner and there it was, a full two blocks down: the intersection where she and Stanley would rendezvous. The blue Mustang was nowhere in sight. She glanced at her watch: 4:44, a minute to docking. Was there trouble? She felt a bird flutter in her stomach. Okay... she would pace herself and arrive at the predetermined corner at 4:45. Where the hell was he?

At precisely 4:43am, Stanley stubbed out the very short butt of the cigarette Lee Ann had smoked in the early hours of the previous morning. The heavy shot of nicotine was lifting the top off his head. Good. He needed a little high here. He turned the ignition key and listened as the Mustang's engine purred into service. Clearing the lot again, he took a left onto Barracks Street and proceeded north to Royal. Just as he was

163

about to make a left, he glanced into the rearview mirror and saw the eyeballs of the Z roll up and out of their sockets— again! Shit! This guy is good. He considered flooring it, but that would throw off the timing, and there really was no time for evasive maneuvers now, but no...no, that wasn't exactly true. He would try one more time to lose his tail. It might put him a few seconds off, but maybe he could confuse the guy and that would give them the time—the precious second it would take to switch drivers. Something they'd agreed to do under any circumstances. He sped up, took a right on Bourbon Street and another on Esplanade and, after a four-and-a-half block circle, arrived back at the entrance to Le Richelieu's parking lot.

Passing the lot this time, he sped to the intersection of Royal and Barracks and just before swinging a hard left, he glanced one more time into the rearview mirror. No lights to the aft. Yes! He'd lost the guy again! He smiled as he looked at his watch: 4:47. He was two minutes late. Two blocks ahead, barely visible in the shadows, he thought he saw an Arab woman. All right, Lee Ann! He pushed heavily on the accelerator now, blinking his headlights three times as he closed the distance between them. She waved. Still no lights from behind.

Lee Ann had reached the corner of Royal and Ursulines at exactly 4:45am.

Stanley hadn't arrived yet, so she'd put the time to good use by using a magic known only to women: that of pinning, unpinning, fastening and unfastening undergarments through the material of overgarments. She'd pinched at the material of the caftan until she'd opened the safety pins holding her unborn pillow. It fell to the street with a *plop*.

She thought of Claire as she gathered up first the pillow, then the pins. Her newborn was really two goose-downs stuffed into one case to simulate the roundness required of an eight-and-a half-months' term. Claire, oh Claire, *she* had been a difficult birth.

Claire had almost killed her.

Lee, closing the pins, looked up and saw a small car come around the corner two blocks to the east. She hoped it was Stanley, and not someone else, coming to pick her up. She gave him a wave as he blinked the headlights three times and kept coming her way. He pulled along side her and, without a word of greeting, executed the prearranged Chinese fire drill. She threw the pillows in the backseat, swung behind the wheel of the idling Mustang, and handed him two safety pins. "It was an easy birth...you're late. You missed it." She floored the car and swung around the corner onto Ursulines.

"Sorry, did you find a substitute breathing coach?"

"No, you beast, I had to do it all alone. Were you being followed? Why were you late?"

"Yes, a Datsun Z, no question about it. When I first left the hotel, he was following, so I drove a circle and ducked back into the lot, waited for a while and then took off again only to..."

"Don't look now," said Lee Ann, eyes flashing between the street and the rearview mirror, "but I think your boy just turned the corner."

He swung round and saw a single pair of headlights following a block and a half to the rear: headlights like the eyes of a prowling shark. "That's him...that's the Z! Beat it, Lee Ann; we've got to lose this guy before we hit the bridge. I mean it!"

"Roger," she snapped as she wheeled the Mustang right onto Bourbon Street and then sped three blocks to Esplanade. The eyes of the shark stayed a block and a half back. She swung left on Esplanade. It was a long block, which gave them enough time to see that their pursuer had increased his speed and in so doing picked up a pursuer of his own. Lee Ann, out ahead by a half-long block, saw the the spinning red and blue lights on the rack of a NOPD cruiser turn the corner a block back and close rapidly on the Z. Her now madly darting eyes seized on something to the right and just ahead.

"All right! A little break here for us!"

"Break?" Stanley gasped.

She swung the car right, down a short alley, doused the headlights, and proceeded a short distance before another deft left brought them to rest in an apartment house garage. A second later the Z growled past, and seconds after that, the squad car's rotating lights splashed down the alley and were gone down Esplanade in pursuit of the pursuer. They looked at each other for a moment in the dim lights of the garage. Then Lee Ann slumped over the wheel.

"Lee Ann?"

"Yes Stanley?" she panted.

"I love you."

"I love you too, honey...oh my God..." She gasped, finally caught her breath, and wheezed. "Now can we do the bridge?"

"In a minute." Stanley had a case of the horns you get after a stiff shot of adrenalin. Apparently she was feeling it too.

He wasn't sure he knew how she did it, but suddenly he found her straddling him on the passenger seat.

"Want to do it right here? Just for old times' sake?"

"Christ, Lee Ann, you know I do...but you're breaking the rules."

"I know, Stanley, but this kind of adrenalin makes me kinda crazy."

"I know...me too. God...whaddayouwantado?"

He felt the heat, a large bubble of it, rise like lava up through his groin. The bubble buoyed him aloft in an instant. Lee Ann, pressed tightly against that groin, felt it too and reached down to free it just as the lights came on.

They pushed away from each other but not apart as they swung around to greet...an elderly black man peering around the door between the stairs to his apartment and the now very well-lit garage. He swung his yellow eyes around and met the dazed deer expression of a couple of middle-aged interlopers who were clearly caught in the act.

"Evenin'," said Lee Ann casually over her shoulder.

The expression of concern on the old man's face melted into sly mirth, "Dammit, don' you folks have a room yous can go to?"

Lee Ann wheezed "...Uh, well, sir, if you'd just give us a minute back in the dark...we'll be going. Right away..."

"Nah dammit, take your time. I'm goin' back to bed." And with that he slammed the screen door behind him and began slowly ascending the creaking steps to his second-story apartment. They looked at each other for a moment, wet dogs under the hose.

In all the excitement and danger of detection, Stanley's little bubble had floated off into the blue, so they waved it good-bye and sat hugging a few minutes in mutual consolation, agreeing that it was a well-timed rescue. Then Lee Ann reversed her acrobatics and slipped back under the steering wheel. "Fun while it lasted, huh?" She sighed and started the engine.

They were free now. Free to take it at their own pace. Free to put the top down and slide like a serpent into the balmy New Orleans morning. Or so they thought.

You can easily exit New Orleans freeways, but just try to get on one. More than one out-of-towner has been seen wandering about on the streets below, screaming epitaphs up at the engineers who created the skyway buzzing along above. And you can look at maps, but even they are short on information as to the location of onramps. Was this some kind of conspiracy wondered the San Franciscans as they joined the other aliens and ended up completely disoriented and frustrated. They finally agreed to drive north up Esplanade for many blocks and then, by dead reckoning only, turn west for a mile or two. And then—there it was—not on any maps but gleaming in the sodium-vapor streetlights: a ramp onto Interstate 10.

It was a few miles to the Causeway Exit where they headed north, arriving shortly at the abandoned tollbooth on the southern portal of the bridge. Pregnant peach hues swelled on the eastern shore.

"God Stanley, this is really surreal out here, isn't it?" Lee Ann, the little kid, was watching the lights of the toll station and those of a waking New Orleans sink like a ship below the waves to the south.

"It gets better," said Stanley, grabbing a bottle of champagne and some glasses from a cooler behind his seat. A couple of quick twists on the wire, a pry, and the cork went flying high into the air and was lost from view as it began its plunge into Pontchartrain.

"Champagne! Stanley, are you too cute or anything?"

"See that emergency bay up ahead? Pull in there and let's put the top up. It's too windy out here to enjoy..."

In mid-sentence she did as he requested. Now, if the Datsun was still following them, he'd have to pass. Can't just hang out on the Lake Pontchartrain Causeway. Within sixty seconds they were speeding along once again, watching sea birds sweeping and darting about the whitecapped waves.

Lee Ann and Stanley, rolling along, sipping champagne and singing cowboy songs in two-part harmony. A couple of canaries for a short time, free of the cat.

18.

Baton Rouge Ryan Metro Airport was humming with the song of worker bees arriving and departing on their respective food-gathering missions. Or so it seemed to Stanley, who had always equated airports with hives. The analogy worked on so many levels.

They parked the car and Lee Ann, now with headscarf draped loosely about her shoulders, went to check in. She rejoined Stanley at the newsstand, and they took the escalator up to a second-floor food service area. It was still an hour before her flight left for Toronto, so they ordered two western omelets to pass the time.

The small dining alcove was completely occupied so they took their trays out to seats overlooking the main tarmac. A white and green twin-engine Corsair executive turboprop was being fueled and prepped directly below their window. Stanley watched these proceedings as he shoveled in his food. "Christ! How can I be so starved?" He swallowed, swiped his mouth with a napkin, and went on.

"Okay, the way I see it, we're juggling events on four separate and quintessential fronts of our lives: Claire, the seaman, Bird, and Us. Can you think of any others?" He looked up at Lee Ann who seemed to be studying him quizzically for some reason.

"Stanley," she began softly, "you really *have* changed."

"I know Lee Ann, but that's under the category of Us, and that's last. We've got some business to do here and time is growing short."

"I mean..." she began and then paused to consider. "I mean...I've been thinking about how we could possibly cover everything we needed to cover before I leave, and couldn't come up with an approach. And you just nail it with a simple agenda: Claire, the seaman, Bird, and Us. That's everything, isn't it? Course there's my work and your work. Work that's not getting done because we're dealing with Claire and the seaman and Bird and Us..."

"That's about it, sweetheart." His pronunciation was flat, slightly lisping. Did she see his Bogart? No, she didn't, or else wasn't in the mood to. He continued in his own voice now. "So where do you want to start? I'd suggest Claire since she is the only real living thing on the roster."

"You know, Stanley, you sound like Woody Allen trying to imitate Bogart."

"Can we leave Woody out of this?"

"Come on get serious...we've got a lot to discuss." She bit off a piece of muffin. "And by the way, Stanley, *Us* is not a real living thing?"

He softened in response. "Of course it is, but Us has got to wait. It's item four."

"So now *you're* in charge of the agenda?"

"Lee Ann, we don't have time for this. Four items, add any you like. Set the order. Choose the opener. Let's get on with it. Time's short."

"Wow, another food fight, huh? We don't get food and we fight. Primal, huh?"

"Claire." He opened with their daughter's name.

"And then...the seaman, Bird, and Us. Go."

"Okay," Stanley said, "you're going to land in Toronto, go to Claire's, call KPIQ and see if the tape has arrived and what they're planning to do with it. You'll be seeing what you need to do to get Claire acquitted, and you'll be delivering my letter to her with seal in virgin condition! And then what, where Claire's concerned?"

"That's about it...have we moved onto the next item then, the seaman?"

"It's all intertwined Lee."

"Boy you can say that again."

"It's all intertwined, Lee."

She shook her head. He went on.

"Let me know when the the tape is going to air, okay? I have a strong inclination to return as soon as possible to Maison Rouge..." he smiled, "okay...I mean Poteet Porcelain...and keep my eyes and ears open. And hopefully arrange to have Jean Paul and Melissa watch that particular edition of *Good Morning San Francisco*. I think it would be good for them to see that, don't you? I think it would be good if I were there to watch them watching it, don't you?"

She lowered her eyes and moved them from side to side as if searching for her napkin. She certainly did need one. She found it, pulled it to her mouth for a quick dab, and stuffed it back at her side. Sutro Tower was generating some kind of strange cacophonous buzz now, a static that was messing up the song they seemed to be singing. Stanley heard the buzzing in his brain and could see that something was bothering Lee Ann. He didn't know what, but he'd known her a long time, could see and hear her aura when it pulsed and buzzed.

"What? What's on your mind?"

She looked up at him from under hooded lids. "I'm not sure how I'm going to handle the Canadian authorities. I guess get a lawyer and go from there. A lawsuit in a foreign country, wow, I'm going to need all the help I can get."

"How're you going to find a lawyer?"

She grew pensive, as if weighing all her options. "Well..." she began and then broke off and then continued, "Jean Paul gave me the name of several who handle this kind of..."

"Jean Paul?" he shot back.

"Yes. While you and Melissa were away at the foundry...her studio... wherever...Jean Paul and I talked at length about how to approach Claire's case. Whose assistance in Toronto I might contract...how generally to, as I said, approach it."

He looked at her in wide-eyed horror. "Lee Ann! Have we forgotten whom we think the stalker might be?" He waited.

"Not to worry, Stan, I told him I'd be doing it all by phone, that I'd be staying in New Orleans with you, 'cause we were havin' so damn much fun it was disgraceful." She hoped her clowning around would throw him off—conceal the fact that she was telling him a bold-faced lie now. That she had accepted more than a small offer of help from Poteet. It worked. He looked relieved.

"Man, there for a moment I thought you'd taken leave of your senses, Lee."

"Nah, Stan, not me, I'm still in the game."

Feeling the seconds pound down on them, they sat finishing their breakfasts and then laid their trays on adjacent seats. "If Poteet is the seaman, and damn, it makes more sense to me every minute, then maybe it would be good to let him help you...draw him into who you are as a real person, not just the personality on the screen..."

"That's one way to look at it." She looked down again, this time not for her napkin. "So, Bird..." she began, just as her flight was called. There was no time to continue. They returned their trays to the buffet area and moved off quickly to her boarding gate.

"I'm going back to Wayfarer's Antiques first thing when I get back to New Orleans, see if I can pick up a trail...any trail," said Stanley.

"I guess that's all you can do." Lee Ann, walking briskly to catch her flight, was wistful.

"I wouldn't hold out too much hope, love." His tone was tender.

"I know," she said as they approached her gate. "But try, Stanley, try *really* hard."

"I will," he said. "And I see, once again, we are being swept into the vortex of life and have no time to talk about Us."

She brightened. "Whaddaya think we've been doing for the last three days Stan?" She pressed herself into his ample frame and gave him a warm, short kiss. "I love you, Stan. That's all I really need to say, isn't it?"

"I love you too, Momma. Give Claire a kiss for me," he said, releasing her and watching her move off to the security check line. She turned and waved a last time. He threw her one last kiss. She returned the gesture.

Stanley made his way to the window of the boarding gate. Her flight would be a few minutes in departing so he entertained himself by watching the proceedings down around the green and white Corsair. A man in a blue uniform was walking around the aircraft, evidently the captain, giving her a final visual inspection. And now he disappeared behind the plane and Stanley could see only the lower half of his body as he greeted someone in a...what? His vantage point was a full one hundred yards farther away than it had been in the food service area, but there was no mistaking it, the captain was greeting someone in a wheel chair. And now that someone was being carried up the ramp and into the passenger compartment by—he couldn't make them out because the boarding door was on the far side of the plane. But wait, the passenger had been loaded aboard now and three tall black men in African garb were waving as the wheel blocks were knocked away and the Corsair taxied off the tarmac and out onto a runway. He forgot about Lee Ann's departure and walked, just short of a jog, in the direction of the terminal entrance. He needed a closer look at this African entourage.

Luckily he entered the main concourse just as they were departing for the parking lot. He stayed a safe distance behind them as he watched them move out into the lot, board a lime-green Bentley, and drive away.

Now how many lime-green Bentleys do you suppose are in this neck of the woods? Stanley steamed to himself. Poteet! That was the car he'd seen parked in the lot at Poteet Porcelain two nights ago. Poteet's car, and those were Poteet's employees, and that was Poteet boarding the Corsair! To go where? He smelled a rat, a big fat *dead* rat. Lee Ann was not telling him everything. Something was going on.

As he moved to his car, he looked up to see a jet bearing Continental's distinct insignias appear out of the roof of the terminal and make that sharp upward tilt for altitude. "Bye, Lee Ann...guess you know what you're doing." He climbed behind the wheel of the Mustang, pulled out of the lot, and moved onto the highway that would take him back to New Orleans. He'd gone about a mile down the road when the white and green Corsair purred overhead, banked, and headed north. That would be the general direction of Canada. "So long, Poteet...we'll meet again soon, I'm sure."

Stanley Hochstetter was ready to wash all this mud from his hands and get them back into a clay that would respond to him and only him. He was ready to get back to work. His work.

As he paid the toll on the north portal and crossed the bridge back into town, he began assembling a piece in his mind. A fanciful upbeat piece, almost silly, but germane to what was going on in his life. Something with a maiden and a dragon. It slowly took form and, by the time he'd reached Wayfarer's Antique Shoppe, all the mental work was done. He would call it Mary Mythe.

In the store a new clerk greeted him. Not the disgruntled woman of the previous morning, but a man in his midtwenties. "Hello," he said, greeting the young man and holding out his hand. The guy didn't offer his. Stanley quickly drew his back— thought, what the fuck? Went on.

"I'm Stanley Hochstetter, and I was in here yesterday morning. There was a woman behind the counter. I bought a maroon-and-lime green fifties-style juice squeezer from her. Do you remember the item I'm referring to?"

"No," said the clerk nasally and said no more.

"Do you know when the lady who sold it to me will be in? I'd like to ask her if she by any chance knows the previous owner."

The young man threw him a "sure you would" look and mewed in a high, flippy alto, "She's gone to *Aaafrica*...won't be back till next week."

"Damn," Stanley grumbled under his breath. As he turned to leave he heard a whiny drawl come from behind him. "Oh...now I remember thaaat one...had a big, long stem...and a handle in the shape of a tongue...maroon and lime-green."

Stanley spun around. "So you know it! Do you know who brought it in? Where it came from? Any information would be much appreciated."

"No," said the clerk nasally and said no more.

For a minute he considered thanking this fruity young man for the mind fuck; then he thought better of it and found out the guy's name and the name of the woman clerk: Bruce and Delilah. He thanked the guy, said he would be back, and walked out the door into the street.

"Great...that's started," he mumbled as he moved off in the direction of his car and the short drive back to Le Richelieu.

Lisa Lynn was tending the late morning bar. She greeted him casually as he walked in with one brick of Melissa's clay under either arm.

"Stan...you're up early, where's the missus? What can I get you?"

"Virgin mary please...you wouldn't believe how early. She's off on a mission."

Lisa smiled. She had some kind of flush about her this morning, as if she'd had an exceptionally good night. "You still want me to show you around this evening? Sorry I didn't call yesterday but got sidetracked, you maught say." Lisa said "...sidetracked you maught say," with a sultry drawl that bordered on the lascivious, but she snapped out of it and asked him about the heavy load under his arms.

"Oh just fifty pounds of mud...ceramic clay I picked up." He looked her over. "Sounds like you were having fun. That's okay, we were too. Yeah, why don't you check by the room when you get off and we'll figure something out."

"Will do."

"Oh...could you bring some margaritas up with you? What time did you say?"

Precious seconds went by for Lisa while he said all this. She was mixing drinks and taking orders and answering the phone. He watched her work, admiring her style. Finally she set up his tomato juice and said.

"Long shift today, won't be off till five. Sure, I can do that."

It was a little too busy in the bar. Lisa was hustling and seemed to be already distracted by whatever was making her glow. So Stanley set the bricks on the floor, threw back his juice, picked them back up, and made his way to the elevators. He wondered again if Lisa would bolt and run when she found out that Lee wouldn't be joining them this evening. Cross that bridge when you get to it he reminded himself as he let himself into his room, rolled up his sleeves, and prepared to go to work.

Stanley could work quickly, pulling forms and masses from clay at an almost stop-action pace. But this late morning he took it slowly, the way he always liked to take it the first time with a new love. Give and take, take and give; and this clay of Melissa's was as fine as its creator. He pulled a block from its plastic wrapper and set it on a circular marble-topped table that sat in one corner of the room. Too cramped. He pulled the table into the center of the room where he could walk around it. Good. Already the block of porcelain white clay looked regal and finished as it rose proudly and solidly from its marble base. Marble to work on, thought Stanley. He'd lucked out. Marble was what he worked on at home. In one minute one could wipe it clean with a sponge, and be cooking on it the next. Sometimes at home, though, he wouldn't wipe it off before he cooked. Have you ever chewed clay? Stanley had, many times.

He sat on the edge of the bed staring at the block—new block—pure block. He heard in his mind, one more time, what Michelangelo had said about sculpture. About the statue inside the block yearning to be free. And he thought again about what an old professor at the San Francisco Academy of Art had told him: "...clay is death, bronze is life, marble is resurrection." So it was fitting then that he be working his death upon a foundation of resurrection. That worked for him. But then again, he didn't feel that clay was death. Maybe it wasn't full-blown life, but it was closer to it, for him, than painting. Painting had frustrated him to the brink of suicide. He'd finally thrown it off his back and gone on to sculpture. He'd tried marble—wonderful results but too slow. He'd tried wood—something too common there. So he'd welded and brazed and poured molten metal. That had been fun, but required some big, hot, gaseous and/or electrical machinery in the kitchen. Not quite right. Finally he'd landed in the mud, and like the pigs he used to wallow with down by the ranch pond, he was in porker heaven. The raw materials were dirt cheap, responded like a fine racing machine, could be worked in the kitchen, and could be molded into not only works of art but useful household objects. Cups, bowls, pots, and dishes to be sure, but he'd gone on to letter holders, jewelry boxes, lamps, and for awhile he'd even done kitchen sinks. They were made of metal and porcelain, materials he knew. So Stanley had made them in all shapes and sizes. He'd made sinks that were a series of waterfall ponds—functioning kitchen sinks! Those kitchen cascades had been well received among the affluent who were building custom homes, because he'd put his art into them, and people could use them and drop his name. But battles ensued over who could outdo whom with their kitchen sink, so he'd stepped back and watched the feeding frenzy as other ceramists filled the orders he didn't. And of course he'd missed his chance to make a bundle of money, which he could have put to good use. But then he'd found it.

"Mud Mythology," he said to the wall. "Why did it take so long?"

History and art, his two cerebral loves, all wrapped up into one ball of clay. And he was glad people accepted the humorous aspect that was a part of his current style. He liked to see people's eyes light up and their smile lines appear when they'd look at one of his Mud Mythologies. No one ever said to him, "Stanley, you're funny," except to mean funny as in odd. Stanley, however, had always envied stand-up comics and wondered, with his Jewish heritage, if he should try it. But, as is the case with millions of others, he'd just never mustered the guts. So when they laughed at his pieces—pointed to various elements and snickered—he felt strangely fulfilled. You do what you can.

Now it was time for him to see what he could do with this block on the table. He snapped a last picture of its virginity—and his—in his mind and laid both hands on it. It was cool to his touch. He caressed it for a moment and then, with a strength known only to him, pulled a large glob from one corner. "Sorry..." he said softly.

He began kneading the material, squeezing and pushing at it with his thumbs and fingers. A piece the size of an egg was pulled from the larger clump. This was not egg shaped, but in seconds it was—a perfect egg. He pinched at the egg, raising ridges off its surface, and was impressed. The clay was fine *and* refined, held a sharp edge and line, and responded beautifully to kneading and forming. It would be a joy to do detail with this material. And Melissa had said it was very forgiving in the kiln.

The ceramist sat for a moment longer experimenting with his new love. Like a musician running through scales and passages, he went through his—put his new instrument through its paces. Handles beautifully! Elation!

Stanley Hochstetter, warming up.

He began massing the piece now, tearing chunks off the block and kneading them into body trunks, arms, legs, heads, undersupports and other rudimentary elements. When he had enough parts constructed, he began pushing them all together to effect the overall composition of a dragon and the maiden, Mary Mythe.

Mary had one arm and hand up over the dragon's slim shoulders. Her other hand was resting softly on the serpent's broad breastplates. She, with only a hint of young breasts, would be clad in a scoop-necked peasant blouse and long, flowing skirt. She would be looking up and smiling at the dragon who would have his neck and head pointed skyward. Somehow he would have to subtly effect the expression of bliss on the creature's scaly face. That might be difficult, but he thought the body attitude of the dragon might say it for him—it seemed to be so far—and he was looking at only a rudimentary massing of the final piece. Good.

Around one, there was a knock on the door. With clay on his hands, he walked over and opened it: room service with a tray of sandwiches, potato salad, and a couple of tomato juices. "I didn't order anything," he said politely to the bellhop.

"Compliments of the lady tending bar."

"How sweet. Thank her for me." He moved to the dresser, fetched a couple of bills for the hop, and sent him on his way.

Two lunches had been sent up, and though it had been only a few short hours since he'd eaten a dinner-sized southern breakfast, he ate both sandwiches, all the potato salad, along with the garnish, and downed both of the juices. It was the traveling munchies, sneaking up from behind to grab him and stick fat on his body in much the same manner as he slapped a belly on some Viking or opulent Greek goddess.

Better watch it, he thought to himself.

Weight problems had always plagued *all* the Hochstetters. And as sedentary as the one named Stanley normally was, he was no exception. He rose from the chair, feeling stiff and almost forty-six again, and walked out onto the deck. What to do, what to do? He wanted to keep working, but he was feeling sluggish and a need to get some air. So he pulled on some sweats and tennis shoes and, taking a back elevator to avoid the bar, left the hotel to wander down and walk and maybe even trot a little along the levee. There would still be time to throw some important details onto Mary and the dragon when he returned to work some magic before Lisa Lynn arrived.

19.

On the flight to Toronto, Lee Ann shoved the possibility that someone might still be trailing her to the back of her mind—it seemed so remote. Besides, she was extremely bored with the stalker's act now. It had become vicious, and she'd dealt with it in the only way she knew how to deal with it. And now it was time to let the cards fall where they may. At least Stanley had had a taste of what it was like to be pursued. At least now he could think about it for a while as they waited for the seaman to make his next move. He had been patient and comforting with her—true—but hadn't really been involved to the extent of feeling it. Now, after their little escape early this morning, she was sure he did feel it. And that was good; she needed a trusted ally who was as soberly impressed with the seriousness of the situation as she was.

The stewardess handed her the ginger ale she'd ordered. She winced and bit the edge of her plastic cup as she thought about the lie—or more accurately, omission of the truth—that she'd committed with Stanley at breakfast this morning when he'd asked her in so many words to what extent Poteet was involved in her quest to free Claire. She *had* lied. What she'd actually told Poteet that evening, alone with him after dinner when they'd exchanged cell phone numbers, *was* that she was headed off to Toronto in the morning—just sort of blurted it out. It was before she'd started suspecting he was her stalker, so it really wasn't stupid on her part, just an ill-timed error.

She considered calling Maureen at KPIQ from the plane phone, but then decided to wait until she arrived at Claire's.

Claire. It would be so good to see her daughter again. It had been almost a year since she'd seen Claire in person, and that had been in San Francisco one evening when Claire had been passing through on her way to Asia on some museum business. But now she would be seeing Claire on her own turf—and—with the addition of Jackie in her life. This might be trying.

Even though she'd had six months to adjust to the reality that her daughter was venturing into lesbianism, that adjustment had been from afar. Now she would be seeing it for the first time, live and in living color. In the flesh, so to speak. She liked Jackie and had talked enough on the phone with her these last six months to know that. Hmm, this would be, as they say, interesting.

The big jetliner hit some turbulence and jostled her ginger ale around on the fold down tray. She grabbed the cup just as it threatened to leap into her lap. The plane passed through the rough air and settled back on course. A lot of rough air in her life of late, she thought. Almost forty-five years of living gave her some assurance that it was just a local disturbance. That all this too would pass. The stalker would at some time in the future find something more entertaining to do with his time. Stan and Claire would bury the hatchet forever—perhaps. And the squeezer would lead them to the long-lost Bird—pleasant possibilities.

"It's all intertwined," she heard Stanley say. And, of course, he was right. And, of course, Claire had been right. It was better now that the cold war with Stanley seemed to be over. Being with Stanley again was making her realize how much she'd repressed the fact that she had, at the bottom of her heart, missed him these past five years.

"Ladies and gentlemen, this is the captain speaking. You'll notice that the seatbelt light has been turned on, as we are about to make our final approach into Toronto's Pearson International Airport. The temperature is a pleasant fifty-nine degrees, a little chilly considering some of you have just come from Houston, but I'm sure it will be a welcome relief. We hope your stay in Toronto is pleasant...I know mine always is. It's been a pleasure serving as your captain today, and I thank you for flying Continental."

The stewardesses and stewards made a last pass with their plastic bags picking up stray drink cups. Lee Ann downed the remainder of her ginger ale and surrendered her cup without a fight. She buckled up and settled back into her seat to await touchdown. The big jet rolled to its right like an airborne whale and locked on for the final approach.

She knew that takeoff was more dangerous than landing as tons of metal and flesh and baggage and jet fuel struggled to take to the air. But she liked takeoff. The feeling of the g's pressing her into her seat as the big jets went to work. Landing? That was cause for some anxiety. All those other planes coming in, the wind vectors, the wheels going from zero to a hundred and fifty miles an hour in a nanosecond, the bounce and crunch as the wheels did just that. And then the negative g's, throwing everyone forward as the pilot splayed the flaps and reversed the thrust. No, you can keep your landings she thought to herself and then went back to thinking about her life.

Poteet had offered to help. Coincidentally he had some business he needed to attend to in Toronto, so he might as well take care of it while she was there. And would she please contact him at CBC when she got in. He'd also given her his number at the Royal York where he would be staying. They could meet, and he would personally introduce her to a very fine attorney he knew who had a good record of acquittals in cases such as these. This guy knew the authorities and could make deals he said.

How could she refuse? It was exactly what she needed: an experienced guide into this jungle. So she'd accepted Poteet's offer with only faint resistance. "Oh, Jean Paul, are you sure you want to get involved in all this?" He, of course, had been his charming gallant self and told her it was the least he could do for her since she'd brightened so many of his late mornings as he'd watched her do her show. She'd laughed then and accepted, and then she'd come home from dinner and found the bouquet and started having second thoughts. But she couldn't tell Stanley that she was going to meet Poteet in Toronto. He would have freaked! No kidding. So she'd lied with omissions during their initial conversations about Poteet being the stalker and then at breakfast this morning.

The Boeing 757 touched down with a stomach-hurling bounce. Lee Ann Barnes, soon to see the daughter she hadn't seen in nearly a year now, felt like shit. Maybe next time she talked to Stanley on the phone she would fess up and get it off her chest. But then he'd start to worry. And Stanley was a worrywart.

Claire in ragtag jeans, a turquoise tank top, black leather jacket, and boots, caught her mother's eye as she came through customs. Her face twinkled with a sweet little girl smile. Claire could be sweet, even if she was one of the toughest young women Lee Ann had ever known. She waved and then, smiling broadly herself, closed the distance to her daughter. Mother and daughter gave each other a long hug. Claire had always had a problem with her dad, but there was no question in her mind—she loved her mom.

"Hi, Mom, sorry about why you're here, but glad you are."

"Hi, honey," Lee Ann returned, then moved back to take her daughter in—see what new fashion jag Claire was on. "It's okay, girl, we'll take care of it. Let me look at you for a sec." And with that, she did, just for a moment, noticing that Claire had returned to her natural blonde hair, and the makeup was soft and tasteful, and all the hard edge that had gone along with the nose ring, including the nose ring, was gone. "You look great," she said, looking Claire straight in her pale-blue eyes.

"So do you, Mom, but I suppose that's your business."

The first hit of Claire's sarcastic sense of humor, thought Lee Ann.

Oh well, she was used to it. She had even copped a few of Claire's punky licks when dealing with a particularly irascible guest. God, it was good to be feasting her eyes on Claire again.

"Mom, this is Jackie. Jackie Garland, this is my mom. I call her Lee Ann, Mom, Blabbermouth, Butthead, a lot of things. You might want to start with Lee Ann and work your way in."

Lee Ann took Jackie's hand and, ignoring Claire's outrageousness, shook it firmly. "Pleasure to be finally meeting you. I've enjoyed our phone exchanges."

"Yes, nice to finally meet Claire's mom. She doesn't talk about you much or anything..." Jackie rushed ahead. "I'm dying to ask you some questions. Communications major...as you know." Jackie had held an imaginary microphone out to her, and then changed it to her left hand so she could shake Lee Ann's. Lee Ann was amused, wondered how many times Jackie had used that one. She sure would in the future.

"Ha! I don't bore people talking about my work or anything, no...never." She was getting into the oblique approach that seemed to be the working mode with these girls. She had a good feeling about this person her daughter had taken for a lover. Jackie was about the same size as Claire, a slim five foot eight or so, and had a springy cloud of black hair that shot out of her head like atomic particles in a cloud chamber. Jackie also wore the obligatory black leather jacket and trashed jeans, but had varied the boot theme and wore sandals. Her face was—Lee Ann considered it—a skewed sort of angelic. She had an easier manner than Claire's. For the first time, seeing the girls together, she had a flash vision of them making love. It was just a flash, but it made her blink. Hard. A blink neither of the girls noticed. She thought about Stanley. She wondered how he would feel about their daughter's current romantic arrangement. Clearly Claire hadn't discussed it with him yet, so she would just leave things be.

They loaded her bags aboard Claire's beat-up Toyota, drove south along 427, and picked up the QEW into town. Dark clouds were drifting in from Lake Ontario. The CN tower tried to snag them as they passed, but even the pride of Toronto wasn't up to the task.

"I had no idea that Toronto had so many huge towers," she shouted over the thrashing of the Toyota's engine.

Claire was driving one hundred kph: the speed limit. This was new. She shouted back, "Old Toronto is the New York of Canada. Economic megacenter. Most of those are bank towers. Like that big white one is Bank of Montreal. The black ones are Toronto Dominion...and that's Scotiabank. Big bucks...big, big bucks."

Lee Ann rubbernecked as Claire exited the QEW and proceeded along backroutes to Queen Street. She was speeding now, it seemed to Lee Ann, driving ten to fifteen kilometers over the limit, and with her usual carefree abandon. Her driving made even a little speeder like Lee Ann slightly nervous. But you didn't comment on Claire's performance behind the wheel and expect to escape some sharp retort. At least now the engine sounded like it was going to survive.

"So how's old Stanley, Mom? How's the old Mud Man? And what made you run away to New Orleans with him after five years of cold war?"

Lee Ann hadn't mentioned the bullet note to Claire in any of their recent phone discussions, and she wouldn't now. "I went down to the opening of his show a couple of nights ago...we got happy on champagne...just sort of did it on a whim, I guess."

Claire smiled wryly as she went on.

"We've been getting along fantastically. God, there's so much to tell you, I don't know where to begin."

"You fucking him again?" Claire said flatly.

"Claire!" Lee Ann reeled. "Jesus...okay...yeah Claire...*no*, I'm not *fucking* him again." She kept her composure, but wasn't pleased about it—sat shaking her head in disbelief.

"Mmm..." said Claire. "Do you want to be? I mean it's been two years since Miguel...no one's getting any younger."

Lee Ann, contrary as it was to her nature, kept her lip zipped and let Claire ramble on.

""Sides, me and the old man been getting along pretty well these past couple of years. Whaddaya know, maybe someday me and Jackie and you and dad'll all be sitting down to Christmas dinner together. Wouldn't *that* be a trip?"

"Yeah, *that* would be a trip, Claire." Lee Ann had iced over.

"Oh...you still pissed about my asking you..."

Lee Ann interrupted. "I guess it's just your shock tactics honey. And if you don't mind..."

Claire softened, "I know, that was punk. I'm glad you and Dad are talking again. Probably better that you're keeping it platonic. You know...not *making love.* There...satisfied?"

Lee Ann glanced sharply at her daughter for a moment and then turned away.

Jackie, who had been taking it all in from the backseat, saw a hole that needed to be filled and jumped in. "So tell me about Stanley. He's getting famous, isn't he? Claire's told me a little bit."

Lee Ann, appreciating the rescue, turned quickly and began filling Jackie and Claire in on Stanley as they made their way into town. About his new-found success. About how he was changing as a person. About how good she felt to have the cold war finally over. Girl talk about a guy.

They turned off Queen Street and began heading north on McCaul. Claire's street. They passed a red brick and glass Bauhaus style building on the the left. "Ta daaaa..." she said pointing. "Home sweet home... Ontario College of Art, OCA. And that's Art Museum of Ontario.

"I worked there. ROM...Royal Ontario Museum is up the road a piece. They're the ones who recently let me go...as you know...but... so...that's my school Mom."

"So how does it feel to be graduated?" Lee Ann asked.

"Well, I guess I still have my major degree in painting. The art restoration minor is pretty much useless, now that I have a record as a poacher." She laughed sardonically.

Lee Ann fell silent, feeling slightly chagrined that Claire had spent the last four years in Toronto, and this would be her first visit to the city. But then Claire had come home for most school vacations or was off on some adventure with her friends.

Her daughter was waving now at a little red brick storefront that housed a bakery and a microbrewery at street level.

"We live above there," she said, pointing to the loft apartment on the second floor.

"I recognize it from the pictures you've sent," Lee Ann said softly.

Claire parked on a side street and the three of them loaded Lee Ann's luggage up the narrow back stairs to the loft. "This place smells sooo good. Do you ever get tired of that bakery aroma?"

"No," said the girls in unison and giggled.

Claire and Jackie's Toronto loft was really just one big high-ceiling room cleverly partitioned off to create a two-bedroom, one bath apartment. With rooms at either end, the central space was windowless, unless you counted two large skylights as windows. A sparse alcove kitchen divided the living and dining area.

"So, whaddaya think?" Claire asked her mother.

Lee Ann, who couldn't decorate her way out of a shoebox, was always somewhat awed by Claire's abilities in that area. "God...I think it's beautiful! As usual."

Claire stepped quickly to Jackie's side. "We did it together. Not too many arguments or anything." She broke away and led her mother in the direction of the study/guest bedroom.

The girls left her for a moment so she could change out of the blue caftan and into some slacks and a bulky wool sweater Claire had laid out on the bed. A worn, brown leather flight jacket lay there also; an old friend she'd reluctantly given Claire several years ago. The jacket and the sweater—two items of clothing Claire knew she hadn't taken to steamy New Orleans. How thoughtful. Claire could be sweet under all that concrete.

They regrouped in the living room where louvered doors opened onto the girls' bedroom and then onto the street. A puffy white queen-sizd bed took up the whole of their bedroom area, except for the closet, and a three foot walkway at the end of the bed. She was glad her room was at the other end of the loft, around the kitchen, in back of the bath. She looked around. What a beautiful place these girls had made for themselves. Their furniture was old but comfortable. Their taste ran to hard-edged industrial, but the lighting was superb, and the loft glowed almost sensuously. Of course, a lover's nest.

Jackie, leaving to do her laundry, was standing with Claire by the front door discussing what sounded like domestic business. Lee Ann walked over and stood studying a recent canvas by her daughter—saw the familiar CH in the lower left-hand corner of the work. Jackie left in a puff of smoke, and after a brief time in the kitchen, Claire, two coffee mugs in hand, walked up behind her mother. "I call it, 'Twilight in Hell'," she said darkly. "Naw, really it doesn't have a title, just 'Composition five point nine in peach and rust'. Ninth painting in my fifth series of color ranges."

Lee Ann studied the work. It was, as Claire had noted, done in shades of twilight colors: light orange, rose, white, and rust, with gradation of those colors into dark gray. Claire had used streaks of corroded copper-green to set all the swirling peach, rust and charcoal grey into motion. It was definitely a sky—but a disembodied sky.

"I did this series to learn these colors," said Claire, holding one of the cups of coffee out to her mother. "It's very difficult to grade orange and peach into grey. The gradations keep showing jumps and smears and tend to get greasy. So I practiced that particular maneuver here. Whaddaya think? How'd I do?"

"Technically, I'd say very good. You must have used a lot of washes. I don't see anything jarring in terms of your transitions. As far as content, I like the tension you've got going between the pastel tranquilities and the dark menacing elements..."

"You are a mouth, aren't you, Mom?" Claire draped an arm over her mother's shoulders.

"I guess so. That's how I eat anyway."

They moved over to the couches. Joao Gilberto sang a sad bossa nova on Claire's stereo. "So, Claire, we should discuss some business before Jackie gets back, and then I've got to make some calls. How's your schedule?"

"Sounds good. I'm not going anywhere soon. As you know ROM's given me my walking papers. Can't have an art smuggler on the staff of a large, well-known, provincial museum now can we?"

"No, suppose not," said Lee Ann pensively. "I'm sorry, honey, sorry about all of this, but fill me in. I'm here to help, and I've got some troops lined up to do battle when that time comes. But right now, I need the story."

Claire was squirming in the cushions. "Okay, but first...I'm dying to know, what's the latest on the seaman? Any more love letters?"

If you only knew, thought Lee Ann. "When did we last discuss *him*...I'm assuming...of course."

"Clever Mom. You think it could possibly be a woman?"

She thought about the bullet note. "No...it's a man."

"Okay...so...last I heard he sent you a fax of a picture of *Venus on the Half Shell*, with a little poem attached. I thought that was cute... anything further?"

"No...that was it." She was lying again. But Claire had enough on her mind without hearing about the bullet note. And she couldn't imagine telling her daughter that the man who was about to help her out of her legal problems was the man she suspected to be the sender of that note.

"That was it?" she heard Claire asking.

"That was it."

"So he's gone away?"

"Hopefully."

Claire saw her mother's mind working, wished she could see the wheels. That mind snapped back and asked.

"So...tell me about your latest perils. Give me the details."

So Claire rambled through the events of her life for the past week. How she had been returning from the dig in Knossos, and how she'd pocketed some small, *very* small figurines, and a not-so-small carved stone altar of some kind. And how she'd tried to ship them along with her return luggage disguised as cheap native crafts, and how there had been a customs check, and a particularly astute customs cop had seen through the acrylic paint that she'd applied over a latex mask: a mask that could be easily peeled off, thereby returning the objects to their original raw marble finish. "How in hell did that guy see through it?" Claire wondered angrily. "So now they have art historians working in *customs!?*"

Lee Ann kept her lip zipped—let Claire go on.

"Shit! Well, this guy suspected something, so he called the museum and had my boss—can you imagine that—*my boss!* come down to inspect and confirm the authenticity of the pieces. All the time I'm sitting there watching them peel the latex off. Oh man! And that was that! Claire Hochstetter, dead meat." Claire pulled her slim twenty-year-old frame into a ball and sunk down into the cushions: a disgruntled young woman, biting her nails.

Lee Ann was silent for a moment. "Bad break," she said, "but one you can learn from. You know, civil disobedience really isn't worth it in the long run. Goes on your record and that's limiting any way you look at it."

"Oh, thanks for reminding me." Claire scowled. "But I know you're right." She shifted in the cushions and continued. "I wasn't going to sell them or anything...just wanted a few items for the private collection. They were so small and beautiful. I wish you could have seen them." She paused for a moment to remember. "And you should have seen the shit I dug up that went to the Greek government! Stuff that would've lain buried in the rubble for all eternity if it hadn't been for little Claire who has a nose for finding that kind of shit. *Shit!* I'm *pissed!*"

"I know you are, Claire, but now we gotta' deal with it." They fell silent for a moment. "Let me tell you about Jean Paul Poteet."

It was Lee Ann's turn to ramble. She told Claire about the dinner party out at the foundry, about Poteet and Melissa and the rhino show and the Kenyans and Poteet's offer of assistance with the Canadian legal system and everything else she could wedge in between Claire's endless questions. Finally the tale was told—still without any mention that she suspected Poteet might be her stalker. "So," she concluded, looking at her watch, "it's six o'clock, time to call your father, and then Mr. Poteet. This could take some time."

"Don't mind...long as I can listen."

"Listen away."

Claire jumped up and set off to build a fire in the tiny wood stove opposite the couches.

Lee Ann retrieved her cell from her handbag and scrolled up room 201 at Le Richelieu. Stanely's sleepy baritone came across the miles in full relief. "Hello."

"Hi, honey, I'm home," she mewed.

"Lee! You safe and sound? On the ground?"

"Couldn't be safer, couldn't be sounder, couldn't be more on the ground."

"You calling from Claire's?"

"Yes, we're sipping coffee, she's building a fire in the stove, and we're settling in for the evening. No events of note on the way up here." She mumbled now. "I think I've lost him."

Stanley who had, moments before the phone rang, greeted Lisa Lynn bearing margaritas, sat on the edge of the bed talking with Lee Ann and watching as Lisa circled his Mary Mythe, studying it from every angle. "That's good," he said. "How's Claire?"

"Oh, a little pissed off but looking great!" She caught her daughter's eyes for a split second as Claire realized they were talking about her.

"Is it going to be difficult? I mean springing her?"

"I don't know yet, Stan, we've only just begun to talk. Her court date isn't until next Wednesday, so tomorrow we're going to see if we can find a counselor and make the necessary connections to make a deal." She was using Poteet's language now and realized it too late.

"Make a deal?" he asked.

She recovered quickly. "Yes, and that could involve time in prison, but I doubt it. I think we can settle with a fine and some kind of deportation agreement."

When had Lee Ann become so astute in the area of plea bargaining? Where had that come in? Stanley wondered. Oh well, sounded like she was on top of it. He asked, "Have you given Claire the bracelet yet? The letter?"

"No, we needed to take care of business first—but I will."

There was a brief silence and then he said, "I stopped at Wayfarer's Antique Shoppe this morning and the lady who sold me the squeezer is in Africa, won't be back until next week. So dead end there until she gets back."

"*Go back* to the store, Stanley. *Find out* how many employees work there. *Talk to* every one of them. *Offer* a reward leading to the discovery of your long-lost son. That's how you get *these* things done."

"Right...sometimes I lack imagination in *these* areas, Lee Ann. Thanks."

"Okay. Will you do that?"

"Def."

"How you doin?"

"Missing you."

"Missing you."

There was silence for a moment, and then Stanley said, "I'm going back out to Poteet's tomorrow, if I can arrange it, and hang around for a bit. It's going to be important to keep in touch with you about when they're going to air your tape...so I can get those two to watch. Have you called KPIQ yet?"

She froze. Tomorrow he would learn from Melissa that Poteet was out of town. Melissa might possibly mention Toronto. She knew the time had come to confess her little omissions. But that might take time, and she had other calls to make.

Stanley knew he was moving her into a box canyon. Would she lie her way out again? This lying thing had come between them before. He decided to cut to the chase—ended a rather long pause with:

"Poteet's in Toronto, isn't he?"

She went cryogenic. How did he know that!?

"Lee Ann? Are you there?"

"How did you know that?" she croaked.

"I'll keep it simple. I saw it when you were lying to me at breakfast this morning, and then I saw Poteet being loaded aboard his little green and white executive Corsair and winging his way north. That's how I know."

"I'm sorry, Stan. Yes, he's in Toronto."

"Sleeping with the enemy?"

"Hardly, Stan. I'm just using his influence and connections to free my daughter. Oh sorry, *our* daughter." She caught Claire's eyes again.

"Let me know how it goes, Lee. I gotta go right now. Sorta tied up."

"I don't think we should end it this way, Stan." She was near tears.

"I'll check in tomorrow. Really gotta go now, kid. Slightly pissed and all that, you know?"

"I know. I love you Stan."

"Yeah, bye." He hung up.

She sat for a moment, stinging. Most lies are told to protect oneself, she'd read somewhere. She had been lying to protect Stanley, to spare him worry. Evidently not the right thing to do. When would she learn?

20.

Raindrops were tapping lightly outside on the deck... pitter- patter...pitter-patter...

Stanley hung up the phone carefully because he felt like slamming it down. What was this! What the hell was this? Was he pissed at Lee Ann for lying? Or was he feeling jealous of Poteet? If he was jealous of Poteet, then that meant he must be falling in love again with Lee Ann—his co-operator in this nasty little business—who was lying to him! Well, maybe she wasn't exactly sleeping with the enemy yet, but she was certainly camping on his doorstep. He wondered if Poteet, maimed as he was, could still do it. The thought that Poteet might not—be able to do it—sent a reptilian shiver down his spine. He was pissed, a compound pissed. This was entirely more complicated than he wanted life to be. And yet, just a few hours ago, he was enjoying the fact that his life was no longer so dull.

Lisa Lynn, who had busied herself circling Mary Mythe, studying it from every angle, had heard the phone fight. Now the guy, Stanley, was still sitting on the bed with his forearms resting on his thighs, hands clasped, staring blankly dead ahead. Rescue time.

"Sure is fun to see a really good artist's work while it's still in progress...before it's finished. Sorta like watching your neighbors courtin'."

Stanley looked up and smiled slightly. "Good analogy," he said quietly. "You write?"

"Not much more than law briefs these days."

"Takes creativity to do it well though, don't you think? I mean write concise, entertaining law briefs?"

"Yes, and it sharpens your writing for when you decide to set it free."

He got up off the bed, moved to the tray of frosty cactus concoctions Lisa had brought up. His hands went out, grabbed two, and held one out to her. "Here's to Lee Ann...Godspeed."

"To Lee Ann...where the hell *is* she?"

"Mmm, right, well, she's flown off to..."—he caught himself—"back to San Francisco...you still want to show me the sights?"

He'd decided to get on with it—move upfront. He didn't want to make this young lady uncomfortable, not if he could possibly avoid it. She was a looker, smart and quick, and was probably the recipient of more than her share of cheap hits.

"So it will be just you and me?" Lisa was all business now.

"Unless you've some friends who want to come along. I need to eat fast. I've got the traveler's munchies."

"I'm hungry too."

"Yes, you know, I've really been starving myself today. Let's see...a dinner-sized southern breakfast and two hotel lunches. Thank you very much, by the way...that was sweet of you..." Lisa nodded, he went on, "and now I'm hankerin for a huge plate of swamphoppers, a couple of Coronas, maybe a big bowl of black beans. Maybe polish it all off with a big mudpie for a midnight snack."

Lisa laughed. She was still over by Mary Mythe. He'd moved off to keep his distance and give her time to think.

"Sure, why not?" she said, "But I should tell you that I'm in love with the guy who we're going to see tonight. Clay Hawkins is his name, and he plays sax. Man does he play." She paused, dropped her eyes. "And so that's where I was yesterday afternoon...with Clay."

"Got yer drift, kid. And I'm in love with Lee Ann...I guess... at the moment. Besides, have you noticed? I'm old enough to be your father."

"I've noticed...strangely attractive...very creative...child-like father."

"Child-like?"

"Yes, it's a compliment. The child in you is very strong. Most people lose their child." She paused. "Me for instance, I'm twenty-seven and law school is beating the kid in me to death."

He was silent for a moment. "Oh, I wouldn't say she's completely dead...yet. Keep playing with her, she'll survive the bar. And thanks, you're right, I'm glad you think the child in me is strong." He raised his glass and took a sip. "And, old child that he is, he'd like you to know he thinks you'd make a very lovely daughter. So give me a daughterly hug and lets get the hell out of here."

The rain outside stopped suddenly. Lisa smiled slightly, set her glass aside, and moved over to him. They clasped hands at arm's length, moved in and gave each other a loose and friendly hug. She backed up, slugged him lightly on the shoulder, and said, "Mount up, cowboy, I hear the chow bell ringin'."

At the Vera Cruz, after they'd ordered, Stanley asked Lisa if she'd seen the bouquet being brought in the other day, the gardenia spray with that sweet little note from the seaman.

But he didn't mention the seaman, even when Lisa told him that, yes, she had seen the delivery and it was by a guy named Audid. A guy who sometimes ran errands for various private investigators in the New Orleans area.

"Audid? Private investigators?" he asked.

"Yes, he's not smart enough to be one, but he likes to hang around the action."

"Any idea what he drives?"

"Yeah...a Datsun Z. Dark green."

Bingo! The lights and bells in Stanley's video arcade went off.

"Sure?"

"Yes, sure, that's all I've ever seen him in. Greasy little guy... never did anything to me...just that he sort of slums around."

Stanley shook his head, pretending to be preoccupied with eating. He was teetering on the brink of taking a risk, a calculated risk, that *Lisa* was not slumming around and infiltrating his ranks on the instructions of Audid who got instruction from some private dick who was no doubt one of Poteet's boys. Oh boy, maybe he had read too much le Carre. le Carre could make you suspect your toothbrush in the morning. He made a decision. Go.

"Lisa..." he began, as she looked up, "wanna hear a story?"

"Story? Sure, I love a good story. What's Audid up to now?"

"Lisa..." he said, sucking another morsel out of a boiled brown crustacean, "Lee Ann is currently the victim of a stalker."

"Really? A celebrity stalker? No shit. Dangerous?"

"We don't know, and I'm taking a little chance here telling you about it." He took a swig of beer, studied her face, and went on. "I know you haven't passed the bar yet, but I need to ask you for some fiduciary trust here. I guess what I'm trying to say is, please keep what I'm about to tell you strictly between us. Can you promise me that?"

"You got it, partner," Lisa said, twitching in her saddle. "That'll be sixty bucks an hour and expenses, with a five-hundred-dollar retainer." She held her hand out for a shake. Stanley, without skipping a beat, reached over a pile of dismembered crawfish and shook it.

"Now you only owe me three hundred. I'm taking it out of the eight hundred you owe me for that unreturned security deposit."

She blushed. "Damn...I'm sorry, Stan." She reached a hand down into a pocket, pulled up a wad of cash, and slid it across the table. He left it where she did.

"Naw, I can't charge you for that...I could get busted. But I would need reimbursement of expenses and guide's gratuity. Cash if you please."

Again, he shrugged and said, "Fine," and then launched into the story, taking it from Lee Ann's arrival at the gallery four nights ago to the present. Stanley, the history buff, rattling off the chronology without getting bogged down in the details. He didn't mention the fact that he and Lee Ann thought Poteet might be the stalker, but when he got to the part about their dinner at Poteet Porcelain, Lisa Lynn broke in and told him she knew, well, *knew of* Poteet.

"Really?" he said. "What's his rep?"

"Benevolent aristocrat," she said, "but there's been some scandal. Some stories of political philanderings. Okay, let's call a spade a spade. He ran for office and lost...but made a lot of friends in the process. Your usual southern good ol' boy shit, you know."

"What kind of scandal?"

"His wife had a lover who turned up with a wire around his neck and" —she gulped—"his nuts cut off. He floated by a wedding reception that was being held on a barge out on Frenchman's Bend. Sort of cast a pall on the party, you might say. A lot of people throwing up wedding cake. The reporters had a ball. Oh sorry, bad pun."

It was Stanley's turn to be stunned. He sat for a long time picking his teeth discreetly—discreetly disguising his terror. Any thoughts about persuing Melissa were running away to four corners with the wind—never to return.

"You don't say? Did they ever implicate Poteet?"

"I hear some DA got close, and then one day it just all went away. Poteet is a ridiculously rich and old bloodline around here. Stories are that his family lineage includes the pirate Lafitte. You know about Jean Lafitte the pirate, Stan? Oh sure you do. You had dinner with his great great great great grandson. Did I get enough greats in there?"

"One too many."

"So what do you think of the man?"

"We think he's the stalker."

Lisa Lynn, who had just taken a swig of beer, came very close to doing a spit take. "No shit! No *shit?*" she said, after swallowing and then choking and pounding her sternum with a clenched fist.

"Yes, listen to this..." And Stanley was off and running again, telling her about all the connections Lee Ann and he had made to date. And why they needed the AV unit this early morning. Somehow the case didn't seem so solid when he told it to a third party—a critical and astute listener. But there was not enough time, nor would there ever be enough time, to explain the nuances that went into the gut feeling both he and Lee Ann had. Poteet was the seaman.

He saw Lisa cooly weighing his words with her fresh legal mind, seeing if the suppositions held up. He could tell he was losing her to some extent so he wrapped it up with another bombshell. "...so that's where Lee Ann is right now, up in Toronto trying to spring our daughter Claire, six years younger than you..." He smiled, she smiled. "Claire's being charged with smuggling Minoan artifacts into Canada. And Poteet is up there right now helping Lee Ann get connected so she can do battle."

"Boy, you two sure don't let any grass grow under your feet, do you?" Lisa sat mopping her mouth with a napkin and shaking her head in disbelief.

He went on. "You know, actually...life has been pretty boring up until now. Or at least since well...the seventies, come to think of it. But now it seems all hell is breaking loose."

"Fair assessment, I'd say." Lisa studied him for a moment.

"Yeah...I feel like the team's broken free of the wagon...I'm headed into a ravine...and my wheel brake just burned out. Should I jump? Should I ride it out? Jump sounds pretty good right now...don't you think?"

"Mmmhuh...know the feelin, partner," Lisa commiserated. "What say we hear some jazz?"

"Always worked for me."

"Let's go."

It was still too early to hit the *Arabesque* and hear Lisa's heart throb, Clay, so they climbed up onto the levee and walked along for some more talk.

"I don't know what I can do for you, Stan, in the investigative department I mean. Do you need any information or research of any kind right at the moment?"

"No. You know...you may have already saved my life."

"Really? How's that?"

"By telling me about Melissa's lover and his fate. As I said, I've met Melissa Frank, Poteet's ex, and spent some time with her. She's shown me her work...I was developing a serious crush on her."

"Whoa," said Lisa.

"Whoa is right. She may be a master ceramist. She may be one of the most beautiful women I've ever laid eyes on...but, oh no...they may be old and tired...I'll keep my nuts, thank you." He concluded all this with a visible shiver.

Lisa cracked up. "Stanley, you better go home. Right now. Right this minute. Pack your bags, do not pass go, do not collect two hundred dollars. Go directly home!" Lisa was bending over, holding her stomach now as they walked along.

"Nice, oh very nice advice, and leave Lee Ann to do it all alone? No, I can't do that...but...thanks for the information you just gave me."

"Yeah, bout five hundred dollars worth."

Stanley, without hesitating, pulled a wad of twenty one hundred dollar bills out of his pocket, peeled off five, and handed them out to her. Lisa, startled by the fact that he would actually be taking her seriously, covered the money with her hand but didn't take it.

"Stanley...c'mon, put it away. I could get busted for prostitution or something if you keep handing me money in public."

"Okay," he said, folding the bills and stuffing them back in his khakis, "but next time you ask for money, mean it, okay?"

Lisa knew her little money joke had become tiresome to him.

"I feel stupid."

"It's okay, but I'm serious about that."

"I know, yeah, sure, it's a deal," she said, and they walked a moment in silence. "'Bout time to hit the club. It's about ten blocks from here. Let's walk and I'll show you some stuff along the way."

"Lead on, Miss Lisa Lynn."

The *Arabesque* was humming, but this time with bees on vacation, slurping up pollen in various flower-shaped glasses.

There was golden pollen served up in tulip-shaped glasses. There was pink-colored pollen swirling about peony-shaped fake crystal. And there was even the specialty of the house, a drink served in a glass the shape of a callalily, complete with yellow stamen. It was billed as a "golden poker." Stanley ordered one, just to stare at the glass and remember the Polaroid shot of the flowers lying in the coffin on the hood of Lee Ann's car. The mixture of liquor and fruit juices was better than he'd expected it would be. Lisa, who didn't feel like drinking and was nursing a tall Sprite, pivoted quickly on her stool as a man climbed onto the stage and the lights went down to blue.

"Ladies and gentlemen...I trust we have at least one or two out there in this mob..." He shielded his eyes from the one white spot that was trained on him and pretended to scan the audience. It brought mild laughter. "The *Arabesque* is pleased to present this evening its own house combo. We hope they will *be* for just a bit longer." Pause and applause. "As you know the group's been away for a few weeks over in Biloxi doing some recording. But we're happy they're back with us this evening and ready to blow the walls out." The audience clapped and cheered. "Without further ado, I give you Turquoise Blue!"

The audience applauded again, as the MC left the stage. Then all fell silent.

From out on the street came the sound of a tenor saxophone. It blew a fluttering and ascending passage, and then came back down and hit the two note opening signature of "Sophisticated Lady."

"They say..."

"I love it when he opens this way," Lisa whispered to Stanley. He smiled and nodded. He'd seen it done before. He liked it too.

A man with a horn appeared at the double doors opening onto the dimly lit street. He was only a silhouette with a flash of light every now and then reflecting off polished brass. The other members of Turquoise Blue now moved to the stage, mounted it, and took their places at their instruments.

As the sax hit the bridge of the song, the other boys in the band came in under.

"Smoking...drinking...never thinking of tomorrow... nonchalant...

Diamonds shining...dancing...dining in some fancy restaurant...

Tell me is that all you really want? Oh no...."

Stanley sang the words to himself. He knew them all. Had played the tune himself but long since forgotten it. But he hadn't forgotten the words, and he could admire how Clay was hanging notes on them, phrasing them. Very good, he thought. Lisa was right; this guy could play.

As the combo came in under him, Clay walked to the stage, climbed onto it, and finished by repeating the opening phrases of the song with a fast ascending and descending run out of time.

"They say into your early life romance came..."

As the crowd came unglued, Clay caught Lisa's eyes for a fleeting second, then Stanley's. Stanley smiled and nodded at Clay as he continued to applaud.

Clay stepped to the mike and waited for some, but not all, of the adulation to subside. "That's one of Duke's little beauties we put on our first CD. Look for it in the bins. Or come back here; we'll have copies for you in a week or two."

Some rude newcomers booed his blatant marketing announcement, but it was countered by another spontaneous round of applause from Clay's fans, who knew how hard the kid had worked to get his first disc produced. Clay continued. "Thank you. Seems we have some people in this audience who don't realize how musicians make a living." Now it's the audience's turn to give the hecklers hell, and they do with so many dirty looks. He went on. "So now that we've taken care of business, let's get back to the music." Applause. "We'd like to do one for you that's an original. We call it, 'Turquoise Me, Light Blue You'. It's a waltz, if you can dig it...fades off into bossa nova. Okay, 'nough said." He nodded to the piano player who opened with some classical figures and then they were off and running. Stanley was impressed as the waltz slowly, masterfully, melded into a bossa nova and then back into an almost innocent sounding little three-quarter time melody. And gently out...

"I see why you love this guy," he leaned over and whispered to the back of Lisa's head. She didn't turn, but he saw her ponytail bob up and down.

He stayed through the first set, thoroughly enthralled. And then at break Lisa introduced him to Clay as "the man who borrowed your camcorder." She said, "Stan's a fantastic sculptor from San Francisco, plays a little sax himself. I'm just out doing a little guide work for the man...showin him the town."

Clay moved over, slipped an arm about her waist, gave her a kiss on the temple, and then shook hands with Stanley, as he listened to the rather large, swarthy man thank him for the use of his AV unit. And now the man called Stan from San Francisco was telling him that he hadn't played in twenty years but had just purchased a mint King alto and was going to take it out in the swamp tomorrow, perhaps never to return.

Clay liked the guy; he had a self-deprecating sense of humor that hovered somewhere between Chill Wills and Woody Allen. So he talked with the man, Stan, about art and music. It was over cigarettes out on the curb in front of the *Arabesque*.

Lisa hung back, not crowding Clay, who seemed to be enjoying a conversation that was being frequently interrupted by a number of side-bars with his fans. Finally, the young musician looked at his watch, whispered something into Lisa's ear, said nice to meet you to Stanley, and moved back into the club to gather the drummer, bassist and piano player back in for the beginning of the second set.

While they were setting up, Stanley told Lisa that he would be leaving after the first number—or shortly thereafter. He told her he needed to roam. "I know you want to stay, so don't worry about me, I'll see you tomorrow. You tending bar?" She said yes, she was, and thanked him for the evening. He thanked her, and reached into his pocket for his cash just as Clay and Turquoise Blue blew into the first few bars of, "Blue Skies."

Somewhere halfway through the second song, another original entitled, "Wiggly Worm" Stanley tapped Lisa on the shoulder and slipped a hundred into her back pocket. She turned her head, shook his hand over her shoulder, and then he was suddenly on the street again—walking—hurrying away from the bright lights and good music.

Clay and the boys, bopping, faded rapidly into the night sounds of the French Quarter.

He felt an immense and unspecific sadness settling in. What was it? As he walked along with head down, he made a futile effort to identify its source.

Was it that he was falling in love again, one too many times, with Lee Ann? Lee Ann, who was now running off with Poteet? Could that be it? Or was it that Lee Ann had lied to him again, tried to conceal the fact that she'd be spending time with Jean Paul in Toronto. Poteet, her alleged, slightly deranged stalker! Lord, that would be enough to bring a man down. And if all that wasn't enough, then he'd add to it the hard realization he'd come to concerning Lisa Lynn. That he was too old for her but, at the same time, felt strongly attracted to her and who she was as a person. So beautiful in her buxom blooming youth. Yes, that could be pouring indigo into his blues. And Lisa *was* in love with Clay; that was obvious. He'd seen the way she'd looked at her hero. And then there was Clay himself, so young and handsome and talented and musically brilliant. Hell, he couldn't even have a mess-around jam with a guy like that. Oh, and let's throw Melissa Frank in there for good measure. He concluded it was probably all of the above. It would take some Herculean effort to dig himself out of this deep 'o fried southern funk.

He thought about his new old sax back at the hotel, wondered if possibly it could help him begin the dig. "Fuck it," he mumbled under his breath, and set off to fetch it.

"Such a sad mon g'wan dare."

Stanley, walking along, plowing a furrow with his brow, heard a voice and wondered if it was addressing him. Caribbean accent, old, probably female. All these descriptions flashed through his mind in the instant just before he looked up and into the white eyes of Jahna Leveau.

"Could be better," he said to those eyes and then focused down to see they illuminated the face of the skinniest, most ancient black woman he'd ever seen. She sat above him in a rocking chair on a small front porch...pipe in one hand.

"K'yan see dat poor chil. Come and talk with Jahna Leveau."

Were there a disproportionate number of people down here in Louisiana named Leveau, or was there some connection he needed to be making here? Leveau, Leveau...light bulb!

"Are you by any chance Claire Leveau's sister?"

"De same..."

Stanley extended his hand up over the porch rail. "Pleased to meet you, Jahna Leveau. Stanley Hochstetter, call me Stan."

21.

After she'd recovered from talking with Stanley and admitted to Claire that her tears were in honor of having told Stanley another lie which he had seen through and which had pissed him off—and that she really didn't need another lecture from Claire concerning the necessity of lying to men—Lee Ann called Poteet's cell and found him at Canadian Broadcast Center: CBC.

"Lee Ann! You are in Toronto, splendid! Yes, yes, I am working ...what? What am I doing? Well, I am editing a new show, or at least directing the editing. Yes, yes, it is my footage... what? Oh marvelous... yes, I know you were so worried about her. Yes, I will call you right away when I am through here and we will discuss tomorrow. You do want to start tomorrow, correct? All right then, within the hour I will call you back." *Click*. He was gone as suddenly as he'd answered..

She settled back feeling a bit better. Claire saw it.

"So you like this Poteet guy?"

Lee Ann reflected a moment. "Yes...yes I do. We're in the same business, he's filthy rich and connected...but he's not obnoxious in the least. And he makes me laugh."

"Go for it."

"Beg your pardon?"

"Go for it, go for the guy, wheelchair and all—what more do you want?"

"Claire," Lee Ann began, "I've got something for you."

Claire could see that her mother was chaffing from her blatantspeak. Oh well, she'd just have to live with it. "So what have you got for me Mom?"

Lee Ann pulled a small bundle of turquoise tissue from her bag and handed it to her daughter; then she dug for Stanley's letter (seal in extra virgin condition) and handed that over too. Maybe she was getting better. She hadn't read it on the plane—though the temptation had been enough to send her to Mail Tamperers Anonymous: MTA.

Claire pulled the tissue off the Kenyan bracelet and held it up for close inspection. "X-quis-it," she said. "You've done it again."

"It's from your father, for your birthday. He picked it out and bought it for you."

Too-cool-for-school Claire looked up wide eyed. "Dad! Dad?"

Lee Ann nodded yes.

"Wow! Man! That's great!"

"The only thing I did was tell him that you'd been looking for one. We found it down in French Market." Lee Ann flashed on her faint two days ago.

She hadn't mentioned that to Claire. Claire had her own problems right now. She didn't need to hear the whole paltry Poteet-the-stalker story, even though, even *Claire* might be amazed at that theory. She teetered on launching into it with Claire but quickly decided against it. Yikes! She needed to contact Maureen. How could she have forgotten about that! It was 7pm Toronto time, that would be 4pm San Francisco time, and Maureen was not available for calls after 4pm: part of her sanity preserving program. Or she claimed.

"Claire, why don't you read your letter? I've got to call the station...just be a minute."

Claire flopped down at the other end of the couch and tore the envelope open as Lee Ann scrolled for KPIQ—more specifically Maureen's private and unlisted office number.

"Yes?" came a husky female voice across the miles. "This better be good, it's four-o-two p.m."

"Maureen, thank God I caught you...it's Lee Ann...what's happening? Did you receive my tape? God, it's good to hear your voice again."

"Not good to hear yours or anything sugarplum. Where the hell are you?"

"Rather not say, but I'm more than okay, and I think I've lost him or found him or both..." She was mumbling now and watching Claire who was smiling at the letter from her dad. "Waaay too complicated to go into here. Anyway things are looking up, and I'm calling to see what's happening with the tape."

"Okay: *First* I want to ask you: Do you really want to take this Kathy Lee Gifford approach and spill the whole thing on the air? I mean it was a professional remote and everything...and we all liked what you said...but we're cutting it up into smaller bits and having Bradley fill in some of the details. Leave others out. Wish you could see it before we air it, but you can't. It's going on day after tomorrow. That would be Monday. Bradley and the writers are having a ball."

"I'm sure they are," said Lee Ann. "Vultures picking my bones? Edit away, I certainly trust your judgement. Did you think it was somewhat Kathy Lee? I..."

"No," interrupted Maureen, "but yes, the boys upstairs *are* chewing on your bones. I've told them to save enough to make a Haitian altar for the foyah." It was Maureen doing her best Israeli. Lee Ann always heard Maureen when she did hers.

She laughed. "How's Tom? How's the old VP in charge of news and entertainment? How's *our* boss?"

"Was having cardiac arrest till the tape came in and he saw how he could make lemonade out of the lemons he thought you were dishing him. He kept saying, '...this is not like Lee Ann to just take off. What the hell's going on, Maureen?'"

"I kept saying, she'll tell you herself tomorrow, next day at the latest. It's an emergency assignment so to speak. You'll see. And then this morning when the tape came in...he did. And now he's happy as a clam in a Bodega tide flat. Not to worry, Maureen is here."

"Thanks, boss."

"You're welcome. And I want you to know that it's not as bloodthirsty as it sounds. We all love ya and want to see this thing over with for you. You still scared shitless?"

Lee Ann faced away from Claire, kept her voice down. "No, as I said, I've either lost him or found him. Too difficult to go into here. But no, either way I'm no longer spooked. Proceeding with caution but not in fear."

"I'm intrigued, can't wait to hear it. Good girl, be careful."

"So it, or the edited version of it, goes on Monday morning? And is Laura sitting in for me now?"

"Yes and yes."

Lee Ann felt the roller coaster reach a crest and begin its plunge; Laura Andrews was dangerous. People liked it when she subbed. She'd have to find a way to get back to work ASAP. "Ratings holding okay then?" She asked a selfish question cloaked in concern.

"Holding steady, but get back here as soon as you can. Laura's not the team player you are, and never will be. So when are you coming in out of the cold?"

"I wish I knew, Maureen. I wish I knew."

"Check in daily; don't cut it so close to four next time. You know I just don't answer...no matter who. And find some way to watch Monday, wherever you are. We'll need your feedback on how we did. Okay, love you sweetie, I'm out of here..."

There was a click at the other end of the line, silence. Maureen was never one to dwell on good-byes. Lee Ann's cell immediately signaled another call coming in. Poteet, it must be Poteet, No time to think. She answered.

Poteet comes on, and before any business is discussed, asks her to dine with him. She says no that she's just arrived and wants to settle in with her daughter. Poteet invites Claire along. Jackie arrives home. She asks Claire if she wants to go to dinner with Poteet and her. Claire asks Jackie if she wants to go and she says. Why not? So she asks Poteet if she can bring both girls along, and he tells her that he is a very lucky man to call for a date and end up with three. Yes, yes of course, the more the merrier. He says he will be around at 8:30pm and to dress casually but probably not in jeans. She asks if it is a posh place because she and the girls can throw together something, but it won't be all that elegant. Oh Lee Ann, so considerate. No, not to worry, it is a fairly formal place but with simple decor and menu. *Winston's,* he says. See you at 8:30 sharp, then, good-bye.

She told Claire and Jackie that they would be dining at *Winston's,* and the two girls high-fived over that. They knew of the place but had never been there. Like a whirlwind they threw themselves together and ended up with a mutual gypsy motif: midcalf skirts, minimal but jangly jewelry, and hair in variations on that old egg-beater wind-tunnel affair. They all agreed: it worked. As promised, Poteet's driver arrived at 8:30pm sharp.

Lee Ann was glad she was going to dine with one backup and one reserve. Always good to have a bit of a fleet when you're sailing out to meet a pirate.

"...and so, Miss Claire Hochstetter, you are a painter...an intern archaeologist...and a failed art smuggler! Such a busy young lady." Poteet was talking as the wine was being poured. Soft bucolic music was floating from the house PA in the dark paneled dining room of *Winston's.*

"Still a painter, but I'm afraid the internship with the archaeologists, including my job at ROM, is over, thanks to my failed career as an art smuggler...as you put it." Claire studied Poteet as she responded to his question. Late forties, ruggedly handsome, he reminded her of Armand Assante, the actor—even had his terse sort of delivery and sardonic sense of humor. Definitely of French descent. She could see that in his occasionally frosty and haughty demeanor.

"It is fortunate that you were apprehended at a rather petty level. I should think that it wouldn't be too difficult to see"— pause for dramatic effect—"that they would go easy on you for this first and somewhat minor offense. He produced a slip of paper from the breast pocket of his dinner jacket, "Here...this is the name of a solicitor who I'm sure will be able to help you. I've taken the liberty of making an appointment with him for eleven tomorrow morning. I've explained your situation, and will be happy to be there to make introductions and discuss what we might do to dispatch this business with haste."

Claire, tough little Claire, tried to act as if it was a normal day, but she couldn't pull it off and blushed as she took the slip of paper from Poteet's hand. He was holding it between his first two fingers as some baroque baron would hold a kerchief. "Many thanks," she said and glanced at her mother—signaling her to come to the rescue. Poteet looked over now to see that Lee Ann was unceremoniously sampling the pinot noir.

"Lee Ann, will eleven tomorrow morning be convenient for you and your daughter? It would be best to settle this thing before arraignment. Harder, you know, to dispatch these things once a court record is established."

"Yes, eleven will be fine," said Lee Ann holding her glass aloft and proposing a toast to their host.

"To Monsieur Jean Paul Poteet, *and* to *One World Incorporated,* may it succeed and live long after he does."

For the flicker of a lash, Poteet processed what she'd just said and then leaned forward and beamed broadly as three women toasted him and his current braintrust. "To *One World Incorporated,*" he repeated, and drank with them to that.

"And now I have a toast of my own," he began. "To Lee Ann and her beautiful daughter, Claire, and the fair Jacqueline...may they realize... their every dream." He raised his glass and drank one short sip. The women toasted each other, and then Poteet leaned back and caught the waiter's eye. "Now, shall we order? I am ravenous."

They were simple, straightforward toasts, but all to the mark. And Poteet's had been almost a couplet. Lee Ann had been impressed, and continued to be, as they ate and talked their way through Chateaubriand, brussels sprouts, and two bottles of pinot noir. Poteet didn't dominate the conversation but rather became one of the diners; always listening intently, letting the conversation drift where it would, asking intelligent and amusing questions of the women in his presence, generally endearing himself to them all.

The white limo deposited them at Claire's door around 11pm. Poteet bid them all a good evening and went sliding off into the night. Lee Ann came in and tried Stanley's number at Le Richelieu, only to find him gone. She bid the girls good-night, agreeing with Claire to be ready to do battle bright and early the next morning. Then she went to her room, changed for bed, and lay in the dark for an hour, tossing and turning, even more confused than she had been before this dinner she'd just had with the man who she felt was quite probably—but then again, could not possibly be—her stalker.

Sleep finally came, and in the early hours of the morning, she dreamed she was a caretaker in a home for people who had been interned for being transformers. That is, people who, when she addressed them, simply turned into other people. The dream ended violently and startled her awake. She pulled herself up and sat, head on her knees, arms about her legs, shivering—rocking and shivering with the nonlocalized but all pervading fear that Poteet was indeed the seaman.

22.

Stanley couldn't believe his luck. Had he just *stumbled* upon Jahna Leveau or had fate inextricably led him to her? With many channels of static jamming his brainwaves, he desperately needed a voice of age, reason, and compassion to come in crystal clear. Presto! Jahna Leveau!

"Mon, you look as though you jes took de straup. Come and sit...talk with Jahna Leveau..I coo you down."

Jahna's accent was not New Orleans. It was distinctively Caribbean—Jamaican? Stanley wondered. Her sister Claire was apparently Creole. He would have to ask her about this.

"We met your sister the other day out at her inn. She took us in out of a southwest squall and told us about you. She said we should look you up and have our fortunes told. And now...I just run into you by accident?"

Jahna continued to rock slowly on the smooth planks of her small front porch. Her eyes narrowed, she cocked her head to one side. "Accident? Hmm. You tink was just by accident?"

Oh, *one of those* thought the somewhat cynical San Franciscan. But he'd liked this woman immediately and decided to play along. "Suppose not...if you feel it's all predetermined anyway."

Jahna didn't reply but fetched a pouch from a side table and began stuffing some kind of herb into the bowl of her pipe. He climbed the stairs to the porch, took a seat beside the old woman, and waited to see what aroma this plug would produce.

Jahna spoke now between puffs as she stoked her bowl. "Forward, backward, future, past, and present, all ri now." The old woman raised a lighted match in her bony fingers and slowly drew large horizontal circles in the air.

Now that was a concept that Stanley's Zen side could embrace. "I know," he said, "but sometimes you see that more clearly than others, don't you think, Jahna?"

"Older you gets...more you see it dat way...aaaw da time."

Old Leveau stared straight ahead, puffed, and rocked back and forth like an ancient shemale. Stanley discreetly sniffed at the blue traces that floated from her pipe. Ah, very fine, the leathery smell of blended spices—no tobacco—possibly some marijuana. He couldn't be sure; the smoke was so layered with other aromas.

"So where is your lady friend? Where is de red headed one? Where is dat Lee Ann?"

He looked up, startled. "How did you know about Lee Ann?"

"Could put you on, but won't. Dat was my blankets you use to pillow her head de udder day when she fain dead away at de market. She mussa taught dat was a gun g'wan off when de palle's fall? Just to fain dead away?"

"Exactly! That's exactly what she thought." Stanley sat shaking his head at his luck in running into this old woman. How long did she have to sit and talk? He was in dire need of a counselor now and Jahna Leveau had the eyes of age to put his misery into perspective.

"You know what a stalker is, Jahna?" he asked.

"Aye!" The old woman's pupils came to rest on her raised bottom lids. "Dats one who follows anudder aroun cause dey'r under dat person's spell."

Yes he thought, that's an original way of looking at it. He decided to hit her with the unelaborated version.

"Lee Ann, the red headed lady is my ex-wife. And she's currently the victim of a stalker."

"Ayeeee!" wailed old Leveau, blowing out smoke and taking in another puff.

He went on. "The stalker, whoever he is, had just recently sent her a note saying that if he couldn't be inside her body, he was going to send a bullet to be there for him. Not very amusing, she thought. The pallets falling might have been a gun sending that bullet on its way..." He paused.

"Whoowee! What some people do aye get attention." Jahna took another pull on her pipe, but this time let the smoke out slowly so that it circled her head for a moment. A whisper of a passing breeze finally coaxed it up and carried it away.

Stanley sat looking on, thinking how much old Leveau reminded him of the caterpillar in *Alice in Wonderland*. "Attention," he said finally, "yeah, that's one way to look at it." He sighed. "You know, I'd really like to tell you the whole story, but I'm not sure who I can trust these days. Lee Ann's gone further into hiding now, and I feel very protective of..."

"Ayeee...I know," the old woman interrupted, "but you just ask anyone roun here, Mista Stanley Hochstetter, dey tell you, trus Jahna Leveau!

"Hmm...well...I could use some advice..." He brightened. "All right then, I will. How'd you like to hear a crazy story?"

"Does it look like I'm g'wan anyplace quick?" Jahna cackled good naturedly. He didn't respond, but straightaway, and for the second time this night, related his tale. This time he started way back in Colorado, so Jahna would get the entire sweep of things. The old woman sat quietly and listened. She nodded yes when he asked her if she knew of Poteet. Nothing more, just a silent nod. He finished up by saying, "...so here I am, talking with you, and I was on my way to play my horn...see if I could take some of my blues out on it."

"How long you g'wan be in New Orleans, Mista Stanley?"

He thought for a moment. "Mmm, not really sure."

"You leave de Richelieu, come move in my place. Save you some money. I c'yan give you large room and bed where you c'yan be safe and work in peace. Forget all de udder folk wid dare complicated li's. For awhile, dey be aw ri. Jahna Leveau c'yan help you find de stalker man, and naw even leave'r rock'n chair. Come, I show you de room."

So he followed her up the stairs and found himself in a small loft that she said could be his. The room faced south and looked as if it might have good light all day. It was a bit cluttered, but clean. Jahna looked on as he looked around.

"De mess will go way fore you move in. I been usin de place to store some tings. Give'm all 'way tomorrow, you say you want it? Tree hun'red a week, flat. An you can reimburse me your calls. Der's a phone over der all hook up. I trust you, Stanleymon."

Stanley smiled. "I'd like to move in tomorrow round noon... would that be possible?" He peeled three hundreds off his roll.

"Is yours, Mista Stanley," she said, stuffing the bills into the pocket of a dress stitched together from twice the amount of material necessary to do the job.

Business completed, they went back down to the porch. He bid his new landlady good evening and said he would be back around noon tomorrow with his things. Jahna called after him.

"Beware Poteet! I will ask questions, we will talk again tomorrow!"

"Till tomorrow then," he called back as he waved one final time and moved off down Esplanade in the direction of Le Richelieu.

As she watched him disappear into the night, Jahna Leveau spoke softly to herself. "Dat boy's g'wan need a whole lotto help. A whole lotto help."

And then she went back to her rocking and her pipe.

Stanley slipped his key card into the door lock just as the phone stopped ringing. He thought it had to have been Lee Ann and considered calling her back. But he was restless. And after that refreshing interlude with Ms. Leveau, felt even more like playing his horn. Not in this cramped hotel room though. Where to play? Out on some street corner? No, he wasn't ready to play on any street corner, let alone a New Orleans street corner—not just yet. And so he found himself walking toward the river, where just hours earlier he'd strolled with Lisa. And before that with Lee Ann. Sure, it might be a little dangerous this time of night, but he'd risk it. It was the perfect place to woodshed.

As he squeezed around the massive steel hurricane gate on the gravel path that led up to the levee, he wondered what he should try to play. Something familiar—something that hopefully was stored somewhere in his rusty fingers.

"When Sunny Gets Blue" headed the list by the time he'd reached the water and cracked the case of the old silver goose. He'd been sucking on a reed ever since he'd left the hotel, and now the bamboo sliver was straight and supple as he clamped it onto the mouthpiece, ran up a scale in the key of D, and settled into the song. He'd blown only a few measures when something stirred in his peripheral vision. He wheeled around to meet the gaze of Melissa Frank. Startled, he pulled the horn from his mouth.

"Jesus! Melissa! Is that you? You scared the p...." He didn't finish—didn't need to—Melissa stepped quickly to his side with a finger to her lips.

"I'm sorry," she whispered, "I didn't mean to startle you. I was just visiting a friend when I saw that it was you." She turned to go but then turned back. "I wanted to say hello. I should have called out. I'm sorry...really must go." Again she turned and started to move off.

"No, Melissa, stay..."

She came to a gliding halt but kept her back to him. "Mr. Hochstetter, it's best that we not talk here." She said it firmly and with precise enunciation.

Mr. Hochstetter? Where had that come from? Two nights ago it had been Stanley this and Melissa that, now we're back to formally addressing one another? He laughed.

"You can call me Stanley, Melissa. Remember, we've talked."

"I know what I'm doing, and what to call people, Mr. Hochstetter." Her tone was brittle.

"Ms. Frank, please stay and speak with me for a moment."

She turned slowly. In the dim light, he couldn't really see her face. Then she moved slowly over to him and he could see even in the moonlight that she'd been crying. "You've been crying, you're shaking. What...?" He unhooked the sax from his neckstrap, lowered it into the case, and moved to take her in his arms. It was getting to be a daily assignment, this taking of seemingly frightened women into his arms. And he'd forgotten all about her dead lover—the one who'd floated by the wedding party. She was in his arms now and seemed to be trembling even more uncontrollably. With arms folded across her breast and her head down, he felt as if he was holding a vibrating barrel. She twisted in his arms.

"No, we can't be doing this. I appreciate your concern and offer of comfort, but..." He released her. She moved quickly to a large stone at the top of the riprap, sat down, and gathered her skirt about her legs. If only he had a guitar player and percussionist, and could still do a decent, "Day in the Life of a Fool." This Latin lady needed bossa nova. But he remained silent and stood studying her in the dim light.

Finally he said, "I was going to call you tomorrow morning and see if I could come out and fire a piece I've nearly completed. I worked with your clay today, and all I can say is... it's miraculous. I see why you love it. Thank you for sharing it with me. I mean that."

"I know you do," Melissa said to her knees. "I wouldn't give it to just anyone..."

"I know you wouldn't, thank you."

"I really must be going. If you want to come out tomorrow, come after noon, anytime after noon, and stay for dinner tomorrow evening. One of our people is having a birthday party; I think you would enjoy it."

She stood, smoothed her skirt, moved over to him, and held out her hand. "I like you, Mr. Hochstetter, I'll even be so bold as to tell you that I like you very much."

He took her hand and, to his utter amazement, lifted it to his lips for a short, soft kiss. "And I will even be so bold as to tell you that I like you...very much." He let go of her hand and she pulled it back slowly to join the other one that was resting over her heart.

"Then you can see why we must be impeccably discreet about these feelings?" Her voice was almost a whisper. "You don't know everything. And I can't tell you everything just yet... but trust me, I know what I'm saying and doing is...right." She fixed on his eyes, whispered without moving her lips. "Someone may be watching...listening."

Stanley felt like covering and concealing his own heart now. A heart that was doing two-hundred-mph laps around his chest. This woman, had just told him that she was...what? Falling for him to the same extent that he was falling for her? She was so beautiful in every way, how could he not love this fellow seeker, this bronze beauty from Rio. He whispered too now. "I know, Melissa. And I may know more than you think. Tomorrow, let's work together down in your studio. We can talk then."

"Fine." She raised her voice above a whisper now, "A little professional association then?"

He smiled. "Yes, a couple of artists at work."

She lightened a shade but still didn't smile. Then a softness came into her face and the fear seemed to melt away. "I feel better. Thank you for..."

"Hanging on to you?" He was whispering again.

"Yes, hanging on. I really must be going now. It's late and I can see you came to play." She looked at the sax waiting in its case. They reached across the distance between them one more time, clasped hands, making sure to keep a polite distance. "Till tomorrow then...goodnight."

"Goodnight, Melissa."

She turned and he watched as she moved off down the levee and out through the hurricane gate. He stood for a moment after she'd disappeared and contemplated again what she'd just told him. Why was it so difficult for him to believe that these feelings of newfound love were mutual? But where could they possibly lead? Would he risk pursuing them—her? The ghost of a man floated by in the river.

All right. It was time to play now. Brother, was it time to play. Music was the one thing he knew that could vent the steam now threatening to blow his boiler. He hooked the sax back on the strap and rewetted the reed. Let's see, where were we? "When Sunny Gets Blue" in D. He opened it again, and a sound came from his center.

"When Sunny gets blue, her eyes get gray and cloudy....

Then the rain begins to fall...

Pitter-patter, pitter-patter, love is gone so what can matter...

No sweet lover man comes to call..."

And on and on he played. And it sounded not so bad, even to his critical ear. Finally his lip gave out, and he polished off with the last stanza.

So hurry new love, hurry here...

To kiss away each lonely tear...

And hold her near...

When Sunny gets blue.

A young man, also a sax player, had finished his evening gig and come down to take some of his blues out on old Mississippi. As he moved around the hurricane gate, he stopped for a moment and listened. Damn, someone else had beaten him to it—and this stretch of the levee could support only one sad sax at a time. He couldn't see the hornplayer—he was over the crest of the embankment—but he could hear him. And what was he playing? He listened for a few seconds. Oh yes, unmistakable now, "When Sunny Gets Blue." He rolled and lit a cigarette, climbed the bank, and sat with only his eyes clearing the top of the levee. The player down by the riprap appeared as a dark silhouette against diamond lights shimmering below the Algiers' shore. The young man smoked and listened.

The silhouette's tone was coarse but soulful. Interesting, thought the listener, he's playing it in D. Most people play it in E-flat. Hmm. Some primal echo reverberated back from long ago—a strange musical deja vu.

The shadow finished up his song and all fell silent for a full six measures. Now only the sounds of the river, round midnight. Slowly then, the shadow bent down, packed his horn away, and sat, head hung down, hands clasped between his knees.

The listener, yards away, considered approaching the player and telling him that he also played sax and very much enjoyed hearing, "Sunny". And how was it that he came to play it in D? But he could see by the posture of the man that he was working on some blues of his own and wanted to be alone.

So the young man snuffed out his cigarette in the mud and set off in the direction of home. As he hurried along now, the sound of that sax rang like a church bell in his head. And though the player's technique had been a bit rough, the tone, *his* tone, had been so full of soul. Like Charlie Parker—reeled in tight. And what was this strange stirring even deeper down inside of him? As though he'd heard this man playing before? He racked his brain but couldn't put anything together. So he widened his stride and walked on down the street—thinking of the player— thinking of Charlie Parker — thinking of the one they called Bird.

23.

Clay arrived home shortly after 2am. Turquoise Blue had started early this evening and so had finished up early. He'd gone down to the river, to play, but someone else had been blowing in his favorite spot.

He turned the key in the lock of his front door and let himself in. Amanda was apparently not home yet from her waitressing job. Cold symptoms were threatening in the back of his throat, so he went to the refrigerator and pulled out three fat oranges. There was nothing like chewing on the skins of oranges to kick an early cold in the butt. A full week's gig at the *Arabesque* wouldn't mesh well with a bout of the flu. And this gig would be paying his share of the rent. He looked at his watch: 2:20am. Amanda must be partying. She often didn't come home at all these days. Well, that was okay, because he didn't either. He and Amanda were drifting apart. They were still roomies though, and because space and funds were so limited for both of them, they were still sleeping in the same bed. But the love they'd once known had gone bye-bye—and they knew it—so they were taking care of each other until they could move on. They'd salvaged, at least, a friendship.

He juggled the three oranges for a full thirty seconds, and then moved over to his squeezer. The squeezer, where was it? Where the hell was his squeezer? He started rummaging through the cabinets, and had just about opened the door to the hall storage closet when, behind him, he heard Amanda entering the house. Saved! He really didn't want to have to attack their one and only storage space—or more accurately—have it attack him.

"Hey Amanda, you're home." He turned and walked back to the kitchen. Amanda was already raiding the fridge for an after-midnight snack.

"Yes, I know that, Clay. I *am* home."

"Uh, you seen the juice squeezer around anyplace? I got a cold coming on." He bounced an orange in one hand.

"Oh, I was weeding out a bunch of stuff and I think it went with that box I sold to the antique store."

Clay stopped bouncing the orange. "You *sold* the squeezer?"

"Yeah, you know, I had to make the rent while you were over in Biloxi. I sold a bunch of stuff and got twenty-five dollars for that thing. Twenty-five dollars is twenty-five dollars *you* didn't have, and..."

"You sold my squeezer?"

Amanda bit off a piece of cold chicken and started chewing it.

"Yes, Clay, I sold it. What's wrong..."

"Where...to whom?"

"Where...to whom...what?"

"Who...*who* did you sell it to?"

"The secondhand...antique store on Royal Street." Amanda could see his panic. Hear it in his voice. "What's wrong? Why are you acting like a little kid?"

"Because *Amanda*"—he spit out his words—"that squeezer has been with me since I *was* a little kid!"

"I...I didn't know. I guess you told me that...but I didn't realize that..."

"Go back there tomorrow, *get it back!* I can't believe you sold it."

"For God's sake, Clay, it was just a weird old squeezer...a machine! And by the way, do you have twenty-five dollars to bail it OUT?"

Clay's frustration peaked. He pulled some bills from his pocket—proceeds from this night's gig—and threw them on the counter. "Forty bucks, kid, *now get that squeezer back!*"

He grabbed his sax, still in the case from its walk home, moved to the entryway, glared at Amanda one last time, and slammed the door as he went out. She stood for a moment collecting her wits. It wasn't like Clay to explode like this. What was so special about a stupid squeezer?

Out on the streets with his horn, Clay walked twelve blocks through a light drizzle, cursing under his breath all the way. He couldn't sleep in the same bed with Amanda tonight—just couldn't. How could she sell his most treasured possession? Hadn't he told her how much that squeezer meant to him?

The light was on in Lisa's apartment. She was probably up late studying. What a slave to the law this girl was. He climbed the stairs to her door and knocked softly.

"Who's there?" he heard her say from inside.

"Clay."

She opened the door and they moved into each others arms. Then moved back to take each other in.

"You look like you just lost your best friend, partner," Lisa said softly, and kissed him. He moved back after the kiss.

"I did," he said, and they disappeared behind her door.

24.

Stanley couldn't sleep. His mind was feverish with flitting images. He felt as though it might short out and burst into flames at any instant. So he rolled out of bed, turned on the lights, walked to his suitcase, and found what he was looking for: a canvas roll with his detailing tools, an iPod, some earphones, and a small silver flask containing cognac. He moved over to the table where Mary Mythe sat no more finished than she had been when Lisa Lynn had come this afternoon, and he'd had his phone tiff across the miles with Lee Ann. He poured a capful of Remy and tipped it back. Good, that was all he needed to cut the tobacco taste that was hanging about his mouth like a cave full of guano. Stanley, the retired smoker, had had a couple with Clay.

A light rain began to fall out on the deck beyond the French doors, cooling the air a few precious degrees. Such a welcome relief. The sound of the rain was all the music he needed, so he laid the earphones aside, undid the tie on the canvas roll, and spread it flat on the marble tabletop.

Contained in various long stitched sleeves were a number of silver and pewter colored detailing tools. He passed over these, and pulled out the only wooden one in the set. He'd fashioned it himself out of rosewood. It was his magic stick.

The hours melted away as Stanley delineated Mary's fine girlish figure and the dragon's many reptilian scales: scales from nostrils to tail.

Dawn found him standing at the doors opening out onto the deck. The rain had stopped and the humidity was back. But along with it were those sweet aromas of wet timbers and rain soaked masonry—coffee brewing everywhere. He stood drinking a glass of ice water, watching the light come up. Thinking of Clay. Thinking about Charlie Parker—thinking about the one they called Bird.

The phone rang on the nightstand. He pulled himself back from a reverie and moved to answer it. It could only be Lee, and he *did* want to talk with her now. They'd left things in shambles yesterday afternoon with that cold good-bye. Now he wanted to hear the latest concerning Claire.

"Hello...Lee Ann, that you?"

"No, Dad, it's your bratty little daughter."

"Claire! Is your mom there?"

"Oh nice, really nice, Pops, I call to say hello and all you can say is, 'is your mom there?' Cheesy, Daddy...here's Mom..."

Lee Ann's husky alto came across the miles now. "Hi, Stan, I'm on too now, wouldn't want you to think I was a snoopy dog."

"Lee, good to hear your voice. Well, girls...what's happening up there?"

There was a moment when Lee Ann and Claire argued about who was going to talk first, each deferring to the other. Lee Ann won, and Claire continued. "We had dinner with Mr. Poteet last night, and he's set up an appointment with a barrister who has the necessary connections to make a deal before the arraignment...which is set for Wednesday next week. We're going for fine and deportation."

"Wow, that's harsh, isn't it?"

"Naw, it's time for a change. I'm ready to come home to the good old USA. Too fucking cold up here for me. I mean the weather and the people. I think I've finally had my fill of the French and their necking in the elevators."

"Know what you mean, Claire."

"So, Dad, you want to talk to Mom? I'll get off here."

"Maybe for just a sec."

"Oh, thanks for the bracelet, I love love love it! And also the letter, I'll be answering it as soon as I bail out of here. Thanks, Dad, bye."

And with that Claire signed off. There was a moment of silence and then Lee Ann said, "You still mad at me, honey?"

"Na...get this. I decided it was half concern for your safety and half jealousy of Poteet that pissed me off the most about your...omissions."

There was another moment of silence on the Canadian end of the line, and then Lee Ann said, "I don't know what to say."

"Say you are madly in love with me again, and you will be with me forever and ever."

"Stanley, I'm not going to repeat all that bullshit."

"I knew it."

Another pause.

"Boy, you and Claire are starting to click a little bit, huh?"

"Yes, and it's somewhat your fault, Lee. How can I ever forgive you? Negotiating our lifetime feud so..."

"Oh, you'll think of something."

"So you and Claire are going to do the legal thing today? What time is your meeting? Will Poteet be there?"

"Yes, eleven am, yes, in that order."

"What are your feelings now about Poteet? How did he seem at dinner?"

"Very cordial, not in the least bit forward. The girls loved him. He's a godsend in this situation. I mean how would I be proceeding with this thing if I wasn't availed of his connections?"

"You'd think of something, Lee." Pause. "When is our remote going to air?"

"Tomorrow morning, nine am San Francisco time, eleven am New Orleans time, noon Toronto time. Maureen confirmed that yesterday afternoon when I talked with her. Can you get Melissa to watch it?"

"I think so."

"Okay...well, get this. I'm going to confront Poteet this afternoon with the big question. We're going sightseeing with the girls after the meeting with the barrister."

"What question?" He felt ice water flooding his veins.

"I'm going to ask him straightaway if he is the seaman."

There was wheeze down in New Orleans. "Do you think that's wise? Shouldn't you be waiting to see his reaction to the show? Ask him then? Can you get it up there?"

"Yes, he's working at CBC doing some editing work. I'm sure they have the necessary link to get KPIQ. And no Stanley, I don't want to wait. I'm going to be with him and the girls, and I'm going to hit him when he's least expecting it, so I can nab his initial reaction. That should tell me...though he is some kind of cool customer."

There was a silence where she waited for him to say something. He didn't, so she went on. "No...I can't wait. I need to get on with this little game." She paused again. "By the way, while we're on the subject...any more messages at the room from our seamy little friend?"

"No, nothing since the flowers. Interesting in itself, don't you think?"

"Yes, very. Let me know immediately if anything shows up."

"I will. And Lee Ann...if you must do this, do it in a public place, okay? I think that would be wise, don't you?"

"Yes, I'll do that...had planned on it. What are you going to be doing today?"

He stalled. "Well...I took a room at Jahna Leveau's rooming house on Esplanade. Hey! I met Claire Leveau's sister, Jahna, last night just by accident. She's a mystic, that's for sure, just as Claire said she is. Boney little black woman who rocks and smokes a long stemmed corncob pipe."

"I can't believe New Orleans, can you, Stan? Don't you love it?"

"Yeah I do. I'm going to stay a couple of weeks at least. I feel there's some unfinished business here. I'm going to check back with Wayfarer's Antiques before I move my stuff over to Leveau's...do what you suggested with the reward for information leading to..."

"Good, keep me posted."

"Certainly will."

"Then what are you going to do?"

"I did a piece with Melissa's clay last night...stayed up all night. It's called Mary Mythe. It's about a dragon and a maiden named Mary. I'm going out to Poteet's and spend the day with Melissa. Snoop around."

"I'll *bet*."

"Oh, that makes me feel better, Lee...now *you're* jealous. We're a couple of funny ones, huh?"

"Yeah I'd say so." She paused. "So Claire is waving frantically at me to get a move on. Have we covered everything? Claire, the seaman, Bird...Us?"

"No, we didn't get to Us again."

"I love you, Stan."

"I love you, Lee."

"Bye."

"Bye."

He placed the receiver gently back on its cradle, and moved back to the open French doors. Ah...that's better, oh so much better. Domestic tranquility was his favorite balm. It seemed to be coming in drums these days. But he was sure that would change.

He stopped in the bar to let Lisa know his plans. She would be his backup now in Lee Ann's absence—and a good one at that. They had a quick briefing as he downed a virgin mary, then it was off, with all his traveling possessions, including Mary Mythe, to Jahna Leveau's. The old sorceress was good on her word; she had jettisoned the junk and cleaned the room—or at least someone had. There were clean sheets on the bed and towels for the bath down the hall. He was happy to see the light in the room was as he'd expected it to be: diffused and pearly. Good, he would be working here for the next two weeks at least.

After he settled in, he questioned the old woman about Wayfarer's Antique Shoppe—asked her if she knew anyone who worked there. She said no, it had new ownership and she hadn't had time to make their acquaintance. Stanley asked her if there was anyone in the Quarter she knew who went by the first or last name of Bird. Jahna scratched her sparsely whiskered chin and said, "No, can sa as I do." Damn, oh well, it was worth a try. He told Jahna that he would tell her about Bird when he got back tomorrow from Poteet's. He said he would like her advice. She said she'd give him a Tarot reading for fifty dollars.

"Deal," he said and slapped the old woman's bony palm. She cackled and beamed with a yellow-toothed grin and then sent him on his way.

He'd told Lee Ann that he was going to the Wayfarer's first, but had decided to check in with Jahna in case she had some connection with the people at that store. No, she hadn't, so he would have to hit it cold.

The bell jingled on the door as he stepped inside and was disappointed to see the man behind the counter was the same snot-nosed fruit he'd questioned yesterday. Oh well, time to exercise restraint. After all, he knew these guys.

"Goodmorning."

"Goodmorning." There was that nasal mew again. Just ignore it.

"I was in here yesterday? And I was inquiring about a juice squeezer that I bought in here the day before yesterday? Do you remember?"

"Yes...I remember." The voice sounded more hospitable this morning (hopefully over our PMS?). Good, thought Stanley, that will make things easier.

"You see, I've come to believe that this squeezer could possibly be the same juice squeezer that disappeared with my son when he was abducted twenty-two years ago, out in San Francisco. And so you can see why I would very much like to know where you people got it. It could lead me to my missing son."

The eyes of the slender man with close-cropped hair grew wide. "You don't say. You *don't* say! San Francisco? Wow, your son?"

Stanley congratulated himself on the blunt approach that had drawn this chilly man racing out of his ice palace into the palm of his hand. He remembered that the man's name was Bruce and that helped as he hurried through the story of Bird. He told Bruce that he would give a reward of one hundred to two hundred dollars to anyone with information leading to the discovery of his son. One hundred dollars personally to Bruce if he would please try to find out who brought the squeezer *in* to this store. Bruce said he would do his best, but that he had been away from his job for several weeks and the woman who had probably bought it, the owner of the store, was presently somewhere in the bush of Africa on a buying trip. She wouldn't be back till next week. Stanley said, "I know, you told me that, but do what you can...I can wait...but you would be a hundred dollars richer if you could find out. And no scams, please. No stand-ins. I want the *real* previous owner."

Bruce smiled sheepishly and said, "Oh...I wouldn't do thaaat."

Stanley gave the guy his best Mickey Rourke closed-lip grin and exited the shoppe.

As he pulled the Mustang out of the parking space and made his way down Royal Street, he saw a dog-eared green Datsun Z parked along the route. The car was empty, its driver apparently elsewhere. Good, he thought. He wasn't in the mood to play cops and robbers this morning.

Such a relief to be out of the city and on his way to Poteet Porcelain. It was hot, but not as humid as it had been the past several days. Gulf skies were clear—pale blue. At the gate the woman told him that Ms. Frank was expecting him and would he please drive directly down to her studio and meet her there. The woman asked him if he knew the way. He said yes and continued down the road through the tunnel of cypress trees, around the mansion, and on down the lane lined with those tidy little cottages surrounded by lazy green lawns. It was good to see it in the light of day.

At the foundry he parked, pulled a cardboard box containing Mary Mythe wrapped in a wet T-shirt out of the trunk, and proceeded to Melissa's studio. The factory was in full swing today. Some large industrial-sized overhead doors had been pulled up to ventilate a work area that bustled with men and women turning out porcelain wares: porcelain for the privileged of the world.

Melissa was working with her back to him when he reached her studio door. He decided to play her trick and stand for a moment watching her before announcing his arrival. No such luck.

"Good day, Mr. Hochstetter," she chimed, without turning from her work.

Does this woman have eyes in the back of her beautiful head?

"Good day," he returned. Melissa still had not turned around. She was roughing out the figures surrounding her dying slave. He stood admiring her back. Her body was as attenuated as the figures she was molding: that high waist, those strong square shoulders, the crown of black hair that now wound up and around her head. He set Mary Mythe on one of the studio pedestals and moved to her side. She continued to work.

"Just give me a moment here, and I'll be with you. Just about have what I want."

"Take your time, I'll wander around. Good to see your work in the light of day. It's *still* captivating."

"Oh, Mr. Hochstetter...you are too kind."

"Ms. Frank? Whatever happened to Melissa and Stanley?"

"We'll get back to them. But today...this evening...we'll be joining all our people for a big patio cookout, and I feel it would be appropriate for them to see us...being formal with one another before they see us as we were the other night. Trust me. I know what I'm doing."

A eunuch in the river floated through Stanley's mind. "Yes, Ms. Frank, I'm sure you do."

Melissa set her tools on a pedestal and turned to face him. Her tan apron was smeared with white clay. She pulled it off and set it aside. Her slim frame shifted easily now beneath a loose cotton dress. Stanley concealed the pleasure he felt when simply setting eyes on her. Oh yes, this would take some restraint. She moved to his side. He took her hand, kissed it shortly, softly.

"I hear Lee Ann and Jean Paul are in the beautiful northern city of Toronto." She almost chirped.

Stanley lost it, jumped back a foot, tried to disguise his surprise. "Yes...how did you know that Lee Ann was ...?"

"I *do* talk with Jean Paul, you know. And he is there," she paused, "and he told me on the phone this morning that he'd had dinner with your daughter and her mother and your daughter's friend..."

"Jackie?"

"Yes, Jacqueline. And that he would be helping your daughter resolve her legal problems. You knew he was there, didn't you? That they were working on this matter at the moment...Stanley?"

He was on data overload. How graciously Melissa was describing it. But, of course, that's because Jean Paul had been perfectly open with her about his intentions with regard to Lee Ann and Claire. Noble intentions indeed. And Melissa didn't know the other factor in the equation. That Jean Paul was currently stalking Lee Ann. Was?...Is?

"...Stanley? Are you there?" Melissa was whispering. She'd called him by his first name. Suddenly he had a sensation that he'd blacked out for a moment.

"Uh...oh...sorry...yes...yes, I knew that Lee and Jean Paul were...as you say...working together to solve Claire's legal problems."

She looked slightly perplexed. "Those two seem to enjoy one another's company as much as we do...wouldn't you say?"

"Yes, I'd say..."

"Is something wrong?"

"No...no, not at all...well..." He felt it was time to change the subject. Fast. "I brought something for you to see."

They turned their attention now to the cardboard box sitting on the pedestal.

"Yes, my first work with your clay. It seemed to call for something full of mirth. So I put my usual brooding self aside and created a Mary Mythe. Here, see what you think." He pulled the assemblage from its container and began carefully peeling off the wet T-shirt. "I didn't have my muslin shrouds with me so had to improvise." She nodded in anticipation. Mary Mythe was now free of her damp wrap. Melissa circled the figure for a look all around. Her expression remained neutral—an artist surveying another artist's work. Finally she said. "Done by a master...most evident..." She paused, looked him straight in the eyes. "Do you think it might not be a bit too frivolous for serious art?"

He glanced up sharply and met her serious gaze. "Don't you think all my work is—a bit too frivolous—for really serious art?"

"No." she replied flatly.

"But you think this is?"

"A shade more figurine than your work in red clay."

"I'll keep that in mind." He sighed, stinging slightly. Mirth was a big part of his bag. Oh well. "So where do we go with this process from here? You said you'd brief me on the drying and firing procedures for your clay."

"Yes...all right, let's take it over to the drying room at the foundry. It's a little room I've created with a barometric control. A slight vacuum in a dry, warm atmosphere hurries the drying time considerably, with no side effects in firing. Come, grab your maiden and her dragon..."

After Mary and Puff had been safely installed in the drying chamber, Melissa and Stanley spent the rest of the afternoon working on her figures. He helped Melissa rough out some of those attending her deathbed slave. She marveled silently at how fast he could work. He marveled silently at how clearly she saw the overall composition, and could direct him gently to see it her way. After years of working alone—always the master in control—he was enjoying taking orders as if he was an apprentice. Perhaps she had some red clay on hand and he could start a work that he'd been building in his mind for some time. He wondered how well she could follow his directions. He wanted to see how gently he could lead. They never got around to that.

About five in the afternoon Melissa doffed her apron for the day and said, "I need to get up to the house now and supervise this dinner we'll be having. You're welcome to stay here as long as you like, but come up and freshen up in time to eat at seven. I think you're going to enjoy this group of people." She smiled and showed him to a bin containing various grades of common red and tan ceramic clay and told him to help himself. He thanked her and said yes, he would like to start something that had been on his mind, and that he'd be up no later than six-thirty. Then she walked on up the road to the house.

He watched her swing lazily up the lane.... let his full desire for her be felt. Wondered how long he could contain it.

Yes, he did want to start a piece of his own now, after spending all day as a slave to a slave. But there was something else he wanted to do a great deal more. And that was spy, snoop around the grounds, the foundry, look for something, anything—he wasn't quite sure what—just anything that might tie some other things together. It was one of the reasons he'd come here today. And now it was time.

He left the studio and walked over to the hulking concrete building that housed Poteet Porcelain. The workers were leaving, so he introduced himself as a friend of Ms. Frank's and said he was a ceramist and would it be all right if he just looked around? The foreman consented amiably. The work crews left, and the foundry fell silent. Stanley poked around the giant kilns first.

Full of blaze for the overnight firing, they hissed and bellowed like captive dragons. He stood for a moment admiring them again, and then made his way around to the back of the large high-bay building where he found refuse neatly piled and ready for disposal. A couple of light- green pedestrian doors led to what? Melissa had said the storage and ancillary rooms of the foundry. He made his way over to one of the doors, turned the handle, let himself in, and turned on the lights. The room was lined with shelves containing various dismembered machines that had at one time, he supposed, served the operation and were now being cannibalized for their spare parts. There were motors and casts and parts of potter's wheels and conveying systems. And what was that over in that dimly lit corner? Some long white containers of some sort? He moved over for a closer look. No...no...this couldn't be...

He felt the blood drain from his brain—swooned—the room began to spin.

Blackness closed in from his peripheral vision as if swallowing him alive. His knees gave out as he grabbed for support from one of the heavy metal shelving units.

He lowered himself slowly onto the cold concrete floor and sat crosslegged, staring blankly—straight ahead—at four miniature white coffins.

25.

Earlier that day, in Toronto, the meeting with Claire's barrister had gone well. An older distinguished gentleman sitting behind a massive walnut desk faced Lee Ann, her daughter, and his old friend Jean Paul Poteet. He'd informed them all that he'd taken the liberty of coming to an arrangement with the Canadian authorities, and had secured a settlement of a $5,000 Canadian dollars fine and a notice of deportation for an unspecified period of time—possibly forever.

Claire, gulping at the figure, asked if it could be reduced in any way since it represented over half of her life's savings. The distinguished gentleman behind the desk said he would see what he could do, but not to hold out any great hope. She said she would accept the deportation clause.

The man behind the desk said, "Excellent then. We have a deal. I'll make the final arrangements and...could you please leave a check with the secretary?" Then, after repeating the much-bandied phrase about how it was so much better to nip these things in the bud before a court record began to form, he moved out from behind his desk, shook hands with Lee Ann and Claire, gave Jean Paul a French peck on each cheek, and showed them to his door.

Claire was steaming and stinging as she made out a check to the Canadian government for $5,000 and gave the secretary her billing address. Jean Paul told them that the gentleman they'd just met with was on retainer to him, and that a billing to Miss Hochstetter would not be necessary. Lee Ann and Claire, somewhat abashed, both said no, they couldn't accept that, but Jean Paul insisted. So they both said, thank you very much, and headed back to Claire's apartment. Claire declined a sightseeing tour of Toronto on the grounds that she needed to go home and lick the wound of losing half her life's savings. Lee Ann and Poteet did not protest. Claire was showing her surly side in all its tarnished glory.

Jackie had seen Poteet's car approaching, so she came downstairs to greet them. The two girls hugged and cried as Claire related the fact that, yes indeed, she was being deported, and they would soon be parting. Jackie didn't want to leave Toronto—it was her home. Lee Ann left the two girls to God only knew what, and sped away with Poteet to their afternoon of touring.

"What is the matter, my dear?" Poteet said as the car pulled away from the curb and swung into traffic.

"Oh...I feel slightly nauseous."

Poteet smiled over at her. He could see that she was trying to gain some kind of composure.

"Jean Paul, I'd like to tell you something"—she looked straight at him—"that I must ask you to keep between...us. Under no circumstances are you to tell Stanley what I am about to tell you. Can you give me your word on that?" It was time to regain control; she knew what she was doing. Poteet nodded graciously and waited.

She took a deep breath. "My daughter and her girlfriend are...are lovers." She said it flatly without removing her eyes from his.

The lines in Poteet's weathered face folded into mirth, and from a warm wide smile, he said, "But my dear Lee Ann, of course, I knew that!"

"What?" She was taken aback. "How? How did you know?"

"Well my dear, I am French, you know. What can I say?"

Lee Ann smiled sheepishly, laughed shortly. "Stanley doesn't know yet. I figure Claire is keeping it from him for some reason. I want them to work it out at their own pace. Promise me you won't slip..."

"Please, Lee Ann, I am a man who keeps many secrets. Yours is safe with me."

She sighed, fell silently into her own thoughts, and watched Toronto slide by the tinted windows of the limo. What was going on here? She wasn't quite sure. Not only did she feel safe with this man who she suspected to be her stalker, but she was growing more and more attracted to his genteel urbanity, his worldly aristocratic manner. Maybe Claire was right. Maybe she should go for it. Plenty of time for that though. There was some serious business to resolve first. So she began plotting in her mind how that should go. How, when, and where should she pop the question? She'd play it by ear.

They spent the afternoon sightseeing around the city. Poteet showed her what he called his hometown away from home. He was a knowledgeable guide, full of stories about this building or that—the person represented in this town statue or that. The driver would pull over and wait as she and Poteet would exit the car. She would push his wheelchair, and he would complain that he could not see her while they were talking, as they browsed museums and other points of historical interest. She was aware of this herself, because when she did ask Poteet straight out if he was the seaman, she wanted to be looking at him straight in the eyes. Something impossible, as long as she pushed him along. She would wait.

They decided an early evening dinner would be in order and pulled into a restaurant overlooking Lake Ontario. The driver let them off at the entrance and proceeded to his long wait. She pushed Poteet into the foyer, and soon they were seated at a table overlooking the water. A gentle fume blanc and some hors d'oeuvres were served while they waited to dine on mussels and steamed vegetables. She felt the time had come, so she braced herself and fixed him with a steady gaze.

"Jean Paul Poteet..." she said and waited for him to look up. He did, and met her calm eyes. "Are *you* the seaman?"

With wine glass raised halfway to his lips, he paused and, with a quizzical expression, responded, "I beg your pardon?"

Damn, she thought, but then, in the next instant, repeated her question. "I said...Jean Paul...are *you* the *seaman?*"

He cocked his head like a spaniel and said, "I'm sorry, my dear, I don't understand what you are asking me. Is this something to do with being a descendent of Lafitte? I..."

Uh oh, she thought, maybe Stanley had been right, maybe she had jumped the gun.

"Never mind. I don't want to explain it now...but could we meet at the station tomorrow morning at eleven-thirty...and watch *Good Morning San Francisco* together? It's very important for you to see tomorrow's show. It will explain my question to you. Would that be possible?" She was blurting now, totally flustered. This was not going well.

"Oh, Lee Ann, this is all *so* mysterious. Yes, of course, if you say it is important. I can arrange that, yes, eleven-thirty you say? Yes, the program airs at noon Toronto time, doesn't it? Yes, I can do that. Should I send the car around about eleven? Would that be convenient? We can have brunch while we're watching."

He was either innocent as a newborn lamb or one of the best liars she had ever encountered, but so far he had passed muster. "No," she said, "I'll be driving myself in tomorrow."

"As you wish, my dear. As you wish. And now I'd like to propose a toast." He raised his glass. "May our newfound friendship benefit us both in the coming years."

"I'll drink to that, Jean Paul." And she did, hoping against hope that would come true. But her keen reporter's instincts kept her still wondering, still questioning, still doubting. Well, they would go another round tomorrow—and that was tomorrow. Tonight she would enjoy this charming man. It could possibly be the last time she could. For if he was the seaman, he was certainly enjoying *his* dream now, and she was too. She was feeling a strong, growing attraction for this descendent of Jean Lafitte.

26.

Buzzing again—like a cloud of giant black locusts again—or was that his brain shorting out forever. He slowly became aware of himself, as slowly—almost imperceptibly—images started to form in his now reopening cone of vision. The blackness that had threatened to swallow him was regurgitating him back into the real—was this the real world? He felt the cold concrete floor pressing up on his backside. All seemed real again—almost—except for that high-pitched buzzing sound. Was that his brain? Oh God, he hoped against hope that it wasn't his brain with a bug in the middle of it. No, now he could tell, the sound was coming from somewhere outside his head. It was a hedge trimmer—no—a lawn mover. Not his brain with circuits fried. Just someone mowing his lawn outside.

He began slowly pulling himself to his feet, checking his clothing as he did. Except for a fine frosting of foundry dust on his backside, his pants were not ripped or damaged. His trip to the floor had been abrupt and less than graceful. He brushed away the dust from the seat of his khakis, and checked the small lump that was beginning to form on the side of his head. He'd hit it on the shelving on his way to the floor at the sight of...there they were...still there...the source of his fall.

Four miniature white coffins.

His mind protested and tried to make them into something else— to make them go away. But they wouldn't. They rested four in a row, leaning against the wall. He glanced at his watch, 5:45pm. Good, plenty of time to decide what to do and still get up to the house. Uppermost in his mind was to get this information to Lee Ann as quickly as possible. Where was she right now? Sightseeing—or dining with her perverted little "new friend?" These coffins were as incriminating as any evidence could be.

And what was this guy Poteet anyway? Some kind of serial stalker? Did he do more than one at a time? Looked like sort of a production line operation leaning there against the wall. Christ.

He felt his first wave of disgust and disappointment that Poteet was indeed the seaman. Petty jealousy aside, in the short evening they'd spent together, he'd grown to like the man. Now there was no possibility of that. Shit.

Should he hide one of the boxes—the coffins? Yes. No. Both seemed like the appropriate response. He pictured a courtroom where evidence was being presented. He was being questioned:

"And so, Mr. Hochstetter, you feel you have the final connection between your ex-wife's stalker and the defendant, Jean Paul Poteet? May we have that evidence please?"

Stanley on the stand: "Well, as you know, entered into evidence is a cell phone shot that Ms. Barnes took of some callalilies lying in a small white coffin on the hood of her car. I believe that's state's evidence, item number three?"

"Correct, Mr. Hochstetter. Please get to the point."

"I am...I propose to show you, secreted away on the Poteet property, a white coffin that I found in the Poteet Porcelain foundry storage room. One of four such coffins I found and hid away for future evidence. I can't tell you where that coffin is at this very moment, but I'll be glad to lead the court-appointed expedition to find it. I'm sure you understand..."

Stanley snapped back to reality. Yes, hide one of the coffins. Do it now! He spotted a spade leaning against the wall of the storage room, seized it and one of the coffins, and hurried down to the edge of the property where the land met the swamp. Pulling his way through an ever-increasing density of underbrush, he came to rest below a mammoth native cypress tree. The ground at the base of the tree was soggy and barely humus. He dug easily to a depth of two feet, lowered the box into the hole and covered it back over. There, he thought, standing back and feeling rivulets of sweat trickle down his back and chest. Evidence.

Even if it was noticed that one of the coffins was missing, who would suspect him? Yes, this was definitely worth the risk.

He cleaned off the spade, replaced it in the storage room, and headed up the road to freshen up for dinner. He definitely needed to do that after his dig. A tall, elderly black man mowing his lawn waved to him. He waved back. Ah yes, the lawn mower—and—there was something familiar about that black man, but the light was coming from behind him so he couldn't see his face.

He was approaching the big house now: 6:15pm. A sudden wave of nausea lifted in his stomach. He found a place in the trees, and sat down to collect his wits and his guts before joining the party. He'd only taken catnaps since he'd arrived in New Orleans, hadn't eaten since last evening with Lisa. This could have something to do with the near faint. And then again the shock of the coffins...

It was finally settling in. Poteet was the seaman! How would he act around Melissa now? How fast could he get to a phone and call Claire? Thankgod he had Claire's number on a slip of paper in his wallet. He felt for his wallet. Yes! Still there. With all the swooning and falling and digging he'd been doing, he was relieved to feel that hard spot still residing on his backside.

"Jambo sana, Mister Stanley." A deep male voice came from behind him. He spun around and looked into the face of Sunjab for the first time.

"Ah!" He let his air out. "You startled me. I've seen you before..."

"Yes, Mister Stanley, I waved to you while I was cotting my lawn."

The accent was a crisp British East African. The accent was Kenyan.

"I know, I know, but I couldn't really see you. The sun was behind you. But I saw you as the driver of the truck that was hit by the rhino, Old Jack. And I saw you again as Melissa's dying slave, though she made you much older and I couldn't really tell for sure. That was you, wasn't it Mr. Sunjab?" He was pulling it all together as he spoke.

"Yes, that was me Sahib... Sunjab." The old man extended an enormous right hand that swallowed his. They shook, but Sunjab did not release his hand. Then he did.

"I feel many things in your grasp Mister Stanley. Many things." Sunjab squatted down on his haunches and started rocking to and fro. Stanley squatted down beside him.

"Sunjab," he began again, "tell me something."

"What, Sahib?"

"I don't know...anything."

Sunjab took Stanley in for a moment, and then realized that this white man was putting him on. He burst into loud black laughter and put an enormous hand across his brow.

"All right, Mister Stanley, I will tell you something. Tonight is my late- born son Mekweto's birthday celebration and I would hope that you would be joining us for that."

"Thank you, I was planning on it, but didn't know it was your son's birthday...how old is he?" Stanley pulled himself to his feet as Sunjab rose straight up from his haunches, on elevator knees, and motioned in the direction of the big house.

"He is ten years old this day."

"Well...I'm looking forward to meeting him."

"Ah yes...he is a fine son."

The two men set off up the road, talking already as old friends. They reached the patio area just as a whole calf was being removed from a large fire pit spit and moved to a cutting board. Melissa was supervising the operation and smiled as Stanley and her old friend Sunjab approached.

"Ah, I see you two have met!"

"Yes, several times now in various ways," said Stanley, taking her in. "He is the model for your most recent piece, am I right?"

"Yes, you are right, Mr Hochstetter." Then Melissa inquired in the most musical of tones, "Sunjab, do you think that

Mr. Hochstetter would be comfortable in the blue room?" She waited for his reply.

"Ah yes, Mimsab," Sunjab said, smiling broadly. "I will show him there?"

"Would you? And see if you could provide him with a fresh change of clothes?"

"Oh...brought my own clothes...down in the car." Stanley suddenly, realized that he'd left his car down the road.

Melissa turned to her first mate. "Sunjab, could you have one of the lads fetch Mr. Hochstetter's car and bring it to the upper lot...take his bags to the blue room?"

"Yes, Mimsab, I will see to that."

"All right then, Mr. Hochstetter, we'll see you soon...for dinner?"

"Soon," he said fetching his car keys out of his pocket and handing them to the one called Sunjab, who then handed them to a young man who was dispatched to retrieve the Mustang. Sunjab led him to the blue room on the second floor of the mansion and showed him in. The room was furnished in masculine materials and motifs and was not large, but very comfortable and well equipped: computer desk, small wet bar, adjoining bath.

The tall Kenyan departed. Stanley went directly to the phone and dialed Claire's number in Toronto...waited through three rings...and got her answering machine. Damn!

"Hi. This is, Claire and Jackie. We aren't here right now, so leave a message at the beep and we'll get back to you...unless we're asleep..beeeep." Beeeep.

"Hi, Claire, this is your dad." He paused. "Claire, I have something extremely important to tell your..."

Claire broke in. "Hi, Dad, I'm avoiding obscene phone calls and letting my machine take them these days. What's up?"

"Claire, thank God you're there. Listen, is your mom there?"

"No, she's out traipsing around with Jean Paul. She hasn't even called in, but I have the number of Poteet's suite at the Royal York. Should I try there? Tell her you want to talk with her?"

"She said she was going to his suite at the hotel!?" He ceased breathing for a moment. The man in the river kept floating by in his mind. He knew almost for certain that Poteet was the stalker now, and Lee Ann was going to his suite!?

"Wow...Dad...settle down. Whew, what the hell's going on...?"

"Much too involved to go into here Claire, but your mom may be in grave danger."

"What? How?" was all Claire could get in before he plunged ahead.

"I know that Lee Ann's told you about her recent dealings with a stalker, right?

"Yeah, the guy who calls himself seaman?"

"Yes, well, I might as well ask you straight out here. Has Lee Ann told you that we have reason to believe...very good reason now to believe...that your mother's stalker might be Poteet?"

There was a gasp on the other end of the line. Cool, streetwise Claire was letting out all her air.

"Shit, oh dear." There was another pause. "You two kids... never a dull moment, huh?"

"Claire, I'm telling you, this is serious. I need to talk to Lee Ann, pronto. I've found something that highly implicates Poteet. You said they might be going over to his suite where?"

"No, Dad. I said that among other telephone numbers Mom's left here on my coffee table is the extension to Mr. Poteet's suite at the Royal York Hotel. I can try that number for you, or you can call directly yourself. What do you want to do?"

He thought for a moment. "I think you'd better call, and if you get her, give her the following message. Ready?"

"Ready."

"Tell her I found four small white coffins down in the foundry storage room and that they're identical to the one you will probably be seeing in the shots your mom is carrying around in her purse." He paused for breath, heard Claire breathing up in Toronto. "See, the stalker sent her this miniature coffin with some callalilies inside and a dark sort of verse enclosed. Have her show you the picture."

"Yeah...I know...she told me about the coffin and the flowers."

He suddenly recalled his conversation with Lee Ann under the magnolia tree that first morning in New Orleans. It all snapped back into his mind. "Right...okay...so you know about that. So...I'm telling you, I found not one but four coffins, identical to that one, down here in Poteet's ceramic foundry."

"Jesus..."

"I know...so...don't have her call me from the suite if you find her there. Tell her to get out of there and come home. Directly home. Got that? I will be calling every hour on the hour, because it would be difficult for her to reach me here— there's a big party going on."

Claire, stunned and amazed, said yes, yes she would keep calling the suite at least until Lee Ann was either found or returned home safely. He asked Claire to repeat the message. She did that, and he could tell by her tone of voice that she could sense the gravity of the situation. He gave her his number in the blue room and said to call him either way within fifteen minutes and give him a report. She said she would and hung up.

There was a knock on his door. The lad sent to fetch his car and baggage handed his keys, satchel, and sax over to him, and left in a hurry, apparently anxious to return to the party forming out on the back veranda. He could hear a band warming up. An African band, complete with brass. He glanced at his sax as he stepped into the bathroom to shower and wash the grime of the day off his body. Damn, he could feel it; he was putting on weight, would have to watch the eating and drinking now. Thoughts of Melissa.

As he was toweling off, the phone rang. He hurried over and picked it up. "Hello?"

"Hello, Dad?

"Yes?"

"There was no answer at Poteet's suite. I left a message at the desk for Mom to call me if she should check in with the man."

There was a silence from the other end of the line. "Dad?"

"Yes Claire, good work. Now, if your mom comes home or contacts you in any way, have her call me immediately. This is not a joke. This is serious. I can't tell you any more. Have her brief you when she gets home. Okay?"

"Okay Dad. I hear you. I will. You say there's a party going on there?"

"Yes, a birthday party for the son of one of the people that works here. Can you hang around your place this evening, at least until we make contact with your mom?"

"Yeah, Jackie and I were planning on staying home anyway. Besides, you've got me totally intrigued and freaking out."

"Good, then you will be mission control. I'm going to be calling every hour on the hour to check in. Your mother could be in grave danger. I'm not kidding, kid."

"I know you're not, Dad. I'll keep trying the suite. Hope mom answers my message...this time."

"Thanks."

"Okay...bye."

"Bye."

Stanley sat for a moment, fully naked on the side of the bed, thinking about keeping Claire's last SOS to her mom in his pocket—just three short days ago. He felt chagrined, but decided that he wouldn't let it blossom into full-blown guilt. Hour by hour, that's how he would have to be taking it now. He said a silent prayer for Lee Ann.

Well, mustn't keep Melissa waiting. As if she was.

A party was in full swing when Stanley, wearing loose-fitting white cottons, joined it on the back veranda. He found himself in a throng of handsome black men and women dressed in various forms of African garb who were eating and dancing to an infectious East African rhythm being supplied by a ten-piece juju band. In the center of this musical ensemble was a young boy holding down a complex rhythm on a double cowbell. He admired the fluid motion of the boy's wrist as he wielded his stick.

"Stanley."

He heard his name being whispered behind him. He turned. Melissa took one step to his side, took his arm, and turned him back around to face the band. He felt that cool rush again as she made polite contact with his arm.

"Melissa," he said.

"That boy playing the cowbell is Mekweto, Sunjab's son. This is his birthday party. You must be starving; come, we'll get you something to eat and then perhaps we can have a dance?"

He considered what it would be like to dance to African music with the Latin Melissa. They certainly had no trouble walking arm in arm. But he was ravenous. So they made their way through the buffet line and found a small table at one side of the festivities, far enough away from the band so they could talk without shouting.

"How long will this go on? The party I mean."

"Oh, several hours at least. Until the band and the dancers weary, and the food is gone." Melissa, in a delicate sweeping motion, raised a salad fork to her mouth. A thing of beauty, thought Stanley. He thought of Lee Ann the devourer.

"Will you be staying over?" she asked, after briefly chewing and swallowing, and going for another bite.

"Yes, I'd like that. Maybe we'll find some time to talk later on?"

"And what would you like to talk about, Mr. Hochstetter?" Melissa smiled.

"Oh...how about Melissa?"

"Oh...how about Stanley?"

They were teasing each other now and it felt good to both of them.

"All right then."

After dinner, and a first dance with Melissa—which went quite well, they both agreed—Stanley said he could stand it no longer and went to fetch his sax. He'd been listening to the horn lines the brass section—one trombone, one trumpet and one baritone sax—were laying down. And they were simple repetitive patterns that worked all through the songs. He could easily play along with that. Melissa seemed delighted as he joined the band on the stand and got down with the Kenyans. He was introduced to Mekweto and began playing off the "riddims" this lad so effortlessly laid in. As he played, he watched Melissa dancing with various partners; her movements were subtle and sinuous, so like her sculpture that he could see where she got her sense of line. The two of them made polite eye contact as often as was discreet. Something was definitely happening now between them, and he wished fervently that the image of the man in the river would float on downstream. But it wouldn't. It was imperative now that he talk with Melissa at the first opportunity about her murdered lover. There could be no more between them until he found out specifically her present attachment to Poteet. Perhaps they'd let each other go in the mateship department—perhaps they hadn't. And if they hadn't, then that would be the end of it. He thought again about how attached he was to his nuts.

The music ended around nine and the musicians, including Stanley, packed away their instruments and rolled up the cords. People were picking up—cleaning up.

During one of the breaks in the music, he'd tried Claire again. She'd told him that she still had not reached her mom. He returned from stowing his sax in his room, moved to the kitchen phone, and tried again. Melissa was off bidding some invited guests goodbye. He watched her out on the veranda as he made his call. Claire came on the line.

"Hullo?"

"Claire, have you reached your mom yet?"

"No. You want me to try again?"

"Yes, I have a few minutes here. I'll be at the number I gave you earlier. Try right now, and call me right back."

"Roger." There was a click on the Toronto end of the line.

He leaned back against the wall to wait.

27.

Warbling...a red-winged blackbird's trill and warble was her ringtone. She heard it in her dreams and then realized she was awake. And there was a hand on her shoulder. It was Poteet's, and he was saying something about...a call for her from her daughter. "Lee Ann...can you take it, or should I tell her that you will call her back?"

Poteet was sitting in his wheelchair alongside the couch where she was lying. She was trying desperately to remember where she was. He was holding her cell out to her, waiting for her to wake up.

She was taking a bit longer snapping to than usual. Brandy sat like molasses in her brain, but finally it came back to her. She and Poteet had returned to his suite shortly after 9pm. She'd helped him out of his chair onto one couch, and then she'd made herself comfortable on another. They'd sipped brandy, talked, and watched a rough cut of the animal show Poteet was currently editing. He'd wanted her professional opinion. It had all been perfectly platonic. He'd not made even the slightest advance. Not asked her over to his couch, not been suggestive of any dalliance in the least. After the animal show, they'd found a movie they both liked and had settled back for more talk, and a flick. She, feeling the effects of the brandy, had drifted off to sleep. She should have called Claire immediately upon receiving her message at the desk, but then she'd been distracted when they'd reached the room, and forgotten. Now her daughter was calling her again and she, with sleepy husky voice, must take the call and talk? It wouldn't sound good.

"Talk to me, Jean Paul...for just a moment here...until I wake up."

He knew what her concern was. "I could tell her you are in the bath and will call back."

"No...too late for that. Peter Piper picked a peck of pickled peppers. Peter Piper picked a peck of pickled peppers. Peter Piper...okay, how does that sound? Awake and with the sparkle of a girl out on a date?"

"Lee Ann, you are a pro." He handed her cell over to her. She punched "talk" and ...

"Hi, honey," she chirped to her waiting daughter.

"Mom...what the hell's going on?"

"Well...Jean Paul and I are looking at some of his recent documentary work on African wildlife. Sorry, I should have called. It slipped my mind. I suppose I'm grounded for a month now." She smiled over at Poteet, who smiled back.

"Listen, Mom, Dad called me with some news you might like to hear. About the seaman?" Lee Ann stopped smiling. Claire continued.

"He was out at Poteet's place today and ran across some small white coffins down in a storage room. Four of them to be exact. And he said they're identical in every respect to the one we know about. Said you should probably know about it as soon as possible. I agreed. He's waiting for my call right now, down at Poteet's, and I think I should be telling him that you've received his message and have left there and are on your way home. What do you think?" Claire was putting the machine-gun mouth she'd inherited from her mother to good use.

Lee Ann had grown ashen. She felt her stomach rise in disgust and fear. She couldn't speak. Couldn't form words.

"Mom? You there? You're probably not going to be able to say much. Keep your cool and get the hell out of there. Tell Poteet that I'm deathly ill, that you have to leave at once...Mom? Lee Ann? Will you do that?"

"Your heart again? Have Jackie call an ambulance, immediately. Claire...do you hear me? Have Jackie leave a message as to where they're taking you. Leave that location on your answering machine. I'm leaving immediately for home." She paused to catch her breath. "Not something to fool around

252

with Claire. Please, will you do that? Breathe...relax...I'm on my way."

"Okay Mom! Good work. See you within the hour. I'll tell dad you're on your way in."

"Okay Claire. Relax now. Breathe. I'm out of here." With that she stood, with cell phone to ear, and turned to face Poteet. He saw the gravity pulling at her face. She retrieved her purse, threw her phone in, and headed for the door.

"I'm sorry, Jean Paul, I must leave immediately."

The Frenchman quickly punched a few commands on his cell and requested that his car be brought up posthaste—that Ms. Barnes would be returning home and that it was an emergency. Then he wheeled over to the foyer mirror where Lee Ann was already hurriedly straightening her clothes and freshening her face—a face grim with concern. She turned to address him.

"I'm sorry, Jean Paul, thank you for a lovely evening...and day. It's Claire's heart; she's always had trouble with it. This latest scrape with the law...I think it's just palpitations brought on by anxiety, but she really can't take any chances. They're taking her in. I need to go to her now. I'll see you at the station tomorrow morning around eleven-thirty?"

Jean Paul was genuinely concerned. "How terrible...yes... yes...go to your daughter. And please, avail yourself of my car and driver to the extent you wish. Yes, I will see you at the station tomorrow morning. Yes, it was a very lovely day and evening. I'm sorry this is happening."

"I am too, Jean Paul." She reached down and offered her hand to him. He took it for a short, gentle kiss, then released it, and she was gone.

Poteet would not sleep this night—would toss and turn—wondering what to do.

Now that Lee Ann knew.

28.

Stanley snatched the receiver off its cradle like a man grabbing a cobra by the neck. "Hello?" he said urgently, "Claire, is that you?"

"Yes, Dad. Relax. I got ahold of Mom. She was up in Poteet's suite watching home movies. I relayed your message. She feigned a heart attack for me and is using that as an excuse to bail out of there. Call me in an hour or so. She'll be home by then, I think." Breathless, she paused to let her father speak.

"Good work. Great work. What's this about a heart attack?"

"Oh, that's what Mom came up with on the spot to get her out of there as fast as possible. You know those show people; they think on their feet."

"Drastic, but yes, that should work. Okay, right, I don't know where I'll be in the next hour, but I'll call you. It's imperative that I talk with your mother before either one of us sleeps. Imperative."

"I hear you, Pops. Be waiting for your call. You havin fun?"

"Hardly a question I can answer at the moment...sure you understand."

"I do."

"Okay...later then...bye."

"Bye."

He replaced the receiver and leaned on the wall for a moment while his own heart settled back to a manageable rhythm. A soft voice came from behind him.

"Are you all right?"

He turned and met the concerned gaze of Melissa. She was standing behind him with her hand on the shoulder of young Mekweto, who was staring up at him with large solemn eyes.

"Yes, okay. I just called my daughter and received some disturbing news. Really don't want to go into it right now, but I'll tell you later. Don't concern yourself...it may all blow over."

"I'm sorry...would you like to be alone?"

"No, that won't be necessary." He turned his attention to the cowbell-playing birthday boy and rubbed his nappy head. "Hey, kid, you beat a mean groove. Really had fun playing with you this evening."

Mekweto's mouth drew up in a large white grin. "Ah yes, Mister Stanley...and I with you!" The two musicians beamed at one another for a moment, then gently brushed palms. Melissa began haltingly.

"Mekweto was wondering...well...he wanted to know if you would be interested in doing him in clay?"

"Right this evening?" asked Stanley incredulously.

"It is still early. And some of the people think it would be a fine way to celebrate his birthday. To have the famous sculptor, Stanley Hochstetter from San Francisco, do a bust of the young Mekweto from Kenya. Of course they said they would understand if you were too tired and wanted to sleep." She was coaxing with all her international charm.

"Where do you propose we do this deed, fair Melissa?" he asked, throwing caution to the wind.

"Some people are bringing a pedestal and some clay over to the foundry. It would be too crowded in my studio, but we can spread out in the big building."

"As if I had a choice. Okay then, lead on, we're off to do Mekweto!"

He threw an arm over the young boy's shoulders and the three of them set off for the highbay building down the road. He glanced at his watch. At 11pm sharp he would have to excuse himself and call Lee Ann. The people would have to wait. This call could not. He was feeling light-headed now from lack of sleep and all that was happening. But he wasn't tired in the least. He was looking forward to later being alone with Melissa. Perhaps they would build a fire in the library. Perhaps they wouldn't.

Mekweto was sitting in a circle of men and women of various ages. Also inside this circle was a man standing at a pedestal supporting a large block of dark brown clay. Stanley Hochstetter, resident sculptor, hard at work. He quickly pulled and pushed on the block until he had the general shape of Mekweto's ovoidally shaped head; then it was on to the features of the lad's face. They seemed to appear as if by magic under his deft fingers. Soon the bald head of Mekweto was facing a semicircle of appreciative onlookers.

"But, Sahib," said Mekweto, looking at Stanley with large solemn eyes, "I am not a bald boy. Where is my hair?"

Stanley stepped back and deferred to Melissa. "Ms. Frank," he said, "do you know how to make this nap? I think you do; I've seen it many places in your work."

Melissa nodded yes, stepped to a side table, and grabbed a melon-sized ball of clay. She moved over to Sunjab who was sitting at one end of the semicircle of people and handed it to him. Without hesitating, he pinched off a marble-sized piece of the melon and passed it on to the next person, who did the same and passed it on again. Soon the last person received a piece and the whole lot of them began to knead and roll their own small snake of earth.

"This will take a few minutes," she said to a puzzled Stanley, who then glanced at his watch: 11:30! Damn, he had become engrossed in his work—once again—and lost track of time. Lee Ann would surely be home by now. He turned to Melissa.

"Is there a phone nearby I could use? I need to call Claire again."

"Yes, there on the other side of the glass, in the foreman's office." She motioned to the unfinished bust. "Is it all right if I start on the hair without you? Will you be long?"

"Yes, I may be. Yes, go ahead, I think I can see what we're doing here. Very clever my dear."

She smiled and met his eyes for a fleeting second before he turned and moved off to the foreman's office and the phone. He dialed Claire's number by heart, and after one ring Lee Ann's husky voice came on the line.

"Hello?"

"Lee Ann, thank God you're home. Safe."

"Stanley. You're late...what's going on? You found coffins?"

"Yes! Listen...I was poking around in one of the storage rooms down here at the foundry this afternoon and I found four, count'm four white coffins that are identical to the one I saw in that cell phone shot you showed me." There was a silence on the other end of the line. "Lee Ann?"

"Yes...I'm here. I heard you. Claire told me. I can't believe this."

There was a long pause, and then he went on. "Did you pop the question this afternoon? Did you ask Poteet if he was the seaman?"

The pause continued in Toronto, then Lee Ann was saying. "Yes, he denied it...oh so convincingly did he deny it. One of the best liars I've ever encountered." Cold tone. Arctic tone.

"Boy...I'm looking forward to hearing that exchange and exactly how it went down, but no time at the moment." He paused, and then went on. "Would you say what I've found is convincing enough evidence to incriminate him? I'd say it was."

"I'd say it was, partner. I'm just sick, literally sick to my stomach right now. I want to kill the slimy fucker." He heard her hissing

"What do you think I should do, Stan? We're going to get together at CBC tomorrow at noon to watch *Good Morning San Francisco*. I guess I'll give him one more chance to fess up...and, if he denies it again, I guess I'll roll in the coffins you found."

"CBC? A TV station? Yes, that's good. Plenty of people around. Yes, go ahead and tell him what I found. And tell him... if you have to...that I've hidden one of the coffins for future evidence if that should become necessary. Tell the bastard that you're going to press charges." He waited. "Are you?"

"No Stan." She paused, "I don't think I'll do that." Another long pause. "I just want him to leave me alone now. That's all." Lee Ann's voice was distant and sad. He could hear it waning over the miles.

"I hear you. I'm sorry. I guess it's so much for these people, huh?"

"Yeah."

There was a long silence. He glanced up to see Melissa supervising the installation of a number of small clay spirals on the crown of Mekweto's clay head. Finally he spoke.

"I wish I could be there to help out, Lee. Will you be careful?"

"Yes, Stanley, I will be careful." She paused again. "Are you going to watch the show with Melissa tomorrow morning?"

"That hasn't been arranged yet, but yes, I think I'll be watching with her. When should we talk again? What are your plans after you leave Toronto? Are you going back to San Francisco?"

"Yes. I need to get back to work as soon as possible. Forget this fiasco." Hostility now.

"I understand...I can understand that. Is Claire going home with you?"

"Yes, we've discussed it, and yes, I think she'll be returning with me...living at home for awhile until she formulates her next move. I guess that's okay with me. She can have her old room back..." She drifted off, as if into a Toronto fog. "Call me tomorrow, Stan, about two pm. I should be home from the station. We'll talk longer then. I'm exhausted. Gotta get some sleep now. Gotta sail out and face Captain Hook tomorrow you know?"

"I know, Lee, stay safe. I'll let you go. Thank Claire for me. Tell her I'm looking forward to seeing her again when we all get back home."

"I will...when are you coming?"

It was his turn to consider. "Well, I've got to follow up on this Bird thing for a few more days, and then when I think I've done as much as I can do, I'll be coming back to San Fran."

"Okay...talk with you tomorrow then."

"Okay hon. Sorry this is happening."

"You're not the only one."

"Okay, bye."

"Bye."

Stanley hung up the receiver and sat for a moment, watching the proceedings out in the high-bay. He was having difficulty sorting out his thoughts. Shitty was the adjective at the top of his list to explain how he felt. He supposed that now he would not get to know Melissa as well as he had hoped to—nor Poteet at all. After a few seconds of blue, he pasted on a happy face and walked out to rejoin the work in progress.

Melissa was using a tool to carefully blend in the many spirals of clay that the Kenyans had fashioned to represent young Mekweto's tight nap. Her technique, with the help of the people, was startlingly effective and realistic. She'd almost finished when Stanley rejoined them.

"That was a long one," said the sculptress. "Is everything all right?"

"Yes, fine," he lied. "This is exquisite, Melissa. And how it came to be fashioned is even more so. You are a genius."

She smiled and let it pass. "Looks like we are about finished here...and not a minute too soon. Ten minutes to midnight, time for Mekweto's birthday song." She turned to the people who were talking among themselves about the finished bust. "We should sing now...the hour is late."

Sunjab nodded and with a deep bass began a calling song in Swahili. A chorus of men and women raised their voices in return and, at the stroke of midnight, filed past Mekweto, shaking his hand and wishing him once again a happy tenth birthday. Still singing in answer to Sunjab's calls, they left the highbay to return to their homes; some with sleeping children in their arms. Stanley and Melissa watched them go. Only Mekweto remained behind. He stood looking up at them with large white eyes.

"Yes, Mekweto?" Melissa asked.

"Yes, Mimsab. I was wondering...could I possibly have this head of mine?"

Melissa looked at Stanley, who rested with arms folded across his chest. "Well," he began, "well, yes, certainly. It is of you. You should be the one to keep you safe. Would you like us to fire it for you? It would be stronger that way, last longer."

Mekweto thought for a moment. "No, Mister Stanley, I don't want to go into the fire. I will keep me safe and dry, just the way I am. Thank you." And with that, the young boy turned and moved off for home. They watched him until he had disappeared through the door and into the darkness. There was a brief moment when they searched one another's eyes, wondering what to do next. Finally, Melissa spoke.

"You must be exhausted. Didn't you tell me that you were up all night last night? Come, let's go back up to the house and tuck you in."

"Amazingly enough, I'm not in the least bit tired, how about you?"

"A little bit. But if you like we can build a fire in the library and have a cognac before bedtime. How does that sound?"

"Read my mind."

29.

He built a small fire in the library fireplace while she poured the Cordon Bleu. She joined him at the hearth and sat on the sofa across from his. Both kicked off their sandals and put bare feet up on the coffee table.

"Ahhh, that's better," said Melissa, settling into the cushions.

Stanley, hearing a shade of a Latin accent in her pronunciation, wondered about something.

"Melissa, you speak several languages, don't you?"

"Some much better than others," she said.

He smiled and swirled the amber fluid in his snifter.

"In what language do you usually think? Dream? Solve problems?"

She considered the question. A Brazilian frown pulled her face down. "Well," she began, "let me think...I guess...I guess I usually try to do my thinking in the language of the country where I currently find myself.

If I don't know that language, then I try to learn it a little bit and do my every day thinking in English. It's very generic, you know." She paused. He waited. "And when I solve problems? Every language I know, I guess. But when I dream"—her eyes drifted off to a far horizon—"I always dream in Portuguese. Brazil is my home, and I love that language. It's like surf whispering to a white sand beach." She settled back into the cushions, deep in reverie.

"Thinking of Rio?"

"Yes."

"Why don't you go back there?"

"I told you...Jean Paul and I are raising our daughters."

"Yes, yes you did."

A long silence passed between them. Then she said.

"So...I suppose you want to know a little bit more about my life with Jean Paul?"

"Hmm...if you feel you can tell me now."

She smiled softly. "Yes, Stanley, you have a right to know. We've probably flirted enough now...I share the responsibility for that. All right then, I'll tell you flat out. Jean Paul is a great deal more attached to me than I am to him. Oh, he's over his jealous rages now, but he does still feel a strong sense of...how should I put it? Owning me? Feeling that as long as I am in this house raising our daughters that I am his. Does this make sense to you?"

"Unfortunately." He paused...asked cautiously, "Is there love?"

She considered it for a moment, wasn't sure she knew what he was referring to. Finally she answered, "No."

"Could there be love?"

"Do you mean, is Jean Paul still...capable?"

"Yes, among other things."

"I honestly don't know...we haven't occupied the same bed since the accident."

Stanley slowly, silently, released a breath that he'd been holding for too long. "Can I ask you a question that you may not care for me to ask? Because I really need to know something before I can continue to sit here by the fire with you..."

"Oh?" It was Melissa's turn to release her breath. "Yes, I suppose so."

"Was that your dead lover you were visiting...crying for... down by the river last night?"

Melissa looked up sharply, wide eyed and frightened. She nodded, yes, and then whispered. "How did you know that?"

"I talk to people, put things together. As you know."

The woman on the opposite sofa drew her knees up under her skirt and formed a loose ball with her body. "Yes, I've noticed. It's what attracts me so much to you. You are a gentle, perceptive man."

It was Stanley's turn to be taken off guard. "And you, my dear, I have noticed, are a very gentle, intelligent woman."

"Does that mean we like each other?"

"I like you..." He was holding back. "I can say that I would very much like to take you in my arms right now, but I have a terrible vision that keeps floating through my mind. Should I tell you what it is, or have you heard enough to know what I'm referring to?" He studied Melissa now, who seemed to be studying her hands and not liking what she was seeing.

"Oh well, no time to play games..." He knew this was going to hurt but knew he had to say it. "I keep seeing your dead lover in the river."

Melissa visibly winced.

"I'm sorry, Melissa."

She cupped her forehead in her hand and left it there. Finally she said, "I should take the girls and get out of here, shouldn't I? I should leave all my clothes and possessions behind and fly to Rio and disappear up"—she gulped—"up the river. That's what I should do, isn't it?"

"I can see why you stay, Melissa. I hope you can see why, as much as I want to come closer, I fear..."

"I know..."

He stood slowly, and moving over to the library doors, closed them slowly; then he returned to the sofa and sat down beside her. "Will we be interrupted now? Has Jean Paul bugged his own house with mics and cameras?"

She let out a little scoffing sound. "No, I don't think it's come to that. Yes, we will be left in private now."

"Come here then." He smiled, throwing caution to the wind. Somehow the man in the river and the sight of Melissa sitting in the firelight balanced each other perfectly on a fulcrum of danger and desire. She moved over slowly and found a place under his arm. Her head came to rest in the crook of his neck.

"Ahhh..." she breathed as she relaxed into him. Stanley's heart began to race. Breath control to the rescue. He measured them now, practiced relaxation response, mentally threw another bucket of ice water over his head. It didn't seem to work as well this time, but it helped.

"Do you want to talk about it now?"

"I don't know...right now...I just want to sit and enjoy the fire. Can we do that?"

"Wouldn't think of spoiling this with any rude conversation."

He felt her face draw into a smile on his shoulder.

"You amuse me, Mr. Hochstetter. All right then, tell me a polite little story." She put a hand on his chest. He could feel his heart slowing by the second. Good.

"What would you like to hear, my dear?"

"About your life? About your family? About your love for Lee Ann? Something juicy and deep." She lifted her head enough to catch his eyes. Both smiled at what they saw.

"With all those possibilities, I'm stumped. Where to begin? Help me out."

"Hmm, well, all right...I've told you about Jean Paul and myself. Now you tell me about Lee Ann and you. I know that you have known each other almost all your lives. That's a long time to know someone...yes?"

Stanley felt slightly uncomfortable now. He would have to tread ever so lightly. But honesty—well-apportioned honesty— seemed to be a good operational mode these days. And he knew that Melissa needed to get her mind off the man whose ashes, he imagined, had long since washed out into the Gulf of Mexico. "Yes..." he began, taking a deep breath, "Yes it is. A long time. And I can say that I guess I've always loved Lee, and probably always will. She's shared my life...we have a daughter together. And we've tried to do right by her. I guess you heard all that the other evening from Lee Ann."

"Yes, I heard how she talks about you. I know that her love is equally strong for you. So why don't you..."

"Get back together?"

"Yes...or maybe you are?"

"Hard to say what together is these days, wouldn't you say?"

"Mmm...okay. So why don't you go back to living with one another?"

"Probably the same reasons you want to run off to Rio."

"What do you mean?"

"I mean, you feel owned here, don't you? I mean, you said you do."

"Oh...I see...yes."

"Lee Ann is a very independent woman. Always sort of has to be her show, or she doesn't go. Not really selfish, she's a great mother to Claire, but she and I have...much different speeds. Our work is different as night and day. Her's is as worldly and extroverted as mine is solitary and introspective. Sometimes our talents mesh, but usually they clash..." He paused for breath. "Need I go on?"

"Is there love?"

Damn, he didn't want to answer that, but now there was no way not to.

"Yes...and no...depending on what period of time you're referring to."

"I see."

"Off and on now for almost the fourteen years we've been divorced there have been periods of love and lovemaking followed by periods of extreme alienation. We try, but we just can't seem to get it right."

"Are you lovers now?" asked Melissa, cutting to the chase.

Stanley breathed a silent sigh of relief at the answer he'd now be giving. "No...we're keeping it platonic...this time around."

"I see." She fell silent for a moment and then asked softly, "Are you tired?"

He took a sip of his cognac, felt her moving off, out from under his arm. She took up her old position at the end of the sofa nearest the fire, arms about her knees. It seemed to him that it was now bedtime—whether he liked it or not.

"Yes, we should get some sleep." He downed the rest of his snifter, stood, and stretched his bruin body. She stood, took his glass from the coffee table, and moved over to the alcove bar.

"Must be lovely knowing someone as well as you and Lee Ann have known each other. To have been going on as long as you two have."

He laughed. "Sometimes it is. And sometimes it isn't. Sometimes it can turn into something resembling sheer hell."

"Somewhere between heaven and hell is where we dwell." Melissa sighed. She moved lazily back over to his side. The two of them exited the library and began climbing the circular stairs to the second floor.

"Somewhere between heaven and hell is where we dwell," Stanley repeated. "Did you say that?"

"I'm sure I wasn't the first, but yes, I did just say that."

She laughed, and it sounded like Chinese wind chimes."

They'd reached the door to her bedroom; the door to the blue room was much farther down the hall.

"We're here," she said, putting her hand on the knob. "I want to kiss you Stanley. And I can tell you would like to kiss me. Unfortunately...we can't do that. I'm sure you understand."

Stanley more than understood.

"You did just kiss me, sweet Melissa," he said.

"Oh, Mister Hochstetter, you are so gallant." She was teasing with all her might.

"Git out of here. Go on git," he twanged and took a wide sweep at her behind—intentionally missing. She opened the door to her room, and suddenly he found himself standing in the hallway. Alone.

"To sleep...to dream. In Portuguese," he mused and moved off to his.

30.

Lee Ann, after spending a short night of fitful sleep and dreams, surveyed her damaged face in Claire's small bathroom mirror. Oh my God, this is not a healthy face at all—half dead!

Exercise: that was the only remedy she knew of to get some blood back under the skin. It was still early. She didn't need to be at the station for another three hours but needed about a half hour to get there, park, and join Poteet. So there was still time to save herself. She borrowed some tennis shoes and sweats from Claire and stepped out into the cold morning air for a run. It hurt; her limbs were leaden, but she knew this was her bitter pill. She began going over in her mind how she would handle this crucial meeting with Poteet. Stanley was such a dear to find that one solid piece of evidence. Without that, Poteet could simply maintain his naive bearing and sail off into the sunset. But with the coffins, she knew she could nail his ass to the yardarm. All right, Stan! Damn, sometimes she loved that man so. And other times? Well, not so much.

Rounding the corner and heading south on McCaul, she looked up, startled—CN Tower rose like a pinnacle of some futuristic city out of the end of the street. CN Tower, like Sutro Tower in San Francisco: beacons of the new age. She couldn't take her eyes off the sky needle as she jogged along—almost stepped on some lady's poodle. "Oh...excuse me...I am sorry," the lady with the dog whined sarcastically. Lee Ann ignored her and plowed on down the street.

CN Tower: Anyone in broadcasting just had to love it.

A woman with unruly red hair stood squinting into a small bathroom mirror. She was applying soft shades of peach to her lips. The face looked better—flushed with the glow of her run and a hot shower. It had worked once again. Thank heaven.

"Are you sure you don't want me to go along with you this morning, Mom?" Claire asked as she came and stood in the doorway of the cubbyhole bath.

"No, Claire, I need to handle this alone. Besides, we're still not out of the woods with your legal business. I don't want to implicate you in what I'm going to have to be doing to Mr. Poteet this morning." Claire nodded. Somehow her mother could talk and put on lipstick at the same time—and maintain perfect diction, a skill that had always amazed Claire. Lee went on, "I'll be okay. It's a TV station...lots of people there. After I'm through with him, I'll just walk out, come home, and we'll beat it back to San Francisco. How's the packing coming?"

"Okay I guess. There's a lot of my stuff that Jackie can use, so I'm not going to have much except canvases and art supplies, clothes, and a few personal items." Lee Ann had finished her face and was heading in the direction of the flight jacket—time to scramble. Claire followed her to the door. "Can we get some kind of storage space when we get back to San Francisco? The paintings take up a lot of room, you know."

"Oh I don't know, maybe well redecorate the place and hang them all over the house."

Claire scoffed. "Oh no, not all of them. Some of them are pieces of shit. I'm only keeping them because I'm going to be painting over..."

"We'll work it out, honey," Lee said, giving her jacket a two-inch zip at the waist. "How do I look? Ready for battle?"

"You're a brave mom, Mom."

"Then why do I feel like such a little chickenshit?"

"Who wouldn't?" Claire handed her mother the Toyota keys. "Be careful."

"Seems a lot of people are saying that to me these days."

"I mean it."

"They all do. Bye, honey."

"Bye, Mom. See you around one or two? If you're not back by then, should I call the Mounties?"

"Yes, as a matter of fact, do just that."

"All right!"

She boarded Claire's rattletrap compact and drove to the CBC building on Front Street West: a modern red and white teched-out structure bristling with satellite dishes and, Lee Ann imagined, some fat cables running underground to the Big Antenna next door. CN Tower rose straight above her, and she couldn't help thinking how phallic it seemed now that she was standing directly below it. She consulted a directory and boarded an elevator to the third floor.

Poteet was already there when she arrived. He greeted her cordially but with some concern. "How is your daughter, Lee Ann?" he wanted to know first thing. "Where did they take her?"

"She's fine, Jean Paul. Just an anxiety attack. They released her, and she came back home last night." You're not the only guy who can lie, she thought as she smiled into his puppy dog French face. "Are we linked up to watch the show?"

"Yes, come, we have a viewing room all to ourselves. I'm having brunch brought in. I hope you like soufflé and chardonnay."

"You're too kind...sounds delicious." She wasn't feeling the least bit hungry. Would her stomach even accept food at a time like this? She had her doubts.

They moved through the studio and into a moderately sized but comfortable viewing room furnished with several rows of couches facing a bank of three oversized television screens. Behind the couches was a small open area that had been set with a breakfast table, replete with white tablecloth, Poteet Porcelain, crystal, silver serving and eating utensils—daffodils and irises.

Poteet wheeled around behind the table and motioned for her to join him at the opposite setting. "So sorry, my dear that I cannot hold your chair, but you understand."

"Certainly," Lee Ann said, sounding nonchalant, as she seated herself, unfolded her napkin, placed it on her lap, and took a sip of ice water. All seemed to occur in one sweeping motion. It was ten minutes to airtime.

Poteet picked up a cordless receiver from the table and ordered their food brought in. With the other hand he pushed a button on the remote that brought the center screen on the far wall to life. He left the sound down, but she could see unmistakably that they were linked to KPIQ in San Francisco. There was her friend Sam Weber, the weatherman doing her old meteorological spiel at the end of the morning newscast. Good, here we go, she thought. It's now or never. She was ready to have this over with—ready to return home, and get back to her job, the job that Laura Andrews would be doing again this morning. Poteet was speaking.

"You have my curiosity honed to a razor's edge, Lee Ann. What could we possibly be going to see here?"

She studied him over her ice water. He was so elegant in his morning coat and tie. So calm and relaxed. Claire was right; he did resemble Armand Assante. "Well, Jean Paul, what we are going to see must all remain a surprise, but I'm sure you will be entertained." She chimed her words, almost chirped them. He listened with raised brows.

The food was brought and served while KPIQ concluded the news, did a few commercials and information spots, and then the familiar theme and opening bumpers of *Good Morning San Francisco* rolled up the screen. Soon Bradley and Laura were on, welcoming the small live audience, and previewing this morning's program segments. Poteet had turned up the sound, and the two of them sat watching, drinking French roast with chicory. Lee Ann had declined the wine. Up on the screen, Laura was speaking:

"...but first, this morning we're going to start with a report from Lee Ann in New Orleans. As you know, for the past week we've been telling you that Lee Ann has been away on special assignment. This is...and is not...exactly the case. You see, our very own Lee Ann Barnes has, quite literally, for the past week or so, been running for her life." Laura faced the camera straight on with green eyes. "You see, Lee Ann is currently the victim of a celebrity stalker...one who has caused her to flee the San Francisco area in hopes of eluding what has become a series of increasingly lethal threats against her life." Laura paused, still looking straight into the camera. Lee Ann glanced at Poteet, who sat with stilled fork and grave face waiting to hear the cohost's next words. Laura continued:

"But maybe it's best that we hear it from Lee Ann herself."

Bradley picked it up. "What you are about to see is an edited version of a tape Lee Ann made several days ago in a hotel room in New Orleans. The tape was shot on a standard camcorder. But we felt we wanted...and Lee Ann wanted...you to hear of her plight directly, in her own words, so that it would become public information, and possibly bring heavy scrutiny on the perpetrator...stalker...who calls himself seaman: s-e-a-m-a-n." The male anchor smiled wryly, almost imperceptibly, and continued. "All right, if you're ready in there, let's roll that tape."

Immediately, Lee Ann's face filled the screen, and she began to speak. "Hi, this is Lee Ann Barnes. I'm speaking to you from New Orleans this evening." A pause. "As you know, for the past week now, Bradley and Laura have been saying that I've been away on special assignment. Well, that's not entirely true...." Lee Ann, live in Toronto, watched her face on the screen telling the viewing audience about her stalker. About the initial approach of the callalilies in the coffin—good they'd left that in—and then on to the note that so chillingly read, "If I can't be inside your body, I'm going to send a bullet to be there for me." She glanced at Poteet as he watched and listened to this part of the presentation. She noted that he showed the surprise, shock, and slight revulsion that anyone who had not heard these words until now would show. He looked quickly over at her and their eyes met for a split second as he shook his head gravely and then returned his attention to the screen. The Lee Ann on the screen was expressing her disgust and revulsion for the note, saying, "...now, Mr. Seaman,

I don't find that amusing, or tasteful, or in the slightest bit romantic. I find that sick."

At that point they stopped the tape and returned to Bradley and Laura. Good, she thought, an excellent edit point. Bradley made some transitional comments to which Laura replied, and then they cut away for a commercial, promising to conclude the piece when they returned.

The two viewers in Toronto swung around to face their plates. Poteet was the first to look up and saw her stirring her soufflé with her fork. Eventually she looked up—straight into his sympathetic and almost sad brown eyes. Oh, this man should have been an actor. But then, she thought, there could only be one Armand Assante. He was the first to speak. He seemed to start in the middle of his thoughts.

"...I see. I see. And so you thought...or you still think that I might be the seaman, dear Lee Ann? This is very disturbing to me. I am such a devoted fan of yours. How could you think that?"

Lee Ann, hazel-eyed news hawk, leveled at Poteet and fired.

"Until last night, when I received that call from my daughter, who had just received a call from her father, Stanley, I'll have to admit that it was all pure conjecture. But that call raised serious concerns, Jean Paul."

"I'm afraid you will have to tell me more, my dear." He sipped daintily at his ice water, biding his time.

Lee Ann knew she'd tipped her ace. Okay, there was now nothing left to do but play it—and watch—watch very closely. "Jean Paul," she took a deep breath, "Stanley was out at your house working with Melissa on a piece he'd completed with the new clay. While going to get something in one of the storage areas down by the foundry (she was covering for him now), he had an occasion to come across some items that are...are highly incriminating. Should I tell you what they are, or would you like to guess?"

Poteet paused for a moment, held her gaze unflinchingly. "Some small white coffins? Ones similar to the one you found full of callalilies lying on the hood of your car with that first message from the seaman?"

She came very close to doing a spit take with her last sip of water. Her eyes narrowed, then widened, then narrowed. "How in hell did you know that?" Her words were clipped—urgently demanding an answer.

Poteet smiled. "I was going to tell you after the show..." He waved a hand in the direction of the screen where Bradley and Laura had returned and were wrapping up the "Lee Ann Exiled in New Orleans" spot. It appeared that they would be skipping Lee Ann's personal appeal to the seaman. Good, she thought. Maureen had been right; it hadn't been all that dignified. But never mind, the segment was concluding, and Poteet was continuing.

"You see, Lee Ann, we make those coffins for the voodoo priests. It's part of their Mardi Gras paraphernalia. We have probably made over a thousand of them over the past ten years. And they, of course, have dispersed to all corners of the...well... possibly the world. They are coveted ritualistically by all the voodoo followers...have always been popular in their ceremonies... or so I've heard. Does that answer your question?" He waited, but she seemed speechless, so he went on. "It's unfortunate that your friend Stanley stumbled across them. In the storage room of the foundry? Yes, I believe that is where we keep them. Yes, I can see how that would not look so good in either of your eyes..." Poteet trailed off. He knew he had said enough.

Lee Ann felt flushed, nauseous, enraged as she studied the napkin in her lap. The contents of her stomach pressed upward in her throat. She took a deep breath, looked up to meet Poteet's eyes, and spoke softly. "Slipped away again, didn't you, Jean Lafitte's many times great-grandson?" She glared now at Poteet. "You know, Jean Paul, if you continue to persist in this masquerade any longer, you are going to start to appear very foolish in my eyes. Is that what you want? To seem ridiculous in the eyes of someone you profess to love and admire?" She was proceeding on pure feminine intuition now. She knew, somehow knew, that he—the man across the table from her—was her stalker. She wanted him to fess up now and be done with it.

"Set me free, Jean Paul. Let me get back to my home and the work I love to do. I'm really weary of this game now." She was pleading, almost in tears. "I promise, if you will just be honest with me, I'll forget the whole thing...consider your help with freeing Claire as compensation for the terror you've caused me. If you love me, as you've professed in all your notes except the last one, then set me free." She dabbed at her eyes with her napkin. Poteet wasn't the only one who could act, but this was only partly an act. How much of an act even she wasn't sure. She did feel exhausted to the point of tears.

Poteet studied her tenderly. "Lee Ann," he began, "there are so many many things I could say to you, but I will say only this. Yes, I feel I am falling in love with you," he was silent for a moment, "but no, you are wrong...I am not the one who calls himself the seaman...how could you think that of me?"

A ball of fire formed in her solar plexus, then dropped to the tips of her toes, then rebounded back up through her body and went blazing off the top of her red head. Her hazel eyes caught some of that fire and glowed now like hot coals. In a voice that was almost a hiss she breathed her next words.

"All right...have it your way, Jean Paul. But please, never attempt to contact me ever again. Because if you do, I will be taking this matter to the authorities. Stanley's hidden one of the coffins...if that should ever become necessary. You made a threat against my life. That my friend is against the law..."

Jean Paul, with a sad, tormented expression, studied her in silence.

"So..." she continued with mock nonchalance now, "if we're finished here? Gotta go."

Poteet was silent. He'd turned misty eyes toward the monitor on the far wall where Bradley and Laura had long since moved on to other segments of *Good Morning San Francisco*. Now he was nodding his large leonine head in the affirmative, still avoiding her eyes, but waving her off with his white napkin: international signal of surrender.

She had signaled a pirate to stand down—and he had.

The object of the seaman's obsession placed her napkin neatly on the table, rose on shaky legs, smoothed her skirt, grabbed her jacket and purse, and turned slowly to go. She heard a voice behind her. Poteet said, "Perhaps...after some time has passed...you will reconsider. If you do, please don't hesitate to call. I'm sorry you are so convinced..." He didn't finish.

Lee Ann hesitated for a moment at the sound of this final plea. Not wishing to respond in any way, she didn't turn but pushed against the door of the viewing room and was gone from Poteet's life forever. Or so she hoped. Call? she thought as she practically ran from the studio. Christmas in hell! Sleigh bells in Hades! The devil as Santa Claus!

31.

The birds awakened Stanley—a symphony of bird songs.

Many of the singers he was sure he'd never heard before, but he heard them now as he lay in half sleep and feeble early light listening, trying to sort out and count them. Fifteen, sixteen, and there was another one, or was that one he'd counted earlier? He marveled that he was again back to full consciousness at this early hour. Nearly 2am when he'd fallen to sleep. And now was it 5? or 6? A heavy arm came from under the sheets; he squinted at his watch: 6:15am. Four and a quarter hours of sleep, after going without for thirty-six? He wondered if this new pace he was adopting for his body was healthy. Stanley loved to sleep, loved to half sleep, loved to dream about sleep when he was awake. Because, you see, many of his ideas came from sleep and half sleep. So many of his works had been conceived in that hypnogogic state between dreaming and waking. Assemblages of forms that had been moving when they'd first trudged through his half-sleeping brain in slow motion would, that very next day, be frozen for all time in clay. And sometimes vice versa. It was useful to have a place where you could watch the sculpture you had created—move.

He rose, took a cool shower, dressed, and walked around the grounds for an hour or so and then found his stomach leading him in the direction of the kitchen. His greeting from those already assembled there was warm and cordial. After blowing with the band and sculpting Mekweto, the San Franciscan had become well known about the place. But now the considerate Kenyans politely offered him coffee, and left him to his morning ritual.

He sat at the big table at one end of the kitchen sipping hot chicory, reading a newspaper, and waiting for the lady of the house to arrive. His mind wasn't really on the news he was reading. He was using that as a guise to disguise his funk. He was thinking about Lee Ann this morning and was feeling more than a little concerned for her. He was even hoping, strangely enough, that Poteet was somehow not the seaman. It had been so lovely last night in the library with Melissa lying close to him...talking...hearing her voice. That voice...

"Good morning," came that same voice from above him. "Did you sleep well?"

He looked up from his paper and made no attempt to conceal the pleasure he always felt when taking Melissa in. She wore another of her delicately patterned light cotton dresses this morning. But this one was more gathered at the waist and complimented her figure in ways he would now have to ignore. Her black hair was done up casually behind her head. She wore no discernible makeup, but he couldn't help wondering, once again, why her skin seemed to glisten, as if she had just stepped out of a tropical mist.

"Good morning...I did sleep well, thank you. Though short. And you?"

"Fitful dreams I'm afraid I have to report." She sat down across from him at the table. A woman in an African sarong brought her a cup of coffee and left with a request for melon and toast.

"Anything you'd like to discuss?" Stanley asked after the woman had left.

"Not really...no." She fell silent. Then she seemed to change her mind. "Dreams of Rio, my family there...the girls... my brother...father...trying to find things...trying to fit things together that resisted fitting together. Things like that." She looked up, slightly confused.

He met her gaze. "I've often had those kinds of dreams. They seem to go on and on and on, don't they?"

"Like life sometimes..." She looked down. "Oh, I'm sorry. It's such a lovely morning, and here I am, sounding so maudlin."

"I understand. They're called frustration dreams. Good idea to listen to what they're telling you...hard as that might seem sometimes."

She nodded. Their melon and toast came. They both thanked the woman who brought them, and then she was gone again. He asked Melissa if she would like some of the paper. She declined saying that she always saved the bad news for later in the day. It was said with a slight smile, and he could see that she was coming out of the mild turmoil of last night's dreams. He felt cruel knowing that he might be causing her even more pain later this morning. He even considered not watching *Good Morning San Francisco* with her, but asking if he could watch it alone. But then he thought that might seem odd to Melissa. No, he'd come this far; it was time to forge ahead with the plan.

"Melissa, is there some way we could watch *Good Morning San Francisco* at eleven this morning? Could you have it sent down to the library by any chance?"

She looked up, slightly puzzled. "Why yes, Sunjab knows how to get the cable down to the library from Jean Paul's study. Anyway, I believe he does...yes."

"Lee Ann, as you know, is in Toronto, but she'll be on via a tape we made the other evening after having dinner with you here. I think it's important that you see the show. I need your reaction to what you'll be seeing."

Melissa's expression shaded to curious concern. "Sounds rather sinister and foreboding." She wasn't smiling.

"I best not say any more now until you watch the show," he said, folding his newspaper and glancing at his watch. "It's ten-o-five. That means we have a little less than an hour to find Sunjab so that he can make the necessary arrangements. Think we can do that?"

"Jambo sana, and good morning, Mr. Stanley, Ms. Melissa." That deep East African bass voice came from somewhere behind him. Sunjab walked into view and stood with large hands clasped in front of him. "You would like to have San Francisco's KPIQ sent down to the library? Consider it done." And without waiting for a response, the towering Kenyan turned and made his way down the broad brightly lit hall that connected the kitchen to the house. Stanley watched him go, marveling at the way he seemed to float rather than walk on his long thin legs. He turned to face Melissa who was smiling darkly.

"You see why we love, Sunjab?" It was a rhetorical question. "So now that that is done, what would you like to do with the time we have until the show comes on?" This was a real question now, asked with a steamy below-the-equator smile. How could such a lady smile like such a vamp? He wondered, and fell in love a little more each time he saw it.

"Perhaps a walk? More talk?"

"Perhaps. Or we could leave you alone to read your paper and I could attend to some things."

"Can they wait?" He was smiling now, but only with his eyes.

"Yes."

"Then let's walk."

They hurriedly finished their breakfast and set out for a walk to her studio, knowing they would no more get there than have to turn around and hike back. But they needed the exercise. Stanley wanted to see the progress she'd made on the dying slave. Melissa laughed, reminding him that even she had to sleep sometimes, and her work hadn't really progressed since the previous afternoon when they'd worked on it together. Stanley shook his head.

"I think things are moving so rapidly these past few weeks, I'm losing track of time."

"I know, but you have to admit, life is more...invigorating... when it seems to be plunging headlong into the future. Don't you think?" Melissa asked.

"Yes...it is," he agreed, "but sometimes the g's of the rocket sled ride make you want to just about pee your pants." He looked over at the woman who had her hand draped discreetly over his forearm. They were approaching her studio. She didn't reply to this, but smiled slightly and nodded from side to side.

They entered the room where she worked, and there they were, just as they'd been left yesterday: all of Melissa's people, gleaming white in the morning light. He stood and marveled again at what he was beholding. Melissa walked over and lifted the shroud off of the old man lying on the cot: the dying slave. She stood looking down at him; a stern expression clouded her face. Stanley moved over and stood close by her side, also looking down. He put his arm around her waist.

Melissa looked up at him. He kept his eyes on the face of the dying man. She turned in his arm and put hers up around his shoulders. And now she did something that sent waves of pleasure coursing through his body. She pressed herself hard into him in the manner of a woman who wishes to be loved. It was a natural reaction, a full embrace; their lips met softly and parted, met again and parted. She laid her head on his shoulder for a moment and then whispered. "I feel safe here. I could never have done that in the house."

"I'm glad we came down here. I've been thinking about doing that from the moment we first met. Or maybe it was the moment after we first met." He was joking, feeling a need to leaven the weight he was now feeling in his shorts. They were still in each other's arms.

"Men," said Melissa flatly.

"Oh I know. We beastly men have such hair triggers when it comes to..."

"The physical part of love?"

"For lack of a better phrase, yes." He smiled. She made a slight movement away from him and he let her go. Things were getting back to normal. "All right, I told you, now you tell me... when did that feeling start for you? I mean that kiss you just gave me was slightly more than a friendly peck on the lips." He was taking a chance here but wanted to know.

"It was a gradual thing..." she began slowly. "First seeing your work, then talking to you that first time on the telephone, and then meeting you, hearing your sense of humor, seeing how you were with Lee Ann, dining and dancing with you, hearing you play, watching you at work..."

"I know, but when did you decide you wanted to kiss me?"

Melissa, who had gone back to studying her dying slave, gave him an irritated look. "Why, just a moment ago. Or maybe two moments ago." She smiled wickedly again, directly at him.

"Ha!" Stanley grabbed her, pulled her hard to him. They kissed again, this time heatedly. He pulled back and buried his face in her neck.

"Oh...wait...wait..." She was resisting. He let up, relaxed his now taut body, let her melt back into his embrace. She stayed there for a moment, then moved back and looked into his eyes. "I..." Was all she could manage.

"It's all right...no need to say it...shhh."

They slowly released one another.

"So much for the physical part of love." He smiled good-naturedly.

Melissa spoke softly. "I feel that for you. I didn't really know how much until just a moment ago. It's been so long, I thought I'd forgotten how to feel that." She moved off in the direction of the door. Stanley followed along behind, admiring her back again. This woman was a moving statue; there was no other way to describe her. He was suddenly sad beyond words that *Good Morning San Francisco* was waiting to smash it. Or was it waiting to preserve it? He supposed both. This paradox served little more than to heap fuel on his melancholy. Melissa was speaking with her back turned to him.

"I guess we should be heading back to the house. What time is it?"

He glanced at his watch. "At the tone, the time will be... ten forty-six."

"Then we best be going."

"Yes."

They headed back up the road, this time walking slightly apart from one another. Stanley spoke softly, almost in a whisper as they moved along the slight grade that led up to the house.

"Melissa...I think I'm falling in love with you..." Melissa kept walking. He kept whispering. "And I want you to know that I want very much...very soon...to hold you through the night and make love with you." He trailed off.

The woman somewhere near his side took a few more steps, absorbing his words, processing them. Then she drew up slowly, stopped, and turned. Stanley halted in response and stood his ground. He let his eyes range around the little cabins and large lawns that lined the road. "But I suppose, as long as you're here...that could never possibly happen."

"No. It couldn't." She looked down. "I'd like to take your hand now, sir, but I don't think it would be wise." She took a deep breath. "But I have to tell you, without touching you, that I feel the same way. You have such a gentle warm manner..." She paused. He knew she wasn't finished. He waited. "Perhaps someday we'll be privileged to indulge these feelings. But... and you're right, this is so difficult to acknowledge...we can't be together...any more than we have been. You understand... don't you?" Her speech was jerky—searching—but the question wasn't really a question.

"Implicitly. I do."

"So then, we'd best hurry...the show goes on in minutes. We mustn't keep Lee Ann waiting." Melissa turned and set off at an energetic pace toward the house. Stanley, slightly out of breath now, for more reasons than one, followed along behind.

As they watched *Good Morning San Francisco* over Earl Grey in the library, Stanley watched Melissa's color fade with each word Lee Ann chose to describe her stalker. At the point where she mentioned the callalilies, Melissa's bronze skin took on an ashen patina that washed to pale green by the end of the spot. She stood on shaky legs and adjusted her dress. Stanley, seeing that the worst had come, hated himself for having to subject her to this. She said she was feeling ill and then, without waiting for him to reply, quickly disappeared behind the door of an adjoining bath. The door was paneled mahogany but not thick enough to muffle the distinct sound of someone retching on the other side. Melissa, losing her breakfast. Long-suffering Melissa. Stanley's fears and suspicions were confirmed. Lee Ann's description of the coffins and Melissa's graphic reaction were enough to tell him that Poteet had done this before—and that Melissa knew something of his modus operandi. Enough that now, seeing him at it once again, she'd become physically ill.

She hadn't come out of the bathroom, and five minutes had elapsed since those unpleasant sounds stopped. Stanley pictured her sitting with the seat down on the commode, head in her hands, waiting. Waiting for what? Waiting for it to pass? Waiting for him to leave? He could understand why she wouldn't want to face him again this morning. He would only be asking questions now. Questions she wouldn't want to be answering.

He found a tablet by the phone, scribbled a message on the top sheet, and laid it on the coffee table. It said simply:

Melissa dear,

I'm sorry—but at some point—you had to know. Perhaps we can talk tomorrow by phone—if only briefly. I'm returning to New Orleans now. This is not the end...

I love you, sweet Melissa.

Stanley

P.S. Might be wise to destroy this note. Think that goes without saying.

Written expressions of love, left for a pirate's lady, in the pirate's house! Stanley, you should have your head examined. But then again, man in the river, or no man in the river, he was getting a little tired of having Poteet ruin his life. First with Lee Ann, and now with Melissa. Fuck him.

He took the elevator to the second floor, walked down to the blue room—aptly named he thought—packed his few belongings, and returned to the library. The door to the bath stood open. The note and Melissa were nowhere to be seen. He stood studying his shoes for a moment. Then, shouldering his gear once again, moved to the Mustang.

What had started out to be a clear blue morning, had now faded into a sullenly sultry afternoon. The road out ahead of him was gray, the sky up above him was gray, the moss hung cypress trees along the highway were gray. A day that had started out so full of colorful promise, had become dull and monochromatic. He wondered as he drove along with the top down, how it had gone in Toronto. Was Lee Ann winging her way home at this very moment after her latest confrontation with Poteet? Or had Poteet somehow once again pleaded innocent? And then what? Would those two now be off on another romp of Toronto? He needed to call Claire now, see if Lee Ann had returned from CBC and to find out what had happened.

Claire Leveau's Inn was just ahead. He pulled in, shut off the engine, and sat for a moment in the heat wondering if he would ever see Melissa again. Well, she still had his Mary Mythe, so that legitimately connected them—at least one more time. Whoa, thought Stanley; he was feeling a heavy crush for this woman. Maybe not such a good thing to cultivate, but then how could he deny it? His heart was speaking, and he'd learned long ago that listening to one's heart was healthy for one who hoped to keep pursuing the arts. Wait and see, he concluded—one more time—wait and see. He climbed out of the car, plucked his sticky shirt off his back, and made his way to the inn.

The roadhouse was air-conditioned—such a blessed relief from the oppressive humidity that was crushing everything outside. Claire Leveau greeted him and inquired after Lee Ann. Stanley told her that Lee had returned home and he was flying solo. He was stopping in for a bite of lunch and to make a call. He looked at a menu hurriedly, ordered a large salad, some bread, and a glass of rhubarb juice; then he moved off to the phones by the restrooms, thinking about the call he'd made there several nights ago. Pretty sure he was going to get a cell one of these days. Soon as he got back to San Francisco.

He dialed Claire's number, and after a single ring, Lee Ann answered. So good to hear her voice. She sounded calm, asked him where he was calling from. He told her that he'd just watched *Good Morning* with Melissa, and she'd become so nauseous that she'd gone into the bath and not come out. Lee Ann said, "Poor woman..." Then she told him that her encounter with Jean Paul over breakfast watching "the show" had gone poorly. He'd denied any connection with the seaman. Stanley asked her if she'd hit him with the coffin evidence, and she told him about the voodoo priests. They both agreed, in light of Melissa's reaction, that he was still lying to save face. Stanley asked her then if she'd told him that he, Stanley, had hidden one of the coffins for future evidence. She said yes, she had, and told Poteet to leave her alone now, or they would produce that evidence and press charges on the basis of his most recent death threat. She thanked him again profusely for finding that evidence.

He said, "Thanks for including me. Yeah, course, I'm in your fleet, Admiral."

"Sound a little ambiguous there, mate."

"Oh I don't know. I guess I just hate to see those two go as friends. I was getting to know the people out there and liking to be around the house. Now, of course, that will all come to an abrupt end."

"You and Melissa been having fun?" she chided.

"Yes, Lee Ann, as a matter of fact we have been...I mean *were* having fun. Probably as much fun as you and Poteet were having before you learned the dismal truth."

"Touché

"We're too old for this, girl. Just a couple of kids from Colorado who got swept up in the malaise of southern aristocracy."

"I'd say that's a fair assessment..."

"But, hey, let's make the best of it. What say you and Claire come on down for a few days; we'll all look for Bird and then pack it up and fly on back to the City by the Bay. Whaddyasay?"

"No...can't do that, Stan. I have got to get back to work before the City by the Bay falls any more in love with Laura Andrews. Know what I mean, jellybean?"

"Unfortunately." He sighed—paused. "Well...I'll probably spend at least another week or two down here and see what I can turn up in the missing child department. Oh, so much else has been happening. I forgot to tell you that I went back to the Wayfarer's Antiques and talked with the man who's filling in for the proprietor..."

"And?"

"And I offered him a hundred bucks if he could turn up the previous owner. Definitely got his attention."

"Good man, Stan. See what a little green flag-waving can do? When will you see him again?"

"Going to check in as soon as I get back to New Orleans, which will be later this afternoon." There was a pause.

"Keep me posted." Another pause, then...

"Say, you suppose you and Claire and I can have dinner some evening when I get back? It's been a long time since we've had all our feet under the same table."

"Course, Stan, it's a date. Call when you get back to town."

"If I turn up anything in the meantime, I'll certainly be calling before that. I miss you..."

"I hope so," she said softly. "Even if you don't. Give me a ring now and then as you wing your way back in. I'm usually home after seven in the evening. Not before though."

"I know, I remember." Now there was a very long pause. "Well, this has been interesting, hasn't it?"

"A little too interesting I'd say," said Lee Ann from far away, "but then I guess some good things have come out of it too, huh?"

"We're talking again."

"That we are, Stan...that we are." Her voice had grown husky. "And you've made some more progress with our daughter." She cleared her throat. "She talks about you all the time now. Says you've changed...that you seem to be a new man."

"She's done some changing too, wouldn't you say? Changes on both our parts that luckily are drawing us together again. I'm happy."

"Me too, darlin'. Me too. Well..."

"Suppose we better get off here; my salad's wilting. I love you, Lee, Godspeed."

"I love you, Stan. Stay away from those bad people out in the swamp now, you hear? They're creeps."

He wasn't in the mood to argue that only one of them was a creep. "I know," he answered. "I'm afraid I will now...be staying away. Take care."

"You too. Bye."

"Bye."

There was a click on the other end of the line, and Lee Ann was lost once again somewhere in Canada. Feeling vacant, he hung up the receiver and leaned on the phone stall for a moment. As had happened too many times before in his life, he'd gone from two women to no women in his life in the space of a few short hours. Did the women have a plan? Were they all somehow subterraneanly and subcutaneously connected by some common psyche that slapped the hand of any man who was arrogant enough to think he could "be with" more than one at a time? The thought of it suddenly cleared the stinging sensation in his sinuses. Amused, he returned to his salad and his rhubarb juice.

After lunch, the inn was nearly empty, so Claire Leveau sat with him for a few minutes and chatted. He told the innkeeper that he'd met her sister Jahna, and taken a room with her. Claire said she knew that since she had talked with Jahna just that morning on the phone. She seemed pleased. The talk wound down quickly, so Stanley, feeling an itch for the blues, asked Claire if he could play his sax out back for an hour or so.

"Are you any good?" she asked matter-of-factly.

"Hmm...I don't think I'll drive your patrons away, if that's what you mean. Promise I'll keep it down."

"Blow away then Monsieur Stanley. And come and play me a song when you are, as they say, warmed up!"

He fetched his sax out of the car, walked out back of the inn, and settled down in the shade of an arching gum tree. Clay's rendition of "Sophisticated Lady," several evenings ago, was stuck in his brain. He'd known that tune at one time so made a pass at it. No such luck; he couldn't remember it for squat, so he dropped back to an old familiar favorite: "A Day in the Life of a Fool". It'd been years since he'd played it, and his fingers, smart as they'd once been, could not seem to conjure it. Terrible noises were now emanating from his horn. It was time for a walk.

Up the asphalt he trudged, running up and down scales in the key of A minor. Then, bar by agonizing bar, he reconstructed the song under his fingers. That was the most expedient way he knew to get back in touch with it. For twenty minutes up the road, and twenty minutes back down, he blew furiously, nodding to passing traffic, building speed by the second. By the time he arrived back at the inn, some facility had settled in again. Claire was standing outside the front door of her establishment smoking a cigarette as he approached and finished up with a mournful ascending and then descending run.

"Ahh now, that sounds much better than when you started," Claire boomed in her big Creole voice.

He lowered the horn from his mouth. "Amazing what a little trip up and down the road will do for your playing. Thanks, and you're right, it does sound better than when I started. Haven't played that song in years."

"You must have been pretty good back then, *mon cher*, if you sound that good after such a long time away from it."

"Not all that good, Claire. But I did play a lot when my son was a young child. Before..." He didn't finish.

"Before he disappeared?"

"Uh, yes, how did you know that?"

"I talk with my sister almost every day. She told me that you are looking for him."

Stanley nodded, remembering he'd mentioned Bird to Jahna, but hadn't said anything about having lost him. But he'd heard about swamp telegraph. These women certainly did have their fingers on the key.

"And she said that you felt you were close, possibly, to finding him. Bird is his name?" Stanley nodded again. "That you had found a toy you believe to be his in a secondhand store in N'awlins?"

"Yes, we...Lee Ann and I did. She told you that?"

"Yes. She wanted to know if I knew of anyone who went by that name...Bird."

"Oh, I see. Do you?"

"No...can't say as I do. But I will ask others for you. We will find him." The innkeeper paused and lowered her voice almost to a whisper. "Jahna...I told you...she can see ahead. And she has seen you being reunited, very soon, with your son. She is often right, more often than not. I must tell you this."

Stanley's jaw hung slack now. "She said that?"

"Yes, but don't tell her I told you. She becomes sooo angry when I get ahead of her magic." Claire did whisper now. "Promise me you will not let her know I told you?"

"All right, certainly. But I'm not sure, knowing all and seeing all as you say she does, that she won't see that I know. That you told me this." He shook his sweaty head. "It's a shock you know...to think that I might see Bird again."

"I know. It has been years hasn't it?"

"Too many long and lonely years of missing him. Yes."

"Return then to New Orleans...have your fortune told. Find your son."

There was a dark mystery and sincerity in Claire Leveau's hushed voice. Her motherly tone of voice gave him an almost childlike sense of confidence. He thanked her for the reassurance, packed his horn away, and drove very swiftly back to the Big Easy.

At Wayfarer's Antique Shoppe, Bruce, once again behind the counter, told him that he'd been asking around and had not been able to locate the source of the squeezer. He told Stanley to be sure and come around tomorrow when Delilah would be back from Africa. Stanley, feeling like he was 0 for 3 at the plate this morning, thanked him and drove back to Leveau's Rooming House for a much needed shower and change of clothes.

And possibly, if Jahna was so inclined, a glimpse into his future.

32.

Lee Ann and Claire spent the afternoon sorting out, thinning down, and separating Claire's belongings from the flat she shared with Jackie. Lee Ann couldn't help feeling that she was witnessing an amicable separation of mates. In the end Claire sat on a pile of ten fully packed banana boxes, with her forearms on her knees, proclaiming that she'd accumulated entirely too much shit for a twenty-year old. Leaning against the wall were several large flat cartons containing paintings she said she could not part with.

Jackie had made a haul. Claire was leaving behind all of her kitchenware, several large paintings—an equal number of smaller ones—some of the clothes the girls had shared, and all of the furniture that belonged to her. Jackie promised to send these along as soon as Claire was resettled. Claire said that could be never because this might be a good time to see the world.

Maybe Claire would be coming back to San Francisco to reconnoiter, but Lee Ann knew it would be little more than a touch-and-go landing. Always fully fueled and ready to scramble, that was Claire.

Packing complete, Lee Ann stood stirring spaghetti sauce at the stove, overhearing some emotional exchange that Claire and Jackie were having in their bedroom. One of many that she'd been overhearing but not quite hearing these last several days, living around two lovers who knew they would soon be parting. Suddenly the conversation—which sounded more like sobbing—ceased. Lee Ann set her spoon aside and moved quietly around a corner to see what was transpiring. Through a narrow crack of vision between the kitchen and the bedroom door, she saw Claire and Jackie in an embrace. And now they were moving back from one another—and now embracing again in a lovers' kiss. She quickly returned to her cooking. So strange, she thought. I guess you're either made that way, or you're not. She wasn't. It was still difficult to accept that her daughter, Claire, evidently was.

But then there had been boys too. Oh lord, had there been a string of boys in Claire's teenage years. And tough young Claire had systematically, or so it had seemed to Lee Ann, broken each and every one of their hearts. Certainly not before some rather heated sexual activity had taken place, however. More than once she'd found spent Sheiks and Trojans languishing about under Claire's bed. At least she'd been careful.

"MOM!"

She snapped out of a not-so-pleasant reverie as Claire's brassy voice bounced about the living room walls."

"YEAH!" she shot back.

"HOW'S DINNER COMIN'? WE'RE ABOUT DONE IN HERE."

She shouted back across the loft, "COME AND GET IT. TABLE NEEDS SETTING."

Jackie, followed by Claire, both a bit flushed, ambled out of the bedroom and joined her in the kitchen. A table was quickly set, and since this was to be their last dinner together—the movers were coming tomorrow, and plane reservations had been made—they had freshly cut flowers on the table and some very fine cabernet sauvignon breathing on a sideboard. Spaghetti and salad were passed, and in went the forks.

"Jackie and I've been talking, Mom."

"I've noticed. Might be more of a news item if you told me you hadn't been. Talking that is."

Good-natured laughter all around. Claire went on.

"Well you know, she will never, ever leave Toronto, but... she was thinking she might come out to San Francisco at the end of the summer for a couple of weeks? And then if we have enough money saved up...head over to France. Her and me."

"She and I. Sure, that'd be fine. I kept the queen-sized bed in your room," she turned to Jackie, "and I could take you in to the studio while you're there. You could watch us doing the show."

Jackie's eyes flashed wide. "Okay then! I'm coming out for sure!" The two girls smiled knowingly at each other.

Lee Ann raised her glass. "To the plan."

In unison: "To the plan."

They finished off the wine with cheesecake for dessert. As they were clearing the table, Lee Ann's cell signaled an incoming call. She picked it up off the counter and saw it was Poteet! After a few rings, some morbid curiosity caused her to answer. "Hello, Jean Paul."

"Lee Ann, I was wondering if you had a moment to talk?"

Her first reaction was to click off. But then the blood froze in her veins and she snapped. "A very brief moment, Jean Paul. I'm having dinner with the girls." And then, almost in a whisper, "You do have some nerve, Mr. Poteet..." She waited.

"Lee Ann, I'm calling you because I am concerned for your safety."

"Mmmhuh...well that's nice. And why is that?"

Poteet didn't respond immediately. She waited. Finally he said. "I've given it a great deal of thought...and I've decided that I must do something I would not, under other circumstances, do..."

"Okay, Jean Paul, I'm listening. The point?"

He skipped a beat and then went on. "You are right." Another long pause. "I am the one who calls himself seaman."

There was a very long pause now as she absorbed this. "Well...I told you...I knew that you were." Her tone of voice was almost motherly now, as if excusing a naughty son. But lead was settling into her knees. She waited, but Poteet didn't go on. So she did. "You know...you are a despicable liar, Jean Paul Poteet. But...thank you for finally coming clean. I think I need to go now. I really don't have anything more to say to you."

"No. Wait! That is only part of the reason I called. Please... don't go...I have something else very important to tell you."

"All right...I'm listening."

What twisted machination was now knotting in Poteet's scurrilous brain, she wondered. He went on.

"Lee Ann, yes, I did send you the callalilies, and the faxes, and the videotape. But...and you must believe me in this...and this is why I decided I needed to call you. I am concerned for your safety."

"Yes, Jean Paul, you said that, but why?"

"Because, dear Lee Ann...because I was not...I did not send you the message that referred to the bullet. I don't remember exactly how it read..."

There was a long pause on Lee Ann's end of the line as she once again processed what he'd just told her.

"Oh, this is *just great*. This is just *wonderful*! You realize what this means, don't you, Jean Paul?"

"Yes, most emphatically, I do. That's why I am concerned for your safety. That's why I am calling...even though you have asked me not to. And I do intend to honor that request in the future...but please tell me...how did the note read?"

Claire, acting as if she was just straightening up the living room, had her ears on eleven.

Lee Ann lowered her voice and mumbled. "It read, 'If I can't be inside your body, I'm going to send a bullet to be there for me.' I can't believe this. I just can't believe it."

Jackie at the sink stopped rattling the dishes and looked on. Lee And motioned them both over. But they waved her off, didn't want to get to close to the laser glare that was emanating from her steely eyes.

"And was that note signed?" asked Poteet after a long pause.

She took a second to recollect and remembered that, indeed, no, no it had not been signed—"seaman"— and it had been constructed out of words and letters snipped from a magazine.

The room started to list slightly as the full implication of what Jean Paul was telling her sunk in: *the possibility that there was another person who had sent it?*

Her voice trembled as she answered. "No...no...it wasn't signed."

"You must believe me, Lee Ann, I did not send you that note. I would never send you such a message, or even think such a thing. It's barbaric."

"You do know what this means, don't you, Jean Paul? It means that I am still very much in danger. Boy, you little boys sure do like to ruin a little girl's day, don't you?"

"Lee Ann, I don't blame you for being irritated with me and what I've done, but if you think back, you will remember that all my correspondence to you under the alias of seaman was loving and non-threatening. Oh, I admit, the coffin was a bit melodramatic, but other than that, wouldn't you say that everything was fairly light and playfully affectionate? Because that is the way I feel toward you..."

Another long pause. "Lee Ann?"

"Yes." Lee Ann said in a barely audible voice. She was not really interested in his pleadings now. Her mind was spinning on out ahead with the possibility that there was a less gentle anonymous suitor out there who would now pick up where the seaman had left off—and continue to make her life miserable. In one deft stroke of will, she decided that this was *not* going to happen.

"Jean Paul, you know..." she began, "I really don't feel much like I can believe a single word that comes out of your mouth. I mean you are such an accomplished liar, aren't you? And you did lie to me twice when I asked you very directly whether you were the seaman. So...I'm going to assume that you *did* send me that note as a desperate move designed to flush me down to your lair, knowing that Stanley was heading your way." She paused for breath, couldn't seem to get her body under control. Poteet waited. So she went on. "No, actually I don't know what I believe, but I'm through running. I'm going home tomorrow...get back to work, see what happens. Fresh out of fear, I'm afraid."

"I understand." Poteet said softly. "But, as I said this morning, if, after you reconsider, you wish to contact me again, for whatever reason, please do that; perhaps I can continue to make up for my foolishness in the past. I wish you no harm. I love you."

"I doubt that will happen...and now...really must get back to my evening. Thanks for ruining my day...again." She didn't wait for his reply, didn't say good-bye, simply punched a button on her cell and stood for a moment with head bowed and heart pumping.

"Boy, what fucking nerve," said Claire finally. "That was *who* I think it was, wasn't it?"

"Poteet," hissed Lee Ann between her teeth.

"Boy, what fucking nerve," Claire repeated.

"Well...he called to say that he didn't send the last message...which you heard me repeating to him...about sending a bullet my way. But the good news is that he admitted that he is the seaman, that he is guilty of all the rest of it."

Claire and Jackie stood shaking their heads, processing what she was saying. She went on wearily. "So either he's lying or I have traded a rather charming dark admirer for a pathological killer. I choose to think he's lying. In either case I'm through running. Through."

The three of them finished up the dishes and, at Lee Ann's insistence, refrained from further conversation about the seaman.

Jackie curled up by the fire stove with a book, and Lee Ann, saying that she was exhausted, retired to the guest room. She sat propped up in bed with her laptop on her knees taking and reviewing some notes for an upcoming show. There was a soft knock on her door.

"Come in."

Claire opened and stuck her head around the door. "Got a minute?" she whispered.

"Sure honey, come in."

Claire stepped around the door and closed it behind her. She was wearing a ratty, full-length flannel nightgown and enormous padded house slippers. Her straight blonde hair hung down around her face. She reminded Lee Ann of the little girl she'd known long ago. Claire walked over, flopped down, and curled herself at the end of the bed. Her hair fell completely across her face. She flipped her head upward and to the side. It fell back down. She gave up and collapsed onto her back, studying the ceiling.

"Man"—big sigh—"this is harrrd."

Lee Ann thought her daughter could be referring to any number of things. "You mean all these changes? Leaving Toronto?"

Claire sighed, was silent for a moment. "Leaving Jackie."

"I can tell...well, you two seem to click. I can see that."

"I love her, Mom. I think we could be together forever."

"Forever? That's a long time."

"I know...I know...I suppose it must seem strange to you, huh? Our arrangement."

"Takes some getting used to, yes."

"I know." Claire sighed again. "I really love her, Mom. More than I've ever loved another person in my life. We've been through some thick shit."

"Well wading through shit can definitely bring people together, or keep them apart. Depends on how they wade...how thick the shit is."

"Ha! You can say that again."

"I could, but I won't."

They were silent for a moment. Lee Ann went on.

"Can I ask you a question? And please don't take offense at this. I'm just curious about something."

"What? I think I know what you're going to say." Claire rolled over onto her side. Her hair fell into her face again. She pulled it back with one hand. "Damn! This HAIR is driving me FUCKING crazy! Do you have a bobby pin or anything?"

"On the dresser, there's a barrette."

Claire leapt to her feet, walked to the dresser, snatched up the clasp, fastened her hair up on one side, returned to the bed, and flopped back down again. "So what do you need to know? Whether I ever want to have a kid by any chance?"

"As a matter of fact, that's is what I was wondering."

Claire considered it for a second. "There're a lot of ways to do that, Mom. Jackie and I could adopt; either one or both of us could be artificially inseminated. We could even find a baby in a basket under a tree!"

Lee Ann smiled sadly over at her daughter. "Yes, I suppose you could. So you don't think that a child really needs a father then?"

"Well...where was old Stan when I was growing up? You pretty much raised me by yourself, didn't you? Look how great I turned out." She clucked wickedly.

Lee Ann, the mouth, wasn't entirely sure how to field all of this brave new world attitude she was hearing from her pioneering young daughter.

Claire continued. "And you know, Mom, there are millions of little orphans out there in the Third World. Maybe we'll go out there and find some of those kids that need raising. I don't know. I don't rule anything out. But having a kid, raising a family, sure isn't all that high on our list of priorities at the moment. I can tell you that. But who knows, sure, maybe some day. Lots of time to decide."

"Oh I know, you're entirely right. I was just curious as to what was on your mind these days in that area. You think you'll ever go back to men?" Lee Ann tacked the loaded question onto the end of her reply.

Claire sat up and crossed her legs, Indian style. She fixed her mother with sapphire eyes. "I doubt it. I doubt it very much. I mean, don't get me wrong, I have nothing against men. I have men friends, a lot of men friends actually." She pulled up a corner of her mouth, stared up at the ceiling. "It's just that when you start sleeping with them, get into a sexual thing with them, it all changes instantaneously. Not that I'm entirely gay or anything you know, sex is fun, different with men. It's just how it changes the way they hold you in their minds that I don't like."

Lee Ann waited. Claire went on. "And it never fails, or at least I've never seen it fail."

"I suppose eventually we're going to have to let your father in on all of this, don't you think? Especially since we will be spending time with him here in the future. You, me, Jackie. You know what I mean?"

It was Claire's turn to remain silent; finally she said, "You haven't even hinted at it yet? To Dad?"

Lee Ann shook her head no.

"I haven't either. What's his problem? He's a San Franciscan. He has gay friends. I know he does. Remember Stacey? And Fredrick? And Harry? A lot of gay friends, both male and female."

"Stacey and Fredrick and Harry are not his daughter, or sons. It's just different when it's your child. It was hard for me when I first knew. It was hard for me when I got here and saw it live and in living color for the first time. It's just different when it's your own kid, that's all I can tell you. Can you understand that?"

Claire nodded, not entirely convinced. Lee Ann went on.

"And if it was hard for me, just think how hard it is going to be for your father. Can you have a little compassion here?" Lee Ann was speaking earnestly now but in a loving, patient tone of voice.

Claire plowed her face into the comforter for a moment as Lee Ann waited for her to process. After a few moments of ostriching, she raised back on her elbows and studied the impression her face had just made. "So..." she began cautiously, "how do you propose that we break the news to dear old Daddy? It isn't going to go away, you know. You're right, he is going to have to know, eventually."

"I don't know Claire, and it isn't like I haven't given that question some thought. I do know that I probably should be the one to tell him. It's just that we've been fielding a whole lot of other things lately, and I just haven't found an opportune time to introduce it into the mix."

"Sorry."

"Oh, nothing to be sorry for. It's just how you feel at this time in your life. I'm adjusted to it. We'll work it out. It's just that I don't want anything to disrupt the delicate balance you've got going with your father at the moment. Isn't it wonderful? After all these years? Don't you think we should try to keep that rolling at all costs? Not so bad having a dad, kid."

"I know...you're right. And he's a long-suffering dad too, isn't he?"

"Well, I don't know why you've done it, but you've both contributed to each other's misery over the years. But aren't you ready to be done with that now? You are both such fine talented artists.

"Oh yeah," said Claire with a lopsided grin. "Fabulous artists!"

"I think you are, both of you."

"Thanks."

End of topic. Time to move on, thought Lee Ann. "Claire... so much has been happening that I haven't felt like I wanted to say anything about this till now...but now seems like a good time."

Claire looked at her mother. "And yet another surprise?"

"Yes. Your dad and I have made an amazing discovery."

"You're going to have a BABY?"

"Ha! Funny you should say that. Yes, possibly, yes. You see we think we may have found one of Bird's old toys. Actually it's a juice squeezer that was his...well, binky. Something he was carrying back from preschool with him when he..." She couldn't finish.

"When he was nabbed?"

"Yes."

"Wow!" Claire was intrigued. "Where'd you find it? What makes you think it was his?"

Lee Ann sat relaxing now as she briefly filled her daughter in on the events surrounding the discovery of the squeezer. She finished up by saying, "...so it occurred to us to scratch the paint and see what was under the maroon and lime-green..."

"Uh huh." Claire was not there. She was floating somewhere, out on another planet. Could it be possible? That she would soon be meeting the mythical Bird?

"...Yes...and can you believe! Under that coat of paint was a coat of blue paint, and under that the original baked-on white enamel! Bird's squeezer had been painted the same shade of blue we found under the maroon and green."

Claire with eyes wide needed some clarification. "Let's see, refresh my memory here, didn't you say he disappeared...you think was abducted...from a supermarket?"

Lee Ann looked down. "Yes, I'd just picked him up from pre-school and had stopped by the market to pick up some things for dinner. Bird had taken his binky, the squeezer, to show-and-tell that day...was carrying it with him in a little gym bag. I let him out of my sight for a second. He walked around a corner"—she drew in a long and audible breath—"he never came back..."

Lee Ann looked somewhere off into space now. Claire brought her back.

"So you think the juicer you found...bought, might be *his*?"

Lee Ann looked up, met her daughter's eyes and thought she saw in that instant all the way to the center of her soul. "What do *you* think?" she managed. "How many juice squeezers of that unusual deco sort of design do you suppose there are that are painted white, blue, and then green and maroon?"

"Pretty unusual. Quite a coincidence if it's not his...I'd have to agree." She considered it all for a moment. "What are you going to do now? Now that you've found it?"

"Stanley's gone back to the store, offered a reward to anyone who can provide any information leading to the identity of the previous owner. The lady who sold it to him is on a trip but will be returning tomorrow. She's our best hope. I've got all my fingers crossed as you might imagine. Don't have my hopes up too high though, who knows where that squeezer has traveled in the last twenty-two years? It's all such a long shot. But..."

"But you're going to pursue it for all its worth, aren't you?"
"Yes."

"And what if by some stroke of luck it should lead you to brother Bird...then what?"

Lee Ann met her daughter's azure gaze. It was her turn to shake her head from side to side. "I honestly don't know, Claire.

Except to say that I certainly have a million questions to ask him. Wouldn't you?"

"Amazing. To think that you might somehow be reunited with the Birdman. And I suppose then that I would have sort-of-a-brother... wouldn't I?"

"Well, he wouldn't be your blood brother in any way. You know, your father and I found him, but yes, he would be your sort-of-brother. As Stanley was mine."

"Wow. How old would he be now?"

"Twenty-seven." Lee grew wistful. "He'd be almost twenty-seven.

"Wow"—very long pause—"this is an amazing development, isn't it?"

"Yes, but as I say, we can't let our hopes get too high. It's all such a shot in the dark."

"I hope we find him. I'd like to know him, hear what his life has been like since he disappeared. Hear what he remembers. Hope he's still..." She didn't finish.

"So do I Claire," said Lee Ann gravely, "so do I." She rubbed her eyes.

"We've got to get some sleep, busy day tomorrow."

"Right," said Claire, rolling to the edge of the bed and pulling herself to her feet. She moved over to her mother and kissed her on the forehead. Lee Ann shut her eyes. A tiny movement of her lashes caused a tear to break and run down her cheek. Claire pulled a tissue from a box on the nightstand and dabbed at her mother's face. Lee Ann kept her eyes shut.

"Thank you darlin'," she whispered huskily.

"Happy tears, huh Mom?" Claire whispered back, feeling her own eyes well up at the sight of her mother's bittersweet lament. Lee Ann nodded yes without saying a word. "'Night, Mom, I love you."

"Night sweetie...I love you." Lee Ann returned in a voice that was barely audible now.

Claire pulled the covers up under her mother's chin, turned out the light on the bed stand, and walked softly from the room.

Part 3: Red Shift

33.

"Ahhh...this is very interesting...very telling," said the ancient seer as she studied a tarot card. "You see dis hangin' mon at de crux of dis cross? You mi tink dat is some ominous forboddin. But no! Lo! Dat is good news for you."

Stanley looked down at the tarot card that showed a young man hanging by one heel from a T-shaped cross. His free leg was in a figure-four position and his hands seemed to be bound behind his back, elbows sticking straight out to his sides. Strangely enough, there was a bright halo about his head. And now as Jahna covered this card crosswise with the next draw, Stanley's heart fibrillated. The crossing card was Death. He gasped.

"Ah! Veery good...veery good...and just as I taught. You are a fortunate man Mista Stanley Hochstetter."

Stanley sank into his wicker chair and covered his eyes. Maybe this wasn't such a good idea, having his fortune told. And what was this woman saying? That The Hanging Man crossed by Death was somehow good fortune? This would take some explanation.

"Oh, can see dat you are a worry mon," sighed Jahna with genuine concern. "Heere, let me explain. You see dis hangin' mon? He is de mon dat waits in pain. He is de mon dat moost remain suspended and in contumplation for an undetermined peeryod of time wid dat nagging question on his mine. But you see dis messenger of death crossing dat mon? He is come to tell de mon dat his waitin' day...soon be over! Someting dat he has been caring for...someting dat you and he have wanted very much to die will soon be dead. You will be free, and dis will bring wid it waves of relief. But now we must consul de udder card to see if we can tell what dat ting is. Do you want to know Stanley mon? Or shou we stop here...let de future unfol as't will?

Stanley remained leaning back in his chair, but lowered his hand from his eyes and breathed deeply. He watched as Jahna took a short puff on her hookah. As she exhaled, he smelled something resembling fresh horseshit. An aroma he'd always found pleasant. He considered her question, wasn't quite ready to answer.

"Could I have a puff of that, Jahna?"

Jahna looked up in alarm. "Such a rude old woman. Rude!" she cackled and handed the mouthpiece of the hookah over to him.

He leaned forward, took the hose, put it to his lips, and pulled up a medium draft. The smoke was pungent, laced with spice and vinegar and musk. He pulled it down into his lungs, held it for a moment, and released it up and out through his nose. "Mmm." He leaned back in his chair again. Jahna followed suit, relaxed back into her rocker, and kept a slow rhythmic pace that seemed to accompany the swirling smoke. People passed by her front porch and mumbled greetings, wanted to say hello, but did not want to interrupt. Finally he said, "So it's not a person who is dying?"

"Aw kinds o' way to die, Stanley mon."

"Mmm. Guess you're right." He looked around. "Okay, let's do the rest of it. I'm ready."

"Good...good," said Jahna, and she leaned forward and laid down the next card of the ancient Celtic Cross. She placed it above The Hanging Man and Death in the position of destiny: it was The Star. Stanley brightened. Jahna beamed. "Dare! You see...your destiny...De Star! Dare! Clear and shining bri in de sky of your ni." Without further elaboration she laid down the other arms of the cross.

The card of the right arm was The Hermit. The card forming the bottom leg was The Moon. The left arm was The Sun. And with The Star in the crowning position, the central cross was fixed. After studying the cards for a moment, she smiled slightly and told him that he was soon to be blessed. He shook his head in wonderment at the darkness in the center of his cross, but couldn't help feeling encouraged by all that light in the arms!

Jahna, between puffs from her water bowl, explained that The Hermit represented the foundation and past. The Hermit: alone and secluded—introspective—but holding up a lantern to the dark—searching with resolve and determination.

He agreed heartily with that description of his life to date.

She went on to explain that The Moon spoke to the recent past.

"...da Moon, weepin' tears dat rain down'n make de ert fertile. An see de woolf and de dog ba'yan below dat crescent slice? Dey speak of de conscious and unconscious mine ba'yan to be free. An de lobster...crawlin from de black water below... watches as dat water mine begins its worl'y flow. An look what is risin on de left arm...

"De Sun!" Jahna screeched, and slapped The Sun card soundly. "Aaaa...aaa...I feel much comfort in dis cross."

He could only nod—transfixed—as she went on.

"Tink of all de good tings you associate wid de sun, Stanley mon. Dese are soon to come to you! Such a lucky mon." Jahna leaned back, puffed on her smoke hose, then leaned forward and handed it over to him. He waved it off and said, "I'm fine, thank you." He sat hunched down and over a table where his tarot cross demanded full attention. Jahna hung the snake on a stirrup and leaned back to listen.

"So the suspended man is soon to die. The self-absorbed hermit, baying at the moon will soon emerge into the sunlight and proceed on to yet another star? Is that the whole of it then?"

"Dat is de call. An you see how de arms circle roun? Dat is de overall cycle of de life you lead. But we mus see now who you are ri now! 'Cause dat will tell us 'bou de whole and how much to take de parts of it all seeryasleee."

Stanley sat mesmerized as she laid down four more cards to the right of the cross. The bottom card was Judgment. Above that came The Lovers. And above that the Wheel of Fortune. The top card of this vertical column was the World.

"Ah ha! You are a mon troubled by matters of romantic love, are you not Mista Stan?" Jahna asked the question in the form of a statement.

"Fascinating." He was moving into it now—his fortune.

Jahna explained that the bottom card, Judgment, was himself—the querent she called him. The man questioning his present and future. The next card up, The Lovers, spoke to his present environment—condition. The Wheel of Fortune spun round at the center of his inner feelings. And The World, up there on top, represented the outcome of all these current conditions. He agreed, that summed it up nicely and wasn't sure what The World was going to be yet, but at least it was a World. And, as Jahna explained, The World was the final card of the Major Arcana. The completion of The Fool's journey. He had a question.

"What about Bird? My missing son? Do you see anything here concerning him?"

Without speaking, Jahna raised a boney finger and laid it squarely down upon the card that spoke to his future: The Sun.

He was silent for a moment, nodding his head and marveling at the oversight. But then Jahna had seen it all along.

"I think ma'am it's time to celebrate, cook dinner? Or should we go out? How about a date?" He reached over and buried Jahna's boney hand in his own. She pulled hers over on top of his and pressed his, palm down on The Sun card. "Come on back de kitchen boy. I got gumbo on, we g'wan spen no money."

He followed her to the back of the house where, as promised, they found an iron pot simmering with juices that sent out an urgent message—they wished to be eaten. He made a salad and heated some bread as Jahna set the table, poured some wine, and ladled out her potion. They settled in for a slow southern dinner.

The sun set while they ate and talked, so Jahna lowered a rude chandelier of hurricane lanterns from the high ceiling, lit the wicks, hoisted it back up, and returned to the table to finish her bowl.

As they ate, she told Stanley about her girlhood. How her father had been Jamaican, so she'd spent her early years there. She considered Jamaica her home; she often went back to visit friends and family. But for the last forty years she'd been living in New Orleans, running the boarding house and Inn that her aunts had left to her and Claire.

"So then your father was a Leveau? And was he somehow related to the famous clairvoyant of the mid–eighteen hundreds, Marie Leveau?" He'd waited long enough to hear the story from the source—Jahna herself.

"Oh no, my mudder was de Leveau, dat was her maiden name. She gave me'r las name because she raise me for de mos par. My fadder was a mon who rarely came down de mountain. He was a cooltivator, but he was a good mon, always saw dat his family had food and clo'ting an de necessities off life." She slurped up another spoonful of gumbo and rice, gummed it a moment, swallowed, and went on. "We live and go to school in Roarin River up de mountain. But den move New Orleans when Claire was college boun. Live here since de sixties. Hard times, but a'ways aye'gets better. Now you see, I live a queen." She swept her knarled hand about to take in her home.

Not bad, not too far from de truth, he thought.

"G'wan down Jamaica next week, up Roarin River way." She paused, looked sideways at him. "You shou come...meet many fine people...get your mine off all dis romance business."

"What river?" he asked.

"Roarin River...up-country Jamaica."

"Where your people are, you say?"

"Yes...many fine people...yes dat is where I spend my early days."

"And your sister Claire...did she grow up in Jamaica too?"

"Oh no, she is my ha'sister. Her fadder was a trappin' mon... French, Choctaw and African. She live with him when she was young...not my mudder. She naw get long wi her fadder so well, so took our mudder's name too...Leveau." She paused to chew her food and then went on. "My mudder was Creole and Irish.

My fadder no ha last name. My mudder had six husbands...lef her a very rich womon." Jahna chuckled.

"That clears things up a bit," he said, pouring them another glass of wine. "I couldn't see how you and Claire could have had the same upbringing, when she is clearly Creole, and you are Jamaican as they come. Couldn't quite sort it out."

"Ah Mista Stanley...now you know."

"Now I know...some gumbo pot of bloodmixes you have in this neck of the woods, Jahna."

"Rich heritage! Thick blood! Yes, mon."

"My people live on the Roaring Fork River...out in Colorado. Sort of a coincidence don't you think? Two people from two probably quite different Roarin Rivers having dinner and striking up a friendship."

"Aye."

"You say you're going up to your Roarin River next week? Are you flying to Jamaica?"

"Aye, dis time I fly. Sometime I take de boat ride ou Gulfport."

"You say there would be room for me at the place you're staying?"

"Aways plenty room in Roarin River...many friends and family."

"Sounds enticing." He plucked a bit of crabshell off of his tongue and set it on his plate. "Well, I better stay around here. I need to keep looking for Bird, you know."

"Mmm, I know dat," Jahna said, and a dark light passed behind her old yellow eyes.

They talked about Bird as they drained the dregs of the wine. Then Stanley asked Jahna if she had heard of the *Arabesque* and would she like to come along with him? The old woman said that, yes, she knew of the place, but didn't get on too well with the owner. Besides she was tired and needed her beauty sleep.

"I don't know, Jahna, you go getting any more beautiful, you're going to start having all those romantic problems I have." Stanley stood and started clearing the dishes. The old woman cackled and shooed him from her kitchen. He went peacefully and retired to his room to rest and reconnoiter.

Jahna had told him during dinner that she had not heard anything substantial in response to her questions about someone who called himself Bird. That had been disappointing, but she reminded him of what the cards had told and reassured him that it was to be soon. He was glad that she was so confident.

Tomorrow he would talk to the owner of the secondhand store. He was keeping his fingers crossed that she would be able to shed some light on his quest. If that didn't pan out, he wasn't sure where he would go with the search other than to give everyone his number in San Francisco and ask them to call him if anything came up.

Potential leads: There was the secondhand storeowner he would bribe handsomely. There was Lisa Lynn who would know people Bird's age. There was Jahna and her sister, Claire, an innkeeper—sisters who apparently knew many people in the region.

With that cross section of people, if something didn't turn up, it wouldn't mean that he hadn't cultivated enough connections. It would simply mean that it wasn't in the cards. And yet he felt so close to Bird right now, so full of hope, that he felt a further need to celebrate. And as Lee Ann had reminded him several days ago, "Hey Stanley! You still in bed? Come *on*, man, New Orleans is out there!"

He considered calling Lee Ann, but knew she would be skeptical of his optimism in light of a card reading, so decided not to dim his glow. A shower, a shave, some fresh light clothes, and he was on the street again, on foot, heading for the *Arabesque* to hear some more of the fine sax of one Clay Hawkins.

At the *Arabesque* Clay and Turquoise Blue were blowing through like a Coltrane. Stanley muscled his way to the bar and watched as someone in charge hopped to the side of the stage and whispered something into the piano player's ear. The player nodded and hit some signal chords that brought the pandemonium to a crescendo and then dropped it fast on its ass. Clay blasted the last bars of the song they were burning

311

and took it out with a two-measure hold on the fourth. A rowdy crowd cheered wildly.

The man with a sax stepped to the mike and waited for the adulation to subside.

Stanley ordered an Irish coffee. He felt a bit lightheaded at stumbling into such a charged atmosphere.

"Okay! Okay!" Clay shouted and brought the restless mob to his attention, and then waited. As soon as he could speak in a normal tone of voice, he continued.

"Okay, that was one off our new CD, a tune we call 'Turnstile.' And the powers that be have asked us to bring it down a bit, so we'd like to do a ballad next." The club had grown quiet now, except for the rattle of glasses and tinkle of ice. The man at the mike went on. "I was walking home last night, taking the long way by the river, and I heard a guy playing this tune. He was playing it in the key of D. We usually play it in Eb, but I liked the dude's riffs, so here it is, 'When Sunny Gets Blue' in D."

Stanley looked up sharply. Clay was talking about him! He had heard him last night down by the river blowing "Sunny" in the key of D—*and now he was going to play it?* The world could have been coming to an end. The ceiling could have been falling in. God could have been speaking to him from on high. Stanley would not have noticed, would not have heard. He was tunneled in now on the bandstand and Clay, who signaled to the piano player, who flourished and ran and came down on the opening bars of "When Sunny Gets Blue."

"When Sunny gets blue...her eyes get gray and cloudy. Then the rain begins to fall."

Clay came in.

"Pitter-patter, pitter-patter, love is gone so what can matter... no sweet lover man comes to call."

The room started to list. Stanley grabbed the edge of the bar, took a sip of his Irish coffee and hung ten. Clay's playing was like a wave, fluid and surging. The young man on the stand was copping his licks, even playing with the rough edge that he, Stanley, had used when stumbling through one of his favorite songs last night by the water. And somewhere near the final bars he felt, no knew, that Clay had heard him before. Somewhere... sometime...long ago. And that's when he felt himself, for the second time in a little more than twenty-four hours, threatening to succumb to unconsciousness.

The lights went out. He fell forward into the darkness.

The faces that greeted him from high above were not the kindly concerned faces that had greeted Lee Ann several mornings ago when she'd regained consciousness and looked up from the cold concrete floor of French Market. No, the swimming sea of expressions that greeted him back into the world from above were twisted and cruel.

"...Fucking drunk...can't hold your booze, pal? Hope you have a designated driver."

And now there was another face. It was Clay's, saying, "Stand back! This man is my friend! Back up!" The crowd quieted slowly and retreated to form a cylinder of towering bodies and mumbling voices. "Are you all right?" Clay's face said into his. "Can you get up, or should we call an ambulance?"

Stanley's slowly revolving mind considered the question; his mouth said. "No...no...I'm okay. Just need some air."

Clay helped him to his feet and the two men made straightaway for the open front door and the refuge of the street. He called over his shoulder that the band would be back in fifteen.

The night was balmy; a slight breeze tamed the humidity that had gripped the city all that day. They found a quiet place on the curb a half block up from the din and settled down for a talk. After a brief silence, Clay asked, "How you feelin?"

"Okay...better...uh...let me explain..."

"No man...'sokay...take it easy."

Stanley sat staring straight ahead, thinking of Lee Ann's embarrassment a few days before—understanding now.

Clay took a pouch of tobacco and some papers from his shirt pocket and began rolling.

"Good thing we met the other night, Christian, otherwise I'd have thrown you to the lions. That's some rowdy crowd in there tonight, huh?" He drifted off.

"Yes, much obliged" They were silent for a moment and then Stanley said, "I think it's just that I haven't had much sleep these last few days and..." He blurted it out. "I was the guy you heard playing 'When Sunny Gets Blue' down by the river last night."

Clay swung round and faced him square on, unlighted, hand-rolled ciggy dangling from his lips. "No shit? *No shit!*"

"The same," said Stanley as he met Clay's high five.

"Man" was all that Clay could think of to say. He lit the torpedo, pulled in a lungfull and blew the smoke up toward the streetlamp. "Damn."

The two men sat for a moment absorbing it. Stanley motioned that he wanted a puff on the cigarette. Clay handed it over.

"Why do you play it in D?"

A reasonable question, thought Stanley; the standard key was indeed, E flat. "Hmm...well...I guess because D major is such a sunny-sounding key. And D minor is, as Nigel in *Spinal Tap* reminds us, the saddest key of all. So it seems to me that, since the song continually modulates so beautifully between major and minor, this juxtapositioning is amplified when you play the song in D."

"I see. Yeah, that's hip. And, man...I've got to tell you, something stirred in me, *deep* inside, last night when I heard you playing it down there by the water. I don't know, maybe because your tone on alto is so reminiscent of Bird's—Charlie Parker. A lot less finesse but..." Clay pulled up, looked at Stanley. "Oh well, you know, no one will ever play like that again. But your intonation, you get that from Bird, don't you?"

Stanley, with forearms on his knees, sat with hands clasped in front of him, looking down at a gum wrapper in the gutter. "Yeah," he said, "Bird is a big hero of mine. I've listened to him from the beginning, I guess."

"Mine too."

"I can tell." He glanced over at Clay, studied him for a moment, searched intently for any feature, any mannerism that might suggest the Bird of long ago.

Clay's hair was brown and bushy. Bird's had been brown and bushy, even from the time he was an infant. But that was no connection; millions of people have brown bushy hair. And the little rounded features of a five-year-old would be more than lost in the face of this man in his late twenties, with deep-set eyes, a prominent aquiline nose and thin cupid's bow mouth. No, there was nothing—either in his features, or his physique, or his movements—that he could in the vaguest way connect with baby Bird. It had all been left somewhere in the past. The only thing he could rely on was a deep gut feeling that this man was his lost son. He was the right age. He was a sax player who said something had stirred in his soul when he'd heard him play.

Stanley had played almost daily during the time Bird had been a toddler, up until the time he'd disappeared. But after he'd gone, Stanley had packed his horn away for what he thought, at that time, might be forever. So baby Bird had heard him often in the first years of his life. And yes, he thought a *mind*, even that young, would viscerally remember the music.

The man still studying a gum wrapper in the gutter wondered. What could he ask Clay that would be some clue to his possible connection with Bird? He decided to start at the beginning.

"Clay...where were you born?"

Clay, who had just finished rolling a second cigarette and placing it between his lips unlit, looked up and over at him. "Where was I *born?*"

"Hey Clay, Stanley!" A booming female voice from half block up heralded the arrival of Lisa Lynn. She came swinging toward them on her Lone Star legs as Clay sprang to his feet, closed the distance to her and scooped her up in his arms. They stood rocking and exchanging a lovers' greeting that Stanley, from ten yards away, couldn't hear. He rose slowly, stiffly, as they turned and, arm-in-arm, walked toward him.

"Hey, Stanley," Lisa said nonchalantly, "I hear you're going to play with Clay."

Play with Clay? This was certainly news to him. Clay and he certainly hadn't discussed it. And now it was a given? He felt a sudden urge to bolt and run.

"Yeah, c'mon, I gotta get back in there." Clay was just as casual.

"C'mon, you can play my alto. I'll play tenor. We'll do a duet of 'Sunny'. It'll be fun. You can redeem yourself with that pack of Mau-Mau's in there. Whaddaya you say?"

Stanley wasn't so sure he was up for all this youthful spontaneity. He hoped that Clay wasn't actually serious. "Yeah, and if I screw up, they can have me for breakfast, right?"

"No, I'm serious. You just do the melody straight ahead. I'll harmonize. And if you feel comfortable with that, then you can take off and run with it for a few bars. Don't worry, I'll keep you covered. C'mon, Stan my man, it's now or never."

And with that Clay threw an arm over his shoulder and with an arm already over Lisa Lynn's, they set off three abreast for the *Arabesque*. There was no way he could get out of this. Clay had made up his mind. This thing was going to happen. Stanley pumped up.

It went surprisingly well. Clay took the stand and rapped to the audience while Stanley wetted the reed on Clay's alto. He explained that the man who was going to be playing was the same man he'd heard last night down by the river.

"...he was so blown away by my imitation of him that it knocked him clean out." The crowd clucked good-naturedly. "Now that's what I call a fan!" And now there was a burst of applause as Stanley strapped on the alto and took the stand.

"So now," he explained, "we're going to do it together. So listen up." The crowd fell silent and settled back for the show. Clay opened it up with a familiar ascending run. The piano, drums, and bass came in, and the two men settled into a literal recitation of the melody of the song. After the bridge, Stanley held down some long notes and let Clay range out. Then the two of them took it out with two-part harmony and some alternating runs to the coda.

The crowd roared its appreciation as Stanley took a modest bow, unhooked the horn, placed it back on its cradle, and stepped down from the bandstand. "More! More!" The audience, appreciating the sound of an alto and a tenor singing so well together, wanted an encore. Clay held his hand out to Stanley who had already taken a place at the bar. He shook his head no. No way.

Clay explained that this was the first time they'd played together and that maybe tomorrow night, after they'd had a little time to feel it out, he could talk the man at the bar into a few more tunes. The audience groaned, but did not boo as he quickly moved on with introducing the next number. Stanley breathed a sigh of relief, grabbed an ice water, and joined Lisa at a table by the stand. She gave him a high five as they settled into the second set.

After the third and final set, Clay was packing away his horns and covering some last-minute strategy with the other members of the band.

"You two want to come over to my place and kick back with a nightcap?" Stanley asked Lisa. "I want to show Clay something, a couple of things actually."

"What?" Lisa asked.

"A surprise. But I'd like you both to be there."

"Sure, it's on our way to my place," Lisa said. "Yeah, we can stop for a minute, but then I've a got a mighty hankerin' for that man tonight. Y'all know what I mean?"

Lisa smiled wickedly and slugged him hard on the shoulder.

Clay joined them. "Am I invited here, or do you two have some business to finish up? Don't get into a slugging match with this woman, Stan, she'll kick your butt."

"Wouldn't think of it," he said moving outside Lisa's reach. "Say...was wondering...would you two like to stop by my place on your way home? Got something I'd like you to see. Can't tell you what it is yet...you've just got to see it."

Clay shrugged. "Yeah, sure, but it'll have to be quick. I'm bushed." He threw a sideways glance at Lisa who smiled back at him.

"Okay then, ready?" They nodded. "We're off."

34.

Jahna was rocking on her front porch, talking on her ancient cordless as the threesome approached. She pushed a button on the handset and laid it on the table.

"Hey, thought you were supposed to be getting your beauty sleep, Madame Leveau." Stanley teased.

"'s no use, don ya know." Jahna was sipping on a pipe, this time a long-stemmed church warden's.

"Do you folks know each other?" Stanley surveyed all their faces in one sweep, saw no recognition. He went on. "Jahna Leveau, this is Lisa Lynn...I'm sorry, you've never told me your last name."

"McKenzie," said Lisa quickly and shook Jahna's hand. "Pleasure to meet you finally. I've heard many things about you."

"Mmm," said Jahna quietly, nodding her head.

"And this is, Clay Hawkins, saxophone player extraordinaire."

Clay looked at him, shrugged good-naturedly, and then took Jahna's hand.

"I think we've waved a time or two as I've been passing. Nice to finally meet you ma'am." Clay took the old seer's hand and held it, did not pump it. They looked at each other for a moment, and Stanley noticed a light shade the old woman's eyes. He felt an even greater impatience now to move things along.

"Jahna, I have something I want to show these two. Would you like to come up and join us for a nightcap?"

"Naah, you folks g'wan bou your business...m' happy sittin here on de rocker." She plugged a Walkman into her ear, and Stanley was sure he heard, for just a split second, Black Sabbath.

"Okay then, here we go," he mumbled almost to himself.

A hard rock drum thumped in his chest as he led Clay and Lisa up the stairs and let them into his room. His eyes fixed immediately on the maroon and lime green contraption sitting on the top of the bureau, conveniently keeping company with a bottle of Remy Martin and some small tumblers. Stanley had put the squeezer there before leaving for the *Arabesque*.

Steady now—pour a couple of cognacs and step back and wait. Holy shit, he really did feel close to another faint as he watched Clay's eyes swing around and lock on the squeezer. Clay did an honest double take, and then his pupils began to glow demonically. And at that very moment, in those fierce glowing eyes...

Stanley saw Bird.

Though there was no physical resemblance to the boy who had wandered off twenty-two years ago, there was no mistaking the ferocity that came into Clay's usually calm brown eyes when he felt his binky was in danger of being taken away from him.

It was Bird.

"Where did you get this?" Clay snapped as he took two strides and came to rest standing beside the bureau. His hand went out and grasped the squeezer by its long green neck. As he turned and fixed on Stanley's eyes, none of the searing intensity had left his.

"It's yours, isn't it?" Stanley said, feeling simultaneously terrified and relieved. And now relief was winning and he felt his sinuses begin to sting.

Clay examined the squeezer carefully, seemed to notice scratches and nicks he recognized. "Yes...it was mine. *Where did you get it?*"

"Clay," said Stanley, trying to calm his own nerves, "take this." He held the tumbler out. Clay took it. "Let's sit down. We need to talk."

Lisa, who had been standing by watching all this, hadn't the slightest idea what was transpiring. She remained silent as the three of them settled into a chair and small sofa grouped about a coffee table. Clay sat by Lisa on the sofa, his glass in one hand, the squeezer grasped like a trophy in the other.

"Clay...you can have the squeezer. It's yours...I know it's yours. If you set it down, you could roll us a cigarette. Share one with you."

Clay smiled hesitantly, realizing that the squeezer was once again safely in his possession. For a moment, since he'd first seen it, he'd been feeling cool panic, wondering how he was going to get it back from this man. But no, this man had just given it back to him. But why? And how had he known it belonged to him? Had always belonged to him.

"Thank you," he said finally, nodding solemnly.

"You can't know how welcome you are."

Lisa, who was not one to be left sitting out on the corral rail for too long at a stretch, repeated Clay's query. "Where did you get it?" She knew that was a question still very much on Clay's mind and hers too.

Stanley took a sip from his glass and leaned back in his chair. The terror had passed, and now waves of almost sensual relief were washing over him. The Sun! He took a deep breath. "The first time I bought it was at a Sausalito flea market, about twenty-five years ago. And then I gave it to my little boy. It was his favorite toy. It was the toy he was carrying with him in a gym bag when he was abducted at age five." He paused, looked at Clay who looked up from licking a hand-rolled. Clay lowered the cigarette from his tongue and began spinning it in his fingers to pack and dry it. His eyes had grown soft again, curious.

"Several days ago, Lee Ann and I found this squeezer sitting in the window of an antique store down on Royal Street. We bought it because it reminded us of the child we'd lost twenty-two years ago. And when we took it back to the hotel and scraped the paint away and found blue under the maroon and green, and the original white enamel under that, well, we knew then that there was a good chance it could have been his...Bird's. You see, it was still painted blue when it disappeared with him. When he was abducted. When did you paint it maroon and green, Bird?"

It was Clay's turn to be in a state of shock, but his hands were steady as he lit the cigarette. Without taking a drag he handed it to Stanley. His brain was scrambling to keep up, connect everything, process what this man was saying to him. And what had he called him? Bird? Something reverberated.

"Bird? Why did you call me, Bird?"

Stanley felt his eyes welling up. "Because that was what we named you. Bird. In honor of Charlie Parker and the fact that you just flew into our lives. You see, you were abandoned in a basket in Golden Gate Park back in nineteen seventy-eight. We found you, sat with you for twenty-four hours, and when no one came to pick you up, we took you home with us. Do you remember anything about your first five years? Anything at all?"

Clay's wheels were spinning, desperately grabbing for traction, any kind of connection. Stanley could almost smell the smoke of burning rubber, hear them squealing. But no, there was only silence and a few street sounds in this deep southern morning.

"I..." he began and then put his hand to his head as if in synaptic pain.

"Take your time, man. You must remember something. You can't know how I need to know what happened. And you may think this sounds strange for me to say...but thank God you are alive and well. Can you imagine what it must feel like to have a child wander off and never come back? Severe mental anguish." Stanley took a drag on the cigarette and followed it with a less-than-polite slug from his tumbler. He looked over at the young man who was still deep in recollection. After twenty-two years or so, Clay began again, haltingly.

"I remember being in a place with hills...streets going up very steep hills. I remember a woman with red hair...very red hair. And feeding geese in a big pond with an orange-colored building at one end of it. It had a dome, like some ancient Roman ruin. I remember a sea with big waves, not like in the Gulf. San Francisco! You're from San Francisco aren't you?!"

Stanley nodded. "And my former wife, your adopted mother, used to be a carrottop natural redhead. You probably remember the Palace of Fine Arts Building down by the Marina...has a big pond with lots of ducks and geese. You used to feed them and then chase them around till they'd take back to the water. And, of course, the waves in the Pacific Ocean are, as you say, not the waves you see in the Gulf."

Lisa laughed. All this time she'd been mumbling to herself as the connections unfolded. "I don't believe this. I can't believe this. This is just too much!" She stood, walked over to the bureau, grabbed the Remy, and returned to the sofa. Sounded to her like they might be in for an all-nighter. She'd all but forgotten what she'd been thinking about earlier. Oh, this was going to be good.

Stanley continued as she refilled the glasses. "Where have you been for the last twenty-two years? Who raised you? Can you remember who took you away?"

"This is weird, really weird, but I only remember Port Arthur and then New Orleans and Pops, my dad. I didn't have a mother, never did. And I went to junior high here in New Orleans, over in Metairie. High school too. The only parent I remember was Pops." Clay paused. "Course I asked him early on where my mother was. He told me she died shortly after I was born. It's strange though. I do remember the point at which I first became aware of Pops. It was on a long drive. A very long drive, mostly at night. And then I was in Port Arthur for grade school, and then New Orleans after that.

"Was he good to you, your dad, Pops?"

"Pops? Oh, he was the best" Clay said with no little nostalgia in his voice. Stanley noticed that Clay's eyes had suddenly grown distant. Well, good, at least the son-of-a-bitch had been a good father and had left Clay with a good feeling for him.

"Where is he now? Your dad? Is he still..."

"Alive?" Clay finished Stanley's dangling question. He looked down into his glass. "Yeah. Yeah, he's still alive." He looked close to a breakdown. Lisa put a hand on his shoulder.

"Clay's dad is in a nursing home. He was a commercial fisherman, suffered a blow to the head about five years ago.

Some free-swinging rigging conked him and put him in a coma. He was in it for three years. He's awake now but still not able to speak, pretty much a vegetable." She trailed off.

"Lisa..." Clay glanced at her sharply.

"I'm sorry, Clay, I forgot." She looked at him for a moment and then went on. "He's severely impaired. He and Clay can only communicate on a mental level. Sorry honey. She put her arm completely around his shoulders and gave him a sideways hug.

"Lisa's right; Pops is getting better, but he'll probably never be totally back." Clay paused; he could see that Stanley was feeling both sympathy, and what was that other thing mixed in, anger? Oh yes, I guess you would feel some anger toward a man who abducted your son, even if that man was now only a vegetable.

"You probably were hoping you could meet Pops, weren't you? Would like to duke him out?"

"Yeah, you might say that. And I wonder, don't you know, I wonder if he really was your dad? Did you ever see your birth certificate?

"Yes, I have a birth certificate; it's at my place. I went down to Guatemala a couple of years ago, got a passport at that time. Didn't have any problem getting it, so the county records must have been good."

"Do you remember who is listed as your father and mother? What was your place of birth?"

"Pops...Clay William Hawkins was the name after father. And Alice Pauline Hawkins was the name after mother. Birthplace? Jefferson County, Port Arthur, Texas, June 16, 1978."

"June 16, 1978? Are you sure?" Clay nodded yes, a little irritated. "Sorry...course you are." Stanley hurried on. "We found our baby on July 30th, 1978, as I said, lying in a laundry basket under a eucalyptus tree in Golden Gate Park. He looked down.

Clay fell silent for a moment letting it all loop.

Lisa saw her opening. "And you just kept the baby? Didn't report it? Weren't you concerned..."

Stanley looked up. "That the parents would come back? That the authorities should be notified?"

"Something like that," wheezed Lisa.

"Well...we sat for twenty-four hours with him and no one came to claim him. Lee Ann had miscarried the baby she'd been carrying when we ran away to San Francisco. We were just a couple of hippy kids who had lost a child...and here was one for the taking. Funny, but we didn't think too much about it." He went on to tell them about the note they had left nailed to the tree and concluded by saying, "We got a few crank calls, but no one claimed Bird." Stanley looked over at Clay. "Do you have any recollection of being called that name?"

Clay said without hesitation, "No."

Stanley nodded. Bird had disappeared in mid-May, 1983. He would have been not quite five years old.

"I wonder how you got all the way to San Francisco from Port Arthur? I wonder why your parents left you to be found. I wonder why your dad, Clay, reclaimed you. I wonder..." Stanley hung his head and shook it from side to side. "I wonder..."

"So do I man. All I can tell you is that Pops told me that my mom died very soon after I was born. I've always wondered if it was somehow connected with birthing me. Pops never said that, but I have a feeling that's what killed her. And you know, maybe they were like you and Lee Ann...is that her name?" Stanley nodded yes. "Maybe they had me in Port Arthur and then put flowers in their hair and ran away to San Francisco." Clay sat up abruptly; a light had come on in his eyes. "Wait! I do remember Pops telling me that Mom's ashes are scattered somewhere around Tucson, Arizona, for some reason. That would fit wouldn't it? Two kids running away with a newborn, the mother gets sick and dies, the father reaches the destination with an infant in his arms, confused and desperate he leaves the baby in a highly public place to be found."

Stanley picked it up. "He watches from a safe distance until he sees who comes to the infant's rescue, follows them home, shadows his child's adoptive parents for four or so years, and then, unable to bear it any longer, snatches his son and beats it back across the country to his home in Port Arthur, Texas. Yeah, that could have happened. It's fantastic, but it works."

"So it also works that I am the person who you called Bird. I mean, my memories of the redheaded woman, early recollections of high hills and a big sea. And of course, the squeezer." Clay reached out and grabbed his machine by the neck, held it up like a trophy again. "The squeezer cinches it. I've had this thing for as long as I can remember."

Stanley nodded and collapsed in his chair.

"I can't believe this! This is all *too* unbelievable. That I should be the one to connect you two. And of course, the squeezer. If it hadn't been for that..." Lisa was cartwheeling with revelations.

"And 'When Sunny Gets Blue', "Clay reminded her. "I can't tell you what stirred in me the other night when I heard you down by the river."

"I used to play that tune often when you were a toddler. I'd get down on my knees and play it, and you'd come over and drop a rubber ball down the bell of my horn. I'd squeak and squawk like a strangled goose. Do you remember that?" Stanley blinked his burning eyes. "Man, we used to have fun."

Clay was silent as he sipped his cognac. "No, I don't remember that. I've told you pretty much all I can recollect clearly that far back."

"But you *do* remember a long drive with your pop? That was one of your first recollections of him?"

"Yes. And feeling that something was not quite right. That I shouldn't be going so far away from home for so long. But you know, Pops was always a charmer, and so kind and reassuring to me, always he was that way with me. I'm sure he pulled it off without too much protest on my part."

"You were always a social little guy," Stanley began, "no fear of strangers at all. Probably got that from Lee Ann." He caught himself. "Oh well, I know you weren't our blood son. I just meant the way she is so outgoing. She raised you that way. You had no fear of talking to absolute strangers."

"Still don't," said Clay. "Hmm, tell me something about your wife, ex-wife I mean, Lee Ann. Where is she right now?"

"Oh, she's a great lady!" Lisa broke in with the promo. Stanley let her roll. "She's a TV morning talk show host out in San Francisco. Wait til you meet her; you'll love her."

"Whoa, the woman who raised me for the first five years of my life, the woman with red hair, a TV talk show host! I've always wanted a mother. Man!"

Stanley jumped in. "You've got one now if you still do. And Lisa's right, she is a great lady, the redheaded woman, as you call her. And you two are both Geminis. I think I'll introduce you and turn around and run like hell."

"So when do I get to meet her? Is she out in San Francisco?"

"As a matter of fact, no, she's in Toronto at the moment with our daughter, Claire, finishing up some business. They're flying back to San Francisco tomorrow, but I'll wager my shorts we could talk them into a little side trip if we called them early enough tomorrow morning."

Clay sat nodding his head, listening. Stanley went on.

"Do you want to meet them? Or do you want to let all this sink in a little bit?" He rushed ahead. "I'm not sure how long I can hold out on Lee Ann; she cried like a baby when we scratched the paint on your squeezer and found blue...found that it was probably yours."

"Do I want to meet them? Of course! Let's give them a ring." Clay looked over at Lisa who was smiling and nodding yes.

"All right then. We'll give them a call about...oh say eight tomorrow morning? And see what they want to do?" Stanley looked at his watch: 2:45am. "'Spose you kids want to get some shuteye, hmm?"

Clay looked over at Lisa Lynn who looked back with hooded lids. She affected a mock yawn. "Mmm yeah, Clay, if we're going to get a run on tomorrow morning, I need to get some shuteye." She stretched her lanky frame like a cat and stood. The woman was a shameless flirt.

"Okay then, what say you drop by Lisa's tomorrow morning for breakfast, about eight, and we'll pick it up from there. Call the girls, drop the bomb as you say." Clay was collecting his sax, his squeezer, and his jacket.

Lisa was scribbling a map to her place as Stanley accepted the invitation. "Sounds good to me," he heard himself saying. He wanted to talk all night, but knew he didn't stand a chance against the new love he saw blooming. The three of them raised their glasses, toasted the grand discovery, and downed the rest of their Remy. Then Stanley walked them down the stairs to the street where they hugged in a tight little circle.

"Man, I can't believe what just happened to me." Clay shook his head, as they all moved back to say a final good-night; none of them really wanted to say goodnight. "I mean, wham! Bam! All of a sudden I have a fam!"

"Kin," said Lisa Lynn. "Now Clay has some kin. And he sure is lucky to have drawn you two. It's just all right as rain."

"Sure is," the two men agreed. A few more celebratory words went around and then they were gone, swallowed by the night. Stanley watched them round a corner two blocks down and turn out of sight. He was actually relieved to be alone. There was something he needed to do.

As he mounted the stairs to the porch, he felt it bubbling up like water from a cave. Collapsing in the chair where, just hours earlier he'd heard his fortune told, he buried his face in his hands and let it come.

But the tears of joy and relief didn't last as long as even he might have wanted them to. His mind was spooling with a thousand questions. Uppermost was to ask Clay where Pops was right now. Was he in New Orleans? Was he in Port Arthur? South America? Who was taking care of the old guy at this very moment? Young Clay? If Clay was still close to his father's care, then that would mean he, Stanley, would inevitably meet Pops. He wasn't sure that he really wanted to do that. At least not until the dust had settled. Old Pops, what a bandit that guy was.

It had occurred to Stanley on a number of occasions during their discoveries this evening to ask Clay more about his father, but early on he'd felt and seen in Clay's reactions how protective he was of his Pops every time he was mentioned. And so he hadn't asked. But tomorrow he would. And if Pops was still alive and kicking, even if it wasn't all that high, he, Stanley, would have no choice but to pay the old man a visit. "Hi, my name is Stanley, and this is Lee Ann. I thought you might like to meet and look into the eyes of two people whose lives you made a living nightmare." And then maybe he'd have Lee Ann shoot the mindfucker between the eyes. He scoffed at the idea. Well, he would have to be changing his attitude about Pops; he knew that.

Clay clearly loved his father.

He'd come full circle with his thoughts. No, he didn't want to meet Pops—ever. He squinted at his watch, could barely read it in this dim light: 3:06am. He'd need to get up about seven to make it to Lisa's by eight. That was less than four hours from now.

Jahna stirred in her sleep as she heard the silent creaking and groaning of Stanley's joints and bones as he pulled his stiff frame up the stairs to his room. How had Lee Ann referred to this coming down from shock? "Man Stan, I feel like I've been marathon bungee jumping." Lee Ann, sleeping soundly in Toronto. Boy was she in for a surprise tomorrow morning.

He laid for nearly an hour in the darkness, marveling at the serendipity of this reunion with his long-lost son. What cosmic power had finally seen fit to illuminate what had been, up until just a few short hours ago, the darkest corner in his life? He didn't know, but he said many silent, heartfelt prayers of thanks to it. And then sleep finally overtook him.

Deep, peaceful sleep.

35.

The phone rang at 9:00am. Toronto time. The girls had been up since six, making final preparations for their 1:00 p.m. departure for San Francisco. Claire answered.

"Hullo...oh hi, Dad, you're up early. Yeah, we're getting ready to shove off up here. Lots of last minute stuff...yeah she's standing right here stirring the oatmeal. You wanna talk with her? Okay." Claire handed the phone to Lee Ann who handed a spoon to Claire.

"Hi, honey, you're up early. You didn't? You did? Yes, but discovery or no discovery, you better be getting some sleep one of these nights or you're going to be falling out of the saddle." Lee Ann moved off to the living room.

"No, I'm not sitting down; should I be?" She walked to the couch and flopped back in the cushions. Claire sensing something was up, set the morning gruel off the burner and came and stood within earshot of her mother.

"Okay, I'm down...what's up? Yes. I'm ready, Stanley, get on with it!" There was a pause.

Claire was watching her mother's face intently now, picking up that old Sutro Tower buzz and crackle. Lee Ann's eyes suddenly snapped wide, her jaw dropped and went slack. What was it? What the hell was going on now! Did these people have no concept of rest?

"Are you *sure?* You are? You are? Looking at him right this very moment?" She put her hand over the phone and gasped, *"Your dad found Bird. He's with him right now!"*

Claire crossed the room in two long strides and pounced on the couch, practically in her mother's lap. She quickly reconsidered, rebounded off the cushions, and made a dash for the bedroom extension.

The four of them talked for over an hour, first Lee Ann and Claire with Stanley, then Clay with Claire, and finally Clay with Lee Ann. Stanley strained to patiently answer a succession of rapid fire questions that came pouring down from Toronto. He recounted for the girls the miraculous series of events that had resulted in his reunion with Clay Hawkins. They, of course, wanted to know all about him: what he looked like, what he did, where he'd been all these years, who had raised him—if he knew who had abducted him. At this point Stanley told Lee Ann that she should probably discuss that with Clay after she'd met him. Lee Ann, finally convinced that Bird had indeed been found, told Stanley in a squeaky voice that she wouldn't be able to talk for a few minutes.

So Claire took over. She told her father she wanted to talk to Clay for a minute. Stanley relinquished the receiver and sat back to catch his breath, watch and listen.

Clay talked briefly with Claire then and suggested that she and Lee Ann postpone their return to San Francisco and take a little side trip to New Orleans. "So we can all get acquainted," he said. He waited as Claire discussed this with her mother. Lee Ann came back on the line and accepted the invitation. They talked for a few more minutes, then Clay closed with "...all right then, Red, we'll see you and Claire tomorrow. This will be fun!" And with that, he handed the receiver back to Stanley.

"Hi, it's me again. Yes...yes, he is very handsome." He looked over at Clay who smiled and shook his head. Stanley listened for a moment and then said. "Can you cancel this late? Just eat the tickets to San Francisco? Uh huh...okay. Lee Ann, yes, of course I want you to come back down. Did you forget the last conversation we had? Okay, all right then. Do you want me to pick you up at the airport? No? I understand. Mmmhmm, uh huh...okay. Me? Well, after we eat breakfast, I'm going to go back over to my place and sleep till you get here. I feel like my wheels are gonna fall off on the next curve."

He gave her his address and phone number at Jahna Leveau's. She'd said she wasn't sure how soon she and Claire could get there, so they would just rent a car and drive on into town from the airport. He repeated again that he was going to sleep until they arrived.

Then they signed off jubilantly, with love, congratulating each other and giving thanks for their good fortune. Stanley replaced the receiver back on its cradle and leaned back in his chair.

Lisa, who had been cooking breakfast and drinking her share of freshly squeezed orange juice during this lengthy exchange, now came over and flopped down in Clay's lap. They squirmed and settled into one another.

"So, that's Lee Ann and Claire," said Stanley.

"They're some kind of whirlwind women, huh?" Clay stirred the air with his index finger.

"Got that right." Stanley looked over at the accumulation of legs growing out of the easy chair across from him. His own limbs suddenly felt leaden. No two ways about it, he was exhausted. "Man, you guys, I appreciate the invitation for breakfast, but I feel like I'm going to keel over in my tracks. Think I've had a total of about twelve hours of sleep in the last six or seven days. I gotta go pass out."

"Nah...Stan, boy I'm gonna shoot you. I cooked this ranch-hand breakfast for y'all, and dadgummit, you boys'r gonna eat eat eat..." Lisa, extended one of those cordial invitations you just couldn't refuse.

Stanley shrugged, dragged himself over to the table and saw just what he needed to eat before he slept for the next twenty-four hours: a big southern-fried breakfast: catfish and hash browns and eggs and grits. Clay was a lucky guy, a kickass cowgirl who could cook. Man it did smell good. He made his way through half a fish, an egg, and a small bowl of grits. Oh maybe just a few potatoes.

The next morning he hardly remembered Clay and Lisa loading him into Lisa's pickup and driving him back to Jahna Leveau's. Jahna told him the following day that he'd stumbled up the stairs and said hello to her, but he didn't remember even that. Somehow he must have changed into his pajamas, because that's what he found himself in later that afternoon.

36.

Time passes like a river.

Reality becomes a dream.

A dream becomes reality.

The Sioux Indians say that dreams are one's wish for the future.

What of nightmares then? What of the alligators swimming in River Time? Big vicious lizards with deadly crushing jaws.

There was a knock on his door. He moved over and opened it. He was startled by the visage of Kathleen. And what was that she was holding? Something wrapped in a blanket.

"Hey Stan, guess what I got for you?"

"Kathleen! God, 's been a long time."

"Sure has, you ol' mud dog. But looky here." She pulled the blanket aside and Stanley was suddenly peering into the face of a tiny cocoa-brown infant. "Stanley Hochstetter, meet your son, Jefferson."

He jumped back a foot—struck by a 440-volt line. "What?"

"That's what I said, Stan, your son, Jefferson Hochstetter the first."

Kathleen held the bundle out to him. She was wearing a carnelian-colored ankle-length dress scooped low at the neck. Her breasts were more full than Stanley remembered them. Well, of course, a nursing mother. And she was more beautiful than he remembered her to be. The rich rust orange of the dress glowed against her dark African skin.

Stanley ever so cautiously moved back in and held his arms out for the sleeping infant. Kathleen handed him over carefully, and soon a warm bundle of baby was snoozing in his arms. The infant, feeling light as a feather, stirred briefly and made little sucking noises with his mouth.

"Kathleen," he began in a whisper, "this is a beautiful baby, but it can't be ours. It's a newborn, and I haven't seen you for over a year."

"Oh, Stan, you are a big bad boy. You got so many girls slipping in and outta your bed, you don't remember that night back last September when I woke you with a knock on the door and, well, sort of stayed over? No, course you don't, sweet darlin. I was gone with the dawn, before you awakened...with little Jefferson on board."

Stanley, recovered from his initial shock, had moved along to an emotion hovering somewhere between panic and indignation. The baby must have felt it too, because suddenly his brown button eyes snapped open and he let out a squall that sounded like a miniature chainsaw springing to life. The less-than-overjoyed father designate instinctively bounced the bundle gently and looked with wide eyes between the tiny angry snarl of Jefferson and the don't-put-me-on expression of Kathleen.

"Where? When? I'm sorry Kathleen you're going to have to refresh my memory here. Last September? You dropped by? Excuse me, but aren't you married to Mr. Assistant DA Jackson Jerek? Could this be his son? Pardon me for asking."

The newborn was revving at full throttle now, so Kathleen moved over, scooped him out of Stanley's arms, dropped a strap of her dress, and plugged him in for a late lunch. The sight of mother and nursing infant stirred something deep inside Stanley. Maybe if he could just have a satisfactory answer as to when and where he and Kathleen had conjured this small person, then maybe he could get into this—a little bit at least. The baby was nursing voraciously now, making little cooing noises. Kathleen looked down at him and tickled his caramel-colored cheek with an index finger. Her nails were painted in the same shade of rust orange as her dress. Kathleen, what style she had. Stanley remembered how much he had—how much he still did—love her style.

There was another knock on the door. Kathleen didn't look up, acted as if she hadn't heard it. Time passed. Another knock, louder this time. Frozen in his tracks, Stanley looked toward the door. Who could *that* be? Jahna? Clay and Lisa? Lee Ann and Claire? The knocking came again, this time louder than before. And suddenly that switch between sleep and waking was thrown and he realized that he'd been dreaming. He surfaced quickly and opened his eyes. Yup, still New Orleans, and the knocking at the door was real. He heard a muffled female voice saying in a loud whisper, "Stanley, Stanley...are you there?"

He ran it through his Rolodex of voices. No mistaking it—that was Melissa Frank. "Line'm up...knock'm down," he mumbled to himself as he rolled out of bed and made his way across the floor to the door. "Just a minute. I'm coming." He reached for the knob and turned it. Suddenly his face was very close to Melissa's.

"Melissa..." he said, rumpling his matted hair. "Sorry. I was sound asleep. Come in, come in."

She walked to the center of the room and turned. Stanley closed the door behind her and turned to take her in. She was dressed as he'd never seen her before—in a putty beige suit and rust-colored silk blouse. Her space-black hair was twisted about her head and secured with two tortoiseshell combs. She wore short heels and pearls, looking as if she was about to fly first class somewhere to attend a power lunch. Stanley liked her better in her loose cotton dresses.

"Tomorrow morning I'm flying to Rio. I'm not sure I will see you again. At least not in the near future. I wanted to see you again. Say thank you, and I'm sorry about the other day."

Stanley stood with one hand on the doorknob, using the other to wipe sleep from his eyes. Melissa's rust-orange blouse was causing some kind of feedback loop to his latest dream. Kathleen draped in her carnelian-colored full length gown was still stuck sideways in his brain. The dream had been so real. Maybe he was still dreaming. No, Melissa was real. "Rio? When? What time is it?"

"It's six-thirty in the afternoon." She paused. "As I said, I'm leaving tomorrow morning, an eleven-thirty flight. I'm staying with some friends here in town. I've just come from my attorney's office...that's why you find me so." She indicated her attire with a downward sweep of both hands. "You look befuddled. Oh, I'm sorry..." She moved over to him and touched the side of his face lightly with an outstretched hand. "You're still asleep aren't you? And I come flying in here and awaken you. I'm sorry."

"Oh...no problem." Stanley smiled weakly. (No problem at all, come and visit me in my pajamas anytime, Melissa.) "I should probably be getting up now anyway. I'm just a little disoriented...was having a nightmare. But now that I think about it, I'm not sure it was a nightmare."

His eyes were still gritty with sleep; there was something strange about Melissa's face, but he couldn't seem to focus. She saw him squinting at her and turned away. "Would you like me to leave and come back? I could do that. Oh, I forgot, I've accepted a dinner invitation this evening."

"No, don't leave. Stay." Stanley heard her urgency, felt a bit of his own. He managed to say, "Uh Melissa, I'm feeling a bit surly. Could you make yourself comfortable while I slip down to the bath and brush my teeth, shave, take a shower? Ten minutes max. Then we can talk. Please stay."

She turned her face sideways to him, smiled, and nodded yes without speaking. He grabbed his khaki pants, a fresh shirt, his dopp kit, and a towel, and walked to the door.

"Okay...see you in ten."

She had already moved over to a small corner desk and was looking for something in her brown leather bag. "Yes, certainly, take your time. I have some beeznez to do."

Yes, certainly...take your time. I have some beeznez to do, thought Stanley as he made his way down the hall to the bath.

Was Melissa already thinking her life in Portuguese? There seemed to be a Latin huskiness coming into her voice and the sound of Astrid Gilberto in her accent. If that is all Melissa had been, simply a disembodied voice, he knew that he would search forever to find the rest of her. But that wasn't necessary; the fully embodied woman was sitting in his room waiting for him.

He was taking his time shaving, concentrating on steadying his hand, making sure not to cut himself. Then it was into the shower with a loaded toothbrush. He let the water, as hot as he could stand it, rain on the nape of his neck as he brushed his teeth with savage rapid strokes. A short blast of cold until he could stand that no longer and then he shut the C tap down. He stood listening to the last of the water gurgle down the drain as it had that morning a week ago when all this had started. Had it been only a week? It seemed like years in the past. What was Melissa up to now? Was she really as delicate and vulnerable as she seemed to be? Or was she just always playing some little game of survival? Survival might be a problem living with Poteet. He was obviously a man who seemed to take liberties with the normal channels that lesser mortals sculled down.

The river.

Some blackwater channels feed in and pollute it, some clear water tributaries flow in and purify and dilute it. He stood on the fire escape landing, wrapped in a bathtowel, cooling down, drying off from his shower—difficult in this humidity.

Melissa had removed her shoes and suit jacket and loosened the button at the neck of her blouse. She was working at the writing desk when he knocked softly and let himself into the room.

"Give me one more moment here," she said, not looking up.

He nodded, moved over to the bureau, and poured himself a drink. "Would you like a cognac? I'm having one."

"Yes, yes...that would be wonderful. The meeting with my attorney was deefficult."

338

He nodded. "So was my dream." A silence passed between them; then he went on. "Are your thoughts...is your thinking...in Portuguese now?"

Melissa looked up. "Why yes...how did you know that?"

"Your accent. I noticed it's becoming more pronounced."

She smiled, recapped an antique fountain pen, folded her day planner, journal, whatever it was, and tucked her business back into her purse.

"You can hear that?"

Suddenly the accent was gone. "Yes, I can. And please, don't change for me. I love the sound of your Portuguese, even if it is just the accent. I love the sound of your voice. I guess I've told you that, haven't I?" He felt unabashed, making this declaration. It would have been difficult to conceal the feelings he was having now, seeing and hearing Melissa here in his room. He poured a second drink for himself and walked over to her with hers. She stretched out her hand to take the glass, and for the first time, with his vision now clear of sleep, he noticed that one of her eyes was smaller than the other. Even her artistry with makeup couldn't conceal the swelling of her left cheek. She could see that he saw it.

"Melissa...what happened?"

She looked away from him. "Should I lie to you and tell you that I ran into a door?"

"You did? You didn't? What?"

"All right then...I ran into a door." She turned back to face him full on and raised her glass. "Here's to renegade doors and careless pedestrians."

He nodded, somewhat skeptical, and sipped his cognac. He'd drunk to crazier things. She tilted her head back and downed the whole short tumbler. She held it out to him. "Another please, if you don't mind?"

"Mmm...you did need that, didn't you?" He took her glass and returned to the bureau. So uncharacteristic of Melissa to toss back her booze. But then she always surprised him. He suddenly wondered how she would be in the country, jeeping up into the Rockies for instance. He would try to make this happen some day.

"No, I'm not going to lie to you, even for your own good," he heard her say behind him. "I'm leaving Jean Paul forever."

Stanley breathed a silent sigh of relief. He turned and returned with another half glass of Remy Martin for her. She took it and set it aside on the writing desk.

"Good decision, don't you think?"

"I didn't know for certain, but then he came home from Toronto in a foul, foul mood and found packing crates being loaded onto a moving van. I'm taking all of Stella and Jacquel's things with me this time...and my projects. I'm not leaving my work this time to be held for ransom."

"Also, good decisions, don't you think? And so Poteet flew into a rage, you argued, and he struck you?"

"Yes. He grabbed me by the wrist, threw me into his lap, hit me with his closed fist. He's very strong in the upper body. I couldn't get away. If it hadn't been for Sunjab, I'm afraid... well...I don't know."

"Sunjab found you? Broke it up?"

"Yes, and thank God it was he. He's the only man alive who can control Jean Paul, wheelchair or no wheelchair. He's a madman when he loses his temper."

"So you got away?"

"Yes, thank God. The movers were closing the doors on the van when Jean Paul arrived. He tried to stop them, but I sent them on. Otherwise, I'm afraid you would be finding me with only the clothes on my back." She paused, took a sip from her glass. Stanley remained silent. "Perhaps it's good that it ended this way; now I have complete resolve to carry through. That's what I was doing at the attorney's office this afternoon, getting a restraining order against Jean Paul. The judge was sympathetic, he knows the history."

"But, and you'll have to forgive me for asking this, how can you be sure that you aren't being followed by one of Jean Paul's little snoops? He has a few, as you well know."

"I can't. All I can tell you is...and I'm taking a chance in doing this...I need your complete confidentiality..."

"You have it. We all seem to be having problems with your ex these days."

"Yes, don't we?" She smiled at him and they drank to that; then she continued in an even tone of voice. "Well Stanley, all I can tell you is that I don't think Jean Paul will be bothering any of us in the future. You see I have some information that could destroy him. It's in a safety-deposit box—has been for several years. My attorney has a key and a sealed letter of instruction. I told Jean Paul about it in a telephone conversation with him this afternoon. I told him that my attorney was listening in. I told him if he didn't let me go, and leave me and my daughters alone, then I would simply make a single phone call and instruct that this information be made public. And that would be that."

"Whew. You two do play some kind of hard ball, don't you?"

Melissa rose, holding her glass, and moved off to the window. She spit her words now with thick Portuguese inflection. "I'm seek of eet. I'm true wid eem. I hate that man."

Stanley considered it a moment. Just a few short hours ago, he was feeling that he had lost both Lee Ann and Melissa. But compared to Poteet, he was the man of the hour. The irony of it nearly made him smile. But now Melissa was looking over at him, and what would she think of him smiling about what she'd just said. He repeated himself. "You're doing the right thing, Melissa. Believe that. Will you be safe in Rio?"

"Yes, I know this is right. I just wanted Stella and Jacquel to have a father. Yes, I will be safe in Rio. My parents live comfortably. It's a big house. There will be plenty of room for the girls and me until I can find a place for us. Yes, I'll be fine." She raised her glass, this time for a ladylike sip.

It had been dusk when he'd been awakened by her knocking. With the setting of the sun, the light in the room had slowly shaded to blue. "Do you mind if I turn on a light?" she asked.

"In a minute." He set his glass aside, moved over to her, and gently put his hands on her shoulders. "I'd like to hold you."

She looked up at him and set her glass on the window ledge. "I'd like for you to hold me." And with that she moved her body into his and slipped her arms up and over his shoulders. He cradled her gently as he felt her settle into him. They stood for a moment without talking, just moving slightly from side to side in a stepless, silent bossa nova. "Stanley..." she whispered against his chest.

"Yes?"

"I feel safe with you. I guess I've told you that before. I don't want to hate men. I..."

"Sshhh...it's okay. I guess we're mutually about as safe as we can be. Poteet is a loose, loaded cannon on both our decks, wouldn't you say?"

Melissa emitted a little scoffing noise, moved back, and smiled up at him.

"You're so beautiful when you smile."

"That's why I love you, Stanley." She searched his eyes. "You make me smile. You make me laugh. It's been so long."

"I'll be your court jester any day baby."

She looked surprised and then realized that he was being sincere, trying to further cheer her. Their eyes met and locked. Their faces moved slowly toward one another until they could move no farther. Lips met softly. She whispered, "Are we going to let this happen?"

He was silent for a moment, then fearful that she would hear his heart pounding. "No hurry," he said.

"No, none. I'll make a call."

"Good. But do I have to let you go for you to do that?"

"Yes, Stanley, you'll have to let me go. But don't forget what we were doing. I'll only be a moment."

He nodded as she slipped from his arms, retrieved her cell from her purse, scrolled to a number and pressed call. He found his glass and sipped while she waited for her party to answer.

"Yes, Angelique, this is Melissa. I've come over to see Mr. Hochstetter, as I mentioned I might. You and Carl go on to

342

dinner without me. I'll see you later. Don't wait up. I have a key. I'll see you in the morning before I depart. Good-bye."

She was obviously talking to a recorder. Good, it would be brief. She hung up. Stanley walked over, picked up her glass, and returned it to her. "To Rio," he toasted.

"To home," she returned. They drank to that and set their glasses aside again.

She moved back into his arms, speaking over his shoulder. "All taken care of. I'm free until..."

"Morning?"

"Yes."

"Can you stay?"

"Yes."

"Should we get comfortable?"

"Yes."

There was only a hint of light from the sky now. Streetlamps were coming on and throwing fleecy patterns of golden light on the walls and ceiling. He moved back and put his fingers on the second button down from the throat of her blouse.

"May I?"

"Yes."

He undid it slowly, and then the next, and the next. And soon there were none left to do, or undo. "I want to feel your body now...all of your body and skin next to mine," he said, his voice barely audible.

Melissa, who had been doing some unbuttoning of her own, slipped her hands out from under his shirt, pulled out the tail of her blouse and slid it off her shoulders. She slowly unzipped her skirt, let it fall to the floor, and stepped out of it. She was still wearing her slip. "This would have been so much easier if I were wearing my usual little cotton frock... wouldn't it?" She smiled. "I'm afraid you're going to have to give me a minute here, Stanley, I have to wear these clothes in the morning."

"I understand. Let me get you some hangers." Stanley, even in this dim light, sucked hard to pull in his ample midsection and moved over to the closet. He gathered some wire frames from the rod and walked back over to her. She had taken off her slip and pantyhose and stood folding things and arranging them on a chair.

She was being so fastidious. He wondered if she was a Virgo.

"I'm glad it's a little dark. I'm terribly shy about this, the first time I mean."

"You're beautiful...don't be nervous." He took the blouse she handed him and carefully buttoned it onto a hanger.

"I think that's all I really need to hang."

He nodded, moved back to the closet, and hung the rust-orange blouse for the night (he hoped). Melissa's voice came from behind him.

"Do you mind if I get into bed like this? I'm very shy."

"Certainly, I understand. So am I. It will pass." He turned around just in time to see her pulling both combs from her hair. It fell in a black shock down her back.

"I know it will." She whispered as she moved over to the bed and quickly slipped in under the sheets. Stanley slid out of his khakis and hung them over the back of a chair. He moved to the bed in his shorts, still trying to conceal the fact that he was pulling in his stomach. Soon he too was under the covers. They lay on their backs, apart, like an old married couple, staring at the ceiling.

"More comfortable now?"

"Yes, yes, I'm very comfortable now. Thank you."

"You're welcome."

Melissa laughed softly.

Their hands met in the space separating them and clasped.

"Whew, Stanley, I feel sort of shaky inside."

"Me too; shall we talk?"

"Mmm."

"I have something I'd like to tell you. Some good news."

"Yes, tell me." And with that she rolled onto her side. He followed suit. They moved into each other's arms and held each other close, but not tightly.

"You feel so good to me...your body. I'd like to sculpt you sometime. Do you think we could possibly work that into our future plans?"

"I hope so. I'd like to see how you see me. But now, tell me your news. I'm curious."

He spoke softly into her ear now. "Do you remember that first night we had dinner, when we were all getting acquainted, and we were telling you and Jean Paul about the early days in San Francisco? How we found a newborn baby, took him home, raised him, and then five years later lost him?"

"Yes, I remember that. Not really the kind of story one can forget."

"Well, my sweet, I found him! Last night we were reunited."

"No!" She moved back to take in his face.

"Yes! Most definitely, I *did* find him."

"Does Lee Ann know yet?"

"Yes, we told her this morning on the phone, Clay and I. That's his name now. We called him Bird, but his given name is Clay Hawkins."

"Before you tell me the story of how you found him...have you made plans to all meet?"

"Yes, we have. Claire and Lee Ann are finishing up some business in Toronto, and then they'll be flying down to New Orleans and we'll all be meeting. Within the next few days, I'd imagine."

"This is amazing Stanley. I can't believe it. I'm so happy for you. It must be such a relief knowing that he is...well...tell me the story now. This is such *good news!*" Melissa wiggled a little closer into his arms. He knew it would be like this.

They took a moment, readjusted their limbs about one another, then he started in. "It really all began when we found a juice squeezer in a secondhand store."

Stanley rambled on with the story as the two of them, lying close together, gently explored each other's backs with their sculptor's hands. Melissa stopped him often to ask questions for clarification or expansion of some detail. He carefully avoided mentioning Lee Ann as he knew it would make her uncomfortable and possibly prompt a specific question about when exactly the big reunion was going to take place. He felt a creeping trepidation about that reunion when she started to nod and drop off to sleep. Could Lee Ann make it to New Orleans by tomorrow morning? And would she be dropping by? Melissa was fading fast now. She was mumbling her responses, entering hypnagogic land. Still clad in her bra and bikini briefs, she felt warm and full next to him. Stanley felt himself fading too. He set his internal alarm for daybreak. He would wake Melissa then, perhaps they would make love, and then he would tell her that they best move along, as he wasn't sure when Lee Ann would be arriving. It was risky, knowing Lee Ann and how fast she could move, but it was a risk worth taking. He wouldn't give up this night with Melissa breathing softly in his arms for all the bossa nova in Brazil. No, this might never happen again. To sleep. To dream with the Portuguese. He fell into a still jungle pool somewhere high in the mist-shrouded hills above Rio.

37.

There was a knocking on the door. Softly at first, then very rapidly, harder and harder knocking. "Stanley! I know you're in there. Wake up! We're here. *Stanleeee!*"

He remembered afterward his first waking thoughts—his first waking words, "Oh God...oh sweet father of Jesus...it happened." He blinked his eyes; yes, yes, there was Melissa still in his arms. It had been a coolish night and they'd stayed close in each other's embrace. And it was still night; the street lamps now threw hard patterns of yellow light on the walls. And Lee Ann was pounding on his door saying something about "...*we're here!*" That could only mean one thing—that Claire was with her! This couldn't be worse. This meant that he was going to die. The Death card flashed like a neon sign at the back of his brain...

Death... death... death...*death*. Shit!

"Stanley! Wake up." More knocking.

"Okay! Hold on, I'm coming."

Melissa hadn't regained his level of consciousness but now was stirring. The first words she heard were from a male voice saying, "*It's Lee Ann...just stay put.*"

Her eyes snapped wide now; she uncoiled her arms and legs from his slowly. One doesn't move too fast when blood turns to ice. She groaned, pulled the sheet over her head, and did as she was told. He made his way over to the door, stumbling and groping on leaden legs "Uh...Lee Ann...is that you?"

"No, Stanley, it's two thin women from Venus come to carry you off in their spaceship."

He wished.

"Stanley...open the door!"

"Lee Ann?"

Long pause.

"What?"

"It's *not* a good time."

"Not?"

"*No.*"

"Oh."

Another long pause.

"Claire's here; she's with me."

"Hi, Daddy, are you being a *baaad* daddy?"

Stanley also remembered later that he just kept thinking—Mother F., this is not fair. This is *just not fair*. "Hi, Claire, how you doing?"

"Just fine, and it seems you are too, *bad* daddy."

He thought he heard Lee Ann telling Claire to shut up. Wasn't sure.

"Lee Ann, we're just going to have to take this up in the morning. I thought you would be calling when you got in."

And now there was a very long pause.

"Lee Ann?"

"Okay Stanley...I guess I understand," Lee Ann finally responded in a very husky voice. "Sorry this had to happen. I should have called. Hope it's Melissa...for your..." She didn't finish. He waited for her to finish. No, she wasn't going to.

"Call in the morning. Okay Claire?"

"Okay." said Claire.

He waited.

"Guess we're leaving now. Are we leaving now, Mom?"

"Okay, Dad, mom says we're leaving now. We'll call in the morning. Have fun." Claire could never resist twisting the blade. He heard them moving away from the door. Two pair of light footsteps echoed down the hall.

38.

He turned and made his way back over to the bed. Melissa was still buried somewhere under the top sheet. He wished he had time to admire the form she was making in the white percale. Unfortunately art didn't seem to be his forte at the moment. He got back into bed, but still she hadn't emerged from her tight white cocoon. "Melissa?" No response. "Melissa, I'm sorry this happened. I asked Lee Ann to call when she and Claire got in. I had no idea they'd be dropping by. What time is it?"

From under the sheets came another husky voice. "It's one-thirty am."

"I should never underestimate how fast Lee Ann can move. I talked with her in Toronto just this morning. I told her to call when she got in." He lied flat out, regretting arduously that he hadn't made that plan, but it certainly hadn't occurred to him that he would be having a woman in his bed this fine evening. He'd gambled and lost. Now he was not only a loser but a liar. Tomorrow, bright and early, he would begin reconstituting his self-esteem.

"Do you have any idea how mortified I am?" came a voice from under the sheet. And then Melissa's face emerged, and he found himself looking into her plaintive eyes. One large one, and one not so large. Yes, she looked mortified and sad and near the edge of emotional devastation. "Can you explain?"

He wasn't sure what she was referring to, but took a stab at it. "You mean how this could have happened? How I could have been so stupid as to let this happen?"

"No," she said quietly. "No, I mean to Lee Ann. She knew it was me. She knew I was here. Did you hear what she said?"

How like Melissa to be thinking of how Lee Ann would be feeling right now. He marveled at her class. "Can I explain? Oh maybe...in ten years or so." He sighed. "Right now I can't help thinking how I would be feeling if I was in Lee Ann's shoes."

"We shouldn't have done this. I shouldn't have done this. I knew...you told me...that you and Lee Ann were getting back together. I seem to have a talent for messing up lives."

"Wait! Wait just a minute." He couldn't let it go that way. "You should talk with Lee Ann before you come to that conclusion. I don't think she would tell you that we were 'getting back together.' I don't think I was feeling that was happening either, or I wouldn't be here with you right now."

"I should go." She rolled to a sitting position and set her feet squarely on the floor.

"You think that's best?" Melissa was silent, so he went on. "Do you have to leave? I mean, the damage has been done. Besides, Lee Ann and I have an agreement."

She spun around and glared at him. "And what ees *that*?"

He recoiled at the sight of her fierce eyes but responded quietly. "No strings attached."

Melissa spat her words now. "You mean you both sleep around? I'm glad we didn't..." She didn't finish.

"Melissa...no...settle down...that's not what I meant at all."

"I'm sorry," she said softening infinitesimally. "Can you explain to me what is going on?"

He considered it a moment—shook his head. "I'm sorry too; can *you* explain to *me* what is going on?"

"No."

They listened to the night sounds for a moment. Stanley couldn't help thinking that if Melissa had been Lee Ann right now, in this very place, under these same circumstances, she wouldn't be here right now. Lee Ann would have been already dressed and out the door. Not Melissa. She sat sleepily on the side of the bed, her hair loose and falling over one shoulder. She no longer seemed to be self-conscious about the fact that she was clad only in her underclothes.

"Should I go?"

"I wish you wouldn't."

"All right then. But I can't tell you how long I'll stay. I'm a little confused."

"Love?"

"What?"

"Love is confusing isn't it?"

She nodded. "Yes...yes it is."

Stanley felt a need to open up, leaven things a bit. It may be now or never; Melissa had seen to that.

"It's funny, isn't it?" whispered Melissa.

"Love?"

"Yes."

"If I don't see her each day, I miss her. Gee, what a thrill... each time I kiss her. Believe me I've got a case...of Nancy with the laughing face."

"What?"

"Those are the words to an old song I used to play. It's called 'Nancy.' I always learned the words to songs I'd play.

Melissa was softening by noticeable degrees now. "And what are the other words?"

He pulled himself up against his pillow. "I don't think I can remember the whole song."

"I liked those words," she said and repeated them. "If I don't see her each day I miss her...and then how does it go?"

"Gee, what a thrill, each time I kiss her."

"Yes, and then what?"

"Believe me I've got a case...of Melissa with the Rio face."

"Stanley..." Melissa pulled her feet off the floor and rearranged herself on her side facing him. Even in the dim light he could see she was smiling now. "You're changing that part, aren't you."

"I am?"

"Yes, you're bad, you know."

"I am? I do?"

She laughed. "Okay, so what are the rest of the words to that song about Nancy with the laughing face?"

"You want to hear them all?"

"Yes, eef you can remember."

Portuguese again. Good she was relaxing.

"Okay, so then it goes, '...She takes the winter...and makes it summer...summer could take some lessons from her. Picture a tomboy in lace. That's Nancy with the laughing face."

"Does that remind you of Lee Ann?"

"No, do you want to hear the rest?"

"Yes."

"Okay...so then it goes to the bridge."

"The what?"

"The place in the song where the interlude begins."

"Yes, the bridge. I'm ready."

Stanley wondered off hand how it would be to go swimming with this woman somewhere on a beach up the coast from Rio.

"Okay, so the bridge goes, 'Do you ever hear mission bells ringing? Well she'll give you the very same glow. When she speaks you would think it was singing, just hear her say hello.'

"Then it goes back to the chorus. 'I swear to goodness you can't resist her, sorry for you, she has no sister...'"

Melissa laughed again.

"'No one can ever replace...my Nancy with the laughing face.'"

"That's it?"

"There's a whole other verse, but I can't remember it."

"He really loved her, didn't he? The man who wrote that song for his Nancy."

"Yes, I'd say he did."

"Who wrote that song?"

"Phil Silvers."

"Silvers...Silvers...I don't know of eem."

"He was really a comedian, late sixties, early seventies. A TV comic...had his own show."

"And he wrote this song?" Melissa's voice had become almost squeaky with huskiness.

"You sound like you're getting laryngitis."

"No, it will be all right as soon as I'm back home."

"Back home?"

"Yes. I don't know, it's too difficult to explain. All I can tell you is that I'm going home. After five years, I'm going home."

"You love Rio."

"Yes, very much."

She'd nudged her way over to him. "Will you come and visit me there?"

"You want me to?"

"Yes, I want you to. I want you to come and meet Jacquel and Stella. And I want you to sculpt me, as you said you would"— she tickled him—"like to do."

"All right then, it's a date. Do we have a when?"

"No. Not yet. I will give you my address. We'll write."

He fell silent thinking about the fact that he hated to write. Especially letters. Was it time to learn? He'd rather be talking with a cordless tucked under his chin, working with his hands on some new creation. The mud. He suddenly realized he was missing the mud.

"Will you write to me?" he heard Melissa ask at his side.

He rolled over to face her. "Yes, we'll write."

"I should go."

Time passes.

"Is it just me, or do I keep hearing an echo in here?"

Melissa laughed huskily. Stanley grabbed her, smothered her mouth with a kiss. She writhed as if to get free, so he relaxed. She fought for a moment longer and then realized that he'd retreated and fallen back. "It would be lovely making love now; what do you think?"

"I don't know...what do you think?"

"I think you should come and sculpt me in Rio."

"Final decision?"

"Kiss me please, gently."

He pulled her to him, found her mouth.

Their lips parted slightly and he tasted her. It lasted a moment and then it was over. "Will you be okay with this? I really don't think it is meant to be just yet. This is not some coy female ploy, Stanley. I just don't. Can you understand?"

All trace of the accent was gone now, except for what he remembered in the beginning, and that was the sleepy southern roll on the telephone—a couple of light-years ago. It was Melissa of the south. He wondered how many men she'd dangled.

"I do understand," he heard himself saying as he swung his legs from the bed. "And now I need a bath."

"You're leaving?"

"Just for a bath."

"Do you want me to stay?"

"If you like."

He'd made a Lee Ann exit as he'd said, "If you like." And suddenly he was on the other side of the door, on his way to the bath. Getting much too complicated in there. Always retake your ground when things begin to get too complicated. It was a little lesson he'd learned somewhere far back on the trail. He locked the door of the small lavatory and turned on the hot tap. Steam rose up and poured through a transom vent. He was surprised to find that a wood casement window still slid in its tracks. Steam now poured out the window but still filled the room. The mirror above the washbasin ran with sweat. It was good to be back in his own reality. Melissa could be a bit too hypnotic at times.

He lowered himself into the hot water. "Gotta get ready for hell, man," he heard himself say. "Gotta feel the heat, get ready for the fire."

She was gone when he let himself back into the room. His eyes locked on the chair where she'd hung her clothes. Gone! And now his eyes swung around and fixed on the writing desk where a note would have been left. Nothing! He moved in for a closer look. Nothing, not one trace that she'd even been there, except for her lingering perfume. Bitch, he thought. She really does like to play games. He felt weak. Emotionally stripped. Empty. How could he ever get in touch with Melissa Frank in Rio de Janeiro. Frank probably wasn't even her parents' name. The Franks of Rio? Just didn't fit. But then again, maybe it did?"

He picked his watch up off the bureau: 2:45am. Two fucking forty-five in the morning and he had to face the wrath of the goddesses bright and early. Any possibility of sleep? Melissa, damn it, a simple note makes such a difference.

He made his way over to the bed, peeling off the towel as he went. The sheets were cool and still strongly scented with woman. As he settled back in the dim light to soothe his indignation, his leg brushed against something scratchy. His hand went down like a shot, seized the leaf, and pulled it up from under the sheets. It was handwriting—had to be Melissa's. He scrambled for the switch on the bedside lamp, nearly knocking it over as he turned it on. And now he read:

Dear Stanley.

I love you very much. You are like no man I have ever known.

I know that you wanted to make love with me, but somehow it was still too soon for me. Please, I hope you can understand. And besides, isn't it precious what we feel? I know we will meet again soon. Here is my address in Rio.

You are dear to my heart.

M.

Below a flowing signature of a single M was her address and telephone number in Brazil. And under that a very soft imprint of her mouth, in a taupe shade of lipstick. Probably not the kind of note one would ever throw away thought Stanley, as the ceiling dissolved and he floated up into a fragile morning sky. A sky now filled with pink cumulus clouds.

39.

Then morning actually did come, too soon, as it often did for Stanley. It couldn't have come sooner for Lee Ann. She hadn't slept a wink.

Could you blame the poor girl? Her brain felt like vermicelli. No matter how many times she told herself that she had no right to feel jealous, she was jealous—and that could mean only one thing. She wanted Stanley back. But she didn't really want Stanley back. Well yes, she did in a sense. Well no, she really didn't, now that she thought about it.

She wrapped up this concise analysis of her feelings by concluding that she was being a blindly possessive female. Oh boy, did she ever need to have a talk with someone. She decided that someone should be Stanley—cut to the chase.

Claire and she had checked into Le Richelieu at 1am this morning and then, at the insistent promptings of Claire, gone over to pay Stan a little surprise visit—probably arouse him from a sound sleep. It had sounded last night like they'd done that. Who in hell had he been with? Stanley had either suddenly discovered street walkers, or else he was having a little tryst with Melissa. Who else could it be? Jeez Stan, that was fast.

Claire ordered breakfast brought up to their room. Lee Ann ate hers hurriedly and then went out onto the deck to pace and fidget. Now she made her way back into the room.

Claire kept her mouth shut while, out of the corner of her eye, she watched her mother reenter. She knew well when her mother was in one of her witchy moods because she had the same moods. Thank God for *The Times Pacayune* and a crunchy

English muffin. She felt her mother looking at her so looked up from her paper.

"What?"

"You know what I'm really pissed off about?"

"Can you get it in before we leave New Orleans?"

Lee Ann cracked and laughed. "That's why I love you sweetie. No, I probably can't."

"Try."

"Okay, so we bust our butts to get down here as soon as possible, and then Stanley is *tied up!* And then we have to wait until morning to hear about Bird...I mean Clay!"

"Do you think she had him tied up? You think Melissa's into that kind of party time?"

"No, Claire, stop clowning, and besides we don't really know that it was Melissa. We don't even know if he was with someone. But for all we know, maybe he's discovered young boys."

"Ma! Stanley? Jesus!"

"Maybe he was in full drag and makeup."

"Ma! I'm trying to eat here... you're making me sick."

"You deserve it. You make me sick some times." She was smiling as she said this.

"Oh, nice, Mother."

"I suppose I should call him now." She shook her head. "But I don't want to call him. I don't want to talk to him or even see him ever again! I had a whole notebook full of questions to ask him before we met Clay today, and he made me wait till morning. I'm going to tie him up and drip water on his forehead for that."

"Can I help?"

"What, drip water on his forehead?"

"Ha...sure...no...want me to call him?" Claire asked.

A little scheduling meeting with Stanley; she could handle that. She walked over to the bed stand and picked up the receiver. Lee Ann had left the number for Jahna Leveau's Rooming House on a scrap of paper by her cell. Claire dialed. It rang six times; she'd give it ten. Maybe he was still in the middle of something.

Maybe he was still in the middle of Melissa. Ha! The thought of it was delicious to her. Something about this southern air was making her hornier than a mink and even voyeuring on sex was ringing her bell. She hoped some day she would get to meet Melissa.

On the tenth ring, she started to lower the receiver when she heard someone pick up and say hello. She raised the receiver quickly back up to her ear.

"Hi, Dad? That you?"

"Claire? Yes, I was down the hall, shaving. I'm out of breath. Just a minute. How's your mom doing?"

"She's pissed."

"I can imagine. You mad at me too?"

"Me? Naw, I'm just along for the ride, as usual. Oh, don't get me wrong; I want to meet my long-lost imaginary brother. I just mean..."

"I know. He's always been some strange mythical creature to you, hasn't he?"

"Could say that."

"You'll be meeting him today, I hope."

"That cracks me up Dad, that his name is Clay. And you a ceramics guy."

"I know, that's occurred to us too." He paused. "I talked with him on the phone just before I went down to shave. He and Lisa, his new girlfriend, want to have some late lunch...early dinner at Brennan's. How's three pm sound?"

"I'll check. Does that mean that we won't be seeing you till then? Might be a good idea to have a little powwow with your ex before we appear bright and shining to the Birdman and his lady friend."

"What's the temperature like over there? I know how I would be feeling right now. I'm sorry this happened."

"What happened?"

"Melissa dropped by late. Did your mom tell you about Melissa?"

"Some."

"She's become a good friend."

"You mean a lover?" If Claire had been a brain surgeon, she would have operated with a chainsaw.

There was a long pause. "No, not lovers in the way you mean."

"Okay, so Melissa dropped by and you fell asleep on the bed talking. And then we came over to play and the shit hit the fan."

"Claire...you're always so concise."

"Saves time."

"Yes, that's what happened, essentially.

"You want me to relay this information?"

"At least it was Melissa." Claire heard her mother mumble behind her.

"Yes. Let her adjust to it and then call me and we'll set a time to meet. Is that a plan?"

"That's a plan, Stan."

"Okay then, bye, Claire."

"Bye, bad Daddy."

Stanley stood wrapped in a towel, breathing deeply. Okay, that hadn't been as bad as he'd expected it to be. And thank you, Claire, for refereeing. He put on his khakis and his last clean shirt and walked around the room, wondering what to do to kill the time until Lee Ann called back. Now it was his turn to wait. He thought about calling Evie Ester at Genoa. He'd been gone a week, and she was probably having second thoughts now about sending him off so jovially to New Orleans: one of her primary current producers was obviously not currently producing. No, he couldn't call Evie; that would tie up the phone. Damn. He wandered over to the writing desk and sat down; there was the faintest trace of Melissa's perfume lingering there.

Business to discuss with Evie:

1. Have someone dig front door out from under ad circulars. Water plants.

2. Tell about new clay—and Mary Mythe.

3. Lie about getting tons of new ideas down here in N. O.

4. Lie about how great things are going with Lee Ann.

5. Tell about Bird.

6. Anymore checks in? Any more sales after the show?

7. ETA San Francisco.

Yes, those were some items. ETA San Francisco? He wasn't sure about that. A week ago he and Lee had bought one-way tickets down here; he supposed it was time to decide now and book his return, but he really wasn't in any hurry to get home. New Orleans was getting hotter and more humid by the day, but he was getting used to it. And Clay had said he'd like to play some more with him. Hell, he thought, he could stay for that alone. And when that wasn't happening, there was plenty of room to work here in this loft apartment. He could take it for another week. It suddenly occurred to him to stay as long as he liked.

The phone rang. He walked over to the bedstand and picked it up.

"Hello."

"Hi."

"Oh, hi." Pause. "How're you doing this morning?"

"Not all that great. I didn't sleep." Long pause. "Stanley, we need to talk. Claire's going to hit French Market solo. I'd like to come over there and then walk on down to meet her. Talk on the way? How does that sound?"

Lee Ann's tone was even...controlled. Maybe a little too even and controlled; like a bomb ticking away quietly, counting off its seconds to self-destruct.

He decided he was being too dramatic.

"That sounds like a plan. Did she tell you about Brennan's at three? I need to let Clay know."

"Yes, well, hopefully we can get things back on track by then."

"What's your prognosis?"

"I don't know, Stan. I'm feeling pretty confused right now about what's going on with me. Not you and me. Just me."

"I understand. Completely. I've been trying to put myself in your place...reverse the situation to see how that felt. Doesn't feel all that good. You're right, we need to talk...alone. When are you coming by? Or do you want me to come over there?"

"No, I want to see your place, possibly meet Jahna, if she's around. Obviously I know how to get there."

"Lee Ann, you've always known how to get there."

"Don't you dare try to make me laugh."

"Wouldn't dream of it. What time?"

"About eleven-thirty...that okay with you?"

"I'll be here."

"Alone?"

"Yes, Lee Ann. I'm alone right now. I'll be alone when you get here. See you at eleven-thirty."

"Goodbye forever."

"Huh? Oh right. Okay; goodbye forever."

She hung up.

Whew, okay, I think we're going to salvage the day after all. He dialed Lisa's number and left a message on her machine. Then, after calling Evie in San Francisco and taking care of business, he walked down to the porch with a sketchpad and a big fat No.2 pencil.

To wait.

40.

"So, it's back to the Blue Hills of Wisconsin, huh?"

Clay and Amanda sat side by side on the doorstep of her dented and rusting VW minivan.

"Yeah, for starters," said Amanda.

"You think this thing will make it?" Clay said, thumping the sad little bus.

"Will unless you beat it to death." Amanda rocked over and bumped his shoulder with hers.

"You got enough money to make it up there and get settled?"

"Yeah, I have a stash. It'll get me there."

"You going to stay with your friends then for awhile?"

"Stop worrying, Clay; it's dear, but I've got plenty of kin and kind in that neck of the woods. I'll be fine." Amanda looked over at him. "You look like a little boy who just got caught with his hand in the cookie jar."

"Ha...yeah."

"It's all right, Clay, you know, we're ending as friends. You know I just about died down here last summer with the heat. I'd have probably left even if you hadn't fallen in love with Lisa Lynn McKenzie."

Clay nodded.

"I like her. I think she'll be good for you." There was a silence. Amanda went on. "She moving in here, or you going to move over there?"

Clay, at her side, flinched. "Uh, neither. That's way ahead of where we are right now. I think I'll try it solo for about twenty years, then we'll see."

They both sat looking at their hands, Clay wishing fervently that he could have a cigarette. But Amanda was a converted non-smoker and had become Pentecostal about his habit. If he rolled one and lit up, she'd probably leave immediately. He wasn't ready to say good-bye, not just yet.

"You're wishing you could have a cigarette?" She'd read his mind.

"Yes, as a matter of fact."

"So am I."

"Good, wouldn't want to suffer all alone."

"Well, now you'll be able to smoke around the house to your heart's content."

"Nah, you've probably cured me of that. Does stink up the place."

"Speaking of stink. Don't forget to wash your socks."

"Oh, thanks, I won't. You're so romantic."

"Mmm." Amanda drifted off. "It was good, wasn't it? I mean our lovin, while it lasted."

Clay slipped his arm around her shoulder and pulled her tight in sideways. "Yeah Mandy, some of the best." And he wasn't kidding.

"I'll send you a postcard with my address in Wisconsin. Will you write to me? Can we stay in touch?"

"I will. We'll stay in touch."

"So I guess it's that time." Amanda stood and smoothed her full-length cotton rag of a dress. She walked around the van and opened the door. Clay followed her and put his hand on her shoulder. She turned, and they took each other in. The hug lasted a long time. Finally Amanda moved back—her eyes were moist. "Okay then... you know I love you, Mr. Blue."

"I love you too, Man."

"Okay then." Amanda leapt up behind the wheel of the van and fired the tiny sewing machine engine. "I'm outta here." She popped the clutch, and the minibus moved out onto the street. Clay watched as she drove down a block—threw him one last kiss—turned the corner, and was gone. He stood for a moment looking at the place where her van had disappeared around the corner, then climbed a half flight of stairs, and walked back into their tiny house. It felt immense.

The phone rang. It was Lisa saying that Stanley left a message on her machine confirming that their tentative plan for Brennan's at three was a go. Clay groaned. Lisa asked him what was wrong. Wasn't he excited about meeting Lee Ann and her daughter?

"I just walked in from saying good-bye to Amanda and now you call to say that I've got to go meet some weird family that I had in the past...that I only at best vaguely remember." There was a silence on the other end of the line. He could tell she wasn't convinced. He went on. "The music isn't going all that well either. We had a lot of problems this morning at rehearsal."

"You're stretched and stressed, Clay Hawkins?"

"You might say that."

"How did it go with Amanda?"

"Fine. We parted with a friendship intact."

"That's good. It was getting pretty rough between you two there toward the end."

"Could say that."

"I'm over at the bar right now. I'm off at one-thirty. You want me to come over there and give you a back rub?"

"No, honey, I appreciate the offer, but you know where that would lead. I think I need to grab the horn, go down by the river. Air out."

"Okay then, come on over to my place around two; we'll head on down to Brennan's"

"All right...sounds good?"

"Okay," Lisa paused. "I was just kind of hoping..."

Clay broke in. "Just need some time to space right now, babe. Before I meet the family this afternoon."

"It'll be fun, Clay. Believe me, you're going to love Lee Ann. And remember darlin', she held you when you were a little baby, changed your diapers n'then lost you. I'd imagine those kinds of memories would stay with a person. Wouldn't you?"

"Thanks, Lisa...needed that."

"Know you did. See you around two over at my place. Blow your brains out."

"You're sweet."

"You are."

"Bye."

"Bye."

He sat for a moment listening to the receiver hum in his ear. That Lisa, what a solid woman she was. He wondered if he was in love with her, concluded that he didn't know about that yet.

41.

A half block up the street she heard the sound of laughter coming from the front porch of Leveau's Rooming House. She slowed her pace and moved along, listening to the animated conversation that was coming from the two people she could see seated there. It was Stanley, with a sketchpad in his lap, but she couldn't make out the person he seemed to be drawing. She could hear her voice though. It was a low contralto, black, she thought, with a lilting Caribbean accent. She still couldn't make out what the woman was saying. Stanley was working intently, smiling at whatever it was.

He looked up and saw her coming down the street in her white madrigal blouse and loose cotton skirt. Her hair was pulled back in a low ponytail, but all around, those recalcitrant wisps hung down. "Hi," she called a little shyly.

"Hi, Lee."

He set his sketchpad aside, excused himself, and walked down the stairs to greet her; wanted to give her a hug, but could see she wasn't in the mood for that. Yes, it was sadness that he saw around her eyes, and Lee Ann didn't fake that. His hand went out and grasped hers.

"C'mon, there's someone I know you've been wanting to meet."

They climbed the stairs still hand in hand, and then she pulled hers back and stood facing the skinniest old black women she'd ever seen.

"Ms. Jahna Leveau, meet Lee Ann Barnes."

Lee Ann moved over quickly and shook Jahna's boney hand. The old woman remained seated in her rocker. "Pleasure to finally meet you; Stanley's told me so much about you. We met your sister the other day."

"Ayeee, she told me. Stanley tells me you will be meeting your long-lost son dis afternoon. De one you called de Bird. You must be joyful."

Lee Ann's eyes snapped wide. "More like scared out of my socks, and I don't know why."

"Are you 'fraid 'e will no like you?"

She considered it a moment. "Maybe that's it. I really don't know. My stomach's been doing cartwheels ever since I heard his voice on the phone for the first time."

"Ahhh...yes...well, you were his mudder when he was a little baby. Did you nurse him?"

Lee Ann glanced at Stanley who smiled warmly. She had fed Bird with formula until her own milk had come. And it hadn't been any too soon. Baby Bird didn't like the Simulac one bit.

"Yes, a woman told me that if I let him nurse after his bottle that my milk would come. And it did...surprisingly fast."

"Ah yes, is a meericle dese cawnections dat life makes for us."

"True." Lee Ann felt a need to change the subject. She had some strange sensual feelings about all this. She wondered if Stanley was having them too. That might be a good way to get into talking about what was going on between them.

She turned toward Stanley. "Could I see the drawing?"

Sculptor turned quick sketch artist had faded back to the sidelines, but now, on cue, he nodded, picked up the tablet, flipped back the cover leaf, and held his work up for the two women to see. He watched Lee Ann's eyes move about the drawing, taking it in.

The sketch was a full body rendering of the old woman seated in her rocking chair. It was done in rapid strokes of a soft graphite pencil. The background suggested the Esplanade with its overhanging gums and elms.

"Haven't lost your touch," she said. "Is it finished?"

"It is for now."

She nodded. "Well, I suppose we ought to be going. I told Claire we'd meet her at the market at noon. Thought you might like to catch up with her news before we headed over to Brennan's."

"That'd be good," said Stanley, knowing they had more than Claire's news to catch up on. Lee Ann was being cool but not in the least hostile.

At least that was a running start.

They bade Jahna farewell and climbed the stairs to his room where she stood looking around rather wistfully. He stowed his sketchpad and loaded some cash into his wallet. As he did this, he watched her out of the corner of his eye. He knew she was thinking about the previous evening, was seeing Melissa in his bed. It was painful for him to see her like this. "Okay, all set. What do you think of the place? Pretty indigenous, wouldn't you say? A room in a rooming house in New Orleans..."

"Yeah," she said flatly as she turned and headed for the stairs.

He followed her back down to the porch where they had some more parting words with Jahna.

**

Moving south down Esplanade in the direction of French Market, they walked a full block side by side without speaking. Finally Lee Ann broke the silence.

"I hate you, Stanley."

"I know."

Silence again for another quarter of a block.

"Bad timing for old Stanley. What's new?"

"Are you with...are you going to be with Melissa now? Are we all going to be sitting down for dinner one of these days real soon?"

"It's not like that, Lee Ann. Melissa's left Jean Paul; she's in the sky, winging her way home to Rio"—he glanced at his watch—"as we speak."

"Left Poteet! Rio?"

"That's what I said. Yes."

"Good for her!"

"Yes, good for her." They walked along in silence another short distance, and then Stanley went on. "Remember my telling you that after we watched your show that morning together she went into the bathroom and was sick? Apparently Jean Paul had pulled this kind of thing before, and seeing him at it again made her physically ill."

"Yes, I remember," Lee Ann shook her head, "poor woman..."

"So then he came home from Toronto in a surly mood and found them closing the doors on a moving van. She'd already decided to leave. They fought; he struck her. She fled into town to finish up her business before flying home. She dropped by my place to say good-bye and ended up staying over."

"He hit her?"

"Yes, I saw her face. She had a big welt under one eye."

"White trash."

"Really..."

"So...you two shack up?"

"Oh so sweet and sensitive. You know, if I didn't know better, I'd say you're sounding more than a little jealous, Lee. What's that all about?"

She looked over at him and frowned. "I'm confused, Stanley. I guess we need to talk this out again."

"Shoot."

"Well, I know we're not lovers, and we're comfortable with our agreement about that. Right?"

"Right."

"So then why am I still feeling possessive of you? Enlighten me. I really need to know."

He slipped an arm around her shoulders—felt the jarring out of sync sensation again and let go.

"Oh, I don't know; maybe we just have too much history for our own good. Maybe we'll always have these feelings for each other no matter how much we try to normalize our *relationship*. God, I hate that word as much as you hate *nice*."

"It's okay...what else could you call it?"

"Hmm, really. Well, you know, you're not the only one with the problem. I'll admit, I was jealous as hell when I knew for sure that you were carousing with Poteet in Canada."

"I know, but you were being sweet about it."

"Wasn't feeling particularly sweet about it, believe me."

"So what are we going to do with these silly feelings we keep having, I mean I'm having at the moment."

"Keep talking about them. The way we are right now and..."

"Are you and Melissa lovers now?"

"Can't let it go, huh? Okay, Yes, yes we are." He seldom lied, wasn't quite sure why he felt it necessary now.

"Ouch!"

"Damn it, Lee Ann, why couldn't you have just let it go?"

She cried her words. "Because you know me, Stanley, little newsperson, Lee Ann. I need to know everything. Oh, make it go away. I don't want it. I don't want this feeling!"

"Lee, let's try to get beyond this. We've got a nice day coming up. We've waited so long for this day. I know you're pissed at me. I'd be mortified right now if you and Jean Paul had..."

She stuck her tongue out, mimed putting her finger down her throat. "Argh! Stanley, you're making me sick!"

"Come on. Claire's waiting. Let's get on down to the market."

"Are you going to see Melissa again?"

"I haven't the slightest idea," said Stanley. And he didn't.

On his way to the river with his horn, Clay wandered through French Market to buy a lemonade. He'd just turned away from the counter and taken his first sip when drifting through the crowd he saw a young woman who caused him to swallow hard. She was wearing sandals, jeans, and a tight turquoise tank top. Slung from one shoulder was an oversized leather handbag. But that's not all she carried. This girl woman, with her short blonde hair and shoulders thrown back, moved with an attitude and an air of confidence that struck him numb. He browsed through the bins of flea market fare, and out of the corner of his eye, watched her do the same. For a moment he teetered on an edge, considering whether or not to approach her in some oblique fashion. But no, his viscera finally protested so violently that he decided it was time to turn around and run—run like hell! He took another sip of his lemonade—one dangerous, long last look—swung around and headed for the river.

It didn't happen all that often to him, the sheer paralysis that can seize a man when he sees a female who turns his insides to queasy goo. But this fox with her fresh haircut and attitude had done that to him. So, as he beat a quick retreat, he grumbled to himself about having enough problems without spending the next several hours with the lingering image of some pretty face and body prickling in his brain. Oh my God! What a body. What carriage! He felt unabashed lust and didn't apologize to anyone one bit for it.

The breeze along the river was balmy and laced with scents of the Gulf. He cracked his case, wetted and fitted a reed, and came fluttering down on "When Sunny Gets Blue."

In D.

42.

Events are shaped long before they happen, shaped in space to occur in time. But that was said earlier, wasn't it? And that voice went on to say; if someone could sit high above and watch in all directions and times at once, then that someone might rule the world, or better yet, write a little novel. Amen, says another voice out there. Who is speaking? Where is there? It might be a voice in another universe feeling that someone is watching them. It might be a voice from the past beseeching someone to see them, acknowledge them. In our case it's just Claire Hochstetter, rummaging through the flea market bins, talking to herself as she searches for the unusual. And, man, was she finding it.

Jackie was very much on her mind. They would be going crazy with each other now over the finds. And who was that guy a little bit earlier who'd passed through and looked her over? She didn't have to look at him, because his gaze, when it came, had burned a hole in her temple. Well, he was cute, and carrying something that looked like a sax case. Yes, he'd looked her over and then left as quickly as he'd come. She was sure she'd seen him before he'd seen her. He was buying some lemonade.

Oh—here are the Kenyan bracelets!

Claire sorted through the bracelets, one of which her father had bought for her only a few days earlier. And now here *she* was, and here *they* were! What a trip. She looked through the entire bin and decided the one she had on her wrist was definitely the hippest. Way to go, Stan!

She saw them before they saw her. It was Mom and Dad approaching, deep in conversation. Good, it appeared that they'd put the fire out, or at least had decided to put a damper on it. Good. She wasn't in the mood to referee this fine first day in New Orleans. The heavy, humid aromas of this place were so sensual they were almost sexual. No fighting, please, she admonished them silently as they approached. No fighting.

"HEY!" At the top of her voice, she shouted to them.

Everyone in the immediate area turned and looked at her, then over at the people she was shouting to, then back to her. Oh well, just some more tourists high on the smell of chicory brewing.

They heard her audibly painful "HEY!" and then saw her, the familiar flash of turquoise that was their daughter Claire.

The three of them closed ranks and met in a three-cornered hug. Claire didn't give them a chance. "Okay, here it is. Dad, you fade out to the flat...right or left...doesn't matter. Mom, you swing round behind me...I fake to you...then I throw to Dad. Okay, you two got that?" She hit them both on the rumps and broke huddle.

It was crack-up time, but they tried to keep it as much as possible to themselves. A few people were still looking on. Lee Ann got it back on track.

"So you had enough market? Want to move on down the street, hear some music?" They could hear a Dixieland combo on the patio to the west.

Claire looked around and sniffed the air. "You know, I'd swear the river was around here somewhere nearby."

"It's over there." Stanley threw a thumb over his shoulder.

"Can we go to the river, oh, can we Daddy?"

"Step right this way," he said.

They made their way across North Peters Street and edged around the hurricane gate that sealed off the levee. A short climb up a slight embankment and suddenly, there it was, spreading all the way to the Algiers shore. The river, broad and leaden in the noonday sun: Mighty Mississippi.

"This is it?" Claire wanted to know. "It looks like just another stretch of water."

"Claire," said Stanley, "you watch too many movies. What did you expect, six or seven paddle wheelers loaded with cotton bales and people singing Negro spirituals?"

"Dad...no...I just thought it would be wider, have some current, more boats and horns and whistles."

Stanley looked at Lee Ann.

She nodded and remained silent, not wanting to get into it.

"Just sit a minute and watch it flow, Claire, you'll see current... plenty of boats...hear the horns and whistles. Maybe even see a paddle wheeler or two, though they're all diesel-powered fakes for the tourists these days."

Everyone was silent now, so he went on. "You know the Mighty Miss is the second longest river in the world, second only to the Nile if you measure its length from the Missouri branch's headwaters in Montana. It has its own timeless rhythm and flow, and though it might not seem that wide at this crossing, that's because its several hundred feet deep out there in the middle."

The two women nodded. He went on.

"And it's been joined by the Missouri and the Illinois and Ohio rivers in its drop through the heartland of America, all the way from Lake Itasca in northern Minnesota down here to the Gulf. Think of the songs and the stories and..."

"Stanley..."

"Yes?"

"Thanks, as always for the promo...now can we listen for the horns and whistles?" Lee Ann patted him on the back. A big freighter coming downstream bellowed deep and low like a bull that had just stepped on its balls.

"Good timing, as always, Lee." He smiled over at her.

Claire stood on top of the levee riprap now, hands on her hips. She was looking off to the opposite shore, wondering what was over there. Eventually the three of them sat down in a line to watch the boats come and go. To watch the river flow. Silence now, except for the call of seagulls, the throb of throaty marine engines, more boat horns, no whistles—waves lapping on the rocks of the shore.

One hundred yards up the levee, Clay sat with his arms circled about his shins. He'd come down to play but had decided to pack it away and tune in to the river. He'd seen three people walk up onto the levee and recognized one of them to be Stanley but hadn't waved to him, not even when Stanley had looked straight at him for a moment and apparently had not spotted him. He hadn't waved because along with Stanley were two women. One woman, middle-aged, with red hair...Lee Ann! And miracles of miracles, he couldn't believe his eyes; the other woman was the girl he'd seen in the market, the self-assured blonde temptress in a turquoise tank top. Claire! That was their daughter, Claire? They hadn't seen him. Good. Time to study them all for a moment. He needed a couple of minutes to adjust. More like twenty-two years.

So he did just that. Watched them to his heart's content as the three of them stood in a line while Stanley pointed this way and that. Now they were sitting down. They still hadn't seen him. Probably because he was pulled into a tight figure four with a Rasta cap on—his case was upstream from their line of sight. What to do? Good lord, Claire, the girl in blue. Clay couldn't believe his luck. Yes! This was going to be a joyous reunion. This family thing might not be so bad after all he mused, as he mustered his cool, stood, pulled off his cap, gathered in his case and his wits, and headed downstream.

There is a time to close, to walk across the years and miles and finally meet—or meet again. Stanley, without his glasses, had seen a man sitting upstream when they'd reached the levee. Now, as he looked around again, he saw him stand and grab a sax case and walk slowly toward them. There was that big bush of brown hair, that lanky stride. Clay? It was Clay.

He collected himself. Hmm, how propitious. What better place for their reunion than down here by The River? Providence was shining brightly again. He watched Clay coming on. He waved to him. Clay waved back. He was closing fast. Stanley put a hand on Lee Ann's shoulder and turned her upstream.

"See that man approaching?" he said softly into her ear. She nodded yes.

"That's Bird."

She swiveled under his hand to fix him with terror-stricken eyes. "Stanley...oh my God!"

"It's all right. Gather yourself. He's seen us. He's coming."

Lee Ann blinked hard, said "Oh Jesus" a couple of times, and turned around to watch Clay close the final distance between them. His eyes locked with hers.

They met once again. On the banks of the Mississippi, in New Orleans. Three people who had once been a family. Now *four* people would once again pick up the beat. Lee Ann was the first to break ranks. She stood and walked towards Clay, matching his slow pace stride for stride. They met—studied each other's faces for a moment—then Clay set his case down, and they moved loosely into each other's arms. He felt her body shudder softly with silent sobs of joy and relief. "Bird..." she cried softly, "you're all grown up...you're so beautiful...just the way I always imagined you'd be..."

Still holding her loosely, he rubbed her back softly, and comforted her through what must have seemed like an eternity for both of them. Finally, she moved back, and with tears streaming down her face, apologized for looking like hell. Clay reassured her that he understood; he could see how beautiful she was. They stood talking quietly then, agreed right off the bat that he would call her Lee Ann. And she would always, from now on, call him Clay. Finally they were done with it and turned to meet the onlooking eyes of Stanley and Claire. Clay stuck his hand out to Claire.

"Claire. I saw you in the market."

"I saw you too...looking at me."

Clay startled.

"That's okay bro. I was checking you out too. Hopin' it was you."

43.

They weren't quite sure what to do with themselves after that, so Stanley spied a passing tourist and asked her to take their picture with his small camera: a memento of this momentous occasion. They all agreed it was a good idea and posed willingly for several shots. Then, at Claire's suggestion, all went back to watching the river. The four of them sitting in a line as they'd been photographed: Lee Ann and Stanley in the middle, Clay and Claire on either side.

"I had a million questions, and now I can't think of a thing to ask," Lee Ann mumbled to her sandaled feet.

"That's a first," said Stanley.

Claire laughed.

"Except to say..."

"See," said Stanley, "just couldn't happen." Lee Ann dug an elbow into his ribs.

"Except to say...thank God you're alive, well, and safe."

Clay was sitting by her side. He took the opportunity to hug her sideways. Lisa had been right; this woman had mothered him as an infant. This is not something one forgets.

"Dad tells me you're a badass sax player," said Claire, jumping in with both feet.

Clay looked around Lee and Stan. "Your dad is pretty good too. Did he tell you we did a number together the other night at the club?"

"Dad! You playing again? Far out!"

"Uh...let's not call it playing...not just yet."

"Hmm, you keep bustin' it out, you'll get it back fast," Clay reassured.

"Can we talk about something other than my nonexistent musical career? What's Lisa up to? Is she going to be joining us?"

"Definitely. But she's over at Le Richelieu till one-thirty." Clay looked at his watch: 12:15. I'll be meeting her and we'll come on over to Brennan's." He paused. Everyone nodded. Then he went on. "You know...we know a place up on Bourbon Street called Patout's Cajun Cabin. Good music, it's open to the street, great gumbo, mudbugs, gator bits, the lot. Might be fun. We could have drinks at Brennan's...then..." Clay dangled it.

It sounded like a plan to everyone; they were all in the mood to hit the streets tonight as a unit. Clay and Lisa were ready to show them their town.

Lee Ann was fidgeting at Stanley's side. "What?" he asked.

"You know time is *so* short."

"Yes?"

"Well, I don't mean to be selfish or anything, but I was wondering if it would be all right if I sat here for awhile and talked with Clay. Do you have time?" She turned to him.

"I'm meeting Lisa at one over at the bar."

Stanley looked sideways at Claire. "Sounds like we've got our walking papers baby. What say we do some shopping? We'll meet you over at Brennan's in a couple of hours or so, say three...okay?"

"You're dears."

"We know." They said it at the same time, exchanged a smile.

After parting remarks, Clay gave Claire a friendly hug, and then Claire and Stanley were on their way down the levee bank—waving one last time as they disappeared around the big green gate.

"You want to walk? Or sit? I'd like to walk," said Lee Ann when they were gone.

"Up the levee?"

"Up the levee."

Clay picked up his horn with one hand and offered the other to Lee Ann. She took it and moved in to take his arm as they set off upstream for a long over-due chat.

"I suppose this is selfish of me, but I was serious when I said I was burning up with questions. And then I realized that I really needed to talk with you...you know...one-on-one. Just us two."

"I understand" Clay said softly at her side.

"I've been away from work for over a week now. I need to get back to my job. I'll be flying out tomorrow afternoon. So time is short. I just thought I'd better grab you while the grabbin' was good."

She squeezed his arm. He pulled her hand closer to his ribs.

"You eating enough?"

"Yeah, Mom...I'm eating fine."

They glanced at one another, smiled.

"It's all right...I understand." Clay went on "I wanted to talk with you alone for awhile too. You have to leave tomorrow, really?" He caught himself. "I understand...work."

"Right...work."

A freighter up the river bellowed once long and low. They walked in silence for a moment listening and letting its deep chord sink into them. Then Lee Ann said "This must seem very strange to you, suddenly encountering two people who think of you as their son. I mean, I've been trying to think how I would feel."

Clay looked down at the woman on his arm. Boy, if you had only one mother in life, this one was worth waiting for. "Well, yes, it is a little strange..." They walked a few more paces. "But I think it's going to be great. You all are some beautiful people. I mean that. I feel fortunate"

"Thanks. Well, we'll just take our time then to adjust to this. Right?"

"Right. You're right. It will take a little while to adjust." He paused, considering. "You know, except for Pops and one sweet old aunt, I don't have any other family. Always wished I did though. Presto: the San Franciscans!"

Lee Ann smiled up at him and pressed on. "Your dad, the one you call Pops, he was good to you? You had a happy childhood?"

"Yeah..." Clay said wistfully. "Pops was...is the greatest. Stanley told you about him?"

"Briefly. I'm sorry he's..."

He nodded and quickly changed the subject. "So tell me about you and Stanley. You two are divorced, but you don't seem like most divorced people I know. You seem to have it worked out."

"Hmm...well...somewhat. I'm glad it shows." She was silent for a beat. "We've had years together, lots of time to work it out." And then we always had Claire to consider."

They walked in silence for awhile, then Clay said, "Can I ask you a rather personal question?"

She looked up at him. "Sure, I think you're entitled."

He smiled and forged ahead. "Why did you and Stanley split the first time? I mean back in the nineties? Was it because of me?"

She looked up sharply, startled by his keen perception and then went back to watching her walking feet. "Oh...it's complicated. But yes, I suppose you were partially the reason we fell apart back then."

"Yes, I've heard from just about every source that parents who've had children abducted will often end up parting ways. Seems strange to me. Seems you'd cling to your mate even closer if that happened. Wouldn't you think?"

She looked up at him for a moment, seeing that he was mildly perplexed. "Well," she began, "it often happens that one party blames the other party for the loss."

He nodded. "Okay, I can see that. Is that what happened to you two?"

"Yes."

He waited for her to go on.

"I was the one you were with when you disappeared. And strangely enough, though Stanley never came right out and said it, I always felt he blamed me."

"Wonderful, I messed up both your lives without even knowing about it."

"Clay...you're kidding...you know it wasn't you darlin'...it was us. We did that to ourselves."

"Yeah, I know; I was just jiving."

She considered for a moment. "Among other things, including but not limited to having our child abducted, Claire was born within a year of that, and Stanley, still mourning the loss of you, never bonded with her as a young child. We were drifting apart over that, and I knew I needed a career, because Stanley was growing more cold and distant by the minute...to both Claire and me." Big breath. "So I buried myself in weather school, and gradually we became strangers and divorced."

"But you worked it out."

"More accurate to say we're always in the process of working it out. Always will be, I guess. You want to sit again? There's a couple of flat rocks down there by the water...see?"

"Sure."

So they sat awhile longer on the banks of the river, dangling bare feet in the muddy water and talking. It was a rambling, free-flowing conversation now, skipping here and there in time. And by the time Clay looked at his watch and told her that he needed to head over to Le Richelieu, they were assured that a new bond had been forged. She told him she wanted to sit a few more minutes and enjoy the river. So they hugged—this time much closer—and then he turned and made his way up and off the levee onto a paved overlook adjoining the street.

He turned, smiled, waved, and blew her a kiss that she blew back. And then he jumped off a ledge and dropped out of view.

Lee Ann stood for a moment watching the place where he'd disappeared. The vision of an empty supermarket aisle flashed through her mind, a vision that had become a mental mantra these last twenty-two long years. She squeezed her eyes tightly shut, made the vision strobe, and then fade slowly away. Waves of sensual relief washed over her quivering body. Wave upon gentle wave. She made her way back down to the water, buried her face in her hands, and let them come.

The sun had passed its zenith and was tilting to the west. A hazy steam of humidity hung like gauze in the air. Claire and Stanley crossed to the shady side of Royal Street.

"I can't believe how good this place smells!" Claire shouted over the tops of passing cars. Stanley was one lane behind her."

"I know! Coffee, booze, southern cooking, wet masonry, and mule shit. What more could you ask for?"

"Right! And there, right there? What is *that* smell?"

"Describe it?"

"Um...I can't."

"Give it a shot."

They were moving at a leisurely pace down the sidewalk now, occasionally stepping single file to let other groups pass. Claire was considering her father's question.

"See, that's the fun of it...before you identify a smell, you're past its source and on to the next one."

"Are you in love?"

Stanley's question threw her off. Not easy to throw Claire off.

"No, no more than usual," she said.

"They say when you're in love, your nose goes crazy. Your olfactory senses start to overload, go into an excited state.

"Makes sense; smell is certainly a big part of the fun." Claire smiled at her father. "So how's your old nose these days, Pop? Sounds like you're sniffing around."

Stanley cracked up, shook his head, pinched the back of Claire's neck.

"Ahh! Don't! You know how I hate that!"

"Feels good though, doesn't it?"

"Yeah, but, you do it too hard, too fast; it's like blitzkrieg neck pinch!"

He patted her back. "I'll keep that in mind."

They walked a few more paces and then Claire said, "Am I ever going to get to meet Melissa?"

Clay wandered around for an hour and then found himself at Lisa's. He'd told the "family" he was going to meet Lisa at Le Richelieu at one so that he could have an hour to recover before he met her over at her place at two. His mind was spinning, almost out of control. He had a family, a whole real live family. And then there was Claire. Oh my God. But it was confusing as hell. There was Lisa to consider. Option overload flashed in his mind. Option overload. Option overload. He really didn't need the confusion, because the music wasn't going for shit. Ever since Turquoise Blue had returned from Biloxi, quarrels had been breaking out. Now that they were recording artists, egos were rising up over "the sound." It was not a happy band at the moment.

He climbed the stairs to Lisa's second-story apartment, and let himself in.

"Hey Lisa, it's just me!" he shouted over the sound of a shower running. He grabbed a beer from the fridge, popped the top, took a long pull.

"Wanna take a shower? I'll leave it running," Lisa shouted back.

Clay pulled the tail of his shirt out and unbuttoned his jeans. "Yeah, I'll be right there." He walked toward the bathroom, dropping various articles of clothing along the way. Lisa's silhouette graced the frosted glass of the shower enclosure. Clay walked to the tub, pulled the door aside, and stepped into the steam.

Back out on Royal Street, Stanley and Claire were approaching Wayfarer's Antique Shoppe. "See that shop up ahead? That's where your mom spotted the juice squeezer the other morning. Did she tell you about the squeezer?"

"Yeah, she did. What a trip that you found that first. Like a note in a bottle, huh?"

They stopped to look at a cluttered shelf beyond the glass. Stanley was pointing.

"A mystic event actually, but then this *is* New Orleans. Hoodoo town. It was sitting right there, right there where those little ceramic cats are now."

"It's really amazing that you found it the way you did." Claire was shaking her head at the serendipity of their find. She went on. "You two from San Francisco are on your way to breakfast one morning, walking along a street in New Orleans, and you find it right there. I mean what are the chances of that?"

"Slim," he said, "and then it wasn't even the juicer that finally brought us together. You know, if there is one living connection in all this, it would have to be Lisa Lynn. She was the one who introduced him to me."

"Wow! This is just amazing, isn't it?" Claire was not often amazed.

She waited while her dad went in and told Bruce that the search was off, that he'd found the previous owner of the squeezer, and it was indeed his long-lost son. Bruce could only say, "Fabulous...this is just toooo faaabulous." Stanley thanked him for his help and turned to see Lee Ann and Claire digging through a stack of dishes over in one corner of the shop. Lee Ann always seemed to pop out of some quantum tunnel. He joined the girls, and after a few brief words of catching up and some more browsing by the three of them, Lee Ann bought two hand-painted teacups as mementos of the store. Stanley said he had his sax. Claire couldn't find anything she really wanted, so they took their leave of Bruce and continued down Royal Street, with Claire buying post cards and trinkets as they closed the distance to Brennan's.

The famous restaurant on Royal was recovering from the lunch crowd and girding itself for the dinner. It was quiet, except for busboys, waiters, and waitresses, shuttling carts laden with china, silver, and linen. The three of them were seated in the fountain area to await the arrival of Clay and Lisa. They ordered three bloody mary's to help pass the time. It was two-thirty, a little early, but they needed the time to cool down and talk.

They cast about for a topic of mutual interest. Stanley bluntly asked Claire if she'd been kicked out of Canada for good. Claire said she really didn't know, but really didn't care. "I mean, it's weird," she said, "to be kicked out of an entire nation." But if that's what they wanted to do, who was she to argue?

"No, you know what really pisses me off?" she continued.

"It's that I'm pretty much washed up as an art restorer, or archaeological assistant. Got a record now. No one wants a poacher on their digs." She looked down into her lap. Her short blonde hair fell forward and nearly covered her face. "Guess I'll just have to become a famous painter. Ha ha."

"You are a famous painter, honey. To me."

"Mom...puleez."

Stanley, realizing that he'd chosen a downer, quickly changed the subject. "Lee Ann, have you heard anything new from your little friend?"

"You mean Poteet? The seaman? Who? Oh, so much has been happening...I forgot to tell you."

He leaned forward in his chair. "What?"

"After I talked with you on Monday when you were having lunch out at Claire Leveau's, and I told you that Poteet was insisting he was not the seaman?"

"Yes?"

"Well, he called later that evening and fessed up."

"He *did?* Why?"

"Because he said he was concerned for my safety. Because he said he was not the one who sent me the bullet note. Said all the other stuff, yes, he'd sent that to me under the alias of the seaman, but that he hadn't sent me the last note. So..."

Claire swung around in her chair. "Bullet note?"

Lee Ann suddenly realized that she hadn't told Claire yet about the bullet note. She decided to cut it off fast. "Never mind, Claire, it's not important now."

Stanley wasn't about to let it go.

"Do you think it was someone else then? Damn." He was feeling the ground shift beneath his feet, much as Lee Ann had felt it slipping and sliding several evenings ago.

"You know what I've decided, Stanley?" She fixed him with slightly angry eyes. "I've decided to forget this whole mess. But in answer to your question, no, I haven't received anything further, and Maureen's been monitoring my mail both at the station and at home. She's supposed to open anything that looks suspicious. And as of this morning, there's been no further contact. Case closed. Let's move on."

"Thank you very much for the wrap around, Ms. Barnes. I seem to recall holding your trembling body a time or two through all this." Stanley knew he had her dead to rights. She did too, decided to end it.

"I'll let you know immediately if anything further shows up."

"Thank you."

The drinks came. They started a tab.

Claire asked "So, when are you going back home, Dad?"

He considered the question, took a first sip of his drink. "I really don't know." A long pause, "I suppose there really is no reason not to go home now. I was only staying here to pursue the Bird thing as far as I could take it. That, as you all know, is work done." Everyone smiled and lifted their tomato juice. He went on. "Clay's asked me to play some more with him. I'd stay just for that, but the novelty would probably wear off pretty quickly for him, for that nonsense. He's in the majors. I'm still playing stickball in the street."

"He's good, huh?" Claire wanted to hear it again.

"Yes, he's good. I don't know if he's playing tonight or not. Sounds like maybe he isn't, but you'll hear him soon. He plays with a soft edge and a round tone that is sensuous as a sax can get."

Claire visibly shivered. They both looked at her. What was this?

She saw them looking at her and moved it along. "Dad, I was wondering, when I get back to San Francisco, do you think I could have a little corner in your studio? You know, over by that south window. Where I could paint?"

"I mean, I'm going to be living at Mom's for awhile, but I can't really work there. You know what I mean?"

He smiled. "Sure. Great. I'll get rid of some of the junk that's in that corner, and you can set up. It's yours."

"Okay, Dad. deal!"

They high-fived on it. Lee Ann was suddenly struck by the fact that she'd waited almost twenty-one long years to see this: Claire and Stanley—grooving. Things were looking up.

Lee Ann saw them coming, all fresh and full with the flush of young love. It was 3:15pm.

"Hi! Sorry we're late. Had some last minute business to clear up," Clay greeted them.

Stanley looked at Lisa, nodded and smiled slightly. She returned the gestures and added an almost imperceptible wink.

Clay was introducing Lisa to Claire. The two girls shook hands and exchanged pleasantries as Clay pulled up two more chairs.

Claire said, "I want to thank you for bringing this guy back around to us."

"It all happened so by accident...can't really take all that much credit," said Lisa.

"Dad says you're working as a bartender...that pay well?"

"It's a living" Lisa shrugged, "Yeah I guess, considering that it's pretty interesting work actually. I get to meet people from all over the world. I guess it pays enough...with tips."

Claire nodded and studied Lisa. Lisa asked, "So you've just come from Toronto? What's that city like?"

"Economic nerve center of Canada, like New York is to the States. City's clean and friendly, but I was finished with art school...it was time to move on. I hear you're in law school."

The girls talked as the five of them settled in for another round of bloody mary's and rambling conversation. Lee Ann turned to Clay.

"Stanley tells me you've just finished work on a CD."

"Yes, as a matter of fact..." He fished in his sport coat, pulling a square plastic box from an inside breast pocket. "...always carry one or two along just in case. Here, this one's for you." He handed the box to Lee Ann.

Everyone except Lisa leaned forward, anxious to have a look at the cover art. Not much to look at but classy: a solid turquoise blue square

— no writing. Along the thin back side of the box was the inscription.

A PATCH OF SKY: TURQUOISE BLUE.

Lee Ann looked at the cover for a moment, then at the writing on the spine, then flipped it over and began reading the information on the backside. Claire tried to grab it away, but her mother was too quick and pulled it back from her grasping hand.

"Mom! Are you going to read the whole thing! Pass it around. We'll give it back. Promise."

Lee Ann gave her daughter a look and passed it over.

Claire flipped it very quickly between the front and back sides, then looked at the thin edge for a moment. "Turquoise Blue, is that the name of your group?" She didn't wait for Clay to respond but pressed the case—blue side out—into her tank top. "Certainly is one of my favorite colors. Probably couldn't tell that." The shades of pale sky-blue matched perfectly.

Lee Ann glanced at Lisa. Neither of them was smiling.

"Nice artwork, who did it for you?" said Claire as she handed the case to Stanley.

"It was our idea to make it all blue. And we came up with the name, 'A Patch of Sky.' The record company had a graphic artist do the actual lay-out."

"Who's your record company?"

"*Wail.*"

"Whale...as in sea mammal?" asked Claire.

"No, Wail, as in cry out. Just a little company over in Biloxi. Good management though, they're easy to work with, so far."

"How's it doing?" Claire sipped her Mary.

"Too soon to know. We only released a couple of weeks ago. People at Wail say its getting some airplay in Chicago, if you can imagine that. They've been trying to get the New Orleans stations to play it, but you know, it's that old thing about local stations not playing local artists."

Stanley broke in. "Yes, I've never understood that one. What's that all about?"

Clay: "I guess if they play one, then everyone wants on. Gets to be a big political struggle with the stations always caught in the middle."

"Yes, that's right," said Lee Ann.

"I want to hear this soon." Stanley handed the case over to Lisa.

She took it and handed it quickly back to Lee Ann. "Yes," she said, "it's good. Not too wild. Well, there are spots..." Clay glanced at her, smiled slightly.

They sat for awhile discussing the music business and the state of jazz. Lee Ann noticed that Lisa seemed to be growing more distant by the minute so she changed the subject and asked her about her roots. Lisa told them about a ranch of a thousand acres, small by west Texas standards, where she grew up. She said she'd had a typical rural upbringing and that she'd always "hankered" to get to the big city. And now, here she was, Tulane law student in New Orleans. Be careful what you wish for, she warned. She missed Texas.

Clay asked Lee Ann and Stanley about their early years together. They told the story in shifts with Claire throwing in a punch line here and there as she was wont to do.

Everyone agreed they were getting hungry, so they raised their glasses, toasted each other one more time, and downed the rest of their drinks. Stanley paid the bill, leaving a generous tip, and soon they were on the pavement again, heading north to Bourbon Street, where bourbon surely flows and will as long as the street does. From a block away they could see it flowing now with the five o'clock crowd, a river of people passing one another on the way to, and coming back from wherever.

Happy hour patrons were packing Patout's Cajun Cabin to the walls. Everyone agreed that Clay should be the one to help them order. He said you couldn't beat a bowl of gumbo, a side order of bread and a salad. Claire said to make that two. Lee Ann said, what the hell, make it three. Stanley went four, with a side order of fried alligator bits. Lisa said she wasn't hungry and ordered a ginger ale. "Lisa, you're going to waste away," teased Clay. "Get some jambalaya or something."

"No Clay. I *said* I'm not hungry."

"Suit yourself."

The tiff passed quickly and everyone went back to shouting over the din of the watering-hole crowd. Lee Ann was the only one to hang back and consider what she'd just seen pass between Lisa and Clay. She looked at Clay, seemingly at ease, talking animatedly to Stanley and then to Claire and then to Stanley and then to Claire. Lee Ann watched Claire's responses to Clay. She noticed a softness she'd never seen before in her daughter's eyes. Claire was actually behaving like a civilized human being. And those blue eyes seemed to be flickering with an icy but warm fire. What the hell was this? She looked at Lisa: take-the-bull-by-the-horns-always-there-with-a-quick-retort Lisa, sitting quietly sipping her ginger ale, taking it all in. Lisa looked up—their eyes met. Before Lee Ann could smile slightly and look away she caught one of those messages that women can pass in a nanosecond. There was no mistaking this message. It was a silent scream for "Help!" She looked back at Claire, Claire with the universe in her eyes, looking straight at Clay as he spoke.

She suddenly felt like she was standing up to her knees in fire ants. Oh, this was going to be a long evening. Hopefully Claire wouldn't become too obvious, at least not until she could get her off in the ladies' room for a little chat. The food came and saved the day. Everyone except Lisa dove in with both hands and devoured what was before them. Good sport she was, she accepted a contribution from everyone's salad plates and sat slowly toying with some lettuce while everyone else ate. Clay looked over at her.

"You okay honey?"

Lee Ann watched as Lisa looked him straight in the eyes and nodded yes, with a bumping up-and-down motion of her head. Then, looking at her watch, she mumbled. "You know, I better git goin. I'm on at the bar in half an hour." She stood abruptly, dropped her napkin onto the table, quickly made some parting remarks, and moved off to the door. Clay excused himself and followed her out into the street. He knew something was very wrong. Those left sitting at the table watched for a moment, then Lee Ann said. "Claire, I'm going to the Ladies' Room. You want to join me?" Her tone of voice wasn't really asking.

Claire caught her mother's eyes, wasn't quite sure what she saw there. She shrugged, polished off her Corona, and said, "Yeah. I could use a leak."

"You can say that again," mumbled Lee Ann under her breath.

Stanley, who had just popped the last gator bit into his mouth, looked up sharply, wondering if his daughter would ever get over talking like a dock worker. The girls departed quickly and were lost in the crowd. Clay returned from the street.

"Is Lisa okay?" Stanley asked.

"Lisa? Oh sure. I think she's got a lot on her mind these days with finals coming up and working and all this new family I've found. She'll be okay."

"I've never seen her so quiet, so demure. Just not the Lisa I've come to know."

"Yeah, know what you mean. She's a kick-ass Texas woman, isn't she?" Clay smiled.

"Yes sir." Stanley smiled. "You're a lucky man. She's a winner that girl. I owe her."

Clay took a swig of his beer. "Yeah, me too."

Claire and Lee Ann returned to the table fresh and watered as a bouquet of daisies. Lee Ann seated herself and didn't waste any time. "Stan, the kids were thinking they'd take off for the evening and drift around on their own. Doesn't sound like it's negotiable." Claire looked at Clay. Stanley looked at Lee Ann. He wanted to protest but knew whatever he said would sound like whining.

"All right. I guess we have some business to attend to anyway, don't we?" He looked at Lee Ann who nodded yes.

Stanley covered the tab, and soon the four of them stood saying good evening out on the street. Stanley thought they'd be exploring together this evening. Apparently not so. He was sure Lee Ann would fill him in when they were alone. Or would she? And now it was his turn to wonder what the hell was going on. Lisa leaving blue and now this...what...? And then it hit him. Uh oh.

They watched "their kids" amble off side by side, talking as they went. Soon those two were swallowed by the crowd that swarmed along bawdy Bourbon Street. Stanley turned to Lee Ann.

"Is what I think is happening, happening? Please, tell me that it's just my overactive imagination."

"Sorry. I can't."

"Oh lord."

44.

Feeling very old and out of control, the two of them stood facing one another, totally befuddled. "What do you want to do?" asked Stanley.

"About what?"

"Good question."

"Maybe we should just stand here for as long as it takes and watch the world go by. We'll think of something."

"Do you have canned rations and flares?"

"No."

"What do you have?"

"A case of bewilderment."

"Want to hit some of these places, or you want to head on back to the hotel?"

"Oh you know, I know you'll find this hard to believe, but I'm actually glad the kids took off. I'm exhausted, Stanley. Aren't you tired?"

"I suppose I could get talked into it."

"Let's walk and talk back to Le Richelieu. I think I'm going to turn in early. Busy day today. Busy day tomorrow; we're booked back to San Francisco."

"You're what? Tomorrow! What time?"

"Five-thirty p.m. United, direct."

"I thought maybe you'd be staying at least a couple of days."

"Like to Stan, but do you realize that I've been away from work now for over a week on this little sortie?"

"A week is a long time in your business, huh?"

"Huh. Especially with little Miss Laura Andrews back there in my chair, charming the viewing audience. No, Stan, not wise to leave your station when the enemy's right there in your fox hole."

"It's war, huh?"

"Yeah, war."

They walked a distance without talking. Lee Ann must have been very tired, thought Stanley. She was staying by his side, and he wasn't walking all that fast. Finally she spoke again.

"You know what really burns me up is that I can't bring *One World Incorporated* in with me when I return. You know, spoils of my little foray and all that. But I just can't. So I'm going to return empty handed. That's what I don't like." She hesitated a moment. "I can't bring it in, can I?"

"How can you even ask?"

"How can I even ask."

"You know, maybe you can bring something in."

"What?"

"A follow-up on the stalker story."

She considered it for a moment. "No, Stanley, I'm going to make a brief statement on the air when I get back and say that I've finished up my business with the seaman and really don't want to think about it anymore. Case closed. Next segment, please. And that is how I feel."

"I know. You can do that, and then you can go on to the next segment, which is what?"

She looked at him. "How should I know? Whatever it is in the litany of endless segments on *Good Morning San Francisco*."

"Why don't you say that in running from your stalker you ran into your long-lost son. And then tell your viewers that story, your story."

Her eyes grew wide for a moment, then she shook her head. "No, you know Stanley, you can only do so much of that Kathy Lee and Cody stuff and then it gets old fast...to your viewers, I mean."

"Lee Ann, this is hardly a Kathy Lee and Cody story. This is a very profound and exceptional thing that's happened to you. Us. I'm sure that even if it wasn't you, people would be warmed by the story."

He could see the media wheels spinning in Lee Ann Barnes's head. "I'd have to discuss this with Clay. He'd have to consent to it, maybe even be on the show."

"What do you think he'd say to that opportunity? To come on his mom's show with his group. Play a number. Plug the disc?"

"Stanley?"

"Yes."

"Will you come to work for me in the creative department. A writer, maybe?"

"No. And I won't marry you again either."

"Whew, that's a relief." Lee Ann pulled her hand across her brow. "Okay, seriously, I'll consider the idea. I mean of the Lee Ann and Clay thing. You want to come on?"

"No."

"Okay." Pause. "Oh no, Stanley, I just thought of something."

"What?"

"I...we...could get busted."

"For what?"

"For finding a lost baby and keeping it and not reporting it."

"Tilt. Mmm, you're right."

They were approaching Wayfarer's Antique Shoppe now. Both turned their heads in the direction of the window ledge as they passed but did not break stride. Finally he said, "You could have someone check out the law. See if there was some statute of limitations on kidnapping. That would be the place to start. Oh, I just thought of something else."

"Yes?"

"Clay is very...I should say *extremely* protective of his, as he calls him, Pops. He probably wouldn't want to do it just for that reason."

"Hmm, what's the deal with his dad anyway?"

"Apparently he's in a nursing home. He suffered a head injury as a commercial fisherman."

"How bad is it? Is he able to communicate?"

"Apparently he's conscious but not all that cognizant. Doesn't sound good, but Clay says he's slowly improving from a three-year coma."

"Jesus." Lee Ann said it like a prayer.

"I know."

"Where is he, where's the nursing home?"

"I don't know."

They walked a distance in silence, and then Stanley said. "After my initial probings into the area of Pops, I learned quickly that it's not something Clay wants to discuss. It will take time."

"We certainly have to respect that."

"Yes, we certainly do."

They were one block from Le Richelieu now.

"Do you think Pops is really Clay's dad?" Lee Ann asked.

"I wondered about that for awhile myself, but the fact that he has a recorded birth certificate in Jefferson County, Texas, makes me think that Pops is indeed Clay's father, yes."

Both were lost in disparate thoughts for a long time. Finally Lee Ann said, "I don't know whether to be sorry for Pops or hate his guts."

"I know. I share the feelings."

"I mean, the gall to first throw his kid to the wolves and then take him back the way he did? Who *is* this guy?"

"We may never know. As a matter of fact, we probably won't...if that helps any."

They'd reached the front steps of the hotel now and stopped to face one another.

"Okay partner, here it is, that old fork in the trail again."

"I know. Lee Ann?"

"Yes?"

"I'm sorry about what happened last night. I mean this morning, early."

She nodded solemnly. "Me too. So you know how I feel then?"

"Always did."

"Yes...of all the people in the world, I'd let you say that."

They gave each other a short, polite, but warm hug and moved back again.

"So what about them kids, huh? What's going on there?" He wanted a final reading.

"It looks...well...all I can say is...*Lisa* knows something is going on. I guess she was the first one to see it. Then I did, in spades, in Claire's melting blue eyes over at the Cajun Cabin. Then you saw it, right?"

"Not until you pointed it out. But you know, Claire always flirts."

She groaned "Yes Stanley, but you should have seen her eyes. I saw something I've never seen in Claire's eyes before. You want me to tell you what it was?"

"Fire away."

"Exactly. I saw a grown woman, firing away."

"Gulp."

"Yeah, gulp," agreed Lee Ann.

"In a way it opens up some interesting possibilities, but I don't think we should get too far ahead of the action here."

"Me either. Just let it unfold. I mean what else would we do?"

"Stand back and watch, you're right."

"I feel bad for Lisa."

"Mmm, me too." Stanley nodded. "I like that girl. Clay and Lisa work for me. I mean, they..."

"I think so too."

"What do you see with Clay? Is he hitting on Claire?"

"Can't quite tell."

"Keep me posted. Like call tomorrow morning maybe? Want to have breakfast?"

"Sure, about eight?"

"Sounds good. You want me to come over here?"

"Yes, come about eight."

They hugged again, this time more warmly. It was difficult saying goodnight, but Stanley knew Lee Ann had more than made up her mind to keep her distance now. He stepped back and looked her straight in the eyes. "I love you."

"I love you too, Stan. Truly. See you in the morning." And with that she disappeared behind the front door of Le Richelieu. Stanley was left standing alone.

He waved to a group of tourists in a mule-drawn tour carriage, stepped out onto Chartres Street, and began walking in the direction of Leveau's Rooming House.

The front porch light was on when he arrived, but Jahna was nowhere to be seen. There were, however, two crates sitting side by side by the front door. He climbed the stairs and looked for some identification on the boxes. Both the larger one and the smaller one had his name printed on the top in bold felt-tip block letters. He took a penknife and slit the tape securing the tops of the cartons. In the smaller box, packed in Styrofoam popcorn, he found his Mary Mythe. No note.

In the larger box he found two twenty-five-pound bags of white porcelain clay. No note. He unwrapped the twisty on one of the bags, pinched off a marble-sized chunk of the putty, and rolled it between his fingers. Melissa's magic mud, no doubt about it. How sweet of her to do this. So like Melissa. He looked in vain for a note.

It took three trips to cart this load up to his room. All that time he continued to wonder who had made the delivery. Melissa was long gone, or she should be. He turned the key in the lock, let himself into his room, moved the boxes to a closet, and walked to the bureau for a cognac. A piece of paper taped to the mirror above the dresser stopped him short. He grabbed his glasses, focused down even tighter and read:

If we ever learn that you have tried to contact Melissa Frank—ever again—you will DIE most unpleasantly.

As some condemned men will do, he felt a sudden urge to laugh hysterically. He didn't. He read the message again to make sure he wasn't hallucinating; then he untaped the single sheet of bond paper from the mirror and read it again. Suddenly his mood swung around to seething anger. He read the note a third time. This was not funny. This was downright criminal, life threatening. Poteet, who the *fuck* did he think he was?

His hand went out for the Remy, poured a half tumbler full, and brought it to his mouth. One gulp. He reloaded his wallet, scribbled a note to Jahna, walked down the stairs, and stuck it in her doorjamb.

Suddenly he found himself walking full stride south on Esplanade, fuming to himself.

This latest love note from Poteet was going to take some thinking, and he wasn't going to sit still while he did it. He wondered if Lisa was still on at Le Richelieu and if she knew where Audid was currently parked. It was time to get in this guy's face.

45.

They hit a couple of bars to hear some of Clay's musical cohorts.

"YOU KNOW," shouted Claire over the throb of a jazz combo. "I DIDN'T GET TO SEE ENOUGH OF THE RIVER!"

The whole club turned around to look at her. The music had come to an abrupt ending, leaving Claire shouting midsentence over the top of a band that was now not playing.

The tenor player heard it, shouted over at them. "TAKE THAT LADY TO THE RIVER!"

The club erupted in laughter and applauded wildly, with catcalls and whistles.

Clay flipped an almost imperceptible bird at the guy with the horn and shouted, "Thanks a lot, Jimmy!"

They moved quickly through the crowd and out onto the street. "So you want to go back down by the river?" Clay asked.

"Yeah, there's just something about it." Claire looked off down Bourbon Street. "This is too hectic."

"Okay, the river, it's quite a ways."

"How far?"

"Nine...ten blocks."

"Wanna run?"

"What?"

"Wanna run?"

He shrugged. "Sure."

She spun around and set up an easy pace in her strap sandals. He set out after her, hoping they wouldn't cross paths with the police. People running after each other in the French Quarter of New Orleans was cause for suspicion. Apparently she didn't know this. His lungs were beginning to burn now, so he pulled up alongside her.

"We have to look like we're jogging," he puffed.

"WHAT?"

"I SAID…WE HAVE TO LOOK LIKE WE'RE OUT FOR A JOG."

"Oh, we sure are dressed for it, aren't we?" She laughed deep in her throat.

"No, we aren't."

They ran side by side now until the sidewalk was too narrow to let people pass. So Claire bounded down into the street and started leaping between moving cars. Fortunately she saw the NOPD cruiser at the same time they saw her so pulled up short—jogging in place. Clay had caught up with her now and followed suit. The cruiser passed with a look from one of the officers. Clay waved. The cop nodded without smiling.

"If we were in sweats"—he puffed—"it would be a different thing. I'm in a sports coat. Get it?" Claire didn't seem to be out of breath. How could this be? Clay questioned the cigarettes.

"Yeah, I suppose it does attract attention."

"Can we walk now?"

"Sure." She reached out and took his hand. He took hers. They set off again at a long stride for the river.

"You smoke a lot?" she asked. "You're out of breath."

"Too much."

"Why?"

"I don't know; don't you have any bad habits?"

She considered it. "Yeah, I guess I do."

"What?"

"I'm a smart-ass."

He laughed. "I hadn't noticed."

"You hadn't?"

"No, I just see you as being more direct than most people."

She nodded. "You been playing sax a long time, huh?"

"Fifteen years. I started when I was twelve."

"Junior high school band?"

"Yes."

"You remember anything about Dad playing to you?"

"No. But I guess I must." He paused. "'Cause when it was time to pick an instrument, they wanted to give me a clarinet, but I said get out of here with that snake charmer, I want that big stack of plumbing over there."

Claire laughed. "Something connected, huh?"

"Must have."

"Do you do anything besides music?"

"A little writing."

"What?"

"Short stories mostly. I started with poetry, got bored fast. I like theme, variation, theme again. You know verse, chorus, verse. Short stories seem more..."

They stopped for a passing motorist. "More what?" she asked, meeting his eyes.

He looked away. "More relevant to what life is really about."

"And poetry isn't?"

"...didn't say that." He gave her a quick sideways glance.

She smiled back at him and set out in the lead. He watched her as she swung along. Yes, indeed, this was some kind of woman. And she was the daughter of...let's see, who was that? Oh yes, two people who kept saying they were his first parents. Lord, this could bend a mind.

They made it to the hurricane gate, squeezed around it, and climbed the levee to the river. Lights on the far shore beckoned Claire.

"What's over there?"

"Not much, it's called the Algiers shore."

"But what?" she insisted

"People. People who live in New Orleans. Mostly blacks."

"Any clubs?"

"Yes, but I only go over there with Jimmy."

She looked up.

"He's the tenor player who embarrassed us tonight. He's a buddy. I can go over there with him." He paused. "I suppose if I played over there it would be different. But we haven't yet."

"I'm not sure I understand this." Claire sat down on a rock at the top of the riprap.

He went on. "There's a lot of racial tension in this city right now. Some places I only go with a native. Need I say more?"

"I get it." Pause. "Could you get Jimmy to take us over there?"

"Like tonight?"

"Yeah."

"No."

"Tomorrow night?"

"Possibly."

"I'd like to go."

He sat down beside her and pulled out his Drum. A quick roll, a lick and a spin, and he had a cigarette between his nimble index finger and thumb. It went up to his lips as he flipped a Cricket and made the tip glow. He handed it her way.

"No thanks."

"You've quit.

"Yes."

"Sorry."

"Oh, no problem. I just can't get started again."

"Understand."

"So you started playing in junior high school...then what?"

"I don't know. I did four years of college."

"Doing what?"

"Anthropology."

"No shit."

"Shit."

"Did you like it?"

"Loved it."

"So."

"So what?"

"So are you ever going to do anything with it?"

"Take a guess."

"Something you like...love more?"

"Right."

"Music?"

"Right."

They sat by the river in silence now. Smelling it, seeing it, thinking their own thoughts.

Finally she asked. "How'd you get your first group together?"

He considered the question. A good one. This girl seemed to know music. She asked the right questions.

"Turquoise Blue picked *me* up. They got me together with them. I'm blessed."

"Lucky, huh?" She turned her head and smiled at him, and then went back to watching the river.

"Yes, lucky. There was this trio of very proficient old jazzbos who had piano, bass, and drums, but they didn't have a voice. They heard me playing on the street and asked me to sit in. The rest is history.

She nodded and thought, yeah, and I suppose you're this lucky all the time.

He seemed to read her mind. "It's not easy, girl. There's a horn on every corner down here in N'awlins." He said it like a native, smiled, and went on.

"So that's how it happened. And we all started to make a living we could live with. And now the CD. I feel something growing."

"Do you have a CD player at your place?"

"Yeah."

"Can I hear it?"

"The CD?"

"Yeah...'A Patch of Sky.'"

"Sure."

Claire expected that they would go back to Clay and Lisa's place. He would put his CD on, and she would listen to it and probably like it, and then Lisa would come home, and they'd have a beer and talk, and then she'd head home to—what was the name of that hotel? Le Rich... something. And that would be the evening. But it didn't work out that way.

Walking along beside Clay now, she could have cared less about where they were or where they were going. She felt confident trusting him to take care of her. And that was reassuring, because it was a strange town. She'd already lost her sense of direction and would need either an escort, or some pretty explicit instruction to get back to the hotel. Clay pointed out Esplanade Street as they crossed it. It was the eastern boundary of the Quarter, he said. She said, "Mmmhmm..." They walked a few more blocks east, and then he was unlocking the front door of a small frame house that was in need of a fresh coat of paint.

"You'll have to excuse this place. My roommate just moved out today. Haven't really been able to regroup yet."

Claire, who always knew every inch of every place she ever decided to sit down in, went on a whirlwind tour of the pad. Shower was clean, no pubes on the stool. Kitchen was clean, a few dishes in the sink, but no big deal. The place was cared for; it even smelled spicy. She wondered if the roommate was the one responsible for that—would need to see and smell the place in a week or two.

"Who were you rooming with?"

"A girl from Wisconsin." Clay was off in the kitchen rummaging for coffee. Damn, Amanda, you better have left some Kona. He found it. What had she asked?

"A woman named Amanda. She left for home this morning."

"Were you lovers?"

He processed it, wasn't sure he liked the question. "Not when she left," he said.

He heard that low throaty laughter again coming from the living room.

"So you don't smoke. Do you drink coffee?" he said loudly.

"You better believe I drink coffee!"

Okay, I guess that answers that. He busied himself with brewing up a pot of Kona with a scoop of chicory for good measure. As he rinsed out some cups, he listened to the noises coming from the other room. It was the girl who had knocked him out this morning in French Market, checking out his house.

"Aha! I found it!"

"What?"

"Another one of those turquoise blue squares of sky. Can I put it on?"

"Sure."

There were sounds of fidgeting and buttons being pushed out in the living room as she loaded in "A Patch of Sky." Silence, then...

...a field of dreams...scintillating aural textures...gulls crying...and out of this ambience...Clay descended on his tenor. He glanced around the corner and saw her sprawled on the couch, bare feet on the coffee table, kicked back for the duration. He only hoped his playing was as good as he remembered it being.

The coffee was brewed. He poured two cups and joined her on the lumpy couch. She was still splayed out, leaning back as far as the cushions would allow, eyes closed, listening. He kicked off his shoes and leaned back too. Damn, the music had reached a point where the drummer had grown flaccid. They were all over the beat, a painful lack of groove, at least to his ears.

"Hey," he said softly.

Claire's eyes snapped open and swiveled in the direction of a man who held out a cup of steaming Kona/chicory brew. "Here."

On the first sip, she burned her upper lip. "Shit! I always do that." She looked over and saw him watching her intently. She soldiered on. "I think it's great, man, I mean, I was drifting off on your sound."

"Uh huh, we put a lot of people to sleep." He took a gingerly sip of his coffee. One does not burn one's lip if one wishes to play saxophone for a living.

Claire giggled. "No, that's not what I meant." She hurried on "How did you get away with using all those natural sounds? Streets...birds....boat horns? You rarely hear that on a jazz album. I've always liked it when they integrate that with the music; I mean, why not? That's music too."

"I agree. And, you know, Wail is very good to work with—fairly enlightened."

"You're lucky to have found them. This is advanced stuff, very listenable and fresh. I hope it makes it."

Clay fell back on the cushions. "Yeah, me too."

About eleven pm Lee Ann's cell rang. It was Claire saying she was still with Clay and that they were having a really good time partying with his friends. There was a possibility she would not be back till morning. She would be staying over with a girlfriend of Clay's.

Lee Ann had heard it all before, but now, in a most predictable way, she welcomed it. Claire was with Clay. The thought of it intrigued her. "Okay, honey, have a good time; you've got a keycard." And then Claire said something about him being "... gloriously beautiful," and hung up.

Lee Ann, who had been sitting up in bed taking notes for a potential show on her big reunion, set her notes aside, doused the bedside lamp, and settled into listening to the night sounds of the French Quarter. Mule hooves clip-clopping on cobblestones, a bird, and what was that, a steam calliope? Claire with Clay? Could that possibly be?

And of course, Stanley is stumbling down Decatur street with three Irish coffees and as many straight shots of brandy under his belt. Driving out to Poteet Porcelain in the morning and asking at the gate to see one Jean Paul Poteet is currently on his agenda. The scenario goes no further unless the guard lets him through and he can drive up to the big house, get out of the car, and act like he knows where he is going. Because let's face it, he's been there before. And he'd walk to the front door. Would it be open as it had been that first time he'd come? Probably not. Somehow, though, he'd find himself face-to-face with Jean Paul, at which time he'd toss the love note on his desk and ask him quietly who the *fuck* he thought he was. Yeah, said his more than slightly greased ganglions. Tha's... wha'm gonna do.

Was it mentioned that Stanley's eyesight wasn't all that good, but that his hearing was excellent? That's what probably saved his life in the next thirty seconds. Because in the next thirty seconds he was crossing Decatur Street heading north, and was hearing it coming on from a half block down—the low growl of a not-so-well-tuned sports car. By the time his brandy-lubricated brain could process the sound and he'd turned to face it, he saw a familiar battered Datzun Z coming straight for his knees, fast! Some instinct in Stanley's primal brain told him he needed altitude, fast! He cocked his knees and, with every reserve of strength, pushed for the sky. The windshield of the car slammed into his left ankle and rotated his body in the air. He'd put a forward vector into his leap so that he landed to the side of the car as it sheared on by him. His clipped ankle was the first part of his body to impact the pavement —then his right hand. He let his elbow absorb most of the shock of contact with the asphalt, but when his head came down full and hard, it lit with stars. People rushed toward him. Those not so close to him, who had seen it all going down, shouted obscenities after the Z as it sliced its way through light congestion down the street.

"You all right brother?" "You need an ambulance?" "Jes take it easy there, brother." "Hey, I know that sonabitch if you want to press charges." He saw a number of faces and heard a number of voices above him. He was pretty sure he hadn't lost consciousness.

Someone was helping him to his feet now. And now he was feeling a burning sensation in his ankle, and now a throb. He twisted it. Might be slightly sprained but definitely not broken. The heel of his hand where he'd landed was scraped and cut, but no blood was oozing out of his body as far as he could see. People called after him as he broke away from his rescuers, limped up Ursulines Street, and was swallowed by a crowd of evening revelers.

"Hey, you ever want to press charges...you come see me..."

He heard someone shouting after him, but the voice faded quickly into the din. His only thought now was to get the hell off the streets as fast as possible.

Suddenly he was back on the front steps of Le Richelieu. His head ached now. He needed about six aspirin. The adrenalin had had a head-on collision with the booze. Lee Ann was probably already asleep. Lisa. That's right, she'd left him a few short hours ago to go to work. It seemed like days. He knew that soon he would need to slow down, way down. Time was beginning to warp and bend back onto itself like a Mobius strip.

He moved through the front lobby of the hotel and limped into the bar. It was empty, except for a beautiful young woman who sat cross legged on one of the stools reading a thick textbook. She saw him coming, smiled only slightly, and closed the book.

"A little light reading this evening?" he asked.

"Business Law: Cases and Precedents."

"Sounds fascinating."

"Actually is, to me. What can I get you?" Her eyes took him in now.

"Whoa...what happened to you? You look like you've been mugged." She slid off the stool, held out her hand, and helped him up onto it.

"Ice water. Yes, I guess you could say I got mugged. Your little friend Audid just tried to take me out with his grungy little Z. You have some aspirin by any chance?"

Lisa moved off quickly for water and aspirin. "Man, that guy is pressing his luck around here." Her ponytail was going back and forth one beat behind her wagging head as she set him up. "You have witnesses? Are you going to go for him? Go for him, Stanley. Everyone around here hates him." She'd been digging in her purse while she said all this, now handed him three aspirin.

He threw them back and took a healthy pull on his tumbler. "No, I think I'm going to follow your earlier advice and get the fuck out of Dodge. Jamaica sounds good, don't you think? Way back up in the hills of Jamaica."

"Not a bad idea, partner. Audid, that little slime ball. Well, tell me how it happened."

So he showed Lisa the note and told her about wandering around getting slightly drunk and wondering whether he should confront Poteet—when out of a glittering French Quarter night, he found himself cartwheeling to the ground. "That bastard, that low life little bastard" and a few other comments from Lisa kept the beat.

She set him up with another ice water. "You know, Jamaica might be a good idea, Stan. At least until Poteet can cool down. Sounds like he's out of control right now."

"You're telling me." He took another swallow of his water and twisted his ankle to see how it was doing. Ouch. Not so good. He was already dreading morning. Lisa made a rather long phone call and then returned and refilled his glass. She looked pensive.

"It's a bitch when you're needin', and you call your man, and he says he's tired, just wants to get some rest."

"That was Clay you just called?"

"Yes, he said he just wanted to hang out, do some writing, go to bed."

Did the fun ever stop in and around the Big Easy? Stanley wondered. Last he saw Clay, he was headed up Bourbon Street with Claire in tow. And now he was home, hanging out by himself? Then where the hell was Claire? Lisa saw his wheels spinning.

"You know something I don't?" she asked.

He looked up and met her fearful eyes.

"No" he said, "I honestly don't."

Lisa backed up a few paces and tried again. "This is hard for me to say. Oh well, I'll just put it straight out." She took a breath. "Is it just me, a jealous lover, or is there something going on between Clay and your daughter?"

"Whew." He took a big gulp of his water this time.

"I knew it. I knew it. Clay just doesn't act that way usually, and he has a lot of women smoking up his tail. Oh damn. Oh shit." Lisa put her hand to her forehead. Stanley knew she was close to tears. What the hell could he say?

"Well, Lisa, if it helps any, Claire and Lee Ann are leaving for San Francisco tomorrow afternoon...reservations in hand."

"That really isn't going to solve anything, is it?" she snapped. Stanley, counting the beats of his throbbing ankle, waited. She went on. "I see how Clay likes having you people in his life. I'm sure we're, or I should say, you and he and your family... daughter...will be crossing paths a fair number of times in the future. Wouldn't you say that's a fair assumption?"

Stanley bowed his head. "I sincerely hope so. You want me to talk with Claire, see what's going on, if anything? I owe you one, you know."

"No, don't do that. I feel so stupid. I hate being in this position. Hate it! Jealous little girlfriend. Shit."

"Believe me, I know the feeling; we've all been there. It comes with the guts and the heart. Can't really control it. Just gotta breathe deep and wait 'till it passes. It will, you know."

"No, I'm not going down without a fight, Stan." Lisa busied herself polishing a bar top that didn't need polishing.

"I wouldn't expect anything less from a gunslinger like you Miss McKenzie."

She looked over at him and smiled sardonically. "It's been nice knowing you, Stan. I mean that."

"Thanks. It's mutual."

"I thought you'd be just another guy passing through town, having your little southern adventure, and then you'd be gone. Then we found a big connection, and I thought awright! I'm going to get to keep knowing this big ol' teddy bear. Through Clay, I mean. Now..."

"Don't jump too far ahead here. Maybe this thing will blow over."

"I want to believe that. I really do. I just got a terrible feeling in my guts that it's not going to."

He was at a loss to console her, knew that her fears were well founded. The fact that his daughter was the antagonist in this triangle made it all the more confounding. He finished his ice water, waved off a refill, and slid slowly, carefully off the stool. His weight came down on the ankle as he ventured a few cautious steps. Good, it wasn't as bad as he thought it was going to be.

"It's late. I need to update Lee Ann. You need to get back to that fascinating reading you were doing before we had this little lonely hearts club meeting. We'll be in touch for sure, Lisa Lynn."

Lisa managed a smile, though he could see she didn't really have her lonely heart in it. "Okay partner, take care of that ankle, get some ice on it. Does wonders."

"I'll do that," he said as he turned and hobbled from the bar.

The night clerk at the front desk connected him with Lee Ann's room. He waited as the phone rang once, twice, three times, then a sleepy voice came on the line. "Claire...is that you?"

"No, it's her dad, were you asleep?"

"Oh, Stanley...it's you." He could hear Lee Ann rustling in the sheets. She went on. "No, just sort of drifting."

"I need to talk with you. It can't wait. I want to show you something. Is Claire back yet?"

"Gods, Stanley, let me get my brain in gear here. No, she called about an hour ago and said she was going to be out all night, staying over with a friend of Clay's. What happened? Is she all right?"

"Mmm. I would imagine she's just fine, Lee Ann. Anyway, I need to talk with you, hon. Right away. It can't wait till morning."

"Are you all right Stanley? What happened? You sound weird."

"I'm down in the lobby. I'm fine, but we need to talk, *now*."

"Okay...come on up."

"I'm on my way."

Click.

Elevators are a great place to think. As it lumbered all that distance from the first to the second floor, he had a moment to sort out his thoughts. So Claire was with Clay, and Clay was lying to Lisa. This didn't look good for Lisa. And perceptive little gal that she was, she was seeing it in spades, as it was happening. Poor Lisa.

And here he was, burdening all these women with his tacky problems. Why was he doing that? Was he taking on allies? Was that it? The more people he told, the less terrified he would need to feel himself? Terror *had* washed through his guts several times as he'd been walking the streets and downing those three Irish coffees, sheer terror. Even before his brush with the Z.

Clearly, Poteet was a man capable of carrying out his threats. The simple solution to all this, of course, was to never see Melissa again, as instructed. He wasn't sure he was going to follow those instructions. Suddenly he was standing at the door to Lee Ann's room. He knocked softly.

"Yes?" came a muffled voice from inside.

"It's Stan."

She opened the door, and he slid around it. She was wearing a green Japanese kimono, tied tightly at the waist. She didn't look nearly as sleepy as she'd sounded. "What's up?"

He took the note from his pocket, unfolded it, handed it out to her and watched her eyes as she read it. "I found this waiting for me when I got home this evening. You saw me lock my door when we left the room this morning. Well, someone must have picked the lock so they could leave this little missile taped to my mirror."

Lee Ann shook her head as she read it a second time. "Stanley, we've got to get the *fuck* out of here. Come home with us tomorrow. This whole situation is making me want to puke."

"I'm thinking about going down to Jamaica."

"Ha! Not a bad idea...way back up in the jungles?"

"I'm not kidding. Jahna asked me to go with her and I said no, I wanted to stick around New Orleans." He shuffled over and sat down in one of the pedestrian chairs. "But that was before I found Bird...Clay...." He paused, winced slightly, went on. "But I left a note on her door before I came over here...told her I wanted to go."

"Are you limping? Why are you limping?"

"You thought the note was enough? Listen to this."

As she made an ice bag for his ankle, he told her about his scrape with the Z. Lee Ann, aghast at the thought of it, flashed like a beacon between concern for him and venomous spite for Poteet.

When he'd finished his tale, she said with chilling objectivity, "I'm really serious, Stanley, this thing has gotten *way* out of hand. Please come home with us tomorrow. Please. This is not funny. This is becoming sick and deadly."

"Tell me about it, baby. No, I'm getting a strong message to hit the tropics for a while. Just kick back and drink some rum and think about how I'm going to handle this thing with Poteet. I've decided I've got to meet with him one more time and talk. Maybe just once, because I can't leave this the way it is right now. Male pride and all that, you know."

"You're serious, aren't you?"

"Deadly serious."

"Please, let's not use that word."

"Yes. I'm going. Down to Jamaica for a week with Jahna, and then back here to see Poteet. Hopefully I'll have figured out what I want to say to him by the time that meeting occurs. But it has to occur."

"Hmm...gee...these are all a bunch of new developments, aren't they?" she said softly. He shifted the icepack to another part of his throbbing ankle and nodded solemnly. She went on.

"Are you going to see, or are you going to contact, Melissa again? Is it worth it? Should I ask?"

"No, you probably shouldn't. But now that you have, I'll tell you. Yes, I probably will. First..."

She asked him if he wanted a drink from the courtesy fridge. He said definitely not.

"So...go on..."

"Firstly, because I want to see her and her work again. And secondly, because I'm sick and tired of Mr. Smarty pants, rich, southern aristocratic, Poopteet, thinking he can get away with this kind of *shit!*" He pointed at the note that had ended up in Lee Ann's hands again.

She looked down at it. "I don't know, Stan, this note doesn't mince words. Are you sure it's worth it?" She paused, he nodded yes, and she went on "I couldn't ask you this question this morning, for obvious reasons, but I guess I need to ask it now. Are you in love with Melissa Frank? Gulp."

He frowned, rubbed his brow. There was that *dumb* question again. Well, he guessed, women just *had* to ask it—*the* question.

"No, right now I'd say I have some kind of high school crush on Melissa. That's a fact, but that's all."

"That bad, huh?"

"Yeah, that bad. And I see absolutely no future in pursuing it any further. Or at least I didn't until I got that goddamn note and was almost run down and left for dead. Now I'm feeling I need to pursue it just as far as I damn well feel like pursuing it."

"He sure does know how to get people pissed off at him, doesn't he?"

"Can say that again...but please don't."

"Okay..." she began, somewhat wistfully "it's your life. It's your call."

"Yeah." he grumbled.

"Mmm." She was ready for a segue. "Jeez, June is bustin' out all over the place it seems."

"Whaddaya mean?"

"I told you Claire called to say she wasn't going to be coming back to the hotel this evening?"

"Yes you did, and...?"

"And she's with Clay...said they were partying, though I didn't hear a party going on. Then she hung up." Lee looked up at the ceiling.

"What?"

"Said she thought he was 'gloriously beautiful.' Her words."

Stanley let out all of his breath. "She said that!?"

"Yes."

He slumped.

"What's wrong?"

"Poor Lisa, she saw it coming."

Lee Ann was silent for a moment. "I wonder what will come of it? I mean Claire and Clay. They're not blood...they could..."

He broke in. "I thought we weren't going to get ahead of the action, Mom."

"You're right, Stan, but just imagine it! What if..."

"Lee Ann."

"Okay. I'll shut up."

"Thank you."

"You're welcome."

"You still want to do breakfast at eight?"

"Sure. You?"

"Sure. Think Claire will be home by then?"

"I have no idea, none whatsoever."

"Mmm. Well, I'm sorry I got you up, Lee. I'm sure you'll sleep better knowing there's a hit out on me."

"Hey, Stan, what're friends for? You certainly did hold my hand there a while back." She looked over at him for a moment. He looked back at her, saw the country girl he loved so much. She went on hesitantly. "You want to stay over here tonight? Claire's not going to be back...there's an empty bed. You shouldn't be walking on that ankle, let alone out on the streets."

He shook his head. "No, you might think this sounds funny, but I need some time alone to think...really. Thanks though, that's dear of you."

They hugged goodnight for the third time that evening, and then he dragged his throbbing ankle home and went to bed.

His note to Jahna was still sticking out of the doorjamb.

46.

Clay was awakened by the sound of a telephone ringing. He scrambled out of his dream and reached out his hand. It landed on the receiver. He pulled it off the cradle and managed a husky, "Hello?"

"Clay?"

Lisa Lynn McKenzie on the other end again. His mind snapped to.

"Mmm...what time is it?"

"The bewitchin' hour, my man. Two am, I'm checking in one more time before I head on home."

Clay was wide awake now. "Uh...oh, man...I got the band tomorrow...little short on sleep. Well get together...tomorrow... really...promise."

Long silence on the Le Richelieu end of the line.

"Tomorrow?"

"Yeah."

Silence.

"Okay?"

"Mmm."

"Okay...night."

Lisa hung up without waiting for a reply and stared vacantly at the liquid blue rectangle that was the lighted swimming pool in the patio area out back. Turquois blue. Heartsick, that was the word she seized on.

She knew.

Clay placed the receiver back on its cradle, rolled over, and put a hand on Claire's shoulder.

"Who was that?" she mumbled.

"A friend" said Clay, and took her in his arms.

47.

Next morning, not so bright, but very early, Claire knocked on Stanley's door.

Maybe it was because he'd had enough knocking on his door. Or maybe it was because he had that death threat still tucked in his shirt pocket. Or maybe it was because he was not a morning person and it was 6:30am. Probably for all these reasons, Stanley, wrenched from his sleep once again, yelled at the top of his lungs. "YEAH! YES! WHO IS IT NOW?"

A short pause. "Me, Daddy."

Now he bolted. Claire? He checked the light—shortly after daybreak. Claire? He threw his legs out of bed, shuffled and limped to the door, and opened it.

Claire, with hair looking like a strawstack, eyes a blur of blue, met his dazed gaze.

"Hi," she said as she breezed into the room—leaving a musky contrail. He closed the door after her.

"Hi" he said.

"They shut the water off over at Clay's! Can you believe that?" Claire was spinning around the room, taking it in.

"I thought you stayed with one of Clay's girlfriends," he said quietly.

The woman ranging about his room was in full bloom. His little daughter Claire, not so little any more.

"We never got there." She looked at him for a moment. "Could I use your bath?"

He walked over, took a towel out of the top drawer of the bureau, and held it out to her.

"*Baaad* daughter." He smirked.

She smirked right back, moved in two steps, took the towel, and walked to the door.

"You and Clay shack up?" he asked, throwing caution to the wind.

She turned, looked at him full on. "Yeah," she said, and then she was gone.

He sat down on the edge of the bed and felt his ankle throb. Poor Lisa. Oh lord, poor Lisa, he heard his mind saying with the rhythm of the pain. Claire had her claws in; he'd seen it one too many times before. When Claire got her claws in, it was a game.

Until Claire said it was over.

He considered calling Lee Ann to give her advance warning, and decided against it. It was Claire's business now; he'd invaded her privacy on a whim and now needed to back off, way off. He slowly climbed back into bed and lay drifting for a few minutes until Claire returned. It wasn't like he didn't have a few things to sort out. Romantic problems? Ha! The tarot had nailed that one dead on the head.

He thought about Melissa. She would be home by now, reunited with her daughters and aging parents. He wished he could be with her to meet them, sit on a veranda somewhere in the morning sun and drink coffee while Stella and Jacquel chattered away in their little girl voices. He was sure they spoke to one another in Portuguese.

There was a soft knock on the door. "Yeah! Come in!"

Lee Ann opened the door, stepped around it, and into the room.

"Lee Ann!" Stanley wheezed.

Her eyes flashed wide at his panicked expression. She turned and headed quickly back through the door, nearly knocking Claire down as she came from the other direction. "Claire!" Lee Ann looked between her daughter and Stanley, total bewilderment in her eyes.

"It's all yours, Claire" was all Stanley could think of to say.

"Hi...mornin, Mom. They shut the water off over at the place where I was staying, so I dropped by here for a shower before I came back over to the hotel. It was a long night."

I'll bet, thought Stanley.

"Oh." Lee Ann had to process it for a second. "Why didn't you just come back to the hotel? We have running water over there, you know. Inside plumbing and all."

Claire laughed. "You know how it is when you need a shower and just can't wait?"

No, baby, but you sure needed one about ten minutes ago, thought a poker-faced Stanley.

"Mmmhmm," said Lee Ann.

"Well, Pop's place was on the way. Besides, I thought you might like to sleep in a little, seeing as how you were a little short on it night before last."

There she goes again, thought Stanley, shifting the attention off herself onto her mother's own little misery. This girl is such a pro.

"How considerate."

"You girls talk among yourselves," he interrupted. "Here's the topic: teal-green is neither the color of a teal, nor a true green. Discuss. I'm off to the shower." And with that he grabbed his dopp kit and his towel, and once again headed for the refuge of the bath.

The women watched him go without saying a word. They seemed to be pondering the assignment he'd just given them.

They walked a few short blocks to a sunny corner cafe that advertised a special of Belgium waffles with fresh berries. Claire asked her father why he was limping and what had happened to his hand. Stanley mumbled something about stumbling off one of the high street curbs that were typical in the Quarter. Claire sympathized with him, and Lee Ann let it go. She assumed he had his reasons for keeping his present troubles to himself.

They kept the conversation light and topical as they ate an early breakfast. Stanley told Claire about his current plan to take a little side trip to Jamaica. Then they talked at some length about Clay and the future they'd all be having with him in their lives now. Stanley kept watching Lee Ann to see if he could tell whether she knew the latest. Had Claire and she discussed it while he was in the bath? Apparently not. Lee Ann seemed to be in a breezy mood as she slowly ate her waffle. About halfway through breakfast, Claire dropped the big one.

"I'm glad we're all together here. I have something I want to tell you both, and what's handier than telling you both at the same time?"

Her parents looked up from their plates.

"I'm not going back to San Francisco right away with you Mom. I'm going to stay in New Orleans for a week or two just to get the feel of the place. I love the feeling around here." She looked over at her mother. "If we can't get a refund or a reschedule on the plane ticket, I'll pay for it."

"Where are you going to stay?" Lee Ann, frowning; she couldn't hide her disappointment. As if the airfare was all she was losing. She'd been looking forward to spending some time with her daughter.

Stanley was still recovering from Claire's latest jibe. Talk about loose cannons.

"I'm going to be staying at brother Clay's, where else? His roommate just moved out, and he says he could use some help with the rent. So it works out fine."

"Will you have your own room?" Lee Ann asked the obvious motherly question.

Stanley methodically shoveled in bits of French toast and sat back, waaay back.

"No. There's only one bedroom at his place. I'll be sleeping on the couch."

Mmmhmm, thought Stanley. If it wasn't for the Lisa complication, he would be enjoying himself immensely right now. But damn it, Lisa was a goner for sure now.

"Well, yes, of course, what can I say...you're a grown woman. I guess it'll save on the phone bill, having you both in the same place." Lee Ann was rambling now, trying to conceal her disappointment.

"So you two must have hit it off famously," said Stanley, calmly biting the end off a link sausage.

Claire didn't meet his eyes as she scooped up a bite of her omelet. "Yeah, he's a totally cool guy. How could you not like him? You guys are lucky, and, hey, think of it this way—you've got to go on with your lives, but I can stay here and really get to know him. Then we can all be one big happy family."

Claire's parents, both nodding, were thinking entirely different thoughts.

They discussed logistics next. Would Claire need any of her clothes or money or anything else Lee Ann could send her? She said, no, she had all her money—what was left of it after Canada had dipped their big fat hand into it. She would start an account in New Orleans, probably buy some new clothes, so no, she had everything she needed.

Oh to be young again, and traveling so lightly, thought Stanley. Then he told Claire that the corner in his studio over by that south window would be waiting for her when she arrived home.

They finished breakfast, picked up Claire's bags at Le Richelieu, and drove over to deposit them at Clay's. He was in a practice session at the club so had given Amanda's key to Claire. She let them in.

Lee Ann wandered around wistfully, looking at every one of Clay's simple possessions. The place was sparse, but clean. She stood in the kitchen caressing his squeezer, now in its old home on his kitchen counter.

Claire stood in the middle of the street waving as her parents sped off down the street in the direction of Le Richelieu. Lee Ann, leaving for San Francisco in a little over six hours, said she needed to rest and collect her wits for reentry into her world there. Stanley dropped her off at the hotel saying he was on his way to check with Jahna about their Jamaican plans. On the drive back to the hotel, they hadn't talked any further about Clay and Claire. So Stanley was left wondering if Lee Ann knew the latest. Probably she did since she was avoiding that topic as much as he was. Also on his wonder list was the question of whether or not to give Lisa some advance warning of Claire's change of plans. No, it was better to butt out completely now. Let the kids handle their own mess. Remember the old rescuer becomes victim syndrome, Stanley? Yes, he did, and how ironic that Lisa would now be remembering it too.

Jahna was rocking and talking on her cordless again as he climbed the stairs to her porch and sat down on the railing. She continued to speak in a pidgin English that was difficult to understand. She held a gnarled finger up to signal that she needed a moment longer to conclude her business. Stanley sat watching a man in rags digging in a pile of refuse across the street. The man found what he was looking for, put it in his mouth, lit it, and walked on down the street. Jahna, concluding her conversation, set the phone back on its cradle.

"So! Mista Stanley mon. You g'wan Jamaica with Jahna!"

"You got my message?"

"Aye, and not only dat, I buy your ticket. We leave dis afternoon. At six!"

"Whoa. That was fast."

"Mmm, well you say in de note...de sooner we leave de better."

"Yes, it's fine...just fine. Are we going up into the mountains as you said?"

"...to see my people in Roarin River, yes mon!"

The old woman was in high spirits, apparently in anticipation of soon being reunited with her kin. He caught the fever. "I guess I best go buy some suntan lotion and pack my bags. This is great news! Thank you. How much do I owe you for the fare?"

"You give Jahna six hundred dollar...dat be all. We g'wan for a week. Dat be irie with you?"

"Yes, fine." He peeled six Franklins off a wad and handed them over. "Anything else I need to know...get...do...before we leave?"

"Nah. four o'clock we start for de airport. Dats it! You got passport and swimmin trunks, Stanley mon?"

Luckily, on Lee Ann's advice, he'd stuck his passport into his bag that night, a week ago, when they'd left San Francisco. Had it been only a week and a day ago? It seemed like twenty years.

Back up in his room, he called Lee Ann and told her that the Jamaican departure had been moved up. They should meet at the airport and have a parting drink. She agreed and then said she needed to get back to her nap. He asked her why she sounded so melancholy. She told him she couldn't answer that question because she really hadn't sorted it all out herself. He said "Get some sleep." She said "I was trying to. I'll see you at the airport." He called Claire at Clay's place. She wasn't there—probably out setting up her life here in Crescent City.

All his clothes were dirty, so he loaded up his travel bag and walked down to a corner Washette. It felt good to be doing his laundry.

The infamous note from last night was still in a shirt pocket. He rescued it at the last minute, thinking it might be more appropriate to send it through the wash. No, he would save this note; he wanted to remember Poteet in a special way.

Laundry clean, folded, and stowed in his bag, he returned to the rooming house and took a short dreamless nap. Then it was time to depart.

He and Jahna loaded their bags into the Mustang, drove to the airport, checked the car in, and took the bus to the terminal. Then they joined Lee Ann for a celebratory drink. The conversation came to an abrupt end as Lee Ann's flight was called. He left Jahna in the bar and walked her to the boarding gate.

"Seems like all we do these days is hang out in airports and say good-bye."

"Yes, does seem that way," Lee Ann mused. She'd seemed distant ever since Claire had dropped the bomb this morning.

"Is anything wrong? Anything we need to talk about?"

"As always, there wouldn't be enough time...even if there was enough time," she said, misting over. "It's just that I feel a big chapter in our lives is closing. Right here. Right now. And chapters closing always make me blue. The bigger, the bluer."

"Turquoise Blue, Lee. Light blue. Bright blue. Think how fine the future is going to be." He paused. They stood rocking. "Think! We no longer have to carry Bird around like some stone in our hearts. We're free of that now."

"I know." She appeared near tears. "I think I'm going to get on the plane, bury my head in a blanket, and cry all the way back to San Francisco. I'm just so relieved...exhausted and relieved."

The PA called her final boarding.

"Okay Stan, I'll see you when you get home. Have a good one in Jamaica. Send me a postcard." She turned her face up. They gave each other a peck on the lips.

"I love you very much, m'dear. We done good."

"Yes...we done good."

She turned and trudged down the tunnel. He watched her until she turned a corner and was gone from view. What was going on in her mind? Why was she so melancholy? As far as he was concerned, everything was coming up roses.

Clay and Claire...lovers? It was still boggling his mind.

Part 4: Nova

48.

Roarin River was everything Stanley had hoped it would be, with cane fields and misty mountain vistas, and beautiful black people everywhere. He saw it now in the first light of day as he stood in the doorway of his shanty: Roarin River, up-country Jamaica.

The plane ride hadn't been as long as he'd expected, three hours.

He remembered when he'd flown down here one time from San Francisco with Jackson, and it had taken the better part of a night. They'd stayed in one of those beachfront compounds and hadn't so much as poked their noses out the gate. But here he was now, with a native, in a native's village. Yes! This was going to be a lolly.

Last night, when he'd disembarked from the plane and was wading through customs, the Caribbean had called to him from somewhere over a sand dune. He'd smelled Montego Bay, more rich layered aromas. It had been balmy; he'd asked Jahna if maybe he could have a swim in the ocean before they headed into the mountains. She'd told him that the man who was coming to drive them was paid by the hour, and it was all arranged. Stanley had taken this to mean that, no, he would not be getting his moonlit dip. He'd booked some time in his mind on the return leg to get that in.

A nappy-headed youth was passing his doorway. "Hey, mon! Harold will be round shortly with coconut and almonds. Breakfast, mon!" The boy didn't break stride as he seemed to glide by. Stanley smiled and nodded. Such hospitality.

His mind drifted back to the previous evening—the driver meandering up a two lane highway on the wrong side of the road. Jamaica! Breetish style, mon! Everywhere men, women, children and goats floating through the headlights. And everywhere reggae bass thumping like a village drummer. It seemed to go on and on as the miles passed. The car threading its way through towns that clung nonchalantly to the sides of mountains. And these followed by stretches of jungle with dips into deep narrow ravines—water rushing everywhere. All seen in the headlights. All up-country Jamaica.

And everywhere the sound of the nocturnal bird, *siffleur de montagne*, peeping its strange pleadings to the night.

This morning he'd awakened to the pleasant sounds of children playing and some cheap Chinese wind chimes jingle-jangling in his window. This was a little slice of what he hoped heaven would be like. And the people, Jahna's people, had been so hospitable as they'd greeted him and shown him, poor weary traveler, to his hut.

He looked around.

It was made of wattle and daub, a woven mat of slim branches turned upright and covered with mud. The roof was a tight trusswork of thicker branches covered with corrugated sheet metal. And the simple dirt floor, trodden by many feet, had a glazed finish. His bed had been comfortable and fresh, and he had a sink with cold running water. He shared a common latrine. Shit, he'd gladly dig his own hole to be here right now.

Jahna emerged from a neighboring house and started his way. She moved forward with a pronounced sideways shuffle. Stanley thought he should sculpt her in mid stride; it would be very striking.

"Goodmarn," she said through a snarl of old teeth—sounded almost Irish.

"Good morning to you."

He gestured to Jamaica. "It's so beautiful..."

"I taught dat you would like it Stanley mon."

Jahna called him Stanley mon almost always now when she addressed him. It seemed to fit with some syllabic modulation she and all these Jamaicans made a part of their daily music.

"And what are you going to be doing today, Madame Leveau?"

"Well, I just be runnin' cool...make some arrangements for a party we havin' toni...hang wid de people."

"Sounds good. Who's the party for?"

"You, Stanley mon!" Jahna flung her arms in the air and cackled. Stanley wondered if he'd just startled a crow.

"All right. I'll be coming."

He spent the day with the children of the village, swimming in a portion of Roarin River that ran through a pasture. It was a grassy swath, wide and green, that raced with the river down through the cane fields. Then it was up to the bridge at the fountainhead of this flow where lily pads swayed in currents created by a gushing of water from an underground stream. A stream rising urgently for its first view of the sun.

There were a few tourists around, exploring a cave somewhere nearby. Harold said they would be seeing it later and set off up the road with Stanley in hot pursuit. Harold had won out among the other boys and become his trusted guide and interpreter. Harold with his nearly bald fourteen-year-old head and clean orange T-shirt with nothing written on it. How could these Jamaicans step out of a steamy, muddy jungle, looking clean and pressed as a fashion plate?

Late in the afternoon, feeling totally relaxed and more than a little bit sunburned, he joined the people on the porch of the house where Jahna was staying. All the kids sat around him as he talked with their parents. The folks wanted to know all about him and about his long-lost son Bird. Jahna had done the advance promotion, bless her heart. They talked for an hour or so; then the people said they "moost be off a dinner" and asked him to please join them.

A small procession of people started to form.

As that group made their way through the village, which was little more than twenty or so neat houses grouped together, others joined the ranks. Everyone carried something: bowls, jugs, coolers, lamps.

The group was talking in a language he couldn't understand. The kids told him it was a patois, a gumbo dialect of the island. He was still surrounded by the kids, but Harold stayed close by his side, ready to interpret, ready to instruct, always ready to philosophize.

"De cave is de mudder of de river. De river is a mon."

He heard the boy's squeaky pubescent voice come across the ages.

"Yes, old man river."

"Yes, mon."

They walked along together for awhile listening to the people chatting among themselves, then Harold said, "So...we g'wan be havin dinner with de mother of ol' mon river toni."

The procession reached the mouth of the cave he'd heard about. Some men lit large torches and others lit gas hurricane lanterns. Past meets present meets future. Right here.

Stanley thought of The Hanged Man.

And now the column of people began making their way down a crude flight of stairs into the darkness. Harold switched on a small flashlight, handed it to Stanley, and then flipped on his own.

"We g'wan on down in de cave to a place de tourist don go. Only veelage people g'wan down there." Harold was whispering now, as was everyone. "Respects to the sleepin' spearits of de cave..."

And so they moved along, threading their way through various chambers and passageways, and eventually found themselves in a large room with a sand floor. Bats hung high above on the damp ceiling. The cave was still alive and sprouting stalagmites and stalactites up and down. Stanley welcomed the sight of some crude wooden furniture that hinted at tables and chairs. It wouldn't be all that comfortable sitting on the damp stone to eat.

Suddenly he felt very old again. And what was this other feeling? Oh yes, *very white.* "Lighten up, Stanley," Lee Ann whispered into his ear.

She would be home by now, going through a mountain of mail over hot soup and salad. Not likely. He'd forgotten that a day had gone by. It was hours earlier in San Francisco. She would still be at KPIQ. What day was it? What time zone? He was losing track fast.

The people were beginning to unpack the food now. One of the kids hauled a boom box off his shoulder and popped in a CD. Prince Fari came on a bit too strong. His dad told him to turn it down. He did. Waaay down his dad said. The kid did, and his father nodded yes.

Stanley was famished, so he got in line with the kids and loaded up on chicken, rice, auki, and a rum punch (or so it seemed) that flowed in an endless stream from five-gallon coolers. The kids were having Kool-Aid.

About halfway through his chicken and rice, he started to see some strange thing—lizards—where he was sure there were no lizards. Shit! What was in that punch? He hoped these flitting images didn't get any worse.

They'd turned out the hurricane lanterns and flashlights and now, in the light of the torches, some people started to dance to a reggae beat coming from the radio. Its owner, a kid named Andy, was DJing the box, gradually—imperceptibly—increasing the volume. Stanley watched to see if the dancers strobed. No. Good. He'd worried for a moment that someone had slipped him a tab. No, the figures, both men and women, were swaying fluidly to a slow reggae bass. He checked to see if he was getting chills—no—and the lizards were gone. If anything, warm brown molasses was now bubbling up through his entire body. It was probably just the rum. He hadn't drunk rum in years, but he remembered some ribald rum dreams.

The kids were still jabbering away, so he lost himself in the music and the shadow of the dancers on the ceiling. Some ceiling. Try and sculpt that, Stanley.

Three young women in their late twenties, dancing together, were looking his way. He watched them, acknowledged them all, and smiled. What else would one do? They motioned for him to join them. He shook his head no. They danced in his direction and all reached down for his hand.

Three Nubian beauties pulled Stanley to his feet.

He tried to match the subtle swaying motion of the lithe young women, but his body was just not built that way, nor had he carried water jugs on his head since the dawn of time. But the girls were playful and smiling and forgiving.

Now he was surrounded by dancing men, women, and children, in a cave, in torchlight, the way everyone remembers it at least once in a life's passage, or wishes they did.

And now the group of dancing men, women, and children began to move in a circle and then a line and then a circle again; coiling and uncoiling like the satellite image of a hurricane when it's run to and fro on the weather map. He'd watched a few. Always fun to watch Lee doing the weather, coiling and uncoiling that tropical depression.

The voices of the girls brought him back. "We g'wan take you swimmin' mon," one of the girls said, and the others giggled. "C'mon n'yaw...follow us."

They took him by both hands and led him over to a passageway that had been hidden in the shadows. The girl in the lead carried a small torch. Stanley, swept along once again and feeling more than a little uneasy about taking a swim in a dark cave, could see, as they approached the end of the passage, a low archway of stone. On the other side was a chamber whose floor was mirror-black water.

They squeezed under the arch and found themselves standing on a broad ledge at the mirror's edge.

"Okay," said the girl who seemed to be a ring leader, "douse de torch."

The girl who held the flame stubbed it out on the damp stone at her feet.

And now total darkness. Only the sound of reggae and people laughing and talking coming from the adjoining chamber. He crouched down in the darkness and scooped at the water. Cave cold but certainly bearable. What the hell he'd swum in the Pacific with its fifty-four degree brine. He could do it.

"Are you afraid?" whispered one of the girls. He'd heard them undressing; now they were stepping down into the water.

"No, I'm fine," he whispered back to the blackness.

The girls were no longer giggling and chattering among themselves. The only sound he heard was a gurgling of water as they stroked out into the pool. He undressed quickly, rolled his clothes, and set them on his thongs. Slowly, he slid down off of the ledge and into the water. It was cold, but the rum was saving his ass in the body heat department.

It was like swimming in outer space with no stars. Such inky blackness was very soothing to the eyes, but he strained to see something—anything.

And where were the girls now? He no longer heard them paddling.

Suddenly something brushed against his feet and then his side and then his other side and then up his back. He tried to spin in the direction of the ledge—but damn! Where was that?

The girls broke the surface all around him giggling and taunting him underwater with their hands. And now he felt them close in and encircle him with their bodies. It lasted for only a moment, a fleeting moment, but one that Stanley would remember for the rest of his life.

The girls were off now, calling for him to follow them to terra firma, teasing and giggling in patois.

None too soon the slippery bottom came up under his feet. There was the faintest glow in the chamber now as someone came down the passageway with a torch. And now, in the dim light, he could see the girls already dressing.

"C'mon mon...we g'wan back now," one of them said as they ducked under the arch.

The light in the chamber came up fast now as a torchbearer, and a group of about ten men, women, and children came from the other direction. They stood greeting him. One of the women held a large white towel in one hand and a white metal teapot in the other. Harold appeared out of the shadows.

"C'mon Stanley. We got a towel for you, some hot tea. Warm you up," he squeaked huskily.

Was this hospitality or what? Stanley abandoned modesty as he pulled his naked albino butt from the water and, in the flickering light of a torch, accepted the towel. It was blessedly warm.

Harold held a battered tin cup for the woman pouring tea.

"Here Stanley. Boosh tea. Warm you up."

Naked Stanley tied the cloth around his waist (generous old waist); then Harold handed him the steaming brew. He carefully slurped up a sip. It was hot, tasted like boiled greens, weeds and twigs. He wouldn't be writing home about the flavor, but at least it was hot. The group of people wanted to know if he'd enjoyed his swim. He said he wouldn't soon forget it. They laughed and chatted him up in Jamaicanspeak, and then motioned for him to follow them back to the party. Harold grabbed his roll of clothes, and one by one, they ducked under the low arch, climbed the adjoining passageway, and soon found themselves once again back with the other members of the group. Everyone seemed to be packing up.

A waxing moon dropped shafts of pallid light into the mouth of the cave as they climbed the final flight of stairs up, out, and into a balmy tropic night. The group stood for a moment at the head of the stairs, shifting their loads and taking a head count of the kids. Then it was off again down a path through a mango grove that led back to the village.

In the grove Stanley started to see strange things again. This time not lizards—but worms. The canopy of trees over the path became a writhing tunnel of grubs. And now rivulets of ice water trickled up his spine, not down. Uh oh. By the time they reached the compound, he'd stopped once along the trail to put on his clothes, and once to throw up. Jahna and Harold, who saw him to his hut, could see he was very ill and afraid. Jahna suggested more bush tea, but he declined adamantly. Harold sat by his side as he wrapped himself as tightly as possible in the thin blankets that covered his bed.

His body felt immense to him now, almost as if he'd been inflated to the bursting point. And now there were hot coals glowing on the ceiling. This is not good—this is not good—this is not good. His mind seized on the words like a mantra. Malaria? His bibulous brain kept thinking. I couldn't have contracted malaria *this* fast. What the hell...?

He saw Jahna's face and large yellow eyes overhead—swimming in the coals on the ceiling. She was asking him to stand up. He did, but not without clutching his blankets fiercely about his now spasmodic body. And now she was helping him out the door through the night to a place in the trees where a large fire burned. And what was that in the sand at the edge of the blaze?

Someone had dug a long shallow pit. He saw people, black faces in the firelight, or was that just his imagination? He was losing it fast; the chills seemed to be winning. Jahna led him to the pit and helped him to lie down in it. She comforted him as he lowered himself onto the warm dry sand. Warmth, oh blessed warmth.

The rest was hazy in his memory. He saw benevolent faces towering above him. And now people were bending down and scooping sand onto his body, filling in the hole over him.

Tepid sand. No—hot sand! Heavy sand! He felt the weight and the warmth of it squeezing persistently at his shivering frame. And then, the last thing he remembered was someone lowering large leaves onto his face, and then someone burying his head—alive.

49.

The Caribbean skies rained in the night. Not a hard-driving rain but a soft drizzle that had left the trees and rocks weeping. Roarin River stood steaming in the first light of dawn.

Stanley saw none of this. He was flying—more like floating—drifting with the breezes high above San Francisco.

It had taken him no little amount of practice to be able to accomplish this. He remembered, as if it was yesterday, those first few times he'd jumped into the air and not come down—right away that is. There seemed to be some more than imagined hang time there at the top of his trajectory. And then he'd found the more he actually believed that it was happening the more it did happen. He'd practiced in private then because he didn't want to frighten anyone. People don't fly. *But he could!*

Air Stanley.

And after enough time of jumping and believing and jumping and believing, one day he just didn't come down at all. And it didn't matter then if he shouted to himself when he was hanging with no visible means of support ten or twelve feet off the ground...

"Christ! I can't believe this really works...I'm really doing this!"

No even that didn't bring him down. He could float! And then, of course, came the problem of how to propel himself now that he could float. He hadn't figured that one out yet so had contented himself with drifting straight up and letting the wind carry him where it would. Now he was at ten thousand feet above San Francisco Bay. At that height no one could see him from the ground. But he knew it was inevitable that someone would, at some future point in time, spot him from an airplane. When that happened he'd decided he would just smile and wave.

"Stanley...Stanley...wake up, mon." He heard a voice come from the light outside his dream. A dream—shit—it was just another dream? It had seemed so real. Where was he? He opened his eyes, wondering if maybe he had taken a quantum leap into yet another universe. For there, filling his full field of vision, was a woman. A black woman, sitting sideways on her legs. She was naked from the waist up, in her early thirties. He could see that in the back of a hand she laid on his arm.

"You g'wan sleep aw day, Stanley?"

He rubbed his eyes; she was coming into focus now, a handsome woman, with full breasts and square shoulders. Her fingers, though long and delicate, showed signs of heavy work. There was a golden glow about her brown-black brow.

It was coming back now. The party in the cave, the rum, the swim, and then bush tea and the chills—and then being buried alive in hot sand. He pulled himself to a sitting position and sat cross-legged, rubbing his head and eyes. Except for a ravenous hunger and a roaring headache, he felt no other unpleasant sensations in his body. No broken bones, and his vision was clear and steady again.

Amazing after last night—he assumed it was last night—when he had been sure he was going to die. "I'm sorry," he said to the woman, "do I know you? Have we met?"

She seemed unaware that she was still uncovered. She flashed a large white smile. Beautiful smile! he thought. Her slim hand came out to him for a shake. "Awfully sorry, Stanley. No we 'ave naw met till now. My name is Cynthia." She stretched out the syllables of her name so that they sounded like a chord being played in arpeggio. It certainly was music to his ears. She went on. "I am de one dey chose to look after you. You were very eel last night. We were veery worried, mon."

Stanley took Cynthia's hand and shook it. "Pleased to meet you, Cynthia. Worried is putting it mildy. I thought I was going to die. How did I get out here?" he asked as he brushed sand off his arms and legs.

"We carried you here. We taught dat you should sleep outside...let dey stars watch over aye and aye."

"Mmmm. Well, thank you. For looking after me."

He looked up into the underside of a thatched hut that was little more than a roof on four poles. Beyond the roof, the meadow was wet with rain, but it was a sunny morning. He squinted his eyes against the brilliant light.

"Ah ha"—gentle laughter from Cynthia—"Stanley...you look as tho you have a tierrible headache. I know someting good for dat." She was smiling wryly now like some coquette of the bush.

"What's that? Bush tea?" he said, wishing now that this woman would cover her breasts. It was becoming increasingly difficult to carry on a relaxed conversation with her. He felt very white again. He wondered how long it would take for this feeling to pass. Cynthia said, "No...tho boosh tea wou be good too. No, I know someting better..." She paused, put a hand to one of her breasts. "Would you like to sex me, Stanley?"

It felt like someone had dunked his head into a bucket of scalding hot water. What the hell had she just asked him?"

"Would I like to *what!?*"

Cynthia was still smiling. "Would you like to sex me? Come inside of me?"

His pulse hit 200. "Well, uh,"—he felt like Butthead about to giggle— "I just met you. Maybe in an hour or two after we've said more than six words to each other...how's that sound?"

This up-country Jamaica life might take some getting used to, but he would certainly give it a go.

"Come, Stanley. Come see my place in de cane." Cynthia stood. Stanley stood, more stiffly than he would like to have, and looked around. They were in the meadow on the bend of the river where he'd been swimming with the kids yesterday. At the edge of the meadow, cane fields ran away to the mountains. Cynthia pulled the cloth that served as her dress up over one shoulder and swung off in the direction of a green wall of clattering grass. She reached the wall, squatted, parted it at the base, and was suddenly gone from view.

He followed her lead and found himself in a short tunnel through a thick mat of stalks. He could see daylight ahead.

When he reached Cynthia's small clearing in the cane, she'd already dropped the cloth from her body and spread it on a bed of flattened chaff. She lay down now and motioned for him to lie down beside her. He tried to keep his eyes from dancing about, but they were not cooperating. Her body was long, lean and strong. She was a full woman there, apparently, for his taking. Shit, oh dear—what now? He propped himself on one elbow beside her.

"Are you a shy mon, Stanley...could not sex me in de meadow? Is this better?"

He put his hand up behind her back and pulled her to him. They kissed softly, then again. And now Cynthia began kneading him gently but to no avail. Nothing was happening down there. Nothing. Hmm, he'd rarely had this problem before. Nature's way of telling him something? He pulled back and said "I'm sorry...you know...I think you are a very beautiful and desirable woman...but I just met you..."

She said "I know, I like you."

"Uh...why don't we just spend some time together and then we'll see what comes up. Right now," he patted his crotch, "it's nadda...that means no go at the moment."

Cynthia laughed and said. "Oh...okay Stanley...later."

She casually donned her sarong. They crawled back out of her small room in the sugarcane and found themselves once again back in the meadow.

"Come Stanley, I cook you some fish for breakfast. You moost be a hungry mon."

You could say that again.

Jamaica, nice place, no problem.

50.

She knew the first day back at work was going to be a heaven-and-hell sort of thing so was relieved to get her feet back on the ground. Her flight touched down at SFO 7:30pm PST. It wasn't late, but she was dog tired so she hailed a cab to her house on Kensington. Sixty bucks well spent. Her house was dark, and when she let herself in, a wave of ten-day-old air hit her squarely in the face. Everything needed airing, but all seemed to have survived.

She'd called Maureen from thirty-five thousand feet over New Mexico. Plane phones rule (she still got a little-girl kick out of using them). Maureen had been her usual motherly self and told Lee Ann she might want to take another day off before she came back in, because when she did, they would be putting in some twelve to sixteen hour days. She told her the mailbags were full of letters to her from women who had experienced what she'd been going through and were sick of it and weren't going to take it anymore. All Lee Ann could say was "Really?" Maureen had gone on to say that she'd sampled some of that tsunami of incoming mail and found the prevailing theme to be man's inhumanity to woman. "Really," said Lee Ann in a less than friendly tone of voice this time. "Really," Maureen said and then told Lee Ann that the power people around KPIQ wanted to milk it a little. Well, more than just a little. They wanted to do a running report on it, make it a regular feature topic on *Good Morning San Francisco*—have a call-in sort of thing. "Really?" said Lee Ann gravely. "Mmm, let me think about that one a little, Maureen. We'll talk Monday. Yes, I'll be in around nine. You can't believe how I'm itching to get back to work."

Maureen said, "...okay, so you've been warned." And then they'd signed off. That was about four hours ago. Now Lee Ann, fresh from her bath and wrapped in a bulky terry robe, sat sipping Satori tea and going through a mountain of mail on her study desk. Most of it consisted of bills and coupon circulars. She went routing and sorting through these looking for correspondence of a personal nature. There was a card-shaped envelope postmarked Glenwood Springs, Colorado. It would be an early birthday greeting from the folks on the ranch: Stanley's folks, her folks, now in their late seventies. They always remembered her birthday. She set the card aside to enjoy on June twelfth and went on sorting.

Ah, there was a battered old envelope that looked like it had been lying in the storage bin of an eighteen-wheeler for one too many trips across the continent. She recognized the tight little scrawl that was her daddy Sherman's and the familiar return address: Sherman Barnes, USA. She tore the envelope open and pulled out two folded sheets of blue-lined notebook paper. Well, this was a rare treat; her daddy Sherman seldom wrote. She read:

5/1/2005

Howdy little darlin,

I'm sitting here at the counter of a greasy spoon in Amarillo drinking some crankcase drip this waitress here swears to god is coffee. I think she's trying to poison me so she can highjack my rig.

Called you earlier this week cause you'd been drifting around my thoughts quite a bit lately. Don't know why—do you? Maybe it's because your forty-fifth is coming up here about this time next month, and I always get to thinking about those years we'd have your birthday there at the Hochstetters' and then light out for a summer on the road. We did have some good times back then, and I think of them often. Guess you get hound-dog sentimental as the years fade off in the ol' wing mirrors. And speaking of that, as you know, come next year when my sixty-fifth rolls around, I'm going to be parking the rig and climbing down for the last time, so have gone ahead and started building a little place out on the Hochstetters' spread. We've only got the slab in so far, but you wouldn't believe how much work goes into that. Rest of it should be a breeze.

Now that I'm going to be settling down, you got to promise me you and that whippersnapper granddaughter of mine will come out for a visit some summer. Be just like old times. Maybe we can talk Stanley into coming out too. You two started talking again? I hope so.

I need to get back on my horse here 'fore this java sets up in my veins and rusts me shut. You know I'm not one for writing too much, but if you get a chance, give me a niner on the old mobile unit here. Let me know what you're up to these days. You got the number.

Signing off here darlin'. Love ya. Think of you often. Hope all is well.

Your Daddy,

Sherman

Lee Ann picked up the desk phone and dialed Sherman's mobile unit. She wondered what highway it was rolling down this time of the early evening. And then again it could be not so early. Maybe old Fancy Dancer (Sherman's Peterbilt) was plying the Jersey Turnpike. He could be anywhere, that old road warrior. She let it ring six times, but there was no answer. Back to sorting the post.

A red envelope came to her attention. The writing on the front was definitely in an adolescent hand. She quickly read the return address.

Pedro and Rosalita Ramone
1071 Green St., Suite 16
San Francisco, CA

Pedro and Lita! Miguel's children. She cut the end off the envelope and pulled out a card with clowns and balloons on the cover. It was another early birthday card from the kids. As she opened the card two small photographs fell out: Pedro and Lita's school pictures. They had always been handsome children, but now they were stunning. She grabbed a tissue, blew her nose, and read the messages inside wishing her a happy birthday, telling her about school, wondering when she would be coming over to see them. Both Pedro and Lita had written, and closed with "I miss you."

She switched off the desk lamp and sat in the dark for a long time and then walked to her bedroom, slipped into her nightgown, and down into her own bed. It felt so good to be in her own bed.

But this night, her first night in from the storm, she would fall to sleep with a heavy heart. Tomorrow she'd call the children and make a date. It had been too long.

Sunday passed like a dream. Pedro and Lita were free for the day, so she picked the children up around eleven and headed over to the Japanese Tea Garden in Golden Gate Park. They walked the paths, threw pennies into the wishing pools, bowed to the Buddha, and finished lunch by feeding fortune cookies to greedy, clamoring squirrels. These were old rituals, some of the children's favorite things to do.

Later, sitting under a eucalyptus, she told the children about finding Bird again in New Orleans. They listened wide eyed and amazed. Both said they wanted to meet him soon. Pedro and Lita cried a little then as they told her how much they missed their father—and the family the four of them had been at one time. It was at that point that Lee Ann looked up and, for a fleeting second, saw her ghost, and the ghost of Miguel, embracing that first time beneath the tree where she now sat with his young children.

Yes, Sunday did seem like a dream as she lay in the dark hours of Monday morning waiting for the clock radio to come on.

It did that at exactly 4am. She swung her slightly stiff legs onto the floor and began trundling through the old morning ritual like a boot camp grunt: stretch, jog, shower, dress, hair, light makeup, oatmeal and juice—no coffee until she arrived at the station. She'd told Maureen she wouldn't be in until nine. Usually it was six to do the show at nine. But she wanted to watch the show from Maureen's office this morning and then sort of slip back into the stream as unobtrusively as possible. The best way to do that was to arrive when everyone was their busiest. That would be nine when the *Good Morning San Francisco* theme jingled out of Sutro Tower.

She parked her Mercedes in the underground garage and took a back elevator up to the studio. The receptionist greeted her with a broad smile and warm handshake, welcoming her back, asking her if she was free of "that guy."

How many times would she be going through this routine today? She couldn't wait until tomorrow when things returned to normal.

"Maureen's expecting me. I'm just going to duck into her office 'till after the show. Yes, it's so good to be back; everything's fine now," she called over her shoulder and hurried off down the hall in the direction of her boss's office.

Maureen gave her a casual welcome, a short hug, and plugged a coffee mug into her hand. They talked, caught up on gossip and work and family and children, all the while watching Bradley and Laura over in the next room do the show.

Then the show was over and it was time for her to hit the beat. It was heaven to be back in the old trench with all the people she knew who whispered in her ear that they were so glad she was back. Laura had always been difficult to work with, and now they'd had to do it for over a week. Some tempers had flared. "So good to have you back, Lee Ann."

And then there was that old teddy bear, Sam Weber, the weatherman, probably her best friend outside of Maureen at KPIQ. They gave each other an extended hug, and he asked her straightaway if this thing with the nutcase was completely over. Lee Ann, still crushed tightly against his enormous body, gasped, "Don't you worry, Sam, it's all over." Before he'd let her go, he made her promise to have lunch with him the next afternoon to fill him in on the details. She promised (fingers crossed), and he released her. Sam—off to monitor the winds of the planet. She missed the weather.

Tom Blake, VP in charge of entertainment, and his crew of mad-dog writers wanted to meet at one to go over some new brainthrust for the "pursued women series." That's when heaven changed to hell. After three hours of discussions, which often bordered on arguments, Lee Ann walked from the room licking her wounds and wondering if she was up to carrying off what Tom and the boys were asking of her. Were they moving the show in the direction of Sally Jesse and Geraldo? It certainly sounded that way. She argued vehemently that even though she had been the target of some rather aberrant behavior and could get into their ideas on a gut level, it seemed they were proposing to take on, on a regular basis, a topic much too serious and complicated to be dealt with on a happy little morning show.

It went around and around with Lee Ann finally agreeing to do two segments to see how it flew. The boys had arranged to have her mailbags sitting off to one side of the conference table during the meeting. That was so Tom could occasionally point to them and say, "We can't ignore this, Lee Ann."

And so Lee Ann and Maureen (thank God she had been there to keep the feeding frenzy moderately civilized) walked down the hall to their offices, cursing to each other about the vaudeville mentality of television marketing *men*.

"Although, in all fairness," whispered Lee Ann, "I guess I opened Pandora's Box."

Maureen nodded. "You know, the irony of this is, if it hadn't been for Poteet, you might never have found your Bird."

447

Yes, that thought had rattled around in her brain, and she supposed it had occurred to Stanley too. But neither of them had come right out and said it. Now leave it to Maureen to call it forward. And, of course, there was no way to deny it. Stanley wouldn't have gone to New Orleans if it hadn't been for the clay. She wouldn't have gone along unless Poteet had flushed her down to his den with his little terrorist tactics.

"Together we found him," she heard Poteet whisper in her ear.

She shivered.

"You all right?" Maureen asked.

"Yeah...I am, but I just heard a pirate laughing."

"I know, gotta watch out for those pirates."

"Well, guess I'll just call him right now and thank him profusely."

"Wait a couple of years...we got work to do."

Lee nodded.

She and Maureen spent the rest of the afternoon and into the early evening hours going over the rally board for the following week's shows. Maureen finished up by asking:

"So, kiddo...you ready to go in there tomorrow? How's your mouth? Up and flapping?"

Lee Ann, starting to feel the fever now, didn't skip a beat. "Okay, it's Monday." Pause. "In the spirit of cohosting, why don't we let Laura do the show tomorrow, and I'll make a little appearance and fill the people in on the fact that I'm back and safe and ready to go to work bright and early Wednesday morning. That would let Laura down easily and ease me back in. What do you think of that plan, Capitan?"

"That's what I like about you, sweetie," rasped Maureen in her whiskey river voice. She grabbed the phone, told someone to let Laura know she was doing one more day. "Tell her Lee Ann's coming on briefly for an update on her story...will be back in full-time the following day...right...Wednesday. Right, goodbye. Done," she said. "Let's get some dinner. I'm ready to prowl out to the nearest waterhole and bring down a wildebeest with my bare teeth...how 'bout you?"

Lee thought about Poteet and his animal club. She decided to tell Maureen about it at dinner, that is, if she got around to it. She and Maureen never—that's never—ran out of things to talk about.

51.

A week had passed. Stanley and Jahna were packing their bags aboard a battered little car with its steering wheel on the wrong side. The same car and driver that brought them here would now be returning them to Montego Bay and "de plane ri," as Jahna called it.

Harold and a couple of his teenage cronies stood off to the side as Stanley said his thanks and goodbyes to Jahna's people. Then he gave Cynthia a hug and a kiss and whispered something in her ear. Harold was last.

"Respects mon," Harold wheezed and grasped his hand.

"Respects. I will see you again soon," Stanley said softly as he wrapped an arm about Harold's slim shoulders. The two of them made their way a short distance to the waiting car. There was some final waving and shouting as the car pulled out of the compound and headed down the road.

"So you be g'wan back to Roarin River?" asked Jahna, even before they'd crossed the stone bridge down by the river.

"Yes...I be g'wan," said Stanley as he watched the village fade around a bend to the rear.

He didn't get his swim in the Caribbean as planned. On the way back to Montego Bay, the car had a slow flat and it had taken two hours to have it repaired: no spare. They made the airport just as their flight was being called. The flight attendants closed the door behind them as they boarded the plane.

Jahna slept on the return flight to New Orleans so he tried to do the same, but he was completely rested so spent the time with eyes closed, watching a week in Roarin River spool through his mind.

The morning Cynthia had taken him back to her house to feed him breakfast, he'd been pleased to discover she was a potter; she made large clay containers for planting herbs and pepper plants and for storing water. And she had her own large walk-in kiln! Was this just luck? He'd wondered. After breakfast she'd told him, in her most innocent way, that the women of the village had decided she should be his woman. It was decided so because she was a widow with a child, and she was the right age for him, and her trade was one that he would appreciate.

"So...aw we ha to know is if you like me, Stanley." She'd smiled warmly and looked straight into his eyes.

He was still reeling from the revelations he'd just been privileged to hear about how these village women conducted business. Straightforward was a word that came to mind. And now Cynthia asked him again.

"You like me? I like you. We will live here and 'ave some chilldren."

He shook his head in amazement. "Well...Cynthia..."

"You don like me?"

"No, certainly I do...you are a beautiful, honest woman...it's just that I have a life in San Francisco. Friends."

"Do you 'ave a womon? Jahna say you no 'ave a womon."

He thought for a moment. "Yes, she's right I no 'ave a womon."

"Ah ha...Stanley...you tease me. You do like me."

"Yes, I do like you...very much...already. And I just met you."

Cynthia beamed.

"But my problem may be, at the moment, that I have *too many* women."

"Oh yes, Stanley, that can be a problem too. Ha!"

"Tell me about it. I mean, I have all these women who profess to love me, tell me how much they love me...and then run away!"

"Ah, well, Stanley, they just like to tease you."

"Well, that's the truth."

"You like to be teased?"

"Not really."

"I no tease you. I no run away."

He walked over and took her loosely in his arms. "Oh Cynthia." He kissed her forehead. "I think you are a beautiful woman...truly. You move like a lazy breeze, and you smile like the morning sun. But let's not start a family just yet. I'm only going to be here for a week.

"I unna'stan you Stanleymon," she'd said, and went off to do the dishes.

The flight attendants came by with the happy cart. He ordered a Beefeater's martini on the rocks, took the tiny thing down in two sips, and leaned back again to listen to the big fans on the wings humming them back to New Orleans.

He'd stayed in his own tiny hut for the rest of the week, but had eaten around the village like a beggar: one night with Harold's grandmother and grandfather, one night with Jahna's people out on their big front porch, one night each with various other households. But it worked out that he ended up eating all his breakfasts with Cynthia and Harold. Fish and rice are nice for breakfast.

Mornings found him swimming in the river with the kids and hanging out down by the cave and the bridge talking with the people and watching a small number of tourists come and go. Always with Harold, his trusted guide and interpreter, by his side. Afternoons Harold went on to his shift as a cave host, so that time of day he spent working with Cynthia in her outdoor studio.

Stanley's ability on the wheel delighted and amazed her as they turned out pot after pot. Together they built some pots that were heads with open mouths and some others that were flower shaped. He tried to do some figures with her clay, but it was too common to hold any kind of detail. Toward the end of the week, though, he finally got the hang of it and did some heavily massed figures of her reclining in the nude and another of her clothed, sitting with Harold.

The villagers enjoyed seeing these, and several people offered to buy them, but Cynthia told them, "Dees statues no for sale."

With protection, he slept with Cynthia on the last night of his stay in Roarin River. He was glad they'd waited because the following morning, amid much kissing and laughter, they agreed they wouldn't mind doing it again. He liked this woman a great deal. She moved like the tops of the swaying palm trees. She was sleepy and slow and clear as the water that bubbled up out of the ground down by the cave.

It was also in her favor that Harold was her son.

Now he was on his way back to New Orleans, but only for a touch and go, only to check in with Claire and Clay, pick up his belongings (including the hundred pounds of Melissa's clay) and then head back to California. He missed home now. He had a million new ideas and wanted to get back to work as soon as possible. Evie would be pleased. Maybe.

"Ladies and gentlemen, would you please fasten your seatbelts as we are making our final descent into New Orleans."

"Jahna...wakeup...we're home."

"Aah...Stanley...I 'ave been awake de 'ole time..."

He'd called Clay yesterday from Roarin River and given him his flight number and ETA at New Orleans International. Clay said he'd try to borrow a car and come out to pick him up, with Claire, of course. "So how you roomies doing?" he'd asked.

"Well...I think I'm in love."

"Who's the lucky girl?" Several possible candidates had occurred to Stanley.

"Your daughter."

"Gulp."

"Yeah, big gulp. I don't know what's come over me. I mean it was infatuation at first sight when I saw her for the first time in French Market. And it's just been getting better ever since. She's a sweetheart."

"Clay?"

"Yes?

"This I will have to see. There are a few hundred adjectives I know apply to my daughter. 'Sweetheart' has never really come to mind."

"Yeah? Well, it's true. Anyway, man, we'll try to get to the airport. If not, can you get a car?"

"Sure, no problem."

He stood looking over the crowd as he emerged from customs with a baggage cart piled high...mostly Jahna's stuff. No kids. He and Jahna proceeded to the National counter, rented a car, and headed back into town. He didn't talk with the old one on the way in; she seemed to be lost in her own reverie, and he certainly was lost in his. They'd spent enough time together now so they felt perfectly comfortable with hours of silence between them. He thought about Lee Ann, knowing that could never happen with her. Lee, the windy little weather girl.

After a shower and much-needed shave, he called Clay's number. Claire answered.

"Hi."

"Hi, yourself. And happy birthday! Happy Twenty-first... this is the old man, home from paradise."

"Dad! Thanks! Where are you? We couldn't find a car to borrow. None of Clay's friends have one. Starving musicians, you know."

He was listening intently to Claire's voice. It was a different voice, full of music and merriment. No trace of the sarcastic nasal snarl. Could this be?

"No problem, I'm flying back to San Francisco in a couple of days, so just as well that I have a rental. How y'all doin? How's it feel to be totally legal now?"

"Surprisingly relieved. How 'bout yourself? How was Jamaica? You marry a native girl and knock her up?"

The tone was merrier now; the brain would always be Claire's. Perceptive, club-wielding Claire.

"Ha! Funny you should say that."

"Daddy! You didn't!"

"Relax, no...I didn't do that...yet."

"So how was it? Did you have fun? How were the people? I hear they're beautiful."

"So many questions, so little time."

"Can I cook you dinner?"

Claire was asking him that?

"Nah, let's celebrate your birthday. How about..."

"THE VERA CRUZ!" she screamed.

"Read my mind. I'll treat."

"Just a minute...let me ask Clay."

There was a brief exchange between his daughter and Clay; he strained to hear. Claire was being girlish, teasing Clay, calling him "honey." This was his daughter?

"Okay he says, welcome back, and that sounds great. About seven? We'll come by there, walk on down?"

"It's a date."

"Okay...bye."

"Bye."

He sat on the edge of the bed in total disbelief. He couldn't wait to see this new Claire with his own eyes. Something was beginning, he could feel it, though wasn't quite sure he knew what *it* was. And though *it* made him profoundly happy, he still couldn't get Lisa out of his mind. He wondered if she was on at Le Richelieu. It was five o'clock and there was plenty of time to drop over for a drink and a chat, but first he'd try Lee Ann at KPIQ, see what her take was on all of this.

Lee Ann was in a meeting—what's new—so he picked up some cash and made his way over to the hotel. Lisa was in a meeting too: a meeting of happy hour revelers. No possible way to talk, but she said she did want to talk, so got a guy to sub for her while she took a short break. They walked out of the hotel and sat on a low stone wall by the front steps. She pulled a Camel out of her battered handbag and lit up.

"I didn't know you smoked."

"I started again." She took a long drag, pulled it down, and blew it out.

"Oh..."

"It's been pure *hell,* Stan. But, hey, enough about me, I've got some news for you."

He looked at Lisa's face. Even from the side it looked drawn and tired. The sparkle had been replaced with a wane pallor that pulled at her skin.

"Claire and Clay?"

"Ha, well I'm sure you've talked with them. I was right; it happened. But that's not the news...here." She handed him a folded *Times Picayune* she'd been carrying with her. "It's three days old, but I saved it for you. Knew you'd want your own memorial copy."

He took the well-handled newspaper and unfolded it flat in his lap. Lisa laid her finger on a sub-headline on the front page. It read simply: "LOCAL CERAMICS MAGNATE SHOT." His eyes quickly dropped down to the first line of copy. It read: "Jean Paul Poteet, owner of Poteet Porcelain and well-known animal conservationist advocate, was shot three times at close range by a woman posing as a florist delivery woman. The incident occurred early yesterday morning at his home...." The article went on, but Stanley slowly folded the paper and sat staring straight ahead.

"I'll read this later," he said softly. "What's the latest? Do you know? Is he still alive? Did they catch the woman?"

"In a manner of speaking. She's in a drawer down at the city morgue."

"Damn. Shot by the police?"

"No, it was a woman named Hattie Devereaux, sister of that man they found floating in the river a couple of years ago. Remember my telling you about that?"

"Yeah, my testicles and I remember that."

Lisa looked over at him and smiled slightly. She told him that Hattie had arrived at the Poteet residence in a white van posing as a singing floral delivery person. She'd presented Poteet with a large spray of gladiolus and then pulled out a gun and shot him three times at close range. Then she'd turned the gun on her own cancer-infested brain and blown *it* away. A suicide note in her coveralls said she'd done it because she knew she was dying and couldn't go without taking some revenge on Poteet for his alleged involvement with her brother's death. Poteet was expected to live, though the newspaper report said one of the bullets narrowly missed his heart. Lisa said she'd done some checking and had heard that, in the last four days, Poteet's condition had been upgraded from critical to stable. Barring the complications that often accompany gunshot wounds, it appeared he was going to make it.

Stanley sat shaking his head in disbelief. In the back of his mind, during the last week in Jamaica, he'd been building resolve to go see the old pirate before he left for San Francisco. Now he wondered.

"I wonder if he can have visitors yet? Ha! I guess now would be a fairly safe time to have a little chat with the old devil."

"I guess it would. Are you really considering it? Going to see him in the hospital?"

"You know, I am. Do you know the name of the hospital where he's recovering?"

Lisa told him it was in Metairie, that it was named in the article. He glanced at the copy and noted it for future reference. They sat in silence for a moment, then Lisa started to twitch, and he knew her break was just about up. But there was still the business he'd come here to do.

"Thanks for saving this for me. I'll communicate it to Lee Ann. I'm sure she'll find it interesting."

"I'm sure she will. I guess Poteet hit the old karmic wall, didn't he? Big splat."

"Yeah, big splat." He looked over at her. "Well, I know you've got to get going here. I just dropped by to say adios, and thank you...and I..."

"Feel somehow responsible for the fact that your little girl took my guy away from me?"

He looked down at his hands and nodded.

She threw an arm over his shoulder, patted him. "Naw, Stan, don't you think it. It was just one of those crazy things that happen. And it *was* crazy wasn't it? The way it happened."

He nodded. Lisa went on. "Thanks for caring, man. I mean you never had to see me again, did you? And you came over to see how I was doing."

"I like you Lisa...I have from the minute we met. And I owe you a big one."

Lisa sat silently staring down at her inch-long cigarette. He went on.

"Just because Clay and my daughter are being totally rude and kicking you out of their lives doesn't mean that I don't want to keep knowing you."

"Thanks." She took a long-last pull on the Camel and stubbed it out in a flower pot.

They sat for a moment in silence. Then she said. "You know, I was the one who went after Clay. As soon as I saw him drifting off from Amanda, I jumped in with both feet...slept with him as soon as I could. I mean you saw that. Remember that day you came into the bar? You'd just come back from taking Lee Ann to the airport? That was the day after the night before, the first time. Win some, lose some. No, I can't say that Clay was as in love with me as I was with him. I think he's in love with Claire though."

"Sounds like it," said Stanley softly.

"You know, it's just that old fucked, gut-sick feeling that only goes away with time. Summer session's starting though. I'll get my mind back on the law, and this will eventually all go away. Isn't like it was my first rodeo. I'm twenty-seven you know."

"I've noticed."

"Thanks again for caring, Stan."

"Love ya like a daughter, Lisa...such a lovely daughter."

She smiled over at him. He hurried on. "So, hey! I've got your address, and I think I'm coming back down in a month or two. Jahna's given me the name of a guy over in Gulfport who sails to Jamaica. I'm going over there tomorrow to check out his operation."

"That sounds great! You lucky guy. Well, come by and say hello when you come back down...before you sail. Okay?"

"Definitely. We'll stay in touch. Maybe this thing will blow over like a Gulf squall. Claire's been known to be a fickle little pickle." He poked her in the ribs with his elbow.

"Naw Stan, I'm movin' on with the storm. It was a nice little cruise, but I'm goin' to marry some successful lawyer and start a firm, have six kids, do the American Dream thing."

"You probably will, Lisa," said Stanley as he pulled himself to his feet. She was already standing with a stubbed-out cigarette still in her hand. It was time to get back to the bar. "Okay then, we'll be in touch." He held his hand out to her. She took it and pulled him in for a short hug.

"You're a darlin', Lisa."

"So are you, Stan."

And then she was through that famous front door of Le Richelieu and gone from view.

Stanley made his way back up Esplanade wondering if he would ever see Lisa Lynn McKenzie again. He concluded that that was probably up to him.

He called Lee Ann when he got back to his room. She'd finished with one meeting and gone on to another. This one apparently not so power packed that she couldn't talk with him for a minute. After a little routing by the receptionist, she came on the line. She asked him first about Jamaica, and he told her they would talk about that over dinner when he got back. He told her briefly that it was what he hoped heaven would be like and that he was going back, soon. Then he told her about Poteet. She made him read the entire *Times Picayune* article word for word. She kept saying, "God, this is extremely confusing. I don't know how to feel about this." He agreed that his feelings were also mixed. Then he asked her if her recent reading on Claire and Clay was the same one he was getting. She said yes, it looked a lot like Love.

There was a knock on his door. The kids, dropping by to pick him up for dinner. Lee said she'd talked to them a few short hours ago, so would let him go see for himself if this was all true. She asked him to call her when he got back from dinner. He said he'd try, and then she was gone, back into her world.

Lee Ann, down in a control room at KPIQ, set the phone back on its console and leaned back in her chair, breathing a sigh of relief. She felt certain now that Stanley would never have to learn about Claire and Jackie, at least not from her. But then again, nothing could ever be taken for granted where Claire was concerned. She'd seen all too often how fast Claire could wind up, come wheeling about, and destroy everything in her path. It had always been like chasing tornadoes, this mothering of Claire.

Dinner with Claire and Clay started off well. And since it was Claire's birthday, they all decided it was only fitting that this be Claire's birthday celebration, May 20, twenty-one years old. The staff of the Vera Cruz gave her a mountainous sizzling chicken enchilada with twenty-one candles sticking out of it, and a margarita that could have served as a washtub. Everyone in the place sang "Happy Birthday". After dinner, on the walk home. Claire and Clay went off into a world of their own. Stanley marched along behind. They reached a corner of Esplanade Street and Stanley signaled that he was going to turn in the direction of Jahna Leveau's.

"You don't want to come by for awhile, cup of chicory or something?" Clay asked.

"Naw, I've got stuff to do...heading home in a couple of days."

They argued about the urgency of that for awhile, but Stanley knew his kids were just being polite. He could see they definitely wanted to be alone. Somehow he managed to make a date with Claire for the following day to go to Gulfport to secure a boat passage to Jamaica. Clay said that would be cool if she went. He had rehearsal at the club all day and didn't think Claire would want to sit around for that. Everyone parted, hugging three ways—then Stanley moved off in the direction of home. Wherever that was? He wondered.

52.

She came bounding down the steps of Clay's place, all twenty-one years of her. His daughter, Claire. He wondered when she was going to change the turquoise tank top. Must be something working for her there. It went with her Mediterranean tan. Claire, she was so beautiful. Was it that she was happy with her life now? No longer felt a need for all the metal that had at one time pierced her body?

And, of course, she was in love. He could relate.

They waved to each other when she was at the top of the stairs, and then suddenly she was throwing her gear bag in the backseat of the Mustang and piling in on the passenger side. It felt so good to be with Claire again. Just Claire, off on an adventure.

"You want to drive? This thing is fun to drive." Stanley offered.

"Oh God, NO!" I'm not so good with new places. Behind the wheel, I mean."

Stanley thought about Lee Ann who would comfortably drive through any kind of chaos. Just give her the next turn.

"But I am a damn good navigator. I can do that. You need that?" Claire brought him back.

"Maps in the glove box."

Claire fished a fresh map of Louisiana out of the box and, after some shuffling, asked "Where's Mississippi? You got Mississippi? Gulfport's in old Miss you know?

"We'll have to stop and pick one up. Didn't know I was going to be headed into Mississippi on this trip."

"Understood" Claire barked over the rumbling of wind starting to build as they headed for the bridge.

"Should we put the top up?" Stanley shouted over the roar.

"YOU KIDDING?"

Okay, guess that answers that. Not going to get too much talking done on this trip out.

The boat and its captain were as steadfast, sturdy, and seaworthy as Jahna told him they would be. She herself had made the trip by sea to Jamaica several times and insisted that he must do it too. The vessel—a fifty-four-foot Alden built ketch christened *Holy Spirit*—was skippered by a man named Flannigan. An ex-Catholic priest who told Stanley he'd found a new savior in the sea. Stanley talked to the burly, suntanned sixty-year-old man long enough to know that he could easily spend four or five days on the same boat with him. Flannigan was well read and had a salty sense of humor. The old priest asked him if he got seasick—didn't want to take him if he did. Stanley said he'd never been susceptible to motion sickness—remembered his many flying dreams.

"All right then, Mr. Hochstetter, you say you want to go in late August? I'm scheduled for a trip around the last week of August. Keep in touch and I'll let you know the exact date of departure. And I require a three hundred dollar non-refundable deposit...good faith money."

Stanley casually pulled three bills off his clip and handed them to Flannigan who just as nonchalantly stuck them into his baggy trousers. They shook on it.

Claire, who had asked permission to wander around the boat while Flannigan and her dad talked business, returned just in time to compliment the captain on his craft and join in the parting remarks. Then they took their leave and went scouting around the waterfront looking for a place to enjoy Gulfport, and some much needed Gulf Coast fare.

A crabshack overlooking the water won out. But with the din of Saturday night diners, there still wasn't time to say quietly what Stanley was waiting patiently to say. Too much catching up to do. Too much hearing from Claire some more about Clay, and how she was fairly smitten—more like totally knocked out.

They'd put the top up before going down to the dock for chow. Now a chill had come down from the north, so they cranked the heater up to ten, and headed west.

A few miles passed with nothing but the music. Then Stanley faded the sound down on a Blondie tune, and the only sound was the rumble and hiss of the Interstate.

"You don't like Blondie?" Claire asked. "I thought you liked Blondie."

"Yes...I like Blondie."

Stanley could wait no longer.

"So, Claire, something's been on my mind."

Claire, lost in a world of her own, looked over at her dad. "Shoot."

There was a long pause.

"Funny you should say that."

"Why?"

Stanley couldn't see why he couldn't just let some miles go by without responding. So he did just that. Claire was into the game so played along. Finally he jumped back in. "Reminds me of the bullet note."

"Yeah, that was weird, wasn't it? That bullet note?"

"When everything was so darkly romantic up to that point... and then a death threat? It really doesn't make sense."

"It really doesn't."

"It really doesn't. But then look at all that's happened! Isn't it amazing? you're in love with the long-lost Bird."

"Yeah...I guess I am. A guy I've hated all my life."

Stanley made little spinning motions at one side of his head with his free hand. The other one, on the wheel, kept them moving in the direction of New Orleans.

"It's bizarro, Dad."
"Bizarro...is an understatement."

"Claire...?"
"Yes, Daddy."
"We need to talk."
"I thought we were."
"Claire...you are an insufferable imp."
"I know, Daddy. What's up?"
Stanley took a deep breath and waded in.
"As I said, I've been doing some thinking."

Claire remained silent, looking over at the green glow of
Stanley in the dash lights. Stanley was taking one of his painfully
long pauses. She was just about to let out a bloodcurdling scream
when he finally went on.

"About when we were younger. About when you were a
little kid. And I wasn't there. Just trying to think how that was
for you."

"Whoa, deep stuff, huh, Dad?"

The Gulf Coast neon slipped by as Claire had to stop and
process what her father was asking. He seemed to read her
mind. She heard him say, "I know, I've never asked you that
before. But now I have. And I really need to know"

She suddenly felt overwhelmed. Man, she thought, I'm
slipping.

Stanley waited. Then— "I never knew what was going on.
I was always scared...I was just a little kid. I mean...

"You really want to know?"
"I really want to know."
Claire went back to her contemplation.

Stanley waited. After a few miles she went on.

"The first part of my life I wasn't sure you even knew I existed. Then you went away when I was eight, and I only saw you off and on. And it seemed to me Mom and I were doing fine. Then you came rolling back in with all your rules and judgements. And here you were, this total stranger, telling me you didn't like my hair, my choice of clothes, my friends. I was getting straight A's, Dad. I mean almost straight A's. And I was actually selling some of my paintings back then. At sixteen years old. Yeah, I was doing some questionable shit, but I felt I was also maintaining. Staying in touch with some kind of fucked reality. I was just out there exploring...like you, Dad." Claire took a deep breath and fell silent.

He felt a sting in his nostrils, could hear Claire beginning to crack.

"Did you even like me, Dad? I mean when I was just a little kid? I didn't think you even liked me. I was always scared. And I..."

Stanley, not so rational now, asked "Of what?"
"Of what what?"
"What were you afraid of?"
"That one day you'd just shove me off the back of the truck.
Or one day. you'd just disappear in the deep end of the pool—although, sometimes I remember thinking, I wished you would. You were some weird sort of strange dude."

Stanley winced.

"You were always pissed off at Mom. And there was a lot of fighting loud voices. Things breaking." Claire seemed to crack. Stanley saw it. And the miles passed, and the years melted away, as Claire tried to control her sobs.

She kept intoning, "Sorry...I'm sorry." Stanley just waved it on and wiped his own nose on a shirttail. "Me too...me too...I'm sorry darlin'." He couldn't see very well behind steamed up glasses, so took an off ramp and turned onto a road spur that took them out over the water. A state park overlook was just ahead. He pulled in and shut off the engine. They sat for a moment listening to the night sounds. Blowing noses and drying eyes.

"Let's walk." They said it in unison, looked at each other and laughed.

Claire grabbed a jacket out of her daypack, leapt out of the car, and moved off in the headlights. Stanley climbed out stiffly and followed.

A full moon was rising in the east. They noticed it but were more interested in a patch of sand down by the water. Stanley sat Indian style while Claire paced around for seashells and driftwood. Finally she came and sat by his side. He was still waiting. She spoke first.

"Well...we certainly do have a couple of hair triggers, don't we."

He relished a second of hearing Claire sounding like Lee Ann.

"What else?" he said.

"What else what?" she asked.

"What else was going on with you?"

"I heard about Bird a lot." Some time passes. "I mean, I heard about all the pain you felt about Bird. Like I didn't matter. Like I just happened to be there."

Claire fell silent but turned to him with very old eyes. "Then I just got pissed" She threw a stick into the sand, jackknife style. "You know the rest."

"Shit" Stanley said softly. "That's how I feel right now...like shit."

Claire bumped his shoulder with hers. "Well you are, you know...a big pile of steaming horseshit."

Had Lee Ann learned her art of segue from Claire? Or had Claire learned it from her mother? Either way, these girls were a team. Stanley took solace in that. He stood, brushed off his khakis, and reached for Claire's hand.

Claire was already on her way back to the car to make sure the heater was still on high when the Mustang made its way back to the Interstate.

Back on the freeway, she looked over at her dad behind the wheel.

"I think we should put some really good music on and not talk anymore till we hit the bridge into town. Whaddaya say? Some more Blondie?"

Stanley hit Play

53.

The next day, back from Gulfport, he consulted a New Orleans map and found the hospital in Metairie where Poteet was recuperating. The nurse at the station buzzed his room, said a few things, nodded and hung up. Stanley, standing with a current issue of *Ceramics* magazine tucked under his arm (a peace offering for Poteet) took the verdict he'd been expecting. Poteet could not see him this day. Check back later. But I'm leaving for San Francisco early tomorrow. I'm sorry, Mr. Poteet isn't taking visitors this afternoon.

Chickenshit, he thought, why couldn't the man just face his failure? But he, with slightly leaden limbs, knew the answer to that. Fear. Embarrassment. Loss of face. What else? Oh yes, add a feeling of helplessness and vulnerability. After all, the man was lying flat on his back recovering from near fatal gunshot wounds.

He made his way back to the elevator and pushed the down arrow. Well, maybe later. Maybe not.

The lift door opened. He held the bumper while they offloaded an androgynously old human being. Think Poteet... you will be this old someday, *if* you're lucky.

From the nurses' station he heard someone call out, "Sir! Sir!" He looked up and saw the nurse in command central washing the air above her head with her hand. She was looking directly at him. He pointed at himself. The nurse nodded her head yes and set down the phone. He released the elevator and made his way back over to the desk.

"Mr. Poteet has reconsidered. He'd like to see you. Room 327C," said the nurse pointing down one of several radiating corridors.

He said thank you, swallowed his stomach, and set off down a hall marked C. The leadenness in his joints was draining away now. He was beginning to relish his mission. That near miss had given him the time he'd needed to regroup. 323...325...327. There it was up ahead, with an armed guard sitting in a chair beside the door.

The guard inspected his California driver's license, loosely patted him down, and motioned for him to enter. Stanley was actually relieved to find a neutral force on duty at the door. He'd halfway expected to find a couple of Poteet's goons stationed there. Wrong. The goons were inside. Poteet, without acknowledging Stanley's presence, waved an index finger, and two men (who looked like they ate pit bull for breakfast) moved in the direction of the door. The men looked at him as they made their way out of the room, but he didn't meet their gaze, just felt a magnetic repulsion as they passed by him. Poteet met his eyes now.

An old man's smile softened his face.

"Sorry, I won't be able to shake your hand, sir, both arms a bit laid up at the moment."

God, thought Stanley, first the legs, now the arms? And suddenly he felt sorry for this man he was a short week beyond wanting to stake over an anthill. Strange. He walked over, laid the copy of *Ceramics* on the side table (without presentation) and stood nodding solemnly. "I'm glad to see you. I'm glad you're alive."

It was the first thing that came out of his mouth, and it was without premeditation.

"Glad to see *you* again, genius. Have you come to finish the job?"

Stanley's face cracked at Poteet's piquant humor. He shook his head no without responding.

"Well then, I assume it's about some unfinished business you feel you have with me." Poteet was not one to waste time.

"Actually, that's exactly why I came."

"Make yourself comfortable. I have a bar set up over there for the visitors. Help yourself and pull up a chair. I'm doing morphine these days so won't be joining you."

"Don't mind if I do." Stanley walked over to the makeshift bar, poured a half tumbler of Glenfiddich, and dropped a couple of cubes into the glass. "So I read in the paper that you were almost dead when they brought you in. What was that like?" He knew how to get to the point too.

"Haven't had so much fun since Old Jack tossed me about."

Stanley wondered if the morphine was fueling Poteet's droll sense of humor. He was already at ease with the man—felt they could talk, fence, whatever it was they were about to do. He walked over to a chair by the bed and sat down. Poteet lay with one arm up in a sling and the other under the covers. It looked as if that arm might be taped to his side. His skin was sallow; there were dark shadows under his eyes, but those eyes still sparkled—down there somewhere at the bottom of his tortured little soul.

They sat for a moment in silence, then Stanley said, "I've been pretty pissed off at you myself lately. I'd like to talk about that."

"Certainly master ceramist, fire away. As you can see, I'm not going anywhere."

Stanley smiled slightly and nodded again. "I can see that." He took a deep breath.

"All right. I don't want to get into your unfinished business with Lee Ann, so I..."

"No, wait" Poteet interrupted, "as long as you opened with that, I have something I need to say."

Stanley remained silent for a moment. Poteet seemed to be having trouble going on. "Okay, shoot."

"Rather cruel choice of words, old man, but all right, let's just get on with it." He winced as he tried to readjust his body. "Yes, I admit it, I fell in love with your...your ex-wife via the television. I admit that. And I admit that I sent her those correspondences that are now more than a part of the public record. The coffin...yes...the DVD...yes...poems...and so forth. All playfully melodramatic, don't you think?"

"Mmm," said Stanley as Poteet winced again in another unsuccessful attempt to readjust his bullet-ridden body. He sighed deeply, let the pain subside, and then went on.

"But I categorically deny sending her the deranged note that referred to a bullet being sent her way. I just wouldn't do that... just not my style. And besides, I think you know, I've fallen in love with the woman. Even more so now that I know her in the flesh."

Stanley glanced up sharply to see Poteet seemingly studying something suspended in the air above him. "Oh well, you know... figure of speech. Would that it could be true." He drifted off.

Jealousy recoiled and retreated back into Stanley's rocks. He said, "Lee Ann tells me that you are a very accomplished liar."

Poteet sighed. "Well, I know...I know. There's really no reason for you to believe me. I'm simply conveying that once again to you so that you can, if you would, relay it to Lee Ann. I..." —his relative humidity rose several percentage points— "I would very much like to see her, talk with her again. I'm concerned for her safety. Tell me she hasn't received any more death threats."

"No, as far as I know. And yes, I will relay your message. Not to worry then, she's a very big girl. As we both know."

"As we both know" Poteet repeated. "Thank you." His eyes seemed to snap back quickly from the edge of some emotional spear pit. "You said you didn't come to talk about Lee Ann. I'm curious, what else could it be? Melissa? Well, of course, Melissa."

"As a matter of fact." Stanley set his drink aside, pulled a folded sheet of bond paper from his coat pocket, unfolded it, and held it up for Poteet to read. "I found this taped to my mirror about a week ago. I assume it was left by the same people who dropped off my Mary Mythe and that load of Melissa's clay. This is a lethal threat by the way." He watched as Poteet's eyes scanned the note. "And then shortly after that I was nearly run down in the street by your man. Audid is his name? Drives a junk-heap Datzun Z?"

Poteet wagged his head solemnly against the pillow. Even this tiny motion was enough to make him visibly wince at the pain it caused.

"Not my man," he gasped between clenched teeth. Stanley waited as Poteet's pain subsided. The pirate's eyes were watering from the sting of it. "Not my man. I sent the clay and your sculpture in to an associate here in New Orleans with instructions to deliver it to your rooming house. But no, I didn't instruct this. But…"

He was breathing deeply now. Stanley felt it might be time to summon someone. "Should I buzz the nurse? Are you all right?"

"Ahhh…" Poteet breathed a final sigh of relief and fell back against the pillows—shut his eyes for a moment. "That's better. No, I'm fine. Just not sure how I can move yet and not suffer for it."

You can say that again, thought Stanley. Poteet went on.

"You see, I keep telling my people to lose this Audid character. He likes to improvise, take liberties. That is all I can tell you."

"Yes, I think that would be a good idea, Jean Paul. Bag this guy.

"He's a loose cannon. As you might imagine, I don't enjoy being tossed into the air by speeding automobiles."

"Ahhh…Mr. Hochstetter, I apologize for all the trouble I have caused you and your family. I'm glad that some good has come out of it. I hear you found your lost son, Bird, I believe you call him? You must be overjoyed and relieved."

Okay, time to move on then, thought Stanley. "I am…and I am. You heard?"

"Yes, yes I did. New Orleans, particularly the French Quarter, is one big ear you know. I know many people."

"Mmm. I know."

"Well, tell me a bit about how you found him. I wasn't informed of the details. It's quite extraordinary."

So Stanley gave Poteet a brief rundown of his reunion with Clay Hawkins, and Jean Paul seemed genuinely amused by the account and the fact that they had been reunited by a juice squeezer. It was good leavening for the otherwise flat batch of bread they had been baking. But there was still some business left and Stanley, after receiving Poteet's profuse congratulations, broached the final item on his agenda.

"Jean Paul," he began, "I've grown very fond of someone... someone who just happens to be *your* ex, Melissa. I intend to continue corresponding with her and letting our professional and personal lives develop as they might." He patted the note that he'd replaced in his breast pocket and went on. "I'll assume, then, that I can disregard this latest notice and I..."

"Yes, yes of course. You two geniuses." Poteet broke in and then trailed off. Stanley waited. Finally Poteet went on. "I still love Melissa very much, but I know she must be free of me now. I'm afraid I've destroyed anything that might have remained in the way of her feelings for me."

"Safe to say that, Jean Paul."

He nodded gravely, then brightened. "Well, sir, it's quite tacky of us don't you think? Engaging in something so banal as ex-wife swapping?"

Stanley laughed out loud once, shortly. "I hadn't really thought about it in that way, but yes, shame on us."

They talked for a few more minutes then and Poteet told him a few more things that Stanley took with a grain of salt. The grand ancestor of the privateer Jean Lafitte told him it was ironic that he had been shot by the sister of the man they'd found in the river. He claimed that Devereaux, a professional gambler, had had a number of enemies and that he'd had nothing whatsoever to do with his murder, either directly or indirectly. Although, he said, in an earlier time he would probably have challenged the cuckolder to a duel. He said he'd always wondered how the very blonde Jacquel, his younger daughter, could have come from two raven-haired parents such as Melissa and himself. It surprised Stanley that Poteet would confide these things in him, but it seemed to be a transformed Jean Paul who was relating them. It was a candidness that seemed to lend credibility to his earlier denials of wrongdoing.

The conversation finally wound down, and Stanley felt it was time to go. Before leaving, though, he asked John Paul what his plans were for the future. He said he'd like to stay in touch.

Poteet seemed pleased and told him that he was going to contract out the ceramics business and devote himself entirely to continuing *One World Incorporated*. And, he added, he'd resolved now to begin the long hours of physical rehabilitation work necessary to rejuvenate his broken body. His goal was to walk again. Stanley told Poteet again that he was glad he hadn't perished and they'd had a chance to clear the air. Poteet agreed. Then suddenly Stanley found himself walking down corridor C, feeling as if he needed to bend over to avoid scraping his head.

The ceiling was only nine feet from the floor.

54.

Gloomy and neglected, that's how his home seemed to him when he turned a key in the deadbolt of a heavy steel door and fell inside. He'd left his studio in shambles that night more than a couple of weeks ago after the show when he'd stopped by with Lee Ann, stuffed some clothes into a bag, and split for New Orleans. He wasn't all that neat, ever, but this place—he wasn't sure he wanted to even claim it—was a disaster! He'd forgotten to flush one of his two toilets. Suddenly pushing that handle down became his first priority.

In the kitchen clean dishes (thank god) sat dry and sparkling in the drainer. Lee Ann must have done them while he'd been packing. He was sure he'd left the sink piled high with plates and pans when he'd departed for the opening. The Genoa opening, with Lee Ann in her slinky green dress. It seemed a lifetime ago.

Time for an air change. He pulled all the blinds aside and opened every window. In the freezer he found some frozen brick of something and popped it into the microwave. Ten minutes later he was wandering around the place lapping up a chunky brown substance out of a Rubbermaid container. Was it stew? He really wasn't sure. Oh my God! Melissa's clay, wrapped in plastic bags and packed in two banana boxes, was sitting in the sun! Christ! He sprang to them and moved them into the shade.

He didn't want the sun's heat causing this delicate porcelain clay any early distress or changes in composition. He had some big plans for it. An idea had been festering in his brain for about ten years now. And now he had the perfect material with which to externalize it. Ironic that it would be Melissa's clay he would be using.

Concepts were like a burr under Stanley's saddle. He saw them in his mind, sometimes drew them, certainly dreamed them. And he'd finally seen this persistent concept, in the flesh, that night a little over two weeks ago at the Genoa opening. Tomorrow he would start on it, and if nothing else, ease it off the mental Rolodex. Move it along as he dug himself out of two weeks of absence and neglect. Evie would come first though— first thing tomorrow morning.

A cool breeze fluttered at the window shades. Fog was rolling in from the Pacific. He thought about New Orleans and how its air made you want to eat, drink, scratch, and well, let's face it, rut. He thought about Jamaica where the air picked you up and rocked you in the tops of the palms. But he loved this Pacific air; it was so laden with negative ions, a balm for the lungs and the poor pithy brain.

Sweet contentment folded around him as he lowered himself into his own bed, pulled the comforter up under his chin, and turned out the light. Within seconds he was teetering on that ledge between waking and sleeping, watching the events of the past two weeks drift through his mind. So much had been accomplished! They'd found Bird! And now the future he saw stretching out ahead of him seemed bathed in light. Tomorrow he would begin the new project. Yes, tomorrow.

Goodnight, sweet Melissa, wherever you are.

Next morning, he was up early and ready to roll. Where to start? So much to do. He decided to follow through with his original plan and drop in at Genoa first.

Evie was in the middle of hanging a show when he walked into her Sutter Street salon. An argument with some painter about a grouping was reaching critical mass. She gave Stanley a one-second finger, and he beat it for the walls. His mounds of mythical mud were still gracing the pedestals out on the floor and would for the rest of the month. He walked around to see if there were any sold stickers on those pieces that hadn't moved at the show. Yes! Two more sales! He couldn't remember how they'd priced these, but it was at least another ten grand. All right Evie! She joined him and gave him a big hug.

"Come on," she said, "I need to get out of here for awhile. Jacob and I are driving each other crazy, aren't we, darling?" She smiled over at a scarecrow of a man who stood towering over a group of paintings that lay strewn unceremoniously about the floor. He waved her off without looking up.

They walked around the corner to a coffee shop and ordered croissants and coffee. She told him they'd grossed another twenty-four thousand. Stanley felt twelve of it bulge in his pocket. He congratulated Evie. She congratulated him. Then she wanted to know all about his travels and whether he and Lee Ann had gotten back together. Was she free of her stalker? So much to tell, so little time. He gave her the very lightest dusting of the past two weeks of his life, and she told him that he should write a book. He laughed and said he'd forgotten how to spell. Then it was time to talk business.

"Evie, I'm going back to Jamaica. I have an idea for a new series."

"Which would be...?"

"Well, I met this woman potter named Cynthia down there, and she has an open-air pottery operation with an old but very large and serviceable kiln. So all I need to do is import some good clay and set up shop in her space. We've worked together some and both enjoyed that, so she's very amenable to the idea."

"Mmmhuh," said Evie, stirring her coffee.

"I want to sculpt the Jamaicans. Here, take a look at this." He pulled a small digital camera out of his coat pocket—studies he'd done of Cynthia and Harold. He wished he'd taken a shot of Mekweto's head. It was his best work on the road.

Evie, holding the sides of her glasses, took the camera and scrolled through the shots, studying them closely. "Hmm."

"Hmm what?"

"Your usual high quality of work, that's evident, but..."

"But what?" he asked softly. He was ready for this.

"But we were doing so well with the mythology. I mean these are beautiful works, but are people going to buy these? I mean the people with money to buy things such as these?"

"You mean are rich white people going to buy sculptures of black Jamaicans?"

"Not exactly that, Stanley. It's more like, why quit a good thing and go on to something chancy? I have to be a realist here."

"I know you do, Evie. I've benefited greatly from your realism."

"I'm just concerned that we might not have as big a market for this." She waved her hand palm up at the camera.

"If I did some myth pieces in Jamaica, could you set up the necessary connections to get them back to the States?"

"Now you're tawlking. For a minute there I thought you'd lost me."

"I would never in a million years lose *you*, Evie Ester. You feed me, girl."

"No problem to ship them back. I don't know about customs, but since they will never have been sold, I'm sure we can say they're your own private collection. Let me check into it. When are you leaving? How long will you be staying?"

"I'm working on a number of fronts right now, Evie, but I think I'm going to prepay the bills for the next six months and stay at least that long. That will give me a big block of time to get another show together for you." He took another bite of croissant and watched as she nodded yes. "Timewise, I can do about five Jamaicans in the time it takes me to detail one Mythical Mountain."

"I hear you," said Evie.

"I'm burning out on the myth thing, you know? I feel this new direction. And besides, eventually, I'll have to move beyond Myth Muffet on her Tuffet."

Evie laughed and dabbed her mouth with a napkin.

Stanley said, "Consider this a transition time."

"I'll keep an open mind." Evie sighed and slipped off her stool. "Well, this is going to be exciting for you. When do you sail?"

"Funny you should ask that."

On the way back to the gallery, he filled her in on his plans to reach Jamaica by sea. She marveled at this and said he was a brave man. She said if she tried that, she'd be sick the whole way down. Funny, thought Stanley, an old art surfer like Evie getting seasick.

He was so glad she was on his team, and he was on hers. The meeting had gone well.

He spent the afternoon digging out the corners of his studio, clearing a space by the south window for Claire and going through the mail he'd picked up from the post office on his way home from the gallery. The clerk handed him his held post in a plastic grocery bag. A quick sort through the junk yielded a card-shaped envelope with a Brazilian return address: Melissa's hand. It sat unopened on the marble island counter where he worked. As soon as he hosed this pit down, he'd let her out of the envelope. That way she wouldn't see how slovenly he'd been living.

About four that afternoon he called Lee Ann at KPIQ and made tentative plans for dinner the following week. "Very tentative" she'd warned. She was swamped. Finally he sat down with a beer, salsa, and corn chips and removed some pale lavender sheets from their traveling sheath. It was a four pager in tight but flowing script, no cross-outs. He thought again that she must be a Virgo woman. He couldn't recall asking her what month she was born, but it just had to be September.

She'd enclosed a photograph of herself standing with people he supposed were her daughters and her mother and father. He studied all the faces carefully. It was a handsome family, very Latin, golden skin, all the beautiful dark eyes smiled. And there was Jacquel with her lemon blonde hair gleaming in the sun. Hmm. He read:

Rio de Janeiro, May15, '05

Stanley love.

I trust this will find you safe and well—home from your travels.

I think about our last night together and sometimes blush, and sometimes laugh out loud to myself. But don't misunderstand me. I hope you were able to explain to Lee Ann and your daughter and repair any damage we might have done there. When I laugh, I laugh at myself. At the end of a day such as I had, to find myself yet again with "the other woman", well, you can see how I might have to shake my head. For now I was "the other woman" to Lee Ann while she was "the other woman" from my point of view. Very confusing. And though I'm sure she feels no malice towards me —I certainly feel none towards her—there we were. Do you understand this? I'm sure you have thought about it too and do. Please update me, if you wouldl.

I think about our last night together, and I would do it all again. I know I'm wearing it out by saying it, but I feel so safe in your arms. The sweet, funny things you say...I love you.

Stanley thought he heard steam coming from the neck of his grungy T-shirt. He took a slug of beer and settled back to continue. Beat heart. Rumba!

And now I too am safe and sound and with my family in the city I love. I'm happy, but my heart aches for my daughters. I've told them that they can visit their father whenever they wish— school permitting—but that I will not be seeing him again. Stella, of course, flew into a rage and actually threw a glass of Coca-Cola down on the tiles. Splat! Broken glass and sticky brown fluid everywhere. She has always been angry with me and blamed me for the fact that she is kept apart from her father. I had a long talk with her and finally had to tell her that Jean Paul was very mean to me—physically mean—and that I was afraid of him now. Of course I didn't tell her about his most recent exploits. You know what I'm referring to. I would prefer that she never finds out about that side of her father. You were right, it had happened before, this stalking business.

Why do I burden you with all this? Because I know that you were part of his latest insanity through your friendship with Lee Ann—and of course me. So that is why I speak of these things, Stanley. I lie by your side in my dreams and whisper them into the night, wishing it was your sweet ear they were filling.

He paused again and took another pull from his long neck. Man, what was it about Melissa? She could turn up the heat from thousands of miles out. He read on.

I've been looking for a house for the girls and me. It's very difficult now with their being in school and all. If it were just me, it would be easy. I would find a little place up the hill and turn the living room into a studio. I guess that I will have to content myself with sketching and conceptualizing my next works until I can once again get my hands back into the clay. I miss it.

The good news is that all my little pets made it home 100 percent intact. And also, surprise! I found a gallery here that has clientele worldwide, and they've consented to offer my work in their next catalogue. I know it will be difficult to see them go. I'm sure you know what I mean. The return, however, will be put to good use. I'm sure you also know what I mean by that. I hope you're doing well in that area. It sounded as though you were.

I'm sending along a picture of my father and mother and me, along with the girls. Thought you might like to see my people. That's Stella on the right with too much lipstick on, and sweet Jacquel in her fiesta dress on the left. If you get a chance, could you send me a picture of your Claire and, of course, a snap of the one you called Bird? Clay is his name now. I think about your good fortune often and once again am struck by the irony of it all. Of course, that's a cliché, I know, to say that. But you have to admit, some strange forces were at work in shaping that reunion. I'm so happy for you and look forward to the latest news. And meeting the rest of your family!

Finally, in closing, I want to thank you for helping me through a very difficult time in my life, and for holding me, and being patient with me all those times we did that. I blush as I write this, but I would like to be your lover some day. Goodness, did I really say that? Yes, I did Stanley love. But I know in my heart of hearts that we will be together sometime in an unforetold future. And so until then, I hope we can write and share our work and our lives and our love.

As usual, I'm saying too much now, so will close here.

Love always,

Melissa

Stanley laid the pages on the table and looked out the window to the south. Somewhere—thousands of miles in that direction—two women were waiting for him. He thought about the note. He thought about the man in the river. He thought about Cynthia and Harold and Lee and Claire and Clay. How was it that all these dear people were in his life after so many years of hermitage?

Feast or famine? It had always been so for him. Part of the job description: hermit artist. Wouldn't have it any other way— or would he?

55.

Honey bees a buzzin', the Queen is in her hive, where do we fly from here?

Who is speaking? Who is watching? A bird? A bee...?

From high above we see...

Lee Ann Barnes leaving KPIQ and beginning a six-block walk south to the Bank of America Building on the corner of Kearny and California streets.

Nearly a month had passed, and she hadn't received any further communication of a threatening nature. So strange, she thought, Poteet denying that he'd sent the bullet note. If not Poteet, then who? Was he lying? Or was that note just some one-time fluke? She knew she would probably never get to the bottom of this mystery, and so she had resolved, with each passing day, to put fear behind her. It felt so good to be walking down the street again without the dread of someone sending a bullet her way—with love. Those little pieces of lead flying by at two thousand feet per second could do some real damage. Well, she'd taken out a buck or two in her time, so she knew.

And what was this *love* thing with the stalkers anyway? John Lennon came to mind. Jodie Foster came to mind. How is it that some people, in their twisted minds, think that to love is to kill. In what dark chamber of the brain does that equate? Stanley would be interrupting now to point out the fact that the Indians of South and North America, all the way to either pole, were wont to apologize to their prey before taking their lives—in the name of love. Yeah, love of their own goddamn stomachs. That's how she would be responding to that. But then she was no vegan. It was very confusing.

She'd reached the B of A Building. Stanley had made reservations for them to dine in the Carnelian Room at the top of this red granite edifice. They'd agreed to meet at the fountain, but he hadn't arrived yet, so she sat down by the water and marveled again at how the shiny black boulder that served as reflecting pool sculpture resembled a giant black heart. Some joke in the boardrooms of B of A? She wondered.

Stanley came around the corner with a small package under his arm. He saw her immediately and waved. She waved back. Good, he looked to be in high spirits as he trundled toward her. It looked as if he'd lost some weight. Must have been that sparse Jamaican diet, lots of fish and rice.

They hugged briefly and welcomed each other back on home turf.

"Man, I was wondering whether we were *ever* going to get together Lee. I've been back for almost three weeks now."

"I know...I'm sorry, hon, this last month I've been back has been a disaster! You wouldn't believe the political struggles that are a-raging over there." She threw her hand off in the direction of KPIQ. "And..." He didn't let her finish.

"Later Lee. Give me another hug, that last one wasn't long enough."

So they stood there in late rush hour pedestrian traffic and hugged again. It felt reassuring to both of them.

"What time did you reserve dinner? It's six-thirty right now, kind of early," she said, looking at her watch over his shoulder.

"Seven," he said into one of her ears, and then moved back to fix on her eyes. "I wanted to meet early so we could toast your birthday. I mean I know it's not 'till the twelfth, but it's taken almost two weeks to get dinner with you, so I thought we should celebrate tonight. I've got a little present for you." He jiggled the package he was carrying. "So let's get up top of this rock."

They made their way hand in hand to the elevator. Hand in hand they could do. Arm in arm? No, Stanley had finally given up on that.

In the bar area on the 52nd floor, they settled in with a couple of Bombay martinis. Far below, and as far out as they could see, commuters were in the later phases of going home for the day. Traffic on the Bay Bridge was flowing smoothly.

"When do I get to open my present?" asked Lee Ann as she fidgeted in her chair and rearranged the cocktail napkin under her drink.

"Later. After dinner. After cake and ice cream."

"I want to open it *now*."

"Lee Ann..."

"What?"

"Will you ever change?"

"Probably not...just get worse in my *old age*. So...okay then... what's the latest on Jamaica? You still getting that trip together?"

"Mmm, there are one or two contingencies, but yes, I'm still moving ahead with it."

"From what you've been telling me these last few weeks, it sounds as if you're locked on."

"Things could change. But yes, I'm anxious to get started in this new direction. I mean sculpting the Jamaicans. I've about run the course with the mythology thing. Lucrative as it's become."

"What does Evie think?"

"She's still not convinced, but that's because she hasn't seen any sales yet. You know Evie, she's a businesswoman. Hey, I've been watching your show since I've been back. Quite a change of pace."

"I know." Lee Ann's face clouded over. "How's it going? I mean how do you think I'm doing?"

"Well..."

"Be honest. I can take it."

"You seem to be a little out of your element. I mean all these angry, harassed women baring their souls at that hour of the morning? I know it's only one segment twice a week, but it seems to...well...it feels sort of like a speed bump to me."

"Good way to put it. You can imagine how I feel about it. The *guys* keep trying to make the show too serious. You know

486

Sally and Geraldo. Maureen and I keep saying...it's wrong...it's the wrong direction...we're not equipped...it's not what people want that hour of the morning...get off of it!"

"They don't listen?"

"No, they have some kind of syndication stars in their eyes. But that's just not going to happen. Power bullshit, you know."

"Mmm."

"Oh, there have been some good moments too—bout two." She paused, took a sip of her drink. "Have you set a date to sail for Jamaica yet? You know late August is the height of hurricane season."

He didn't have a chance to answer. The waitress came by to check for refills. Then they heard their name being called for dinner.

They spent the next two hours enjoying each other's company. The subject of Claire and Clay came up often. In the last two weeks since he'd been home, Lee Ann and he had talked often on the phone to their kids in New Orleans and then called each other to exchange the latest developments. It seemed to them that everything was still coming up roses in Crescent City.

Lee Ann, despite insistent warning from Stanley, was prone to project her hopes for the future. She'd just asked him again where he thought this would all lead. Were they possibly looking at grandchildren? He found himself once again hauling on the reins.

"But just think, Stanley. Just think!"

"There you go again, Lee."

"C'mon, Pops, indulge me a little grandmotherly fantasy."

"Okay, you want me to say it? I will. Someday we may be bouncing a little bundle on our lap, courtesy of Claire and Clay. There, satisfied?"

"YES!" she shrieked, and everyone—that's everyone in the room—many of whom had been trying to be respectful of their privacy and act as if they hadn't recognized Lee Ann's familiar face, now turned and stared.

"We're going to have a *baby!* "she said to all the eyes she could take in, then quickly reconsidered as everyone clapped and cheered. "I mean, some friends of ours are going to have a baby." The crowd clapped and cheered it one more time to let her know they were still happy for her.

"Quick thinking Lee. I can see Leah Garchik tomorrow, '... and overheard at the top of the lift at Kearny and California streets, Lee Ann Barnes, comely cohost of KPIQ's *Good Morning San Francisco* is soon to bounce her and her ex-husband's baby on her knee...while in other news, dot, dot, dot.'"

"You're right Stanley. I just sort of just lose it when I think about it."

"And you probably will if you do."

"I want my present now."

"Good timing...speaking of Claire and Clay." He reached down by the side of his chair, pulled up a flat rectangular package, and handed it over to her. "Happy birthday. Sorry, I looked for a card, but they're all dumb."

She nodded, took the package, and tore off the wrapping. It was a framed photograph of Claire and Clay and the two of them sitting together on the riprap down by the river where they'd all first met.

"Oh Stan," a soft light came into her eyes, "this is fantastic! You couldn't have given me anything...okay I'll say it...nicer."

"Atta girl, Lee...nice is a nice word. Yes, I've got one just like it on my kitchen counter. And I sent two just like it to Claire and Clay for Clay's birthday. You know his birthday is on the sixteenth... in just a few days."

Lee Ann had gone off on another one of her misty trips. It looked as if she was about to dissolve into tears.

"Do I know what's wrong now, Lee?"

"We should go to New Orleans, Stanley. We should go to New Orleans..." She wiped her nose on a rose-colored Carnelian Room napkin.

Time passed between them, as it often did these days.

"You mean..." Stanley started.

"Yeah, I'll just make up another story why I should be leaving town again. You hang up your mud and fame, and we'll just fly back down to New Orleans and spend a fifth birthday with our Bird...twenty-seven for him." Now she did dissolve into silent tears.

"We should do that." Was about all Stanley could say. "But we probably can't"

The waiter came to inquire about dessert and coffee. Lee Ann motioned with her hand and mumbled something about the check. He could tell something was happening between these two so bowed once and backed off.

"So...it's agreed. We both feel punk that we can't get to our son's twenty-seventh?"

Stanley nodded yes into his napkin.

"Well...Claire is there."

"Yes...Claire is there."

They held hands over the dirty dishes for a moment; then the check came and it was time to go.

The sun had set, lights were coming on, there was a cool breeze coming up from the bay. They were feeling uncomfortably full, so decided to get the blood moving and walked briskly down California Street to the Embarcadero, crossing it without mentioning its significance in their lives. A pedestrian pier, secreting itself between what was left of the wharfside warehouses, beckoned. They made their way out to the end of it and settled on a bench. Large freighters sliding under the Bay Bridge headed out to the Golden Gate. None were coming in.

"Boy, look at that, one after another, a whole flotilla's sailing out."

"THE MARKET YELLS! SELL! SELL!" Lee Ann jumped up and went screaming down the pier. Stanley pulled his jacket collar up against the stiff sea breeze and set out at a leisurely pace to follow her.

"AMERICA...AMERICA...NOW HERE'S SOME GOODS FROM THEE!" Lee Ann was singing her own version of an old song at the top of her lungs. And now she was rocking dangerously close to the breaking point over a heavy wood railing.

Her legs suddenly shot straight up in the air. Stanley froze in mid- stride and then broke into a dead sprint as she screamed, lost her balance completely, and disappeared from view. Some part of his brain registered relief as he heard a loud splash in the water below. At least she'd not landed on a piling. And now he was looking over the rail, searching in the dim light for a white face.

Lee Ann broke the surface in a pool of bubbles and began screaming again at the top of her lungs. He shouted to her to swim over and hold onto a piling. She was a strong swimmer, so she did this easily enough, but now there was the problem of how to get her back up onto the pier, twelve feet above the water.

"Lee Ann! Do you see a ladder, anything you can climb up on?"

"Oh God, Stanley! This water is freezing! Oh god!"

"Stay calm, Lee Ann; you've got to stay calm. Look around... find something to crawl up on. A cross bar...anything..."

"It's dark down here, and there's slimy goo all over everything. No wait, there's a ledge inside this post here. I think I can get up on that. I'm going to have to take this skirt off though. I can't climb..."

His heart fluttered as he saw her head disappear below the inky black surface of the water. She was under for several seconds and then reappeared.

"Are you okay, Lee? speak to me."

"Yeah...I'm okay...I took my skirt and jacket off...so I can climb...oh god, Stanley this water is FREEZING!"

"I know...get out of it, and then we'll figure out how to get you up."

She swam under the pier and was out of sight for a moment. He heard sounds of exertion as she apparently struggled up onto a crossbeam. Fifteen heart-stopping seconds went by, and then, still out of view, he heard her shout up to him. "Okay...I'm out... just behind this post. Now what? I'm freezing to death, Stanley! Go for help now!"

"Okay! I'm parked a couple of blocks from here," he shouted down to the liquid darkness. "I've got a rope in the car. If I get it, do you think you could climb up if I was pulling you? Or should I find a phone and call 911. What do you think?"

There was silence for a moment. "I don't want a rescue team, Stanley. Yeah, go get the rope, but for God sake, hurry! I feel like I'm going into convulsions, I'm shaking so badly."

"Okay. I'll be back in two or three minutes. Hang on!"

"Okay...okay! Go!"

He set out at a full sprint for his car two blocks away. By the time he reached it, he'd cut it back to a brisk trot. His out-of-shape heart was sending him stern warning signals. But he quickly fetched a coil of rope and a sleeping bag from the trunk, slammed it shut, and set off at a jog to return to the pier. He spotted a pay phone, and noted it for future reference—in case their little rescue plan should fail. Suddenly he found himself lowering a loop of rope over the railing to a now whimpering Lee Ann. He saw her hand reach around the piling and catch the loop and pull it out of sight. Within five minutes after much effort, exertion, and cursing, she stood barefoot once again on the pier clad only in her slip and blouse—drenched and shivering. Stanley unzipped the sleeping bag and pulled it close around her shoulders.

"So much for a nine-hundred-dollar suit," she managed through clenched teeth. "Why...why do these things happen to me, Stanley?"

"Just be glad you're alive, girl. You could have impaled yourself on something down there." He shook his head and gave silent thanks as they half walked, half stumbled back to his car.

"And I lost the picture too! I dropped it when I hit the water. Stanley, I lost it!"

"Don't worry about that, Lee. I'll get you another one. No problem." He pulled her in tightly as they walked along, felt her body shivering uncontrollably. They reached the car. None too soon for Lee Ann, he thought. She was practically doubled over with the shakes. But seconds later they were speeding down Embarcadero with the heater on full blast.

He looked over at her—wrapped tightly in the sleeping bag with only her wet head sticking out of the top. She resembled an emerging chrysalis.

"How're you doing? Warming up a little bit?"

"Yeah...a little...but..." her voice was little more than a scratchy rasp. "I've gone color blind. Everything is gray and white and black. Exposure...exposure...exposure"

"Whoa...really? Do you want to go to a hospital?"

"No, let's go to your place. I'll take a hot bath. I'll be okay." She made a little scoffing noise. "You know, Stanley, I've got to stay away from the Embarcadero. That place just doesn't agree with me." And then she added in almost a whisper "I love you, Stan. Thanks for taking care of me again. I'm sorry."

Somehow they'd just come full circle.

His place off Valencia was miles closer than her house out on Kensington, so they decided to go there to regroup. After a half hour in a scalding hot tub, Lee Ann pulled on some of his old sweats, bundled herself in his terry robe, and joined him by the firestove.

He held a tumbler of cognac out to her. "Feeling better? How's your vision?"

"Okay, I've got my color sight back. That's happened to me before. I mean losing color sight. Symptom of hypothermia, they say. God, Stanley, that water was *freezing!*"

"Yeah, I know, mid-fifties year round. That's cold."

She flopped down on the sofa beside him and moved in under one of his arms. "So once again you have to rescue Lee Ann. You must be getting tired of that."

"Naw...what else would I do with my life? But you're right, never a dull moment with you around." He bumped heads with her. "What happened back there on the pier? You lost your balance or something?"

"Yeah, I had the picture in my hand, so I only had one to balance with. My hand slipped, and rather than let go of the picture, I..."

"Well, don't worry. I'll get you another one. I'm just glad you weren't hurt. Falling off a twelve-foot-high pier can be hazardous to one's health."

"Tell me about it."

They were silent for a moment, listening to the fire crackle in the stove. Lee Ann laid her head on his chest, just under his chin. He brushed the back of his hand lightly across her cheek.

"Stanley..." she whispered huskily.

"Yeah, shooter..."

"I love you."

He didn't respond for a moment, so she lifted her head to look at him in the flickering firelight.

"I love you too, Lee, always have."

She laid her head back on his chest. He went on. "And it's funny you should be saying that right now."

She sat up at his side now, looked him in the eyes. "What do you mean?"

"What do *you* mean?"

"Stanley, stop." She smiled. "Ask your question."

"Well...what do you mean exactly when you say 'I love you?'"

She shook her head but remained smiling. "Oh man, Stan, are we all the way back to go?"

"Unfortunately."

She waited. He went on.

"So...you're all the time saying those words, Lee, but what do you really mean when you say, 'Stanley, I love you?'"

"I can't *believe* you insist on asking this question." She patted herself on the heart. "Hey, Stanley, it's me, Lee Ann."

"I know." He smiled and rubbed his chin. "Okay, well a lot of things are happening in my life right now, Lee. I've got to make a"—he paused—"some big decisions about direction. And I need to know what you mean about the love thing. You know, now, in light of what's happening in our family...Claire and Clay..." He drifted off.

"What do you want me to say?" She searched his eyes earnestly.

"Okay, sorry, I'll lay it on the line." He sighed. "Lee Ann, do you ever, in any of your future scenarios, see us living together again?"

She hadn't seen this one coming. He heard her letting out her air, and then she was silent. When she spoke again, and not too much time had gone by, she said, "I thought we talked about this in New Orleans. I thought we agreed, one day at a time. Do you ever see yourself living with me again? You? The hermit monk of all time?"

"I would."

"You would?"

"Yes."

"Why? It'd be a full-time job...always rescuing me."

He laughed. She went on.

"Holy cow, Stanley, this is...well...I hadn't expected this!" She shook her head. "When would you propose this merger? Would we live here? Would we live at my place? How do you see this?"

"I've given it some thought, and the way I think it might work out nicely is if I keep the studio and work here, and then I come home to your house every night...or most nights...cook you dinner...we spend an evening together...we sleep together... and then we'd get up the next morning and do it all again."

"You mean like shack up?"

"Jesus, Lee Ann. Now you want me to propose?"

"No. I'm sorry. I've been spending too much time around Claire."

"Really."

"Jeez...I don't know? Can you let me think about it some?"

"Think away, but let me know before I leave for Jamaica. May have something to do with how long I plan to stay."

"That sounds slightly menacing."

"Well, you know, okay, well, just give it some consideration, that's all." He felt a need to change the subject. "Are you going into work tomorrow?"

"Not till afternoon."

"What are you going to be doing on Sunday...your birthday?"

"Oh...we're doing a show on the San Francisco Symphony on Monday. And they're going to give me a birthday cake as we go off, with the whole orchestra and staff playing and singing 'Happy Birthday'. Corny, I know, but they want to run through some things."

"Why don't you stay over here tonight? I'll take you back down to the station in the morning."

"Well..."

"Come on, we've had enough excitement for one evening. Let's kick back."

So she did, and they did, talking for several hours in front of the fire about everything from A to Z, brushing every once in awhile on his latest madcap notion to live together again. She felt shaky. He said after five years of monkdom he was very weary of living alone, working alone, eating alone. She told him that after a day at work constantly surrounded by people, she didn't mind coming home to some solitude. And so as the evening progressed, he could see that she was being gentle with him as she convinced herself that the final answer would be no. The hour grew late so they settled into his king-size bed and fell asleep watching Letterman.

In the dark hours of the morning, with a light rain padding about on the roof, they found themselves in each other's arms making love. Feeling okay about it. Feeling more than okay about it. Making love was something they'd always done very well together. This time was no exception.

At the break of dawn, he awoke to find her fidgeting by his side. She said she was getting "really nervous," and needed to get to the station earlier than she'd said. He offered to cook her some breakfast, but she declined. She was still wearing his sweats when he gave her a peck on the mouth and let her off at her Kensington address. There was a last minute flurry of promises to stay in close touch concerning all the latest breaking news from New Orleans. Then he was around a corner and heading home.

Little did he know it would be the last time he would be with Lee Ann Barnes. Little did she.

56.

Oh, he would watch her on TV for the next couple of months or so, and he would talk with her on the telephone at least twice a week, but he wouldn't see her in the flesh again. And when he called her just before he left for Jamaica in the month of August of that year, she'd told him that NBC was once again lighting signal fires to bring her in and she was swamped with those negotiations and the work at the station never let up, and she would love ever so much to be able to have dinner and another quiet evening, but it would have to be when he got back from his trip.

"You mean at the end of six months?"

"Are you really going to stay there that long, Stanley? I don't believe you're going to be there that long. You're going to miss San Francisco. I know you are. You'll be back in two, bet you ten."

"You're on, Miss Smartypants. It's going to be six. Evie and I've put a lot of planning into this. I've got to push through with a series I've promised. It will be six."

"I'll miss you."

"Oh, you mean like you have for the last couple of months we haven't seen each other?"

"Right."

"I'll call...you call. It's just Jamaica you know. They *do* have phones."

"Okay, Stan, you take care of yourself. Get a lot of work done. I promise we'll spend some time when you get back. Okay, Stan, gotta go...love you forever."

"Love you, Lee."

"Bon voyage."

"Yeah, big bon. Big voyage."

There was a click as she hung up. And then he hung up.

"Close, but no cigar," he mumbled to himself as he popped a Miller's, switched on TV, and settled back for some baseball. His bags, his boxes, a letter from Melissa, and a one-way airline ticket to New Orleans sat in a neat pile by the front door.

57.

Losing Claire had not been easy on Jackie.

Claire told Stanley that she'd "shacked up" with Clay the morning after they'd fallen asleep on his bed playfully making out. She'd decided to let her father think they'd made it right away because Stanley had been so rude as to ask her straight out if she and Clay had done that: "shacked up." In actuality, Claire and Clay waited until after Claire came back from picking up her Toyota in Chicago. Jackie had ferried it below the Canadian border for deported Claire. Art Smuggler.

And that trip to Chicago came after Stanley had returned from Jamaica with Jahna and had gone back to San Francisco. So in truth, Clay and Claire had waited until after Claire finished her business with Jackie to, as they say, consummate their relationship.

Jackie smiled sadly as she watched Claire come down the hall to baggage claim. It was hard on both girls when they hugged for the first time as friends. Claire would be starting her drive back to New Orleans the following afternoon, so they had only twenty-four hours to talk. And once they started in, it didn't seem like that would be enough time to cover everything. They sat now in a bar overlooking the Loop, sipping beer, munching tapas, and catching up.

On the phone, during the two weeks they'd talked over the miles between New Orleans and Toronto, Claire tactfully (as far as Claire was capable of being tactful) let Jackie know there was something brewing with Clay. Or at least Jackie had picked it up, and Claire had then been honest about her feelings. She was continuing to be so as Jackie asked for the axe.

"So, CH, are you in love with this guy?"

Claire looked up sharply, met Jackie's hurting eyes. "Hmm, do I have to answer that right now?"

"Let me put it another way. Are you falling in love with this guy?

Claire held eye contact. "Mmmhuh...I think so."

"Are you lovers?"

"Boy, you don't let up do you?"

"I think I have a right to know."

"You do, even though you say you will never leave Toronto, and I may never be able to venture above the border again for the rest of my natural born life—stuffy fucking Canada. But, to answer your question Jackie Garland, no. No, Clay and I aren't lovers...*yet*. I wanted to talk with you first. I told him that, and he said, okay, he would wait, but to do it soon. So here I am, asking your blessing. I want to be Clay's lover, and I still love you, but we can't be together now. It's the way life has it worked out at this point in time. I ..."

"You sure do have a lot of I's in your speech these days." Jackie was clearly stinging.

"I know...I know...I do."

They looked around at the crowd now as Claire let Jackie absorb this latest salvo. A couple of guys came up to the table and asked to join them. They said no, heap big powwow going on here. Maybe later, much later.

"Like the next ice age," Jackie mumbled under her breath as the men moved back into the crowd.

"So Jackie, sweet Jackie, I'm still waiting. Let's get beyond this so we can have some fun. Time's short."

Jackie was teetering on some totter between anger and anguish. She looked up into Claire's bottomless blues. "You don't need my permission or my blessing CH; you know you're going to go for it no matter what I say. Even if it was no."

"I'll take that as a yes then." Claire smiled slightly.

"Don't piss me off, girl. Don't condescend." Jackie paused now to take back some ground. "Sounds like a great guy, this long-lost adopted sorta brother of yours. Tell me about him."

And so Claire launched into the story, taking it from the very beginning. She told Jackie things now she for some reason hadn't told her in their six months living together. Maybe they were things she'd wanted to forget but now wanted to remember. She told Jackie that she'd always been—for as long as she could remember—intensely jealous of the mythical Bird. How, as the years passed, she'd come to realize that her father blamed her mother for having lost him. And though he'd never come right out and said it, she'd strongly sensed that. But it was only later, after several sessions of therapy, that she came to realize her father's coldness to her was really no more than a manifestation of the sense of loss he felt for his missing son. It helped to know that, at sixteen, she finally had words to describe why her father and she were so estranged and alienated from one another. It helped, but it didn't make it go away.

"And now, here I am, falling in love with a guy I've hated all my life. Such a *strange concept*...Bird..." Claire faded off.

"Strange bird. Yeah, he sounds great from what you've told me." Jackie was ready to move on with it.

"He's fabulously beautiful, I think. Very gentle. Devilishly playful. Serious about his music and his writing. Sometimes too serious. But that's okay. I take my painting seriously too."

"Are you going to get married or anything weird like that?"

"Jesus, I hope not. Besides, I still gotta check out his action. So far so good, but well, you know?"

"No, I don't...I'm gay...you're bi...remember?"

"Right, but hey, you ought to check it out again, Jack. Just for the sake of research. Good little journalism slash media person you."

"Not even curious. I'm happy. Or at least I was a couple of weeks ago."

"I'm sorry, love." Claire met Jackie's eyes. "I do still love you, girl."

"I know."

Claire felt a need to change the subject. And she had just the item with which to accomplish that. Boy, did she have an item. Jackie was Catholic. She understood confession, and Claire was feeling a strong urgency to download her karma.

"Jackie...need to tell you something here. Something I don't want anyone else to know. Something I'd need for you to keep between us. Can you promise that?"

Jackie looked up and smiled. "Smuggling wasn't enough... you murdered someone?"

"No, but I threatened to."

"What! Who?"

"My mother."

"Claire! Lee Ann!?"

"Yeah, Lee Ann."

"When...where...why...what...how...etcetera...you know the drill. Shoot."

"Okay, here goes...big breath...uh...well...you know when Lee Ann was being stalked by Poteet and went on her show and told all of San Francisco about the romantically dark things the stalker had sent her way? Until the last *thing?* A note that read, 'If I can't be inside your body, I'm going to send a bullet to be there for me?' You remember that?"

"I didn't see the show, but I read about it on the web." Jackie sat bolt upright; her reporter's instincts put two and two together in an instant. "No! Claire!, You didn't! *You* sent that note...you? Why?" She sat shaking her black, spin-curled head from side to side in total disbelief.

"It was a desperate act."

"Ha...I'd say *that's* an understatement." Jackie was recovering from her initial shock. All she wanted to know now was why. "What was your motive, Claire? Does Lee Ann know this? No, you said you were the only one who knew."

"And Serg, my old, retired coke dealing buddy in San Francisco. He delivered the black granite egg to Mom's doorstep. Remember, the note was delivered in that egg?"

"Yes, and it came short hours before your mom decided to leave town with your dad. But I still don't understand why. Didn't you...don't you think...it was a *cruel,* not to mention dangerous, thing to do?"

"Maybe. But see, I had several reasons actually. I need to give you a little background here before you can understand those."

Claire told Jackie that Lee Ann had confided in her from the beginning about her stalker. Her mother called her one night when she was in Crete, on the Minoan dig, and told her she'd received a rather dark but beautiful gift from an anonymous person.

"That was the callalilies in the coffin. Remember?"

"Yes," said Jackie, picking it up, "and then I believe there was the DVD and several faxes and so forth?"

"Yeah, everything you might expect from a guy like Poteet, aristocrat that he is. Classy and mysterious, but nothing life threatening. Anyway, mom told me about these things as she was receiving them. And she kept asking me whether she should be concerned. I told her no, the guy didn't seem dangerous in his communications. Oh well, no more dangerous than a fixated man can be. I told her not to worry. Just wait it out."

"Oh nice...and then you send her a death threat! Don't worry Mom, but here, let me fuck with your mind."

"Not exactly on the mark, Jack, but let me go on."

"Please do."

Claire told Jackie while all this was going on, her mother had been talking with her about Stanley, how she felt—and Claire agreed—the time had come to end the cold war. Stanley had sent Lee Ann an invitation to his next opening and she was considering doing it that way. Simply arriving unannounced and what did she think about that? Claire told Jackie she'd strongly encouraged her mother to go but knew that Lee Ann would probably chicken out. She said her mother needed a good hard shove because down at the bottom of it all, she felt guilty about the way she'd treated Stanley, and she would probably continue to avoid him. So Claire bought the egg and composed the note and sent it off from Crete via private carrier to Serg in San Francisco. And by telephone she made a deal with him to be the mule. He owed her a few, she said.

"I can't believe you did that, Claire. I'm numbstruck..."

"Oh, you'll get used to the idea the more you think about it. And you don't...I mean you didn't...have to grow up with their nonsense. They always seemed like a couple of spoiled, emotional teenagers to me. I'd had it with their crap. I was sick of it. I'd lost patience. So I used a little terror tactic to shake them up. And it worked. It drove Mom straight into Dad's waiting arms. Think about it Jackie G. Desperate yes, but effective."

Claire was clearly enjoying some long overdue return on her lifelong frustration with her parents. And Jackie was gradually beginning to see the logic, if not the light, in it now.

"So your folks get together, thaw out their affairs, find their long-lost son...who you have always been intensely jealous of and who has kept you and your father from coming together all these years and then...will miracles never cease...you fall in love with the lost son to boot." Jackie paused for breath, noticing that Claire was shaking her head in the affirmative, obviously very pleased with herself.

"But what if it had backfired? What if your mom had harmed herself somehow, fleeing, as you knew she would. What if?"

"A calculated risk for a highly improbable event. I took it knowing that Mom wasn't really in danger. She just needed to think she was. The thing that blows my mind is that it actually delivered her to her real stalker, Poteet. But then Poteet was courting Stanley with Melissa's clay and so would have eventually met Mom through that association. So it was only a matter of timing really."

"It's pretty amazing. It would make a good story."

"I know. Clay's taking notes. Believe me, is he *ever* taking notes."

"But he doesn't know about this part of the puzzle, right?" Jackie looked over at Claire who was taking another pull on her beer and shaking her head no. "Are you going to tell him? Are you going to tell your folks?"

Claire set the bottle down and swallowed. "Naw." Pause. "What purpose would it serve? I came close to telling Mom that night in Toronto after Poteet called and insisted that he hadn't sent the last note...my note. She was whispering under her breath but I heard her mention the bullet note. I went in to tell her but then decided it was still too early."

"I remember that night. Jeez, you just about told your mom then?

What changed your mind?"

"Oh, you know, as I said, it was still too early. The folks still had some things to resolve. And anyway, I knew they'd just get pissed off at me again, or at least Dad would. And then we'd have to go another round."

Jackie nodded but remained silent. Claire went on. "As far as Clay goes? No, I'm not going to tell him. Again, it's too soon. Maybe someday."

"So, you're going to be his? When you get back?"

"Yes."

"Go for it."

"I'm going to."

58.

It was a dark and stormy night. Not really. The weather in San Francisco was everything an eighty-degree day in late August can bring: fashion plate San Franciscans frolicking in the parks.

No, the storm was much farther east and not really yet a storm, just a little baby tropical depression forming off the Bahamas. Lee Ann was standing in the middle of Sam Weber's weather monitors talking to the big man when she happened to glance to the right and saw something that made her lock on. A technician was spooling a satellite image back and forth and seeing patterns that had caught both his and Lee Ann's attention.

"Just a minute, Sam," she'd said and stepped around him, positioning herself over the tech's left shoulder. "Is that what I think it is, Jack?"

"Yeah, looks like we might have us a little baby hurricane."

"Jesus! I warned him about this, but he just wouldn't LISTEN!" Lee Ann's voice went from a gasp to a shriek.

"What? Who?" Sam wanted to know.

"Stanley! Damn him. I told him not to sail off into the Gulf right in the middle of fricking hurricane season." Lee Ann's face resembled a spastic traffic light now: first red, then green, then yellow.

Sam said, "Let's have a look at this, Jack." He turned to face the monitors. "Has this hit the net yet?"

"I don't know, but I doubt it. It's still just a baby."

Sam walked over to the phone and called a number in Denver, had a short conversation with them, and they told him the word was out on a depression, but it was being passed more like a rumor. It had no status as yet. Coast Guards had been notified but not alerted. Most of them had said, "Thanks...we've been watching it too."

Lee Ann's world hung suspended for the next six hours as she monitored the storm's movement westward. She camped out by Jack's desk with a deli sandwich some V8 juice, and a telephone—pouncing and ready to pounce. She called Claire, and after Claire searched her cell for Jahna's number, she called Jahna in New Orleans and got the name and number of a man named Flannigan in Gulfport. Jahna said he was the skipper of the boat Stanley had sailed on. Lee Ann called that number and found it was the Holy Family Foster Home and that she was talking to one of Father Flannigan's coworkers, a Sister Bartholemew. She explained her concern for her friend who was currently out at sea with Father Flannigan. The nun seemed knowledgeable and told her that Flannigan's boat was equipped with both radio and satcom positioning equipment. And, no, Flannigan had not called her since he'd left early that morning.

Now what? She watched as the coil of clouds pulled tighter and tighter and kept up its relentless march for the barrel of sea between Florida and Cuba. At 5pm the National Hurricane Center issued its first advisory of a tropical depression. She didn't need to make any more phone calls; she could see what was happening. She knew exactly what was going on now on the airwaves of the southeastern seaboard. Storm warnings were going up. The Coast Guard was sending out an alert to all small crafts to put in at the nearest landfall. The snake was coiling, getting ready to strike.

Praying came to mind: Stanley, if you're out there, hope to God your radio is turned on and you're not too far from landfall...any landfall. Hit Cuba if you need to but put in now, Stanley...do it now! Stanley...can you hear me...it's Lee Ann... turn your radio on. And on and on into the night Lee Ann, half heartsick, watched the maps and heard the reports coming in as the tropical storm was updated to hurricane status: Katrina was born. And she was coming on with a vengeance.

At 1am the following morning, after twelve hours of feeling slightly sick to her stomach, she found herself realizing that she was going on the air in six hours. She drove home, took a bath, dozed for a couple of hours, and drove back to the station, listening to reports come in on the storm.

The eye had decided to thread the needle between south-shore Florida and north-shore Cuba. The National Hurricane Center had confirmed her name would be Katrina. And she was headed right toward the course Stanley and Father Flannigan were taking south to Jamaica. Unless he and Flannigan had heard the warnings and turned back, or more likely made a sharp right turn and headed for the Yucatan. There were so many possible scenarios. They just had to be listening out there.

Back at the station she tried Sister Bartholemew in Gulfport and learned that Flannigan had not called in yet. Either there or in Montego Bay. Not good. So much for the Yucatan theory. But then it could still be valid. Phone lines and all communication channels would be burning up in that region of the world at this hour of the storm.

A map of the Caribbean was now indelibly etched in her mind. On that map was drawn Stanley and Flannigan's most logical course from Gulfport to Montego Bay. It was a line that coincided exactly with Katrina's predicted path. She didn't like the collision that was occurring in time, in her mind— not good at all.

Lee had asked the good sister if she would call her first thing at her private number if any word came in. Sister Bartholemew said certainly, she would, and hung up reminding her to pray. I have been, Sister. I have been...

Another forty-eight hours passed as she watched Katrina pass over South Florida, weaken, and then head back out into the Gulf and pick up steam again as she turned north toward

Louisiana. Stanley and Father Flannigan still had not yet called in, but surely they would have heard the warnings and headed west out of Katrina's relentless march. Why had they not called in? She couldn't come up with a logical explanation

And then she went on the air. Highly distracted, she flubbed a couple of teleprompter readings, but in true form said, "I'm sorry, my mouth is willin' but my brain's just not engaged." And then, horror of horrors, she broke down and cried right in front of one hundred thousand viewers. Bradley, of course, told everyone that Lee Ann had a friend who was out at sea in Katrina's path and that friend, as of now, had not radioed in. She recovered quickly, apologized, and then Bradley said something philosophical, and they cut to Sam doing a special report on the Southeast's oncoming storm.

Big Sam nearly obliterated the green screen as he walked in front of it. "...Okay...Miss Katrina's eye has cleared the coasts of South Florida with some severe property damage and as yet unconfirmed death count. And now, back over warm water, she is once again gaining strength. Governors Blanco of Louisiana and Barbour of Mississippi have declared a state of emergency and advised their citizens to start boarding up and preparing for the worst. People along the south coast of those states hardly need to be warned. They've been getting ready now for the past eighteen or so hours, hanging plywood, and stocking shelves. And it appears they're ready to let'r rip. Now,"— he swept his hand over the map— "if we project Katrina's path, we can see that she is probably going to hit New Orleans, Gulfport, and Biloxi with a lethal broadside. Her steering winds suggest just such a landfall."

Lee Ann tuned it out and began perusing her notes for the upcoming segment. Okay, her little scene was forgiven today, but that would have to be the end of that kind of behavior. Sam's spot was concluding. She came down hard on herself and hit her next cue running.

"We've got a story for you this morning from up in Mellow Marin."

As soon as she came off the air, she called Gulfport again and again Sister Bartholemew told her there was no message from *Holy Spirit*. You can say that again, she mumbled under her breath. Sister went on to say that she had acquaintances in the Coast Guard who also knew Flannigan and they'd said yes, they had a notice on their register concerning his planned voyage and would contact her immediately when they had any word at all on, or from, the boat. "They're very busy right now, but are our friends so we have the best connections possible... along with the Lord, of course."

Her voice jingled as she said this, and for a moment Lee Ann was uplifted. She thanked the good sister and assured her once again that she had been praying. Sister said, "Of course..." and "I will call you immediately when I receive word." Then she told Lee Ann that she was very busy and must excuse her now as they were battening down the hatches around the compound. Lee Ann said, "Thank you very much, Sister, Godspeed" and hung up. What else could she possibly do now but wait and listen—and pray.

She sat at her desk in her office with head in hands—pulse climbing steadily. Even the Coast Guard hadn't heard from *Holy Spirit*. Which craft, if holding on its planned course, would be in the eye of Katrina about right now! Surely the crew of the boat must have monitored the warnings and headed west, but then why hadn't they called in? Not good...not good...not good...

The message beeped in her brain like defunct Morse code. Panic time—she needed to talk to someone. And she knew that Maureen was that person. She dialed her friend's office thirty feet up the hall.

"Palmer...this is my direct line...better be good."

"Maureen, do you have five minutes? I'm redlining...need to talk."

"Again? You did fine today...cry a little...they loved you... what's the problem?"

"Tomorrow."

"Always is, sweetie. I'm swamped, but you don't sound so good. Come on down...I'll get the nitrous out."

She didn't have the heart to laugh—felt physically ill now, so said, "Okay...be right down," grabbed her bag, and headed for help.

"You look as if you just saw a ghost," said Maureen when her star player walked into her office and collapsed in a chair.

"Funny you should say that. What I'd really like to see or hear from is the *Holy Spirit*."

"I didn't know you were Catholic," said Maureen, handing her a glass of water and some white tablets.

"I'm not. What are these?"

"Aspirin, sweetie...real high-powered stuff."

Lee threw them back and chased them with half the water.

"The *Holy Spirit*?" asked Maureen.

"Stanley. You saw it this morning...the little breakdown on the air?"

"Yes...no problem...so it's your Stanley who's out there?"

"Mmmhuh."

"Oy vey," whispered Maureen.

Lee Ann went on. "He's sailing to Jamaica with an ex-Catholic priest on a boat named *Holy Spirit*. They're two...almost three days out of Gulfport, Mississippi. And, if holding on their probable course to Montego Bay, would probably be just south of the eye of the damn hurricane about"— she glanced at her watch— "now."

Maureen let out a little wheezing gasp, remained silent for a moment, and then said. "Who have you talked with down there so far?"

So Lee Ann rattled through her story from the time she saw the first sign of the spiral several days ago until now. Maureen asked:

"Does this Sister Bartholemew have the number of the Jamaican end of the Holy Family?"

"Yes, she gave that to me. And it sounds like she has a direct connection to the Coast Guard. And they are well aware that

Holy Spirit is out there. Said they would call her and she would call me when any word came in."

"You've done all you can...now pray." Maureen cut it down to size.

"I've been reminded to do that, thank you. Remember, these are God's people I've been dealing with."

"Right," said Maureen, "now I'm telling you."

Lee Ann nodded silently and then almost whispered "I feel so helpless. I feel like there's something else I could be doing... if I could just think of it."

"How much do you know about this Father Flannigan? Is his boat equipped with all the latest little eyes and ears? Communication, I'm tawlking?"

"Yes, Stanley said it was...asked about that himself. The boat has short wave and satcom both. And Claire confirmed that. She toured the bridge when she and Stanley went over to make reservations for the passage."

"I'm sure they'd keep monitoring the weather as they sailed along, wouldn't you?"

"Yes...they could have turned in at a number of spots along the way. Florida, Yucatan, Cuba."

"Yikes."

"Yeah, Cuba. But I'm sure there are arrangements for this kind of emergency with old Fidel."

"And you say no word...or communication as of now? Mmm...I'd be concerned. But you have to have faith that a boat with a name like *Holy Spirit*, being piloted by an ex-Catholic priest, is going to get through."

"Mmmhuh..." Lee Ann mumbled. "It's the ex part that's got me worried."

"You don't sound convinced."

"I'm a meteorologist, Maureen. What can I say? I know how fast the weather can shift and move and put people into a squeeze play. Toss'm to and fro, especially out at sea. I'd imagine—and this is a big system— even if they are on the edge of it, it could be..."

Maureen cut in. "I know...but you gotta get a grip on now, girl. It's not like the last time when I covered your tush. We can't afford to miss your smiling face around here in the near future. People liked Laura Andrews a little more than you might like to know. I know you may think this sounds cold hearted now, but Lee, you gotta pull some professional muscle here and rally. Get your mind back on business..." She spoke slowly, kindly, and dangled her last words in the air as if to keep them off of Lee Ann's already heavily burdened back. There was a long silence while Lee Ann stared off to the southeast. Then a deep breath and...

"Thanks, coach."

"You're welcome."

"Lunch? I could sure use some company even if it's just in here."

"That's where it's going to be. As I said, I'm up to my ankles in snakes at the moment. We'll talk about the ones that concern you at lunch. That way I won't waste my time or yours either. You have to think extremely positively right now, Lee Ann. You can't let the boogie man get you again."

Lee laughed halfheartedly. "Okay, see you for lunch. One?"

"Yes, I'll order. Don't worry, I know what you like. Outta here, girl, I got some shows to do and so do you."

Lee Ann stepped back into the hall feeling juvenile. Of course the boat would have heard the warnings and put in, or headed for the Yucatan. She'd get a call from Gulfport. It would come in this evening around 6 or 7 o'clock. That would happen.

And with that resolved, she set off in the direction of Sam Weber's office, down by the eyes and the ears of the weather.

Katrina did her work. She came screaming into New Orleans on the morning of August 29, overtopping the levees of the 17th Street Canal, and flooding a vast majority of the city—including the now famous Lower Ninth Ward. 20,000 people, stranded by a mass exodus from the city, took refuge and languished in the Superdome for days with limited food and water. Along with flooding New Orleans, she leveled Biloxi and Gulfport, Mississippi, and proceeded to spawn tornadoes as far north as Pennsylvania. As Katrina finally spun herself out, she left in her wake over eighteen hundred dead, and tens of billions of dollars in property damage. And as the days passed, some boats went into the Coast Guard registry as missing at sea. Among them was *Holy Spirit*.

The first week was the most difficult for Lee Ann. She, by prior arrangement, called Sister Bartholemew daily at noon for a status report. The first day after Katrina had passed over, Sister had told her to keep praying, that there was still no word. Second day, Sister told her to have faith in the Lord, that there was still no word. Third day, she finally heard concern in the nun's voice as she told her there still was no word from *Holy Spirit*. On the fourth day, she told Lee Ann that the craft was listed officially as missing, along with several others that had been in Katrina's path.

Sister Bartholemew agreed that Lee Ann could call daily if she wished but that she would call Lee Ann immediately when she received any word of any kind. Lee Ann thanked the good sister quietly, said good-bye, and hung up the phone.

At that precise moment, she let herself imagine—for the first time—the worst. That Stanley might be gone.

59.

Clay sat staring out the south window of Stanley's studio. He found he sat here often as the first anniversary of Stanley's disappearance approached. Claire's easel was here along with her meticulously kept rolling side carts of paints and brushes. She was working in blues and blacks and greens these days, painting things that could only be described as huge tidal waves of color. It never ceased to amaze him how Claire could charge a four-by-six-foot rectangle of canvas with such fury. She was a passionate one—Lee Ann and Stanley's daughter.

Stanley, oh Stanley, you and your wind-torn illusions. You with your raging mud mythologies. "So you perished at sea, did you..." Clay spoke the words out loud to no one. "Mmm...well we still wonder, and it has been almost a year." It felt good to be speaking out loud now, as if, sitting here in Stanley's own home, the latent image of the ceramist would hear him and possibly respond.

He'd felt Stanley's presence many times since that first day he and Claire had come to the studio and never left—except to close out their affairs in New Orleans and move to San Francisco. But it had never occurred to him to speak directly to the man of the house, wherever his spirit might be.

"People have theories. You want to hear some of them?"
Silence. The birds singing.

"They say you might have forgotten to take a left at Jamaica and just headed on south, to Rio, maybe? Ha! Stanley, you old mud dog!"

Clay felt a strange tingling in his scalp. Yes, this speaking out loud directly to his lost friend, Stanley, was helping. Everyone in the family was feeling a little blue lately as the first anniversary of Katrina approached. He walked over, turned on the radio, tuned in KJAZ, and returned to his chair and his stare. No, he suddenly veered off course; it was better to keep moving—moving and talking.

"Oh, and there's the theory that you had another run-in with Poteet and his blazing cannons, and Cynthia and Harold and you beat it up into the Cockpit Country of Jamaica and are living in jungle bliss. Those are some juicy theories, don't you think? You with all your women in waiting?"

Clay listened. Out on the street he heard laughter and animated conversation, but no Stanley.

His mind wandered now, recalling all the detective work they'd done this last year. He thought of the letters that he'd read from Melissa to Stanley and the letters Stanley had written to Melissa. Stanley had made copies. They were all in chronological order in a file drawer by his desk. Good read.

And after peeking into their affairs, Clay wrote to Melissa to apprise her of the situation. She was shaken by the news. She called Clay from Rio, and they'd talked for some time. No, Stanley had not shown up down there—yet. But she would call at first sign of him. "Oh dear...oh lord...ees terrible..." she kept saying. He hadn't even been able to comfort her because he still felt too much pain himself. That call was about a month after *Holy Spirit* was listed as missing at sea. He'd talked to Melissa several times by phone as the months passed. But still no word on either end. So much for the: Stanley-and-Melissa-in Rio theory.

And Jahna and Lee Ann had kept in touch. Jahna had told her Cynthia and Harold had moved back farther into the mountains after Katrina and lived where there were no phones. So Stanley could have slipped through the back door into Jamaica and gone into hiding with Cynthia in a badass region of heartland Jamaica?

But where then was Father Flannigan and *Holy Spirit*?"

"So Stanley, you talked Father Flannigan into it and sailed south, did you? Just like Lafitte?"

Clay smiled, glanced at his watch: 5:33pm 8/24. "Almost a year now. Must be getting pretty spacey in the jungle." In his imagination he saw Stanley sitting on a rock above a black jungle pool. Cynthia and Harold were on either side of him. People were swimming below. Steam was rising up and shafts of sunlight were streaming down through a dark canopy of mango trees. Pleasant thought.

The phone rang. It was Claire calling from Genoa to say she would be home around seven and did they need anything from the market? And what was he doing? He told her no, they had everything they needed for dinner, and he was just sitting and thinking.

"About what?" she asked.

"Mostly Stanley."

"Yeah, me too...we sold the last of his myth pieces just this afternoon. It was punk to see it go...really hurt."

"I love you" they'd said to each other, and then hung up.

Claire, that girl of his. How strange was this? His adoptive parents introduce him to their daughter and six months later he marries her. Whoa. Clay always shook his head in disbelief when he thought of this.

"And you want to hear something else, STANLEY? We're going to have a little Libra running around here this October. So why don't you COME ON BACK FOR THAT? He was almost shouting now, but no one heard.

Wind rattled the blinds.

"Twenty-eight years old...yeah, I can do a kid...don't you think, Stan?" Clay felt his nostrils begin to sting, his head swell. He never knew when it was going to come on, these sudden bursts of melancholy that came over him when he'd let himself think about Stanley. And here it was again, out of the blue.

He walked into the kitchen, grabbed a Calistoga from the fridge, and made his way out into the small backyard. It was in need of some maintenance; fall was coming. Claire had planted some cactus. She loved cactus. She said they reminded her of herself. He had to agree. He liked cactus too.

"So, Stanley, you're not all that conversant today, are you?"

A siren went by.

He smiled slightly as his eyes ranged over to a row of ceramic faces that hung along the top rail of a fence. Egyptian, Grecian, Roman, Nordic, Gothic, Celtic: all were represented. Clay had seen a great deal of Stanley's work, and photographs of his work, this past year. These heads were all archetypical of that work. If he had anything to do with it, they would never be sold.

Another siren went by, this time accompanied by the bull-bleating horn of a fire engine. He smiled again. "Still blowin', Stanley?"

He pictured the man Stan, sitting in a fenced compound on a cocaine plantation in Columbia, playing sax for his fellow slaves who were providing wicked Latin rhythms on plastic water carboys and assorted tin cans and bottles.

"Who knows, maybe you even get to play up at the big house on occasion. Do you, Stanley?"

Claire's theory:

Stanley and Father Flannigan were blown off course by Katrina and ended up off the coast of South America where their boat was highjacked and pirated by yachting drug lords who took them back to their cocoa plantations and forced them into servitude. Leave it to Claire to come up with that one, though sometimes her psychic abilities amazed him. And she insisted that that's what she was going to believe —at least for a few more years.

"So, Stanley, you a slave boy now?" He listened. The city hummed its song. No line from Stanley. "Well, better than dead. I know you'll work it to your advantage man, eventually."

He walked inside and called Lee Ann at KPIQ. She told him she had a couple of writing assignments for him and she'd drop them by later that evening. She said people in the say very much liked his work lately, and he could certainly expect more if he wanted it. Well, that was good, because the music he'd been able to find in San Francisco wasn't quite paying his share of the rent. And it was always fun to write for Lee Ann. She kept the beat.

The phone rang. It was Lee Ann calling back, asking him if he could get down to the station tomorrow morning with the stuff she would be bringing over for him that evening. She told him she thought he could get it done by then.

"With an all-nighter," he said.

"Do you mind?"

"No, I'll do it, no problem."

The fact that he was a night-owl musician was working to his advantage where this budding writing for television career was concerned. And Claire had a solid job with Evie at Genoa and was taking the bull by the horns, as only Taurus Claire could. She liked her job.

"So every little thing is just hunky-dory here in Baghdad by the Bay.

"YOU'D LIKE IT!" Clay shouted up to the rafters.

Maybe Stanley was floating about up there. He was a Pan sort of guy. Clay's nostrils began to sting again; he continued to pace, mind drifting off to over a year ago, the day after Stanley had come back from Gulfport, having just secured his berth on *Holy Spirit*—bound for Jamaica in late August. He was as happy as a little kid with a baby gator in his washtub. He said he'd always wanted to sail down to the Caribbean...and now, he'd shouted, "I'm doing it!"

Claire had gone out looking for work that afternoon in New Orleans when it was all still so new. So he and Stanley spent the afternoon sitting down by the river playing a few tunes and talking about his time in Jamaica, about Cynthia and Harold and all the fine new friends he'd met there.

By the time they took him to the airport the next day, to return to San Francisco, Clay felt blessed to have this older friend who had, at one time, changed his diapers and given him his squeezer. Stanley gave Claire a hug first and then a warm one to him. He must have still been feeling Jamaica mellow because Clay saw a deep contentment in the eyes that glanced one last time into his.

And, oh yes, a few stars.

Then his new friend made that long trudge down to the boarding gate, waving one last time as he turned a corner and was gone from view. Off to see if Lee Ann would live with him again.

They'd only seen each other again briefly when Stanley was passing through in August, on his way back to Gulfport to begin his passage to Jamaica.

"Hey, Stanley...if you're out there...call home. We love you."

60.

Moving back in time now...to sometime in late September, 2005

Stanley was gone. At first it was for a few days. Then the days grew into weeks. Lee Ann couldn't seem to accept the reality of that. Oh, she carried on with her work, and to watch her do her show, you'd never know the profound sadness that lived behind her professionally sparkling eyes. In the weeks following Stanley's disappearance, she'd learned the meaning of acting, and finally realized why people had always told her she was such a natural as a host. That's because she *had* been herself—said what was on her mind at the moment—and fielded things as they came her way. But now it was different. Now the joking with Bradley and the guests came from someone outside of herself. It was as if she was watching herself from the audience, doing what that person in the audience expected her to do. She didn't like what was happening to her. She was becoming a phony.

And those nights she found herself circling home, driving by Stanley's place just off Valencia, hoping she'd see a light on in the front window. He'd been there almost three months putting things in order to return to Roarin River for his extended stay, and she hadn't been able to get over once except for that one time after he'd pulled her out of the bay. She felt the whip of guilt sting her back; she felt like saying, "Do that again; it feels so good." She wondered how long Stanley would remain missing, how many times in her life she'd have to lose someone down a black hole of uncertainty—not knowing if they were dead or alive. First Bird, then Manuel, and now Stanley.

Finally one evening, about three weeks after Katrina had blown over, she braced herself and dropped by Genoa Gallery.

Evie was in her counting house, counting all her money, but she dropped everything when she saw Lee Ann standing in her doorway. Streetwise Evie thought at first she was seeing a woman who had just come from hard time: drawn, haggard, hard around the eyes,

Lee said. "Evie, I'm about at the end of my rope. You got a minute?"

Evie, of course, did; the money could wait. Stanley had grossed another $50,000. She got up, walked over, and stuck out her hand, immediately realizing that Lee Ann needed more than a hand. She took her in her arms and held her then as Lee's body started to jerk with an effort to muffle her sobs. Evie led her to a couch and sat down beside her and put her arm around her shoulders. Then it was a good two minutes of release while the two women commiserated over their loss. Finally Lee asked Evie if she could have a key to Stanley's place because she might find something that would give her a clue as to his whereabouts. Also, eventually someone would have to take responsibility for his affairs, and she thought that she was the most likely candidate. Evie nodded gravely and moved to her desk to get the key ring.

"You know Stanley paid his rent for six months in advance, don't you, Lee Ann?"

"Yes, he did tell me that. Also that our kids could stay there when they come out next week. I mean, I know you're watching the place while he's gone, but I could take over those responsibilities now in light of..."

"I understand," said Evie, and she went over to her desk again to get Stanley's small pile of bills and other mail."

The two women talked a few more minutes about the need to keep the faith and then, realists that they were, had to admit he was probably gone: he'd been three weeks missing at sea. They parted then with solemn faces and only a brief mention of wills and legal matters to close Stanley's affairs. They decided it was entirely too soon to even think about that.

Lee Ann left Genoa and drove over to Stanley's studio, but she still couldn't bring herself to go in. So she drove home and called New Orleans. Claire answered.

"Hello."

"Hi," she heard herself say from somewhere far away.

"Oh...hi, Mom. You don't sound so good."

"I'm not feeling so good."

"Are you sick?"

"At heart."

"I know. I know. I've just been going around with this big lead brick in my chest too. Any word from your contacts? Jahna? Sister Barth?"

"No, but I did pick up Stanley's mail from the woman who was sort of his business manager. Oh boy, there's that past tense again."

"It's okay, Ma, go on."

"In that stack of mail is a letter from Melissa. I don't feel right about opening it. As a matter of fact, I don't know how to feel about starting to take over his affairs; it's very confusing."

"I know. Well, the old Claire would probably have told you to rip that sucker open. But the new Claire would tell you to slowly and carefully slit the seam and take a peek."

"That's progress, Claire."

"Yes, I think so. Oh, speaking of Sister Bartholemew, Clay drove over to Gulfport this afternoon to talk with her at Holy Family Foster Home. Flannigan's home base, as you know."

"Yes?"

"Yes, he wanted to get to know those people for future reference and to ask the nun about Flannigan's sailing skills. He wanted to verify what communications he had on board and just find out about the man in general. For instance, did he also have a girlfriend in Rio?"

"Can't hurt, but you know how protective the Holy Family is of their own don't you, Claire? I'm not sure what he'll find out even if some connection does exist."

"Hmm, well, Clay has his way. Those sad little puppy dog eyes of his."

"Yes, Claire, I've noticed."

"GOD! I LOVE THAT MAN," Claire screamed like she was having an orgasm.

Lee Ann pulled the receiver away from her ear, and then moved it back slowly. "I can tell." She paused. "Are you two still coming out at the end of next week? I mean, I hope that's still on; I need help."

"What kind of help? Yes, we're coming; thanks for the tickets."

"You're welcome. I just picked up a key to Stanley's place from Evie, his manager."

"Yeah...?"

"And I was going to drop in there on my way home. But I just couldn't bring myself to do it. I was thinking I might wait till you guys get here for moral support."

"Totally understand. You got it. Wait, place ain't goin' nowhere."

"I know, thanks."

"We're there for ya, Moms. Clay's feeling just as heartsick as the rest of us. But he's really looking forward to seeing San Francisco again. He wants to see what happens in his brain. We'll help you out any way we can. Don't worry."

"Thanks, Claire. I'm still a little numb you know."

"Hey, he's my Pops! We were just starting to groove. Bird was back in the nest...what can I say...it's fucked."

"Yeah, I'd agree with that. Well, I'm starving, so I'm going to put some soup on and try to get some letters written. We'll talk before you come next week. Let me know what Clay finds out, okay?"

"Will do, Mom...same if you get any word."

"Course...well..."

"Take care of yourself, hear?"

"Usually do."

"Yeah, you usually do. I love you. Bye."

"I love you Claire. Give my love to Clay."

"Will do, bye."

"Bye."

Lee Ann placed the receiver back on the cradle and stared at the pale lavender envelope postmarked Rio de Janeiro sitting on the top of Stanley's mail.

A week and a half flew by, and then one bright Saturday afternoon in early October, Lee Ann found herself driving south on Highway 101 to the airport to pick up her kids coming in from New Orleans. Suddenly she realized that her heart was not aching. She was feeling relaxed, excited, light hearted. She passed Candlestick Park on her left. She thought of Stanley, baseball, and the afternoons they'd spent there with the Giants. Then the hammer came down again.

What a pleasant three or four minutes out of a month of unrelenting anguish. She hoped, maybe soon, she could get it back again. Stanley would want that.

Claire and Clay came down the escalator to baggage claim with their arms draped over one another. It was the first time she'd seen them like this, and Stanley was right, they were the Parisian lovers on a fashion-plate spread. They were striking together. Just the fact that they were together still astonished her. She hugged Claire first and then Clay.

"Let me look at you two. You're beautiful, you know. Course I could be accused of being prejudiced."

"You, Mom? Thanks, you're beautiful too."

"Second it," said Clay.

Claire said she wanted to show Clay the Pacific first thing. And he agreed he wanted to see it "again" too. So Lee drove over the hill and picked up Highway 1 Northbound. The surf was up and trailing rooster tails off its crests. Clay was riding up front with her. Claire was in the backseat giving a running commentary on all her high school adventures along this stretch of road.

"Man...man oh man," he marveled, "big waves, not like you see in the Gulf."

They drove into Golden Gate Park, parked, got out, and walked to the base of a towering eucalyptus.

"This is it," said Lee Ann, "right here. Right in this very spot is where we found you, Clay."

The three of them remained silent for a few moments and then Claire said, "Let's show Clay the house and neighborhood where we lived back in the nineties. Maybe he'll recognize something."

"Read my mind," Lee Ann softly.

They drove down to the panhandle of the park and up Baker Street. "There. There it is." She pointed to a house that was wedged into a block of gingerbread Victorians. "Course this whole street has been repainted, probably several times since we lived here with you, Clay."

"You know, just being around in this area, I have intense déjà vu. I have been here before."

"Yes, you have," Lee's voice was barely audible.

The Palace of Fine Arts Building, floating on a reflecting pool in all its Greco Roman grandeur, was the last stop on their tour. Clay walked around saying yes, definitely, he remembered this place. And the birds.

Someone had thrown half a deli sandwich into a trash barrel. Lee Ann looked on with vacant eyes—feeling outside of herself— as Clay walked among hungry begging geese and ducks dropping crumbs here and there. Then he clapped his hands twice, loudly, and they all made a mad dash back to the water. Bird had done that too.

The time had come to move along and get settled at Stanley's.

About six o'clock they unlocked, and let themselves through, the heavy steel front door of his studio. Lee Ann was in the lead. She hadn't been over here since that last night she'd spent with him after her unexpected dip in the bay. The place was more Spartan than it had been on that evening. All the knickknacks had disappeared. The walls were bare of paintings. It looked almost Japanese in its austerity, as if his personality had left with him. Almost as if he knew he wouldn't be coming back? All the furniture remained, though, and the bed was made with clean sheets. He'd known that Clay and Claire would be sleeping there during his absence.

There was, however, one piece of sculpture that greeted them as they entered the kitchen. It was sitting dead center on the marble-topped island counter. It was a statue of a young girl and a dragon. A note was tucked under one corner. Lee Ann walked over slowly, picked it up and read.

Hello everyone. Lee, Claire, Clay.

Welcome to my humble abode. You'll find it sparse, but functional. I took this opportunity to get rid of a lot of junk that was weighing me down. I did this little fanciful piece while in New Orleans. It's called Mary Mythe. It was the first thing I did with Melissa's clay. I'd like to give it to you, Claire and Clay, if you'd like it. If not, give it to Evie. She'll sell it and give you some money.

Such a deal I have for you.

I did another piece with the clay before I left for Jamaica. This one is for you, Lee Ann. You'll find it in a wooden crate in the bedroom. Be very careful when you lift it out. It has some very delicate elements. Hope you like it, my dear.

You guys, make yourself totally at home here. Claire, I've set an easel up over by your south window. Perhaps do a painting while you're here, if you find time? Wish I was there, but I'm not. Next time for sure.

Enjoy. I love you guys,

S.

Lee Ann closed her eyes and handed the note off sideways to Claire. She stood with her back to them as they read it. After a few moments of silence she heard her daughter speaking softly behind her.

"Let's go see what's in that box."

"Yes, let's...." Lee Ann whispered.

She'd seen the wooden crate sitting in the bedroom on their first pass through that area and thought little of it. Now, as she rounded the corner into Stanley's bedroom, the crate seemed to jump out at her. Her heart was racing, and she didn't know why.

"Clay," she said, "I don't want to open it in here. Can you move it out to the living room? And I don't know about you guys, but I need a drink. I know where the cabinet is. Any orders?"

"Whatever you're having," said Claire.

"Yes, I'll have one too." Clay walked over to test the weight of the box. "This isn't all that heavy, I can get it." He lifted it easily and started for the living room.

Lee Ann went to the kitchen and found a bottle of cognac similar to the one she and Stanley had been drinking that night (it seemed like yesterday) when they'd fallen asleep watching Letterman. She didn't know how much longer she was going to be able to contain the cry that was screaming like a little kid locked in a closet. But she bucked up and returned to the living area with the bottle and three glasses.

"Cognac all right?"

"Fine."

"Sure...fitting actually," said Clay. "That's the same thing we were drinking the night Stanley and I reconnected. Remy." He drifted off for a second. "Okay, let's see what we've got here."

He untied the cord and lifted the top off of the crate. The box was completely filled with styrofoam popcorn. He carefully started removing the pellets, a handful at a time, setting them on the floor. Fastidious Claire found a cardboard box and transferred them into it.

Lee Ann stood looking out the south window at the small yard area to the rear of the studio. She nursed her drink as her damp eyes ranged around, fixing one by one on some old familiar objects. There was a piece from the disembodied organs phase of Stanley's work. And there was one of his kitchen sinks, now serving as a fountain and birdbath. And there, out along the top rail of the back fence, were those faces of the ages that stared back at her with frozen, blank expressions. And now she heard Clay pulling whatever it was from the pellets. Claire gasped as she realized what it was.

"I can't look. I just can't bring myself to look. Set it on this table here by the window, Clay. And when it's there, I'll look. Okay?" She turned her head so that she couldn't see them and walked to the middle of the room.

Claire was still oohing and aahing. "You're going to *love* this, Mom. You can't believe how beautiful this is. Be careful honey... it's so delicate."

"Believe me, I will."

She heard them moving to the table, setting something on it. Her heart was not keeping very good time now. She wondered if they could hear it. She certainly could.

"Okay, ready when you are," Clay said softly.

She turned slowly and looked.

The light had grown pastel with the setting sun. An amber-rose glow filled the room. Lee Ann found herself staring into her own face. Stanley's gift to her was a full-size bust of her head and shoulders. Melissa's clay had indeed been a wonderful choice for this work, with its pearly luster, its ability to embrace and hold fine detail.

The bust was of a younger Lee, a more perfect Lee, sculpted with an almost baroque felicity. Her shoulders were bare, her neck slender and long. A faint smile played about the corners of her mouth and eyes. And her hair—that hair—that wind-tunnel, egg-beater affair, all wound round her head, with wisps here and there... hanging down.

J.Q. Gustin is a retired architect who lives in Sebastopol, California with his imaginary cat, Mr. Twinkle. This is his second novel.

www.ingramcontent.com/pod-product-compliance
Lightning Source LLC
Chambersburg PA
CBHW030843030726
47495CB00005B/1342